D0571563

Nauti Intentions

Nauti
Intentions

Lora Leigh

B
BERKLEY SENSATION, NEW YORK

THE BERKLEY PUBLISHING GROUP
Published by the Penguin Group
Penguin Group (USA) Inc.
375 Hudson Street, New York, New York 10014, USA
Penguin Group (Canada), 90 Eglinton Avenue East, Suite 700, Toronto, Ontario M4P 2Y3, Canada
(a division of Pearson Penguin Canada Inc.)
Penguin Books Ltd., 80 Strand, London WC2R 0RL, England
Penguin Group Ireland, 25 St. Stephen's Green, Dublin 2, Ireland (a division of Penguin Books Ltd.)
Penguin Group (Australia), 250 Camberwell Road, Camberwell, Victoria 3124, Australia
(a division of Pearson Australia Group Pty. Ltd.)
Penguin Books India Pvt. Ltd., 11 Community Centre, Panchsheel Park, New Delhi—110 017, India
Penguin Group (NZ), 67 Apollo Drive, Rosedale, North Shore 0632, New Zealand
(a division of Pearson New Zealand Ltd.)
Penguin Books (South Africa) (Pty.) Ltd., 24 Sturdee Avenue, Rosebank, Johannesburg 2196,
South Africa

Penguin Books Ltd., Registered Offices: 80 Strand, London WC2R 0RL, England

This book is an original publication of The Berkley Publishing Group.

This is a work of fiction. Names, characters, places, and incidents either are the product of the author's imagination or are used fictitiously, and any resemblance to actual persons, living or dead, business establishments, events, or locales is entirely coincidental. The publisher does not have any control over and does not assume any responsibility for author or third-party websites or their content.

ISBN 978-1-60751-957-7
PRINTED IN THE UNITED STATES OF AMERICA

A special thank-you to Natalie.
You help me keep my sanity,
and there's not enough thanks for that.
You go above and beyond and make life easier.
And my appreciation
for that knows no bounds.

For everything you do, thank you!

PROLOGUE

Janey Mackay should have known something was wrong when Dayle Mackay, the man who'd donated the seed for her conception, left the message on her cell phone that her brother, Natches, was hurt and she needed to come home.

She should have called someone else, but who was there to call? After all, Dayle had made certain Janey was as isolated from the rest of her family as possible. Private girls' schools until college, and even then, she knew she was being watched. She was always watched.

She should have been suspicious because Dayle hated Natches, his only son. Hated him so much, and feared him to such an extent that Janey knew it was the only reason she was in college rather than married to one of his fanatical friends. Or dead, because she would have killed herself first.

But she hadn't been. Her only thought had been of Natches, the brother she had never been able to really get to know, but the one she knew protected her. She knew, because he'd always managed to get little notes to her through the years. He'd always found ways to contact her, to let her know he was there if she needed him.

She had needed him. But it wasn't a life-or-death need, and she knew if she defied Dayle Mackay and publicly chose Natches over him, then it would end in blood. Possibly her brother's blood.

Her father had her booked on a red-eye flight into Lexington from the college in California that he'd had no choice but to allow her to attend. She arrived after midnight, and Dayle and her aunt Nadine were waiting on her.

After that, things got a little hazy. But that could have had something to do with the nasty-smelling cloth Nadine had capped over her mouth and nose after they were on their way to Somerset. Or the pills Dayle had shoved down her throat before she could fight him, as her lashes fluttered open later.

Yeah, she had a pretty good idea that was the reason. And she couldn't seem to clear her mind enough to think. She needed to think. Dayle was a monster, twisted and evil, and Nadine was his perfect match. His "soul mate," Dayle called his sister.

Janey stared up at the ceiling above the bed her body felt weighted to. She wasn't tied down, but they hadn't had to tie her; whatever they had given her made her so sluggish, made her feel so heavy she couldn't move. She could feel the tears that fell from her eyes, though she didn't want to cry.

Shame twisted inside her, congealed into a sick ball in the pit of her stomach as her skin crawled with the horror of the past hours.

She hadn't begged.

She'd always imagined what it would be like if her father did something this vile to her—and yes, there were times she had expected it—and she'd imagined she would beg. Call him "Daddy" and plead with him to make it stop.

But the words had choked in her throat. She had stared at the ceiling, hating him, hating her aunt. Hating that bitch's hands as they touched her.

Her breath hitched on a silent sob. He'd let that old slut touch her. He'd laughed with amused indulgence as Nadine had pleaded like a little girl to have just a "little fun."

As though Janey were a toy. A toy to be used.

Nadine hadn't had time to do much, but even a little sickened Janey. She'd nearly thrown up on the bitch.

She turned her head into the pillow and tried to dry her tears. She didn't want Nadine or Dayle to see her crying. To know they had hurt her. It would only make them worse. They thrived on pain. It amused them. Empowered them.

And she had to stop crying. She had to fight past the blanketing haze that fogged her brain. She needed to just get up. If she could just make herself get up, then she could get out of here. She could find help. If she could get out of here, Alex's house wasn't far away. Alex would help her. He would take her to Natches and Natches would make it all go away.

She sobbed at the thought. Alex would take care of her. Maybe he'd even put his arms around her. She would like that. Just for a minute. Just long enough to make her feel safe. There was something about him, something that warmed her in the dead of night when she was alone and cold.

Another sob broke from her. She swore she could hear Natches's voice now. She was hallucinating. She had to be. Oh God, she had to get out of here before they gave her more of those damned drugs.

Making her limbs work, making her brain clear enough to force her legs, her arms, to move, had her breaking out in a cold sweat.

If she stayed here, something would happen to Natches. She'd heard them talking about it. She couldn't remember what would happen to him, but she couldn't let them hurt him. He had protected her. He was her older brother. And he loved her.

Breathing harshly, sweat pouring along her face, she managed to roll to the side of the bed. The floor looked as though it were miles below her.

Hell.

She swallowed tightly and blinked the sweat from her eyes. She could do this. She could. If she could roll to the side of the bed, then she could get up on her damned feet. She could do this.

She forced herself to believe she could do it. It felt as though it took years, but she managed to sit up, swaying, swallowing back the bile in her stomach as the room spun on her.

Hell yeah.

She could do this. She could feel her feet on the floor. She struggled to pull her T-shirt down, over her breasts, shuddering at the memory of why it was up there.

Oh man, she was so gonna puke if she had to think about that now.

Janey shook her head, slowly. The fog eased a little. Bracing herself, she forced herself to her feet and went to her knees.

Shit, that hurt.

She bit back a moan, panted, and dragged herself up the side of the bed. She stumbled; her ankle nearly collapsed. The door looked so far away. But she knew it wasn't. She just had to get there.

Natches. She had to think about Natches. The night Dayle had beaten him, nearly senseless, until he was bloodied and almost unconscious, trying to protect her. He had protected her. She had to protect Natches.

She reached the dresser, hung on tight, and made herself move. She was gripping the corner when the door opened and Nadine stood there. Surprised. Surprised and amused.

"Well, hello there, baby girl." The sound was a hiss of evil as she smoothed her hand over her dress.

Janey watched her, that bile rising again. Wouldn't Nadine just hate it when Janey puked all over her perfect white carpet?

Nadine moved to the chest by the door and pulled out a drawer. Janey's breath caught on a sob. *Don't cry. Don't cry.* If they were going to kill her, it wouldn't do any good to cry.

"Come on, sweetheart." Nadine approached her, and she couldn't run.

She stumbled, trying to get away from the old hag. Nadine was surprisingly strong. Her arm hooked around Janey's neck, choking her as she hauled her up against her.

"You feel good, Janey," Nadine breathed at her ear. "Come on, let's go see if Natches is going to be a good boy. If he is, then you're nice and safe. Otherwise . . ." She laid the barrel of the gun against Janey's neck as she forced her from the room. "Otherwise, I get to pop your little head just like that bastard popped Johnny's. I have a feeling I'll get to pop your little head, baby."

Janey stumbled and received a vicious pinch in her side. By the time Nadine pulled her to a stop, the fog was so thick, mixed with sickness and vertigo.

She heard Natches, but she couldn't find him. She blinked at the window across from her. Blinked and fought to focus. There was the tiniest crack in Nadine's curtains. Just a little one in the sheer panels.

She focused there. She could hear Natches talking now. His voice sounded so heavy, so resigned. It was her fault. She blinked. All her fault. If she had just thought.

She blinked again when something moved. Focused on the curtains, she almost smiled at her flight of fancy. Those drugs her father had forced down her throat after they arrived last night were some damned good shit. Because now she was having hallucinations.

Alex.

Alex was on the roof of the house that she could see. And Alex didn't climb roofs. He didn't lie down on them. She watched, knew him. He was too far away for her to see his features, but this was her hallucination; she knew who he was.

He lowered his head and she imagined their eyes met as he rested it against his arm. Like she dreamed of sometimes. That he was lying beside her, staring at her with those dark gray eyes of his.

Pop!

She heard the sound, felt something splatter against her, and she was falling. Falling. Crumpling to the floor as an enraged scream seemed to echo around her.

Her nails dug into the carpet and she smelled blood. Was it her blood? God, she wouldn't know if they cut her head off right now. *Don't do drugs.* Now she knew why. This was some serious fucked-up shit. And she had to figure out what the hell was going on.

She tried to shake her head, but she couldn't move it. She lay there, the feel of Nadine behind her like a sick weight. Bitch. Someone needed to pop her little head. She was like a rabid dog, always determined to bite something. Or someone.

A sob lodged in Janey's throat, the memory of Nadine's bites searing her mind again.

If she puked, she was going to kick that bitch when she had a chance. Janey hated throwing up. Hated it. She dug her nails into the carpet and tried to pull herself away.

Glass crashing, enraged yells, grunts, groans—they cascaded around her. She could hear sirens, see shadows. Maybe if she closed her eyes, just for a minute. Just for a minute . . .

Major Alexander Jansen stepped through the hall-way to the two fallen women. Nadine Grace was dead. The back of her skull was splattered around the area. Her arm was still locked around Janey Mackay's neck, the gun lying to her side.

He kicked the gun aside, sparing a moment to check Natches's progress in the fight against Dayle Mackay. The younger man was winning; the house was surrounded and law enforcement officials filled the entrance to the room. This was contained.

Dayle Mackay had betrayed his family and his nation. A home-grown terrorist who had aided in the hijacking of four missiles and the death of the soldier transporting them. He had conspired to sell those missiles to terrorists and, along with the group he worked with, conspired against his own government in a plot to strike against the nation's capital.

There was no remorse in Dayle. There never had been. Bringing him down and tearing apart the organization he was a part of would be the highlight of Alex's career, simply because he hated the bastard. But what Alex felt for the daughter was nothing resembling hatred.

Janey.

Fuck, his hands were shaking.

He knelt beside her and checked her quickly for any broken bones or wounds, before lifting her into his arms.

Ragged pain twisted his guts, surged through him. She was so tiny. Barely five-five, all that long black hair flowing around her, splattered with blood. Her face was white, eyes dazed, but they were open.

"Alex." She whispered his name. Did she try to burrow closer?

He'd seen more death than any one man should have to see in his lifetime, but nothing, at no time, had ever pierced his soul as the sight of Janey pierced it now.

He checked the room quickly, his gaze meeting one of the federal agents. Chaya Dane, Natches's lover. She was calling for a car for immediate transport to the hospital.

Alex turned and rushed through the back of the house. Clasping Janey to him, feeling emotions he didn't want to feel. Anger, grief, loss, fuck this, loneliness. Because he'd let this happen. He should have made certain she was at school. He should have checked on Janey.

A car screamed to a stop in front of the house as Alex loped across the yard, the sniper rifle slung across his back, Janey in his arms.

"Major. Here." One of his men jumped from the front of the car and raced to the back passenger door.

Throwing it open, the other man took the rifle and rushed back to the driver's seat as Alex slid into the back, holding Janey.

One hand pressed her head to his chest. She was weak, unable to hold herself in place.

"I have you, Janey." He pushed the hair back from her blood-splattered face, checked her eyes. They were dilated. Dazed.

"My hallucination," she slurred.

"Okay. It's all yours," he murmured, checking her pulse, the weakness in her limbs.

"You kiss me."

Alex froze. His eyes lifted to the foggy depths of hers.

"What?"

"My hallucination." She stumbled over and slurred the word. "You kiss me. This is mine. You just said."

The sergeant was racing through town, a siren blaring from the car, rushing her to the hospital.

"Janey."

"Mine." Her eyes filled with tears. "It doesn't all have to be ugly, does it?"

Ah Christ. His heart was breaking apart. He was fearless. Tough. Yet this one tiny, almost-broken young woman was stealing his soul with the simplest request.

"All yours, Janey."

He ignored the sergeant. He cupped her face, stared at those perfect, pretty lips. Pale pink, her lower lip lush and tempting. He touched it with his thumb, then lowered his head to give her something that wasn't ugly. Something that wouldn't hurt her.

His lips whispered across hers, and he realized this would never be enough. The memory of this would never be enough. He wanted to sink into those beautiful, warm lips and feel her moving with him, against him, as hungry for him as he was for her.

She sighed against the light caress, her lashes fluttering open to meet his gaze. Sleepy, drugged. The light green of her eyes was nearly overtaken by the dilation of her pupils. Whatever they had pumped inside her was too powerful, too much. She was too fucking tiny.

"Sergeant, you're moving too slow," he snapped, pulling Janey to his chest again, realizing his voice was a rough rasp, unlike the cold, hard tone he normally used. "Put some lead in your fucking foot."

"We have traffic, Major," the sergeant warned him, but he pressed his foot to the gas and began shooting around the cars ahead of them.

"Hurry, Sergeant." He stared down at Janey. Her eyes were closed, her breathing more shallow. Her pulse was weaker. "Ah God," he whispered, more to himself than to the sergeant, who he knew was already pushing the limit. "Hurry."

He'd waited too long. He'd watched her from afar. He'd helped Natches protect her, not because Natches was his friend, not because his sister, Crista, was married to Natches's cousin Dawg. He'd watched over her, because watching her was something he couldn't stop doing anyway. Because he was depraved. A bastard. He was obviously more warped than he had ever believed he was.

Because he'd been watching her since she was seventeen, aching for her, and he knew, God help him, he knew, if she survived this, he might not be able to stay away from her the next chance he had to touch her.

She was twenty-three years old. He was thirty-seven. Older than her brother, nearly old enough to qualify as her father. And he was sick. Because there was nothing paternal, nothing brotherly, friendly, or otherwise platonic in anything he felt for her.

And it terrified him.

Janey could touch him. And that was something he hadn't allowed anyone, outside his sister, to do in too many years. No one was allowed to touch the heart of Alex Jansen.

Until Janey Mackay turned those pretty green eyes up at him six years ago, and pouted a kiss across the distance. Her normally somber expression had turned teasing, dancing with laughter and life and fun. And Alex had known then, just as he knew now. He was a dead man.

Because Natches would kill him.

ONE

Janey stood in front of the hostess station, her expression carefully bland, her body controlled. She'd learned a lot about control in the past five months. And it had prepared her for this night, she was certain.

Alex Jansen.

It took more strength than she'd ever imagined she could have to look him in the eye, to smile.

"Alex, your table is waiting." She smiled her bland smile, deliberately met his gaze, then nodded to his companion. Some slinky blond thing dressed as though she were in New York City rather than Kentucky. A black calf-length silk gown? Give her a break. Where did he find this one?

It was anger. She knew it was. Facing Alex again, after the events that happened six months before, wasn't easy. It was damned hard.

"Janey, you're looking well." His sensual, wide lips quirked at one side. Full lips. Did he even remember touching those lips to hers when she all but begged?

"And you're looking like you're healing well." She collected two menus.

"I'm taking very good care of him," the Marilyn Monroe wannabe cooed with pouty red lips.

"Good." She shot them another cool, polite smile. "If you'll follow me, I'll show you to your table."

"You did reserve us one of the private tables, didn't you, Alex, honey?" If the blonde's purr got any better, then she would be lapping up cream.

"They were already reserved, Catherine," Alex murmured. "I believe I mentioned that."

The sound of his voice stroked down Janey's spine. And it shouldn't have. She shouldn't have any reaction at all to a man she couldn't have.

"All it takes is the right tip." Catherine laughed, a silky, smug sound, as Janey turned at the small table marked for Alex and his date.

"Your server's name is Tina. I hope you enjoy your meal." She smiled at them, let the curve freeze in place, and tensed as Catherine's finger touched her wrist.

"This table won't do," Catherine murmured as she slid a fifty against the back of Janey's hand. "Could you fix that for us?"

Janey glanced at the fifty, to the woman, then to Alex as he watched the scene silently, his brows darkening.

"I'm sorry." She drew back from the other woman's touch, stifling a shudder. "This is the best we have. Enjoy your meal."

"Perhaps we should find another place to eat, Alex." Catherine's smile was cold.

"You're welcome to that option." Janey nodded at Alex. "I'll even waive the cancellation fee, Alex."

"Catherine can do as she pleases." He shrugged his wide shoulders. "I'll be staying."

Catherine pouted, but as he pulled her chair out, she huffed and took her seat before casting Janey a glare from beneath her lashes. Her blue eyes spat anger.

"I'll send Tina over." Janey nodded. "Enjoy your dinner."

"She's uppity for the daughter of a traitor," Janey heard Catherine murmur.

Janey kept going. Shaking inside, feeling something crawl into her chest and rake at it with ragged claws.

"Tina, I need you to—"

"We won't be staying."

Janey swung around at the touch of Alex's hand on her arm. He looked furious. His gray eyes were darker than normal, his brows lowered and nostrils flared. Janey's gaze moved behind him. Catherine was flushed, furious.

"If she means so much to you, then perhaps you should stay, Alex," the blonde sneered. "Though I'd have chosen better for a man of your rank. Patriotism is to be applauded."

Alex's jaw clenched. His hand snapped out, encased Catherine's wrist in firm fingers.

"I'm sorry, Janey," he said softly. "It won't happen again."

"Of course it will." Janey smiled stiffly. "It happens several times a night, Alex. But I'm sure I can fill the table." She nodded to Catherine. "Have a good night."

She turned away from them, marked their name from the list, and kept her head down as Alex pulled Catherine toward the door.

She did lift her lashes just enough to sneak a peak at that gorgeous male ass, though. She was all for being cool, composed, and all the good stuff that kept the restaurant running, but some sights a woman didn't miss out on. No matter how uncomfortable she felt at the sight of this man with another woman.

Well, perhaps more than uncomfortable. She was damned mad and she didn't have a right to be. She was hurt, and again, she didn't have a right to be.

It was one kiss, because she had begged. Because he felt sorry for her. And the last thing she wanted was Alex Jansen's pity.

"Ms. Mackay, there's a couple waiting in the reception area that was requesting a table a few moments ago." Her manager, Hoyt Napier, stepped from the register.

Hoyt was just a few inches taller than Janey in her heels. At five-eleven, he was slender, dark-haired. Twenty-four years old and sometimes, she swore, her lifesaver, despite his sometimes melancholic intensity. Deep brown eyes were surrounded with thick brown lashes, and tobacco brown hair was brushed neatly back from his broad forehead. Between him and her brother's adopted son, Faisal, she managed to keep her sanity.

Everything about Hoyt was neat. His hair, his clothes, the way he helped her run the restaurant, and how he often tried to shield her from the snide comments directed at her. Even Hoyt's mother, Augusta, it seemed, wasn't pleased that Janey had come home.

"Let them know we have a table ready, then." Janey nodded, turning back to the reservation book and staring at Alex's crossed-out name pensively.

There was no time to dwell on the event, or the woman Alex had with him. But that didn't keep her from doing it. From imagining him with the curvy blonde. Janey knew he was angry, but Catherine would purr her way out of trouble. Janey was certain.

So why did that thought hurt so damned bad that it made the rest of the night more difficult to endure than normal? As she had told Alex, that wasn't the first snipe of the night that she had heard, and it wouldn't be the last. Being the daughter of a traitor, a man who had fooled almost everyone he knew into believing he was patriotic, kind, and to be respected, wasn't going to be easy.

The fact that she had taken over his thriving business, and the sensationalism of the arrests and events that had occurred six months before, grated on people's pride. It was a damned wonder someone hadn't killed her.

Sometimes she thought the only reason they hadn't tried was because of her brother, Natches, and their cousins, Rowdy and Dawg. And Uncle Ray. Who had stayed at her side in the hospital for more than a week. His wife, Maria, had babied her as though she had raised her. And Natches's twenty-one-year-old adopted son—and that one still amazed the hell out of her—was normally at her back like a guard dog. Thankfully, her chef had taken him into the kitchen this week. Faisal took his duties seriously while he was at the restaurant, and he considered her family. Evidently, he saw the family the same way Natches did. Worth killing for. It was scary how much alike her brother and his adopted son were.

Too bad Faisal hadn't been around the night Dayle Mackay had literally kidnapped her.

She barely remembered her uncle Ray shedding tears three days after she was admitted into the hospital. Where the doctors had confirmed that the rape kit had shown none of the signs of rape that were consistent with the bite marks on her breasts.

No, she hadn't been raped, but what Nadine had done to her had scarred her in other ways.

She didn't sleep well. Not that she ever had, but the insomnia was sometimes worse now. The nightmares could be brutal.

Natches knew. When she looked in his eyes at that hospital, she'd seen the grief there, the fury. He knew, and there had been no one left to strike out at.

She'd had the restaurant for three months now, ever since the Department of Homeland Security turned it over to her and her brother, and it was thriving. Because she let the customers snipe. Because she played the perfect little robot. Just as she had before her father's death.

"Another full night," Hoyt murmured as they cashed the last

customer out at nearly midnight and locked the doors behind them. "The kitchen staff is nearly ready to leave unless you require anything."

Janey shook her head as she rubbed her lower back and turned to stare at the huge dining room. There were several private screened areas that could be enlarged or made smaller. There was a banquet room that was normally closed except to large parties and would have to be reserved well in advance.

"I don't require anything, Hoyt." She finally shook her head. "You can go ahead and leave. Has Faisal left yet?"

Hoyt nodded. "Your cousin picked him up a few minutes ago." He paused. "I heard what some of the customers said tonight." He frowned lightly. "You act like it doesn't bother you."

It tore a strip from her every time it happened.

"What can I do?" She sighed. "Dayle was what he was. Nothing is going to change that."

"Does that mean you're to blame?" Hoyt asked her heatedly. "You didn't do it."

"But I'm here to blame." Janey shrugged. "Grab something from the kitchen to take home to your mother. There's plenty in there. I'll see you tomorrow evening."

He shook his head and moved to the kitchen. When he left by way of the back doors, Janey locked up behind him, then checked the front doors again as well.

Augusta Hoyt had been ill lately; Janey hoped some of the food that the chef put back in the refrigerator for their lunches the next day would cheer her up. She never came to the restaurant, refused to associate with "the traitor's daughter." Janey was damned lucky everyone else was too nosy and gossipy to feel that way.

But that was a small town for you. Somerset was a tight-knit community. Most everyone knew everyone else, and the controversy only made them more curious. They loved their hometown heroes, and her brother was one of those heroes. As were her cousins. That meant she was "almost" part of the community, therefore not "completely" to blame. She was the one they could snipe at, because Dayle Mackay was no longer there to punish and Natches had captured him, seen him arrested, imprisoned. He was their hero. Janey was their scapegoat.

Small towns were amazingly supportive in some ways. Amazingly cruel in others. And it was home. A home she loved, one she had missed in the years she had been forced to live away from it.

Sighing at the thought, she moved through the dining room and headed to her office.

The restaurant was eerie, too silent. She turned in the middle of the dimly lit room and stared around her. It had not been as busy as it was ever since she had taken over, but she expected the rush to slacken once the sensationalism wore off. Once the newspapers stopped reporting and the tabloids stopped gossiping. Or would that never happen?

She moved to the hall on the far side of the room and then into her office. Janey closed the door behind her. Pulling the hem of her shirt from the narrow skirt she wore, she kicked off her heels and moved to the small refrigerator that sat in the back corner.

She poured a glass of wine and sat down in the heavy leather chair behind the old scarred desk she had moved into the room.

She pulled out the bottom drawer, slapped a pillow on top of it, and propped up her feet before closing her eyes and sinking into the chair.

She meant to relax; she didn't mean to feel the ghostly touch of male lips against hers. A dazed memory of a kiss, butterfly soft, probably so he wouldn't have to touch her too much.

"No." She shook her head, lifting herself, her feet thumping to the floor as she rested her elbows on her knees and pushed her fingers through her hair.

She couldn't let herself think that. It was the only memory she had that wasn't tainted and somehow dirty. The touch of his lips, warm, gentle. That was what they had been, she told herself. Just gentle. So he wouldn't hurt her.

And he had held her tight. Prayed, maybe. She could have sworn she had heard a prayer. Or maybe it was a curse.

She sat back in the chair and lifted the wineglass, tipping it to her lips and swallowing a healthy sip. Well, probably more like a drink, she thought as she rubbed at the back of her neck. If she didn't manage to relax, she would never get to sleep tonight.

She was taking another sip—drink—when a heavy knock landed on the outside door.

Natches. Or one of her cousins. They checked up on her often.

She finished the wine quickly, wiping her lips as she moved around the desk.

"Just because the lights are on doesn't mean someone's home." She pasted on a fake smile.

It froze on her lips. Because it wasn't Natches or one of her cousins. It wasn't even her uncle Ray or the overprotective Faisal.

It was Alex.

He stared down at her, his expression as stoic as always, his brows heavy over his thunderous gray eyes, his brown and dark blond hair a little longer than it had been six months before.

He moved into the office, the slightest limp betraying the wound he had come home with.

"Restaurant's closed," she told him, turning to face him, still holding the door open. "Or did you somehow miss the sign in front?" She widened her eyes innocently. "I forgot to put one on the back door, huh? Geez, who knew customers could get turned around that easy."

"Don't be a smart-ass, Janey." He sighed, running his hand over his short hair. It wasn't quite a buzz cut anymore, but it was close.

And he was too damned sexy for words. Dark flesh that always looked tanned. Those dark, stormy gray eyes and lashes thick enough to make a woman want to kill for them.

She closed the door. Slowly. Quietly. She wasn't going to give in to the need to slam it. Robots didn't slam doors, did they?

"Fine. So tell me what kind of problem you had with locked doors and closed signs." She moved around him back to the desk, poured another half glass of wine, and faced him.

She had a feeling a bottle of whiskey wouldn't be enough to numb her against Alex.

He shoved his hands into the pockets of his dark slacks, his lips quirking with a small grimace as he looked around the office, before his gaze moved back to hers.

"I'm sorry about Catherine," he finally said.

Janey rolled her eyes. "You going to apologize for the rest of the night, too?" She shook her head and sighed wearily. "Hell, Alex, she wasn't the first. She won't be the last."

He was silent, staring back at her, his expression heavy.

"Why are you here?" She waved the wineglass toward the room. "It's after midnight. Didn't Catherine want to put out after you made her leave?"

His frown deepened. "Maybe I was the one that didn't want to put out."

"Oh. I'm sure." She sat on the corner of the desk, pushing back until her feet dangled off the cold floor as she sipped at her wine. "Still hurting from that leg wound?"

She nodded to the hard thigh muscle—hell, she shouldn't have looked there—where he had taken a bullet to his leg in Iraq. Alex was always getting shot, knifed, or almost blown up. He'd come home for a while, heal, and be back at it.

"The leg doesn't stop me from putting out, Janey," he drawled, that quirk of his lips turning into a half smile. "And I don't need excuses not to spend a night with a woman. Catherine was being a bitch and she knew it."

She widened her eyes mockingly. "You said the B word, Alex. Bad boy. You should never call a woman a bitch."

He grunted at that.

"You've been in the military too long," she told him.

"Probably." He looked around the office again. "Do you live here, Janey? Shouldn't you be upstairs relaxing instead of hanging around the office?"

"Shouldn't you tell me why you care?" She arched her brow. "Really, Alex, your girlfriend didn't hurt my feelings. You can go give her a little nasty with a clear conscience now."

"What makes you think I wouldn't be fucking her if that was what I wanted to do?" he growled.

Janey widened her eyes again, pretending to be scandalized. "Your language, Alex."

Actually, she might be having fun.

"I don't beat around the bush, Janey." He pulled his hands from his pants pockets and folded them across that mile-wide chest of his. "You want to talk sex, I'm all for it. But don't expect me to get flowery over it. And don't think I forgot about the question I asked you."

Why the hell was he here? Janey stared back at him, trying to make sense of his presence. Six months since he had pulled her out of Nadine's house, a month since he'd come home, and she hadn't seen him. Why now? Why like this?

"I just closed up." She lifted the wine and sipped at it. "I was relaxing a few moments before I had to haul my tired butt up those stairs."

"Lock up. I'll carry you up."

He was serious. Janey blinked up at him, then forced herself to finish the wine before sliding off the edge of the desk. She could feel the tension now. It was coming off him in waves. Sexual tension.

"Just because I may have somehow caused you to miss out on a little piece of tail tonight doesn't mean I'm willing to substitute myself for her." She slid her shoes back on, the three-inch heels giving her almost enough added height that she didn't feel as though he was towering over her.

She could feel that tightening in her chest again. But it wasn't claws tearing at her; it was a sense of excitement. And she didn't need it.

"Did I ask you to fuck me?"

Her stomach clenched at the sound of his voice. He might not be asking for it, but she had a feeling he was thinking about it. And she was thinking about it. And she was stepping into seven different kinds of trouble if she dared to mess with this man.

"Good thing you didn't," she told him softly, staring back at him regretfully. "I don't think you'd have much fun."

"Really?" he drawled.

"Yeah. I hear virgins are a bore to men of your advanced years, Alex. Go find your girlfriend. She'll give you better sport."

Alex stared back at her. Years of training kept his expression from slackening in total shock. And a superhuman effort kept his hands from reaching out for her and jerking her against him.

"A virgin?"

"See? I'm not even fair game," she told him as she collected her purse and keys. "Are you ready to leave now? Because I'm kind of tired."

She opened the door, forcing herself not to shiver as the cold February air whipped around her stocking-clad legs.

"I'll walk you up."

He looked determined, implacable.

"Alex, I don't need another guard dog." She sighed as he stepped out.

She set the alarm and closed the door, locking it quickly behind her before moving up the wide, wood steps to the small balcony and apartment door upstairs.

"There's no inside entrance?" Alex asked behind her.

"Only in my dreams." She felt like groaning. She hated walking these stairs every night.

Alex watched her walk, watched her cute, tight little ass bunch and her hips sway. He was rock hard; images of taking her, seeing the innocence in her eyes as he filled her, were torturing him.

She was right; he should have been turned off. The thought of a virgin should have him running for the hills. The hell if he should be following her to her apartment like an obedient hound.

He could have sat in his truck and watched her to the door.

But, he told himself, that wouldn't mean she was safe. Someone could have gotten into the apartment.

Yeah right. Sitting in the truck wasn't going to get him under that skirt of hers. And knowing she was a virgin wasn't helping things.

It sent a shaft of possessiveness burning through him. And that, he didn't want to feel. He didn't feel possessive about women. It wasn't allowed and it wasn't part of his life.

So why the hell was he standing on her balcony now, watching as she unlocked the door and stepped inside? She disabled the security, closed the door behind them, and flipped on the lights.

He watched as she kicked off her shoes; spiky black heels, they made her legs look sexier than hell. She dropped her purse on the little table just beside the door and moved into the wide living room before turning on a lamp and turning to face him.

"See, I'm safe." She lifted her arms out to indicate the room, the apartment.

Alex shook his head slowly. Safe from everything but him. "You know what I want, don't you, Janey?"

Her arms dropped to her side. For a second, just a second, she lost that unemotional, cool expression she had worn every time she had seen him in the past month since he had returned home. He saw her eyes flare with interest, with need, a hint of fear. Then, just as quickly, they were gone.

"No, I don't know what you want, Alex." There was a thread of anger there now. "Do I owe you something? Is there something here that belongs to you?" Her lips quirked mockingly. "I don't think there is, I don't think there's anything here that you want to do more than play with."

And she wasn't a toy. The implication was there, and he knew, son of a bitch, fury searing his guts, he knew what Nadine had done to her. How she had asked Dayle to let her just "play" with Janey for a while.

The doctor's report, Janey's recollection of it—it had all been in Chaya's report to Timothy Cranston, the agent in charge of that investigation last year.

Alex had read it. He had forced himself to read it. To look at the pictures the hospital had taken of the bite marks on her breasts. Janey wouldn't tell them if the bitch had touched her anywhere else. For months Alex had dreamed he had killed Nadine slowly, slow and painfully, rather than the quick death he had given her.

"There's many different kinds of play, Janey," he told her softly. "There's nothing vindictive or painful in what I want. You know that."

She turned away from him, one hand propped on her curvy hip, the other lifted. From where he stood he could see her chewing on her thumbnail, and he almost smiled. That was a "Janey" trait. It wasn't a good sign. She was trying to hold back, anger, pain— whatever emotions Janey didn't like to deal with.

He knew her. Sometimes he thought he knew her better than Natches did. Because there were times when he hadn't been on as- signment but had watched Janey, wherever she was, instead.

From that day on the lake, six years before, when Janey had teased when she shouldn't have teased. When she had awakened a hunger he hadn't known lived inside him, though she had always brought out a possessiveness he hadn't known he had. And he had worried about her. Worried to the extent that several times a year he had shadowed her, watched her, kept tabs on her when he wasn't there. Until this past year. Shit had gone to hell with the operation in Somerset, and he'd let himself get distracted. He'd pulled the tail off her to gather intel on other subjects instead. And this was what had happened.

Janey had nearly paid with her life.

She turned back to him.

"Leave." Her mask was back. That cool, professional, I-don't-feel-a-fucking-thing mask. She was protecting herself and her emotions, and no one understood the need to do that more than Alex did.

Alex grimaced and nodded. "I can do that."

But his feet weren't moving. He wasn't turning and heading for the door. Because he couldn't. Because he had waited too long, wanted for too many years. Walking away now seemed impossible.

"So why aren't you?" Her gaze flickered again.

She wasn't nearly as cool as she wanted him to think. Emotions seethed inside Janey; he could see them, feel them. He wanted to taste the hunger he had glimpsed in her eyes; he wanted to feel it burning him.

"I want that kiss, Janey."

Her green eyes seemed to darken, almost. Just a shade, maybe. And it wasn't anger.

"What kiss?" Her breathing was heavier now, deeper. Her breasts lifted and fell, pressing against her white blouse with tempting promise. And her nipples were hard. The sight of those tight little peaks held him entranced.

"That kiss you teased me with the day I pulled you out of Nadine's." He moved toward her, stepped behind her.

Alex let the scent of her wash through his senses. An essential smell of feminine warmth, of sweet heat. The smell of a woman, mixed with the peachy scent of soap and the delicate fragrance of shampoo. The scent of her shouldn't have been as arousing as it was.

She had cut her hair. It was straight, tamed, framing her face like black silk ribbons, instead of long and filled with the riotous curls that tempted his hands. This hair was tempting, too, though. So damned tame and restrained that it made him wonder exactly what she was trying so damned hard to hide within herself.

The pulse was throbbing at the side of her neck, almost as hard as the pulse in his dick, and the urge to taste her sweet flesh was nearly overwhelming. He wanted to lick her from head to toes. He wanted to taste her, grow drunk and wild on her.

"You kissed me." Her voice was weaker now. "I remember it."

"Do you call that a kiss, Janey?" He lowered his head. He didn't touch her any other way. Not with his hands, or his body, just his cheek against her hair. "That wasn't a kiss, baby. That was a tease. You owe me a real kiss."

She licked her lips, and he nearly groaned. Her expression wasn't cool now; her profile was flushed, and yes, her eyes were darker.

"Why now?"

"Because the thought of it has me crazy wild, sweetheart. I want to taste you, while you're conscious, while you know whose lips are on yours and whose tongue is in your mouth. I want that kiss, Janey." He let his hands settle at her thighs, then smooth to her hips. "And by God, I want it now."

TWO

Fuck Natches. Fuck dying. Alex had lived dangerously all his adult life; he didn't see a reason to stop now.

Alex knew if Natches caught him fooling around with his baby sister, then death would be the least of Alex's worries. But like an addict, like a man addicted to the scent, the taste of one woman, Alex found himself enthralled. He found himself unable to walk away.

Fourteen years separated their ages, but nothing separated the desire he could feel burning between them except the clothes they were wearing.

She was as wary as a doe, standing before him, poised to run, quivering, uncertain about the next touch to come. She ached as much as he did. Something about that knowledge almost humbled him. That the same hunger that filled him could fill her as well. Just as strong. Just as deep, despite the distance in their ages.

If she hadn't told him she was a virgin, he would have suspected it now. She didn't know if she should stay or run, if she should allow him to touch or if she should fight it. Fear and need battled within her, and Alex had to force himself to rein in his lusts, the hard-core center of his hunger, to give her a chance to come to terms with what he sensed was unfamiliar ground to her.

"Natches will kill me for this." He let his lips touch her ear, and she jerked, inhaling a harsh breath as she swallowed with a tight reflex of her throat. "He warned me, Janey. Six years ago. Not to touch you."

Natches had threatened to cut Alex's dick off if he ever touched Janey.

"I can tell you're really scared of my brother," she said, her voice breathless, her expression intent as she stared straight in front of her, obviously battling whatever emotions, or needs, were rising inside her.

"I stayed away," he breathed against her ear. "Six years, almost seven, Janey. I stayed away."

He moved in closer to her, his hands tightening on her hips as he pressed his hips against her, letting her feel the hardened state of his cock beneath his slacks.

She gave her head a little shake and shuddered.

"Why are you doing this?" Her hands moved to his wrists.

Small, graceful hands. Her nails dug into his flesh as she held on to him. She didn't relax against him, but she wasn't fighting him either. Like a creature unused to any touch that didn't involve pain, she was debating what would come next. If the gentleness would dissolve.

Alex wasn't surprised by the fury that rose inside him, but he was surprised by the fact that the hunger rising inside him was overriding it. Christ, he needed to touch her. If he didn't, then the pressure building inside his balls was going to destroy him.

And if he did, the need was only going to get worse.

He could feel it. It was one of the reasons he'd left town

immediately after her rescue. It was one of the reasons he hadn't returned until he was forced to. Because staying away from Janey had been damned hard before. He had a feeling it was going to be impossible now.

"Janey, I'm not going to force you," he told her, letting his lips drift over the shell of her ear.

Her breathing was harder, faster. Her lashes drifted over her eyes and he watched her face flush, slowly. Need made her skin take on a rosy glow, made her lips look poutier, prettier. He almost groaned at the need to feel them under his.

Her hands tightened on his wrists. "I don't know what to do. I don't know what you want from me."

He turned her slowly, slowly, in case she wanted to run, in case she needed to run. Tipping her chin up, he stared down at her with a sudden gentleness he hadn't known he was capable of feeling.

"Whatever you want to do," he told her softly. "We can do whatever you want to do, Janey. But we start right here."

And his head lowered.

Janey's breath caught in her throat. She stared up at him, eyes wide, caught, held, like a deer in headlights, as she watched his face lower. One hand threaded in her hair, pulling her head back for him. His arm curved around her hips, lifting her to him.

She had never seen his expression like this. Tight with lust, his eyes flinty with it, brows lowered, brooding. When his lips touched hers, she felt something inside her explode. A radiant heat, a need, cascaded through her, filling her senses as her lips parted, her hands gripping his arms, trying to lift closer to him. Trying to draw herself into him. Trying to take as much of this feeling, this sensation racing through her, as she could consume.

Her lips parted as his slanted over them. His hand gripped the back of her head, one arm anchored her back, and she just wanted to crawl into him. She wanted to be closer, wanted more. She whimpered with the need, feeling his lips grow harder, hungrier, in response.

Oh yes. This was what she needed. His lips opening over hers and his tongue pressing against hers. Deep, hard kisses that burned her lips and filled her body with sensations she hadn't expected.

There was no fear allowed here. This was her kiss, her first kiss, her first real kiss that swamped her with such blazing pleasure that she couldn't fight it. She didn't want to fight it.

She could feel years of need exploding inside her. Years of fantasies and dreams about this one man. The one man she had always known she could never have. It wasn't their ages; it had been the danger Dayle represented to anyone she would care for.

And now that danger was gone. She could have; she could have this man. Her hands tightened on him, her need for his kiss growing more desperate. She could have so many things she couldn't have had six months ago.

"God! Janey." Alex lifted his head, only to lower it again.

His lips moved over her jaw, beneath it. Her arms tightened around his neck and she tried to get closer, tried to steal the kiss back.

Then he was bending closer, his hands gripping her rear and lifting her, pulling her against him.

"Put your legs around my waist," he growled. "Hold on to me, baby. Hold on tight, and I'll give you what you need."

She obeyed instinctively, then cried out when her skirt bunched at her hips, and she felt hard, muscled abs between her thighs.

But his lips were on hers again. His hands kneaded her butt, his lips ground against hers, tongue curling over hers. Driving explosions of light erupted behind her closed eyelids. She could feel him in every cell of her skin and she wanted to feel him deeper.

Between her thighs, she could feel herself growing wet, swollen. Throbbing sensation pounded at her clit, inside her vagina. She was a mass of sudden internal explosions of need, and nothing mattered but this wild crescendo of pleasure now pounding through her.

The sensations were frightening, exhilarating. They burned over her flesh, seared her insides. She felt herself growing dazed, sensually weak and unable to sate the need for more and more sensation.

"Alex." She moaned his name when his head jerked back, the strong column of his neck flexing with strength as she heard him inhale, hissing a breath from between his teeth as he gripped her rear and lowered her. Lowered her just enough to allow the thick wedge of his erection to press between her thighs.

He was huge.

Janey stiffened, her eyes widening, staring into his narrowed gaze as he moved her against him, stroking the soft silk of her panties against the distended knot of her clitoris.

Technically, she knew exactly what he was doing. Technically, she knew exactly where this was heading, where over the years, she had rarely gone past the fantasy of just this kiss.

"You know what I want." His voice was hard, his gaze fierce.

No, she didn't know what he wanted. Technically, yeah, she knew. Physically, emotionally, she was suddenly terrified of the need whipping through her. Burning her. Because it didn't make sense. Because it went too deep, was too blinding. Because it made her feel weak, dazed. Unable to fight against the swirling flames building inside her.

"Let me go!" She was pushing at his shoulders when she didn't mean to.

Suddenly, a sense of panic overwhelmed her. Not fear of Alex, but fear of herself. Fear of the sensations, the emotions she couldn't quite grasp.

"Let me go, Alex!" She struggled out of his grip, stumbling as he set her back on her feet, his expression dark, forbidding, as she pushed away from him, almost falling before she steadied herself by the couch and jerked her skirt back down over her thighs.

"Leave. Please." She kept her back to him.

She was shaking. Quivering from the inside out and she couldn't make sense of it. She was hot and cold at the same time, spiked with energy and yet lethargic.

"It's natural, Janey." He spoke as though he knew.

Janey swung around, glaring at him. "You don't know what I feel, Alex. Don't pretend you do."

His eyes were steely gray but calm as somber determination lined his face and his expression grew heavy.

"You're twenty-three years old," he said. "You lived in a vacuum of no touch, no affection for too many years. And then you had to suffer through the hell Nadine and Dayle put you through. A man's touch will be scary at first. Frightening. But it will ease."

Janey shook her head at his confidence, his sheer arrogance.

"And of course you're the man to get me past that fear," she said harshly. "Why didn't I come up with that on my own?"

His lips quirked at her mockery. "Maybe your senses are a little off balance right now," he suggested. "I'm sure, in time, you would have considered it."

She glared at him. "Why don't you just go home, or go find your little blond piece of fluff and leave me alone?"

"That's no longer an option." His voice hardened. "The blond fluff, that is. I've developed a taste for you, Janey. And I want more."

Janey felt as though her head were spinning. He couldn't be serious. She stared up at him. He was over six feet, broad, so muscular he made her mouth water. Powerful. And large in every way.

This wasn't a nice, steady, unassuming man. This was Alex. Bold. Larger than life. A warrior who knew who and what he was and how to use that perfect body of his. In a variety of ways.

"What if I don't want more?"

Oh yeah, she saw that one happening. She was going to be fantasizing about that damned kiss for the rest of her natural life.

He almost smirked. That little tug at his kiss-swollen lips clenched her stomach.

"You want more right now," he told her, his gaze flickering over her. "Don't bother lying about it either. Your nipples are still pointed hard beneath your shirt and your face is still flushed. I'm not some kid you can lie to, Janey. I know your pussy is hot and probably so damned wet I could drown in it." His voice turned to a growl; his lashes lowered. "I want to drown in it. I want to run my tongue through all those hot juices and eat you until you're screaming for more."

Oh God. Her knees were weak. Her legs were going to collapse right beneath her and leave her a puddle on the floor moaning just for that.

"Then maybe I need someone younger," she bit out. "Maybe I don't like where all that knowledge of yours came from."

He grinned. It wasn't an amused grin either. It was knowing.

"You've been touched by a man now, Janey. A kid isn't going to still that fire inside you. You'd grown past that at seventeen and we both know it. That day at the lake, the boys rumbling around there, twittering and playing their damned games for your attention didn't faze you. Nothing did. Until you caught me staring at you."

She hated the fact that he was right. That somehow, something inside her had matured past the "boys" her own age a long damned time ago. And any chance she would have had to experiment with men was snatched from her grasp with a single phone call from Dayle. A warning. She had been under his control and he didn't let her forget it.

"Why are you doing this?" She shook her head, confused now, uncertain.

Alex was more than just a man. He was more than just physically powerful. There was a confidence, a dark edge inside him that made her wary.

She had a feeling Alex would push boundaries she'd never

imagined. He'd demand more than she had to give, and sometimes she feared she had very little to give anyone.

Janey had learned early just how easily everything she cared about could be sucked right out of her life. She didn't think she could bear to lose anything more.

"I don't have time for you." She shook her head. "I don't have the strength for you, Alex."

"Then you better find it, Janey." He moved, a ripple of strength, and as she watched he was crossing the room and moving to the back door. "Because I have a taste for you now. But even more, you have one for me. It won't be that easy to forget." He paused at the door. "And don't make the mistake of thinking just any man is going to fill that taste. I wouldn't be happy."

"Threatening violence, Alex?" Her heart thudded with sudden wariness.

He shook his head, that grin sending a surge of anger through her.

"I'd never hurt you, Janey," he promised, his voice raspy, graveled. "But if you want a chance to navigate your own way through this, then don't pull another man into the battle. Or I'll keep you in my bed for a week and show you just why that won't do." His expression shifted, became harder, more sexual, darker. "Oh, baby, I'll show you exactly why no other man will do."

Her lips parted to blast him. Yell at him. Curse him. And she would have. She'd never done that in her life, but she would have, if he hadn't slipped out the door and closed it behind him, leaving her staring at it in dumbfounded fury.

Arrogant. Conceited. Overconfident. Prick.

"Asshole," she spat into the empty room before clamping her lips closed.

God. She never called anyone names. She never confronted anyone. She never got too close to the fire. And what the hell was she doing now?

She lifted her hand, touched her sensitive lips, and closed her eyes against the pleasure. Then she couldn't help herself. Her fingers trailed down her neck, over the curve of her breast, to the hard points of her nipple.

She gasped. A surge of feeling rushed from the hardened point straight to her clit and exploded in a detonation of need before she jerked her hand back.

Once, a long time ago, Janey had known how to touch herself at least. She was a woman. And she'd ached for touch, anyone's touch, and had been too frightened to defy Dayle by accepting a lover.

So she had touched herself. Something she hadn't done since Dayle had allowed Nadine to touch her.

She bit her lip and paced to the kitchen. She fought the memories, but they were there. The way Nadine pulled her T-shirt over her breasts, loosened her jeans. And Janey hadn't been able to fight her.

She leaned against the table, pressing her hand over her mouth to hold back the instinctive need to be sick. She could barely tolerate touch since that, even her own. Until tonight. And tonight, nothing had filled her head but Alex's touch.

There had never been anything more frightening in her life than being unable to move, unable to fight, forced to let that evil bitch touch her.

And Dayle had just watched.

A sob tore from her throat. He had just watched, amused, indulging his depraved sister with affectionate humor.

"I hate you!" She yelled the words, her hand jerking a kitchen chair from the table and slinging it with jerky strength across the floor.

It crashed into the wall as she pressed her fists into her stomach and fought the tears that would have fallen from her eyes.

She wasn't crying. She hadn't cried since the day it happened, and she wouldn't cry now. She would be okay. By morning, she'd have her control back in place, she'd bury the hurt and the pain and force that mask on her face, and she'd do all the things Dayle had refused to allow her to do as she grew up.

Tomorrow, the restaurant was closed. She had a girls' night out with one of the few people she had ever connected with as a friend. Drinks and snacks at the local bar. She'd never been to a bar. Music and wild men acting like fools, she was told.

The thought was terrifying, but she would do it. Because she wasn't dead. Because there was so much she had never done, and she needed to learn how to live.

She didn't need to learn how to want Alex Jansen, though. That was a recipe for disaster.

As she stood there, she heard a plaintive meow from outside, a demanding sound and the pad of soft little paws against the door as the monster stray tapped impatiently.

"Decide to come visit me again?" Janey called out in a shaky voice as she moved to the door and opened it to allow into the house the mangy, overgrown cat that had somehow managed to target her.

She shook her head as he moved to the food bowl in the corner of the room. As he ate, she showered, changed into loose pajamas, and returned to the living room, where the large orange male cat was curled up on her couch.

She knew the routine. She sat down on the other side, turned on the television, and waited.

Still wary, the cat crept across the couch, watching her from slitted, narrowed eyes. Warning her not to dare to touch him. She watched the news, one arm propped on the arm of the couch, watching the animal from the corner of her eye.

He was beautiful. Scarred, ragged. The tip of one ear was missing; his nose had a thin scar through it. But his fur wasn't matted anymore. He had cleaned himself up nice, and she had managed to secure a flea collar around his neck a week ago.

He growled as he neared her, and she ignored him, because she knew he was all bluff. If she moved her arm or shifted to him, he'd take a swipe at her, but otherwise, it was all for show.

Finally, he moved against her. Watched her. Then took a heavy paw and patted at her hand. She lifted her arm and a second later he was curled in her lap, allowing her fingers to shift through his fur as he purred against her and settled down for a nap.

He was finally fattening up. He'd been bedraggled, skinny, when he first showed up more than two months before. He'd been in one too many fights, and pride and hunger had glittered in his topaz eyes as she set out a bowl of cat food mixed with hamburger.

Now, in the past weeks, he was demanding more than just food. He was demanding affection. Nothing and no one had ever demanded affection from her. Before the cat, she had just lain on the couch until she couldn't hold her eyes open any longer, then trudged to her cold bed.

Now she stayed here until the animal grew tired of her petting.

The cat was safe, she decided. All he wanted was the food and a few strokes over his heavy body for a while, then he was good to go.

But tonight, he didn't go. He lay there and lay there, until Janey couldn't hold her eyes open another moment.

"Come on, Fat Cat." She pushed at his heavy butt. "I have to sleep."

Surprisingly, he didn't scratch her for her daring. He rose, stretched, and hopped off the couch, looking at her expectantly.

"Time to go have fun, huh?" She moved to the door, then paused. He wasn't moving behind her. "Do you want out?" He blinked those yellow eyes back at her sleepily. "Last chance." She yawned. "I'm going to bed."

When he didn't move, she shrugged, checked the litter box she kept on hand, then checked the security system, and moved to the bedroom.

She turned down the heavy quilt, flipped the light on low, and moved into the bed. As she pulled the quilt over her, she was surprised to feel a heavy thump at the bottom of the bed.

Lifting, she stared down at the cat as he curled at her feet, his eyes blinking back at her. Wary. Warning. And her lips quirked as he growled at her.

"Night, Fat Cat," she murmured, rather enjoying the warmth against her feet.

She could get used to this, she thought. Just a little bit of affection. It felt good. As she drifted off to sleep, the thought floated through her mind that she somehow knew Alex would demand so much more.

More than that kiss.

More than just a little sex.

A lot of sex.

She didn't know if she should be frightened or excited. But as sleep took her and the dreams began to filter through her head, for once they weren't nightmares. They were Alex. Kissing, stroking her. Alex murmuring against her flesh. Alex. Demanding.

Alex sat in his truck and watched the apartment far longer than he should have. The street had cleared of traffic, the old center of town was empty, all but deserted at this time of the night, and he was sitting there staring at a woman's window like a lovesick fool.

Hell, how had he let himself come to this? He hadn't even done this crap when he was a dumb-fuck teenager. And it looked like he was about to get caught.

Hell. Sheriff Mayes's cruiser eased up behind his truck as Alex laid his head back against the seat and hit the electronic locks to release them. A second later, Zeke was sliding into the pickup, his sheriff's hat in his hand, watching Alex with a considering expression.

"I've sat out here a time or two and talked to Natches, one of his cousins, or his uncle Ray. But this one is a first for you, Jansen." He leaned back against the door. "Something I should know about?"

Alex stared up at Janey's window. "I'm a fucking dead man." He sighed.

He trusted Zeke. Trusted him more than the Mackay boys did, and had no doubt anything he said would stay with Zeke. Another slipup. A year ago, he wouldn't have given a damn. Nothing would have induced him to tell the sheriff anything personal.

Zeke turned his head, looked up at the window, then back at Alex, and let out a soundless whistle.

"Damn, Alex. Natches is as protective over that little girl as he is his new wife and that skinny kid he had brought out of Iraq. Are you sure about this?"

"No." He was damned sure he was going to end up fucking her, no matter what he told Zeke.

"You're fourteen years older than she is, Alex. That's a lot of years. If you don't have more in mind than a few hot nights, then you better watch your ass. Or your head. Because Natches is damned good with a sniper rifle himself."

Actually, Natches was better at it than Alex.

"Yeah. I better be careful." But not because of Natches. Fighting Natches wasn't what worried him. Hurting Janey. The thought of that bit at him.

Zeke sat silently then, staring up at the window with Alex.

"She tell you about the notes?" Zeke asked then.

Alex lifted his head slowly. He and Zeke were more than just friends. Before Zeke got out of the military, they'd fought together a time or two. They had more of a connection than Zeke had with the Mackay boys. Alex knew when Zeke was telling him something sensitive.

"What notes?" he asked carefully.

"Yeah, I was afraid she was keeping it to herself, especially after she made it a point to make me swear to investigate it myself. Hell. Damned Mackays. Every one of them is trouble in one way or the other."

"What notes, Zeke?" Alex could feel the tension tightening in his body then, the hairs at the back of his neck lifting in warning.

"There's been three in the past two months. Words cut out of the newspaper and taped to plain white paper. No prints, nothing unusual, no way to trace it. Always left somewhere she won't miss them. The first was taped to the door of her apartment. The second shoved under the front door of the restaurant. The third was shoved under her apartment door. All three warning her to get out of town. That a traitor's slut wasn't wanted in Somerset."

Damn. Alex felt his hands curling around the steering wheel, tightening. Violence raged through his body, and the need to exact vengeance slammed inside him.

"Natches doesn't know?"

"She made me swear I wouldn't tell a single Mackay." Zeke smiled at that thought of that. "I haven't told a single Mackay."

No, he was telling Alex. Alex slid him a furious glance. The bastard.

"So I get to spread all the good news?"

Zeke shrugged before pulling a plastic envelope from inside his jacket. "I was out looking for you tonight anyway. I was waiting for you to heal up a little bit before we talked. You're still officially deputized with DHS last I heard, so this is your business."

Alex took the envelopes. "Copies?"

Zeke nodded. "All three of them as well as the report where we dusted for prints. We didn't find anything. But I don't like the tone of those letters, Alex," he admitted. "They worry me."

They worried Alex now. And what worried him even more was

the fact that Janey wasn't telling her family about them. They could protect her, help watch out for her. Yet she was taking it on alone.

"You weren't able to find out anything?" Alex asked again, even though he knew Zeke would have told him if he had.

"Nothing. And I'm worried about her. I hear the crap that goes on in this county. And I've been in that restaurant to hear some of the comments she gets. She's like a damned robot in there, and people can be mean. They keep striking until they see blood. Janey doesn't show blood. It could end up getting her hurt worse."

Natches was going to have to know about this. If Zeke thought the youngest Mackay cousin would kill him for fooling with his sister, it was nothing compared to what Natches would do if Janey ended up hurt and he'd had no idea there was a threat against her.

"Natches is going to be pissed at you, Zeke," Alex warned him. "He'll know you held back on him."

Zeke shrugged. "It won't be the first time, will it?" His voice was filled with amusement. "Be careful, though, Alex. Janey's not the play-around type. She's been hurt a lot in her young life. There's no sense in adding to it."

No. There wasn't. But damned if he could stay away from her now.

"I know that, Zeke." He knew it clear to the bottom of his soul.

Zeke nodded and left the truck, leaving Alex to stare up at that damned window as the light went out. She was going to bed. His body clenched at that thought of it. Did she sleep naked? Somehow, he doubted she did. She was young, a virgin; had she learned how sensual the sheets could feel against her naked flesh?

He would show her. Show her how erotic it could be to sleep naked, curled against his body, his hands petting her through the night.

He closed his eyes and breathed out roughly. His cock was pounding in his slacks, fully engorged and torturing him with the need for sex. Not just any sex either. Oh hell now, it had to wait thirty-seven years to get picky and decide it was getting hard for only one woman.

One younger woman.

He was hooked on her kisses, and he had a feeling he was about to get hooked on much more than those perfect sweet lips.

He groaned at that thought. Natches would kill him for sure, but after that kiss earlier, Alex decided, it just might be worth it.

THREE

Alex pulled into the marina parking lot a little after seven the next morning. It was damned cold on the water in February. Those Mackays were frickin' insane. All three of them were still on the houseboats, all of them with very pregnant wives.

Certi-fucking-fiable. That was all he could think. One of those very pregnant wives was his sister, Crista, and Alex was still ready to blow Dawg's head off for not having that house ready yet. If it weren't for the fact that Crista was the one holding things up, he and Dawg would have already fought.

He looked around and saw Ray Mackay's pickup in front of the marina office, though he knew Ray wasn't there. He'd called the other man that morning and asked him to meet him at Natches's.

Shit. This wasn't going to be easy. Natches had just gotten his sister back, thought she was finally safe and secure, and now this crap. And Janey, Alex knew, hadn't mentioned a word to her brother.

He stepped out of the pickup, tense, wary. Dealing with the

Mackays all at once wasn't a fun time to be had, and bringing news like this?

He couldn't get those letters out of his head, though. They were brutal, filthy trash. No wonder Janey was so damned wary, almost frightened, last night. She couldn't know who was doing this to her; she would suspect everyone, and he couldn't blame her.

He moved quickly from the parking lot along the docks. As he neared the *Nauti Dreams*, Natches's houseboat, the door opened and Natches stepped out. He was still as wild as the wind, Alex thought. Dressed in jeans and a T-shirt and bare feet. His black hair was mussed, his dark green gaze sharp despite the drowsy look on his face.

"You're working early, Major," Natches drawled as Alex stepped onto the boat. "Playing Cranston's lapdog again?"

Alex sighed. He'd been working with Cranston for years. His team was one of the agent's favorites to call out for the hairier assignments. Alex had already been called before a review board twice because of the insanity that was Cranston. But damn if the agent didn't make life interesting.

They called him the Rabid Leprechaun, and Cranston was inordinately pleased with that title. So much so that his agents and Alex's team worried that he took it a little too seriously. The thing about Cranston that the Mackays never understood, though, was that it wasn't about the manipulations he conspired to do; for Timothy, it was all about the past and everything he had ever lost. It was about retribution. And in ways, it had been for Alex as well. He understood that. For Alex, though, the thoughts of retribution were melting away beneath thoughts of Janey.

"Not this time, Natches." He shook his head as he stopped in front of his friend. "We need to talk."

Natches's eyes narrowed dangerously before he inclined his head into the houseboat. "Well, we're all here as you asked. Keep your voice down, though; Chaya's still sleeping."

Evidently, all the Mackay women were sleeping. Ray, his son, Rowdy, Dawg, and Natches were waiting, but Crista, Kelly, and Chaya were absent.

He stepped into the wide front room and stared at the men huddled around the table at the side, a pot of coffee between them.

"Alex, good to see you." Ray Mackay, Rowdy's father, with his sharp Mackay green eyes and graying black hair, waved him over. "Get a seat, son. We have a cup for you." He poured coffee into a cup as Alex stepped over to the table.

He didn't sit down. Neither did Natches.

"Seven in the morning," Natches commented with a drawl. "Must be trouble."

"Trouble follows Alex," Rowdy grunted. Evidently he didn't like getting up early anymore either.

"So does Cranston," Dawg commented mockingly. Another less-than-polite Mackay. Hell, they were nicer than this before they decided monogamy was the spice of life.

"No Cranston this time." Alex pulled the letters from inside his jacket, unfolded them, and handed them to Natches. "I got these last night. They've come in the past two months, to Janey."

Natches took the letters slowly, his gaze locking with Alex's. He could feel the sense of danger, the ragged, burning fury already building as he stared into the other man's gray eyes.

When his eyes moved to the letters, his blood began to boil.

Traitor's whore. Slut. You're not wanted. Get out of town before you're carried out in a casket.

Traitor bitches aren't wanted. You dirtied yourself with daddy and auntie. Did you moan for them? Did you beg like the bitch you are? Take your dirty ass out of town before you're taken out.

Fucking daddy and auntie isn't nice, little bitch. Get the fuck out!

Natches could feel the fury burning, building.

"She didn't tell me about these." Natches handed them to Dawg and Rowdy, knowing what was coming once they read them. "She would have told me."

Fear was balling in Natches's gut now. This was what Janey had been keeping from him for months? Was this why she had moved from the marina to that apartment in town, so he wouldn't find out?

God, she didn't even trust him, her brother, to help her? But why should she? He hadn't been able to help her in all the years Dayle had controlled her. What would make her think he could help her now?

"She made Zeke swear not to tell you about them. It was the only way she agreed to turn them over. I'm still officially on the investigation from last year. He turned them over to me instead."

Natches turned away and reached for his boots. He and Janey were going to have a talk. Now. This wasn't happening. Damn whoever had written those letters to hell. He wasn't letting anything else destroy his sister.

"Where are you going, son?" Ray rose from the table.

"To get Janey."

It was the only solution. Get her back in the middle of the Mackay clan where she could be watched, protected. There was no other choice.

Alex watched him. He understood Natches's determination, but he'd also seen Janey's last night in that apartment. She would fight her brother, draw further away from her family. That wasn't the answer. He had the answer; he just had to let everyone see it in their own way.

"And do what? Lock her in a box?" Alex asked him. "Show her she's still a child with no control over her own life?"

Natches paused, one boot on, one off, his expression twisting in disbelief. "You think I'm going to let some fucking crackpot threaten her?" His voice rose. "Did you read that trash, Alex? What if it were Crista?"

Alex ran his hand over his hair. "I thought of that." He nodded. "I'd go after her. And we'd fight. And she'd push me as far away from her as she could if she thought she could handle it. I talked to Zeke again before I came in this morning. Janey thinks it's pranks. She's not going to budge."

Natches's expression twisted in fury.

"That's not pranks," Natches yelled. "Dammit, Alex. You know that. That's not pranks."

"You're not going to convince her of that," Alex warned him.

"Are the three of you going with me?" Natches turned to his cousins, his uncle.

They were already getting ready to go. Their expressions were hard, murderous. And Alex couldn't blame them. Janey was still a kid to these men, unprotected, terrorized her entire life, and she was still standing. They wanted her to have peace, not more fear.

"Thanks for the tip," Natches snarled. "You can go home now."

Alex arched his brow. "Get fucked, Natches. This is my business, too. Or did you forget who you tagged years ago to help keep an eye on her?"

This was going to get dicey as hell, because he knew damned good and well Janey wasn't going to let Natches lock her up.

"Every one of you has lost his mind."

They swung around as Chaya moved from the back bedroom, the mound of her stomach barely poking against the T-shirt she wore over her pajama bottoms.

"How the hell did I know you wouldn't sleep through this?" Natches grimaced at his wife as she moved into his arms. "Go back to bed."

"Not on your life." She shook her head. "And you better think before you go to Janey screaming your little heart out. She's just like you, Natches. She's going to go her own way, no matter what you want."

And that was pretty much Alex's opinion of the entire situation.

"She's smaller than me," Natches informed her. "She's coming back here. Period."

"Bet me."

Alex could see the ragged rage and pain in Natches's face, and he understood it more than the other man knew. Alex had nearly lost his own sister to this bullshit. When Johnny Grace, Nadine Grace's son, had impersonated Crista and stolen government missiles. Johnny had realized no one believed it was Crista, and his lover had kidnapped her and Johnny had nearly killed her.

It was Natches who had saved her. He'd killed his own cousin with a sniper rifle as Johnny had tried to kill Crista. Yeah, Alex knew exactly how he felt, but now Natches was going to see what Alex had known even then. Sisters didn't always do what you wanted them to do. No matter how dangerous their way turned out to be.

"I have to try, Chaya." Natches moved away from her, grabbed his leather jacket from the hook on the wall, and turned back to the rest of them. "Ready?"

"Ready!" Dawg, Ray, and Rowdy already had their coats on and were heading for the door.

"Natches," Chaya called out as he opened the door to the houseboat. "Don't push her too hard. You'll regret it."

He stared back at her, his eyes alive with the anger burning inside him.

"I'll do what I have to do to protect her, Chaya."

She smiled at that. "You'll do what you *can* do, Natches. What she lets you do. Remember that."

Alex watched the other man's jaw tense, a sure sign he was grinding his teeth, and if the situation hadn't been as serious as it was, Alex would have grinned.

Instead, he followed the other men out and up the docks to the vehicles. He got in his truck as the others got in theirs, and damned if he didn't feel sorry for Janey this morning.

This was too dangerous, though, to let it go. Too dangerous not to let her family know about it. Losing Janey wasn't an option. And if he didn't let the Mackays know, and something happened to her, then he would never be able to look his own sister in the eye again.

They drove, four pickups in a row, into town and then along the town square. Mackay's was in a converted office building at the end of the block, near the town square. Parking was on the street, a large lot at the side, and in the back. Lately, there hadn't been enough parking.

It was closed now, the windows dark. Alex pulled his truck in beside Natches's on the private side of the building. Rowdy, Ray, and Dawg parked on the street. Alex saw the curtains in the apartment over the restaurant flutter, and felt Janey staring down at the street. Shit was going to hit the fan now, and Alex had a feeling he was right in the line of fire.

He made sure he was behind the other four as they moved up the stairs. As they reached the landing, Alex wasn't the least surprised when the door was jerked open and Janey stood there glaring at all five of them.

"Zeke has a big mouth," she snapped before turning and stomping back into the apartment.

"Why the hell didn't you tell me, Janey?"

Janey heard the edge of hurt in her brother's voice and turned to him, raking her fingers through her hair and glaring at him.

"Because of this." She waved her hand at the Mackays and Alex. Shooting Alex a look of retribution, she sneered. "Let me guess, you were the little messenger boy?"

"First a lapdog, now a messenger boy." His smile was tight.

"I'm going to start showing y'all just how well I make decisions on my own."

"We'd have to give you a decision to make first," Janey snapped, crossing her arms over her breasts and staring back at the men.

Damn. She had cute cousins, but they didn't look cute this morning as they frowned at her. And Uncle Ray didn't look happy at all.

"You could have told us about the letters, little girl," Ray berated her gently. "You think we're going to stand by and let someone hurt you?"

"Evidently she does." Natches's voice was quiet, but rough with anger. "Is this what you think of me, Janey?"

She shook her head slowly. "No, I never thought that, Natches. I thought exactly what I see. The four of you coming down on me like a ton of bricks just before you demand I come back to the boat and live with you."

His eyes narrowed. "It's the only way to protect you properly."

It was the sure way to drive her slowly insane. There was no way she was living with Natches and Chaya again.

She glanced at Alex. He should be fixing this, not leaning against her damned wall like an amused mannequin.

His brow arched, the condescension in his expression causing her to grind her teeth.

"I'm not leaving." She made the statement firm, flat.

She cleared her face, pushed back the fear and the pain, especially the fear that she would disappoint or hurt the family she'd never had a chance to love except from afar.

"You can move in with me and Maria," Ray offered. "That would be a good alternative."

"No, it wouldn't." It would steal the independence she had fought so hard for. "I'm not moving in with anyone, Uncle Ray."

She forced herself not to show any nervousness. She clasped her

hands in front of her and faced five of the strongest, most determined men she had ever known or heard of in her life.

"This is not acceptable, Janey." Natches's voice rose. He didn't
yell or scream, but the anger in his face caused her to flinch.

"Enough, Natches." Alex shifted from the wall. "Contain that
temper of yours or get the hell away from her."

Janey threw him a surprised look before she jumped in front of
Natches, her hands on his chest as he moved for Alex.

"Are you going to hit him?" she asked quietly.

"Right in the face," Natches snarled.

"Would you really do that to me, Natches?" she asked. "Would
you hit a friend, a man who saved my life six months ago, just because you were out of line?"

His expression twisted. Fury, concern, and love—he stared at
her with all those emotions, and it made her feel like slime. Like
the lousiest sister in the world.

"Janey." His hands clasped her shoulders. "I read those letters,
honey. Whoever wrote them is dangerous."

"Whoever wrote them is a coward," she told him, moving away
from him, rubbing her arms as she forced back a shiver of dread at
the thought of those letters. "Let it go. I'm handling it."

"Let it go?" Dawg beat Natches to the exclamation. "On what
planet were you raised, Janey, that you think we're going to let this
go? You're family. Do you think we're going to let someone hurt
you? Terrorize you? Again?"

"I think you can't really stop it." She shrugged, hiding the shame,
the bitterness at the thought of those letters. "None of us can.
They'll get bored and stop."

"And then what?" Natches demanded. "Let me tell you, Janey.
Then they get dangerous. Then they start taking shots at you."

She curled her lips bitterly. "And you want me to let you stand
in front of me. Again? I'm not eight anymore, Natches. And Dayle

is dead. Even then, I learned how to fight my own battles. I'll fight this one, too."

"Son of a bitch, Janey!" He reached for her again, and the swift strike of fear that filled her must have shown on her face, because he stopped. His brows lowered in agony, his lips tightened. "Did you think I'd hit you, Janey?"

"No, dammit, I don't think you'll hit me." She was so tense now she felt as though the slightest touch would shatter her. "You moved too fast, Natches. It freaked me out. Okay?"

The quick, predatory action of her brother's body often had her forcing herself to contain her reactions to it. Dayle had always been quick, quick to hit, to push, to backhand her if he thought she were in the least resistant to what he wanted.

Learning to control her reactions around men, any man, had been her hardest battle in the past months.

"Janey, we're family," Rowdy said then. "If you won't come to the boats where we can watch you, or to Dad's, then we'll have to take turns staying here with you. It would be easier if you'd stay with one of us."

She lifted her gaze beseechingly to Rowdy. He was usually the sane one. The one the others listened to.

"Rowdy, I'll be okay. I can't just leave."

"And, Janey, we haven't had you back with us long enough to take that risk," he told her gently. "Hell, if we had raised you ourselves, we couldn't take that risk, sweetheart. You're family."

And she felt that; she did. It made her chest tighten with emotion, made her want to run to Natches and have him hug her, hold her, just 'cause he made her feel this way. That he cared that she was safe. That their cousins cared that she was safe. She wanted to hug all of them. But hugs had never been a part of Janey's life, and taking one for herself now wasn't that easy.

"You're too damned stubborn, Janey," Natches accused her.

"So says the kettle to the pot?" she asked sweetly.

Fat Cat chose that moment to walk arrogantly into the room, his rumbling growl directed at the men before he crouched and gave them all a little hiss. His orange fur seemed to bristle, and he gave all the appearance of a grouchy, ill-tempered male that didn't want to deal with socializing that morning.

His head turned to Janey, topaz eyes glittering as though blaming her for all the testosterone parked in her living room. Or maybe he considered it his living room.

"What the hell is that?" Natches glared back at the cat.

"That's Fat Cat." She grinned.

Walking over to the cat, she lifted his heavy body into her arms and moved to the door. "Come on, vicious. Time for you to go outside."

Fat Cat rumbled a protest as she opened the door. Setting him on the balcony, she received a hard slap at her hand by his sheathed paw, and a hiss before he jumped up on the railing and stared at her with feline anger.

"Be good." She wagged her finger back at him. "Or I'll forget the hamburger in your cat food tonight."

His whiskers twitched as his slitted eyes narrowed back at her. Janey turned back and closed the door behind her. Just what she needed, another pissed-off male.

"So, Uncle Ray, do I get to bring my cat when I come to stay with you?"

Ray looked at the door skeptically. "Only if you have to."

Janey almost snorted at that. Cats and water didn't always go together, so she doubted the male Mackays had much experience with cats. Especially fat cats. She was going to have to put him on a diet soon. He was getting heavy.

If she had to leave, he would end up hungry again. This was his territory, where he was comfortable. And Janey had found that, in ways, it was hers as well. She was comfortable here. She had a routine, the semblance of a life.

"Look, I'm not leaving." She shook her head at them as she moved to the coffee cup. Dealing with a roomful of Mackays and one Jansen mountain wasn't her idea of morning fun.

"Then we'll take turns staying here. There's five of us including Alex. You'll be taken care of," Dawg decided.

She swung around. "Unacceptable."

"Highly acceptable, except for the Alex part," Natches bit out. "Don't push me, Janey. I'm still having fucking nightmares due to Dayle and Nadine. I don't need this right now."

"And you think I need this?" She waved her hand at the five of them furiously. "Fine. You want someone to play babysitter, then he can do it." She stabbed her finger at Alex. "If he wants to play tattletale, then he can also play night watch."

Alex's brow arched, his gray eyes filled with amusement.

"No!" Natches barked. "He's not staying."

"Then no one is." She shrugged. "Been great seeing you this morning, bro. Tell Chaya I said hi, and give that little bundle she's carrying a pat from me. Close the door on your way out."

She could feel five male gazes on her, searing her, trying to see past her expression. She stared back at them calmly.

Natches was frankly furious. Alex was amused. The others ranged from simply pissed to disbelieving. They were all too big and too stubborn and too determined to run her life. Hell, she had known when that first letter showed up exactly what was going to happen if Natches found out about it. She'd have to let Sheriff Mayes know exactly what she thought of his promises.

"This won't work, Janey," Natches bit out.

"Of course it will. He can show up after I'm finished at the restaurant at night and leave the next morning. No problem." She shrugged.

"And the rest of the day?" Natches pushed the words past gritted teeth. "You think from midnight to dawn is the only time you're in danger?"

"It's the only time those letters have shown up," she said. "He can do it my way, or you can forget it."

"You don't mean this! Janey, tell me you don't mean this!" Natches's expression was blank with shock now, his eyes brighter in his sun-darkened face, and that wasn't normally a good sign. He was outraged.

Alex watched Janey coolly. Her expression, as calm, as remote as it appeared, hid much more than anyone in that room could guess. Her bravery was boundless. Her courage was terrifying. But he already knew that. He'd figured that out over the years while watching her.

She was pissed. She was stubborn as hell. And she was about to make every damned one of them pay for coming here and backing her into a corner. He almost grinned as he watched her maneuver the Mackays. And she thought she was maneuvering him as well.

She had no clue.

He'd known when he pulled into the parking lot of the marina where this would go. He'd already weighed out the possibilities and come to one conclusion. Hell, he'd managed to do that while he was sitting on the street outside last night.

Leaning against the wall now, his expression controlled, arms crossed over his chest, he watched her play her brother and her cousins with a confidence and sheer daring that only a Mackay could muster. When one of the males of that family used it, it never failed to piss him off. But watching Janey do it, he was hard as a rock and praying to hide it. Thankfully, he'd left his jacket on. Because sure as hell, if Natches had a clue just how hard Alex was for his baby sister, blood would be spilled.

"Tell her how insane this idea is!" Natches turned on him when Janey refused to listen.

Alex grimaced and rubbed at the outside of his thigh. "I am wounded, Janey," he informed her. "I might not be your best bet."

Her expression was almost smug. "Too bad." She turned to Natches. "Do you guys want coffee before you leave?"

Everyone looked back at Alex.

He scratched his jaw and stared back at Janey, eyes narrowed.

"Why him?" Natches turned back to her suspiciously.

"Because I don't have to put up with all the moaning and groaning at night like I would if it were one of you." She rolled her eyes back at him. "Really, Natches, all that marital bliss is too sweet for words."

All three of the younger Mackay men developed an almost smug look on their faces as Alex finally winced. He didn't want to hear about their marital bliss, because one of them was married to his sister.

"I don't like it," Natches muttered, plowing his fingers through his hair again. "Damm it, Janey. You need someone around the clock. Not a night watchman."

"If anything other than letters happen, I'll consider it," she promised him.

The fear was there. Alex saw it, even if she did think she was hiding it from her brother. Those letters had her spooked, and rightfully so. But guts and courage were Mackay traits, even if they were mixed with pure hardheaded stubbornness.

"How long is your leave?" Natches clearly wasn't happy.

Alex arched his brows. "I have extended leave right now. I'm clear."

He could feel the other men watching him closely.

"I don't like this," Natches muttered again.

"Look at it this way," Janey chirped. "You get what you want." She turned to Alex, tilted her head, and smiled with a tight little curve to her lips. "And he gets to pay for it."

FOUR

Alex followed the others from the apartment almost an hour later, carefully keeping his expression calm and his mouth shut. If he wasn't careful, he was going to chuckle. And that chuckle could risk *his* carefully laid plans.

It wasn't often a man could claim he'd managed to maneuver not just one intrepid little Mackay female, but her brother and two cousins as well. Though, he wasn't so sure about the cousins. Or the uncle. The three of them were a little too quiet, and a little too amused.

Mackays could be subtle when the situation called for it. It just had to suit them to do so. Now, Natches, he wasn't so subtle.

"Touch her. Just one time. Even dare to touch her, Alex, and I'll cut your dick off," Natches warned him as they reached the trucks, his cousins and uncle trailing behind them.

Alex turned to him, staring back at Natches's furious green eyes curiously. "Hell of a warning to give me, buddy," he snorted. "I'm doing you a favor here, not the other way around."

Natches was right up in his face and, under most circumstances, would have found himself flat on his ass for his trouble. Problem was, it he hit Natches, he would have three others just as mean he'd have to fight, and then all his planning would go to hell.

"You don't do anyone favors," Natches informed him heatedly. "And don't think I forgot how you were watching her six years ago." He gave Alex a disgusted look. "She was a baby."

Alex stared back at him coolly. Janey had been seventeen at the time, which didn't excuse him, but she hadn't been a baby.

"I've done the Mackays plenty of favors," he reminded Natches. "The past six years I've busted my ass and my team's to not just do our job, but cover her when we're not on assignment. When on assignment, I've invariably managed to find backup, Natches." He sneered the other man's name. "That was a hell of a favor, buddy."

"From a man lusting after a kid," Natches charged.

Alex had control. He'd majored in control. He was the king of control. But it snapped. Before he realized what he was doing, he had Natches's jacket in his fists, throwing the other man against the side of the building.

"Don't cross the line, fucker!" Alex snarled in his face. "Don't even cross that line."

He was surprised the others hadn't jumped in. He was even more surprised when Natches's expression lost its fury. His hands came up, not to hit, but to jerk Alex's hands back.

"Christ!" Natches dug his fingers into his neck, shook his head. "Hell, Alex. I didn't mean that, man."

Alex stepped back, fury and guilt, more guilt than fury, pumping through his veins as he retreated.

"You're right." Natches ran his hand over his face and shook his head again. "You're right. You've been in this all along, watching out for her. More than I was." Torment creased Natches's face. "You did what I couldn't."

And Alex had lusted. Every year it had grown, surged inside him until now. But Janey wasn't a baby. She was a grown woman. An innocent, seductive young woman. And he was old enough to know better.

"Fuck it." Alex moved back to his truck. "I'll be here after dark. Hell!" He got into his truck and waited. He let Natches pull out first, then, as Dawg moved to the window, he hit the control and lowered the glass.

Dawg leaned against the door, watched Natches leave, then turned back to Alex.

"I know what he doesn't." Dawg nodded after Natches.

"And that is?"

"You want her too fucking bad to walk away." Dawg turned back to Alex, his gaze steely. "And that's okay. She's a damned pretty *woman*." His voice hardened. "And a damned vulnerable one. Break her heart, Alex, and brother-in-law or not, we'll take you apart."

Alex stared back as Dawg nodded, then moved away. Hell, Mackays were a pain in the ass.

He looked up at the apartment, and, standing there in the chill morning air, that cat cradled in her arms, was Janey. How much had she seen? Heard? From the look on her face, probably all of it. He knew the look of a pissed-off Mackay, and she definitely had that look. The only difference was, on her, it looked damn fine.

He lifted his fingers in a lingering salute and shot her a mocking smile before backing out of the parking space and heading down the street.

His things were already packed at home. He was prepared. He'd return in a few hours. And then what? He frowned at that question.

What? Seduce her? Show her how nasty he could get, then walk out on her later?

Hell. What was in his mind? What made him think Janey was anything like the other women who understood that when morning came, he would be gone?

So why wasn't his dick listening? Hell, why wasn't his head listening? He couldn't stop thinking about her, remembering that kiss. The innocence was killing him, and God only knew, he thought innocence was a damned fine thing in a woman. So why did he want to destroy Janey's?

Because it was his. He wasn't even going to let himself think *she* was his, just her innocence. He wasn't going there, he promised himself. He had never let himself get mired in the quicksand of false love, and he wasn't going to let it happen now.

Janey was more grounded than her brothers or her cousins thought she was. More mature than any of them believed. He had seen that in her, felt it in her. Or he was just fooling himself and creating an excuse to allow himself into her bed.

For a second, just a second, he prayed she was strong enough to keep him out of it. Otherwise, he had a feeling he would end up destroying both of them.

Janey was waiting when Alex arrived that evening. She'd called Rogue and rescheduled their girls' night out. She hadn't given the other woman an explanation and Rogue hadn't asked for one. Janey had been torn, though. She wanted that night out. She'd never been dancing. She had never gotten tipsy in her life. She wanted to do both.

She wanted to sway to the music, laugh and have fun. She wanted to be female. Feminine. She wanted to wear makeup and that new skirt Rogue had talked her into buying.

This evening, she wore a pair of cotton running pants and a T-shirt. She hadn't straightened her hair, so the loose curls feathered around her face, almost to her shoulders.

She'd had it cut immediately after coming out of the hospital months before. The long strands had hung nearly to her waist, and every time she felt the weight of it she'd been reminded of how often Dayle and Nadine had used her hair to drag her around.

Now it was shorter, easier to keep up with, and Janey actually liked the way it framed the almost narrow lines of her face.

She was twirling one of those curls around her finger as she sat on the couch going through bills for the restaurant and waiting on Alex. Yet when his firm knock sounded on the door, she jumped, startled.

She excused the reaction. In the two months she had lived there, she had rarely had anyone knock on her apartment door.

Standing, she moved to the door and looked out the privacy peephole to see him standing there. As if it would be anyone else. Opening the door, she stood aside as he walked in, a duffel on one shoulder, a hard, long, narrow case in the other.

Looking into the parking lot, she frowned when she didn't see his truck.

"Where did you park?"

"I didn't." He moved through the apartment to the short hall, and directly to the spare bedroom, as Janey closed and locked the door.

"What do you mean you didn't? Did you walk?" she questioned as she followed him.

"Zeke picked me up at the marina and drove me in. He'll pick me up in the morning when he goes back on shift. It would be best if no one knew I was here with you."

Janey froze in the hall as he spoke from the bedroom. She was surprised at the hard surge of hurt and betrayal that struck her at his words. Of course it would be better if no one knew he was here. He was considered one of Somerset's favorite sons. He was in the Special Forces, part of the investigation that destroyed the homegrown terrorist group Dayle Mackay had been a part of. It just wouldn't do for people to know he was living with a traitor's daughter, would it?

She turned and moved back into the living room, to her place on the couch. She wished that damned cat would show back up. She would have had something to distract her from the sudden pain building inside her chest.

She punched the numbers into the adding machine for the next bill, wishing she could throw the damned thing at the wall instead.

It was best that people didn't know he was staying there? Oh yeah, she could definitely understand that. Why hadn't she thought about that? She should have. When she was trying to put all those big, tough males in their places this morning, she should have considered more than her own pride. She should have considered Alex's reputation.

"Clean sheets?" Alex stood in the doorway now, his tone cool, the typical remote Alex tone.

"Closet in the hall," she told him, her voice low, just as cool. She knew the robot tone, too.

She hadn't made up a bed for him. Somehow. She frowned. Had she actually considered that he would try to talk his way into her bed again? The aberration that was last night flitted through her head. His touch, his kiss, the hunger she had felt blazing within him. Obviously, he had reconsidered that moment of insane lust. She should have done the same. She should have never canceled her girls' night out. She should have left him here doing his damned job and gone out and had fun.

She pushed the adding machine back on the coffee table and tossed the bills back in their pile before rising to her feet and pacing the living room. If it wasn't for him, she wouldn't be here. She could have been in the restaurant doing her job properly or out having fun. She hated vegetating in this apartment as she had done in the apartment in California.

If she had known how worried he was about anyone knowing

he was here, she would have done just that. Instead, she moved into the kitchen, pulled open the refrigerator door, and pulled her wine out.

One glass. That was all she allowed herself a day. Well, sometimes a glass and a half. Tonight, just one glass. She poured the pale liquid before shoving the cork back in the bottle and returning it to the refrigerator.

So much for changing the sheets on her bed. That was wasted effort.

She moved back to the couch and looked at the clock. Hell. It was barely six thirty in the evening. She had at least another eight hours before she went to bed herself.

"Are we having dinner?" he asked as he moved into the kitchen.

"If you're fixing it." She lifted her glass and sipped as she stared at the curtained window across from her. "Or ordering it. Whichever you want to do."

She sure as hell wasn't ordering it for him. And she bet her ass he wasn't going to order anything. That would require actually letting someone know he was there.

He didn't say another word.

"Whatever." She rose to her feet and moved to the phone. "Burgers or pizza?"

His expression was stoic, dark. He watched her, like she'd seen Fat Cat watch a mouse once. Pondering. Considering. Was it really worth his time?

"How 'bout both?"

She nodded and picked up the phone. She ordered enough food for her brother and her cousins to share. She'd done that before. They'd just assume Natches and the others were going to be there tonight.

There. His nice, pristine reputation was still intact. And she felt as though something had shattered inside her.

"Janey." He caught her arm as she moved past him, pulling her to a stop. "What's wrong?"

"What would be wrong?" She blinked back at him with false innocence. "My big, bad-assed brother and cousins decided I needed a watchdog, and I was stupid enough to agree to let you stay. Hell, I thought you'd at least protest."

"Why would I do that?" he asked quietly. "I don't want to see you hurt. Those letters are serious, Janey. Someone wants to hurt you."

"Someone wants to hurt my feelings and run me out of town," she argued, fighting to keep her tone placid. "You're the one that ran to Natches and the others like a damned spy."

"So I'm the one being punished?" He stroked her arm as he released her, running the backs of his fingers down it, and nothing more.

He stepped back. As though he remembered he shouldn't touch her.

"Yeah. Something like that." She moved away from him.

She made it as far as the couch.

"How long did they give you for the food?" he asked.

"Forty minutes." She shrugged, sliding back into her seat and reaching for her wine.

"Enough time."

Her head jerked up at the sound of his voice. He was stalking toward the couch. He'd shed his jacket; the dark T-shirt stretched across powerful shoulders and biceps. His jeans were snug, clearly revealing the erection she had refused to check for earlier.

"For what?" Her voice was weak, breathless.

She was a fool. She should put her foot down right now, let him know she wasn't going to be a toy for him any more than she would be for anyone else.

But then he knelt in front of her. Slowly, his hands cupped over her knees and drew her thighs apart, wide enough for him to slide between them.

"Don't do this." Her hands moved to his shoulders, but she wasn't pushing him away.

What he did to her should be illegal. He made her weak, made her unwilling to fight.

"I don't think I can help it, Janey." He slid his hands up her thighs, the heat of his palms burning her through the cotton pants she wore. "I didn't sleep worth shit last night."

That made two of them. But this wasn't going to help either of them sleep at night, and it sure as hell wasn't going to help her keep her heart shielded against him.

"You were too busy plotting to sleep," she accused him. "You didn't have to tell Natches about those letters."

"Yeah, I did." His gray eyes were darker, his lashes surrounding them like a heavy shadow. "I won't let you be hurt."

Janey pressed back into the couch cushions behind her. She could smell him, and she needed to escape the dark, heated scent.

"Take your shirt off for me, Janey," he whispered. "Let me see you. Just a little bit."

Her nipples peaked harder than they were before.

She licked her lips, her breathing becoming rougher, harder, as his gaze latched on to that action.

"I dare you," he challenged her. "Come on, Janey. Tease me. I give you permission."

"Tease you?" she repeated. "I have a feeling it would be like a lamb teasing a wolf, Alex. We've already established the fact that you can make me respond."

"Make you respond?" His thumbs rotated inside her thighs. "Do I force you to respond, Janey?"

"Don't play word games with me," she protested, hating this response to him, hating herself for being so weak.

His lips quirked. She loved his lips when he did that. The wide, sensually full shape of them made her hungry to taste them. Made her desperate to feel them.

"Can I take your T-shirt off, then?" He leaned closer, his lips touching her jaw as Janey felt her lashes flutter at the warmth of the caress. "I'd do it slow and easy. Give you time to protest. I'd unwrap you like the prettiest present."

She felt his fingers move beneath the hem of her shirt, lift it. She shook, felt herself trembling as the material cleared her stomach, then eased over her breasts.

Memories, stark and brutal, clashed with the need rising, sharp and hot, inside her.

"You're so pretty, Janey." His voice was like a sigh, breaking through the fear that would have risen inside her. "I've wanted to tell you for years how pretty you were, and I knew better. I knew I had no business wanting you, thinking about you."

Her arms lifted as he drew the shirt over her head and dropped it to the couch beside her.

She was breathing hard and fast now, her breasts rising and falling, framed by the white lace of the demi bra she wore. Her nipples were hard, sensitive, pressing into the thin cups as he stared at her, his expression tight, his lips parted as his own breathing roughened.

"It should be a sin for a woman as pretty as you to be a virgin," he told her. "You should have been loved slow and easy. Taken all night long. Licked from the sweet curves of your lips to the tips of your toes."

She was enthralled. His hands pressed against her sides, moved up until they paused just beneath the swollen curves of her breasts.

Janey watched him carefully. Her breasts were tender, sensitive. They had been ever since Nadine had bruised them. The bruising had been deep, but the mental scars had gone deeper.

"I know what she did," he whispered, as though reading her mind.

Janey cringed at Alex's words and tried to push him away from her.

"No, Janey," he whispered. "No secrets between us. Not like this. I won't hurt you."

"Yes, you will," she protested, her voice hoarse. She couldn't seem to maintain that veil of cool disinterest with Alex as she did with everyone else. "You won't be able to help it."

He lifted his eyes from her breasts to her face. "Do you think I'm that rough?" he asked her.

"You could probably make me beg you for any touch you wanted to give me," she admitted. "But I can't handle you, Alex. Not right now. Not like this."

He grimaced. "No games, Janey. I promise. I'm too old for games. We agree to just this, and no one gets hurt."

Just this? Just sex?

She watched him, miserably aware that she wanted him with a strength that was going to destroy her. She knew it would. She could feel it coming.

When his lips touched hers, there was no fight left in her. Except the fight to see how much deeper she could make him kiss her. Her lips parted beneath his, a moan slipping past her throat as her nails dug into the material covering his shoulders.

Tongues dueled. Licked. Tasted. One hand moved from beneath her breasts to cup her neck. His hand was so large that his palm and fingers curled from the side of her neck all the way around the back of it. His fingers were calloused, rasping against her flesh.

He was so big, so hard. She wanted to feel him over her, around her, surrounding her. Her arms wrapped around his neck, her hands flattening to feel the flex and power of his muscles beneath them.

God, that turned her on. The way he kissed her, the way his muscles tensed as the kiss deepened, the way he groaned into their kiss, a sound as hungry as her own. But it was darker, sexier.

"Damn, I love your lips, Janey." He sipped at them, nipped at them. "They fit me, baby."

Janey forced her eyes open in time to watch his head lower.

She stiffened as his tongue stroked over her collarbone.

"I'm dying to taste your nipples," he rasped, his hand moving from her neck back below the breast, where it had rested before. "I want to feel them hard and hot against my tongue. I bet they're sweet. As sweet as candy."

His hands moved, drawing the straps of her bra from her shoulders, easing the cups just beneath her nipples.

"Alex. Alex. I don't know about this." She couldn't breathe. She couldn't seem to draw enough oxygen into her lungs. Couldn't find the strength to push him away.

"Are you scared of me, Janey?" He breathed the words over one nipple. "Do you think I'm going to hurt you?"

She shook her head, but she didn't know if that was an answer.

"Watch me, darlin'," he crooned, looking up at her, his lips lowering farther. "Watch me love this pretty nipple. See what it's supposed to feel like."

At the first touch of his lips, sensation tore through her nipple to her clit. Janey arched, driving the tip between his lips, against the moist, hot flesh of his tongue as he licked over it.

She froze. She swore the ability to breathe was forgotten as she felt the pleasure erupt inside her. Like flames. Like tiny explosions set off beneath her flesh and searing her with their heat.

"How pretty," he murmured, pursing his lips and kissing the tip before sucking it gently, easily, back into his mouth.

Just her nipple. He licked it with his tongue as he sucked it slow and easy. His palm cupped her breast, nearly swallowing the curve before she could even consider fear. Calloused palm and fingers, just holding the swollen flesh. Cupping it. Framing it as he sucked at the hard, sensitive tip.

"Alex." She was breathing again, rougher than before. She felt fevered, too hot, too sensitive. She had been cold earlier. She shouldn't be hot now.

His head lifted, but only to move to her other nipple. As he treated it to the same careful caresses, Janey closed her eyes and fought to hold on to her senses. She was sure there was a reason why she shouldn't be allowing this. She knew there was, but the reason slipped beneath the pleasure.

Her hands held the back of his head now, trying to force him closer as she arched to him, watched his lips drawing on her, the way his cheeks hollowed as he suckled her. He kissed the hard nipples. Let her watch him lick them.

Oh, that was so good. Watching his tongue lick over the hard tip, curl against it. Her thighs clenched as sensation tore across her nerve endings again, shattering between her thighs, filling her clit, the aching depths of her pussy. She didn't know how to fight this. She didn't want to fight it. She wanted it to continue forever.

"I knew how sweet your pretty nipples would be." He kissed one peak, then the other. "Hard against my tongue. Like sugar candy."

Her nails dug into the back of his head, wanting him there again, wanting her flesh in his mouth again.

"I'm going to kiss your clit just like that, Janey. Kiss it slow and sweet. Draw it into my mouth and lick it nice and soft while I suck all its sweetness."

She wasn't going to survive this. She was going to melt into a puddle of pure need at his feet if he didn't stop saying these things to her.

"Then I'm going to push my tongue into your tight pussy." His expression tightened, lust flaring hard and deep in his eyes. "I'm starving for you, Janey. For every touch, every fucking taste."

She was going to orgasm from his words alone. She was going to flame out of control and scream out in need if he didn't do something. Fast. She could feel herself peaking, feel the pleasure building and tearing through her until she didn't think she would survive the culmination of it.

His hands gripped the band of her pants, drew them down as she lifted to him. She needed this, too. She wanted it. Wanted his mouth on her. Wanted the pleasure and the torturous heat tearing through her.

Her lips parted to beg. Her breath had gathered to push the words out, when a hard, loud knock sounded at the door.

"Delivery, Ms. Mackay," a young male voice called out. "Hey, hurry. Your cat's growling at me."

Janey flinched. Alex moved.

He pushed the straps and cups of her bra back in place and had her shirt over her head before she could blink. His expression was no longer sensual, no longer filled with lust. It was tighter now, harder.

She pushed her arms slowly through the shirtsleeves and readjusted her pants. Yeah, now she remembered why she should have never allowed him to touch her.

Shame burned through her. Jerking from the couch, she moved quickly to the kitchen, aware of him behind her, sliding to the side of the door. He checked the privacy peephole before moving to the side, where he wouldn't be seen.

Damn him. Damn Dayle Mackay and this town and her own stupid, traitorous body.

She jerked several bills from the kitchen drawer where she kept extra cash and moved to the door. She shot Alex a glare, hating him as much as she hated herself at that moment.

She swung the door open, pasting a smile on her face for the young delivery boy. Fat Cat shot into the house, sliding past her legs and heading for his food bowl, no doubt.

She handed the boy the money. "Keep the change, Robby," she told him as she took the food.

"Wow, thanks, Miss Mackay. And tell your family I said hey. Natches was in the pizza house last week right at closing. He had to sweet-talk the owner into opening the kitchen long enough to bake his wife one of those pizzas she's been craving."

Another forced smile, a little laugh. "Chaya likes her pizza."

"Yeah. And always right at or right after closing." Robby grinned. "They always give Natches grief, but he talks them into it."

"He can be a charmer," Janey agreed.

"Night, then, Miss Mackay." Robby nodded his shaggy head. "Take care."

"Good night, Robby."

She closed the door and locked it. She paused for a second, then turned, tossed the food to the table, and faced Alex.

"There's your damned food. What you don't want, put in the fridge. You can eat it tomorrow night. I'm going to bed."

And he let her go. She felt his eyes on her, felt the hunger behind her, but he let her go. Only Fat Cat followed, meowing softly as he jumped up on her bed and stared at her as though questioning why she wasn't watching the news. Why she was crying.

And yes, there were tears. For just a moment. As she sat at the edge of the bed, risked Fat Cat's displeasure, and pulled him into her arms.

His fur caught her tears, but the ragged sobs were contained inside her chest. Where they had always been contained, all her life.

The man she had always fantasized about had touched her, and he was ashamed of her. Now just how was that for hell?

FIVE

"Faisal, Desmond needs more cilantro for the dinner course this evening. I need you to run to the grocery and pick up whatever you can find." Janey caught Natches's adopted son as he entered the restaurant several days later.

The young man, dressed in black slacks and a white shirt for waiting tables, moved to her quickly, his black eyes and desert-dark skin a sharp contrast to the white shirt.

"Janey, Mary Lee just called in sick," Hoyt called out from the register counter. "I'm calling Tabitha back in if she can make it."

Janey shoved the cash into Faisal's hands. "Do that, Hoyt," she called out before turning back to Faisal.

"Jane, Natches says I am to stay here. I'm not to take my eyes from you," Faisal told her softly, concern reflecting in his dark eyes. "He will be upset if I go to the grocery."

"I'll be more upset if you don't go," she told him impatiently.

"Look at this place, Faisal. Who would be crazy enough to try to attack me in this chaos?"

Waitresses were moving around preparing the tables and waiting stations. There was pandemonium, as usual, just an hour from opening.

"I need that cilantro and I need you to go after it now, before Desmond has a meltdown in the back. If that happens, I'm going to tell him it's your fault."

Indecision and a flicker of wariness flitted through Faisal's dark gaze. Everyone was scared of Desmond's wrath, even Janey.

"Go." She pushed at his shoulders. "Natches will never know. Cross my heart."

He went reluctantly, casting a worried look over his shoulder as he headed out. Janey smoothed her hands down her pencil-slim skirt and moved quickly to help the waitresses prepare for the first rush of customers. Once the dining room was prepared and the doors opened, it was a madhouse of keeping service and quality at perfected levels while ignoring the jibes and comments of many of the customers.

"Hoyt, we're going to need more flowers from the florist." She moved quickly to the register and wrote the sticky note before taping it into the memo program of the register computer. "We'll be in sorry shape if we don't have them first thing."

The assortment of small flowers in a tiny vase at each table was a personal touch that she knew would be missed if they weren't there.

"I can pick them up on my way in." Hoyt nodded, making a note in his PDA as well. "I should have the morning clear. The nurse will be with Mother in the morning."

A frown creased his forehead as he made the note.

"How is she doing?" Janey paused to lay her hand on Hoyt's shoulder. He'd lost his father in Iraq several years before, and now, with his mother's illness, the young man seemed more worn with each passing week.

"Her medication seems to be working better." He gave her a thankful smile. "Hopefully, she'll rest this week."

"I hope so . . ."

"Janey, this simply will not do." Desmond was rushing from the kitchen, a frown on his dark Italian face, his brown eyes snapping with ire as he waved a limp stalk of celery in her face. "This produce is inferior."

"Call Faisal's cell. He's at the grocery." Her lips tightened at the sight of the celery. "I'll call the produce company in the morning and take care of it."

Desmond's lips thinned. "You will call a different produce company and demand a quality product," he ordered her. "This company, they do not know quality and deliberately give us their worst."

Story of her life.

"I'll take care of it in the morning, but produce could be later arriving in the day," she warned him.

"Rather later than this inferiority." Desmond raged as he turned back to the kitchen. "I have had enough of this. I will call a produce provider." He threw her a furious look over her shoulder. "You are too nice. You do not yell when you need to. I will take care of this."

Janey sighed, shaking her head before turning back to the register counter and smiling at Hoyt. "He's probably right."

"Probably." Hoyt's smile was tentative.

She returned to the tables, preparing for the dinner crowd, knowing exactly why she was getting inferior produce from the local vendors. Maybe she should talk to Natches about it, but he had made it clear he wanted nothing to do with the restaurant. He'd just as soon see it burn to the ground.

Besides, she had promised herself she would fight her own battles; Natches had fought enough of them when she was younger, and he had the scars to prove it.

"I'm here, Miss Mackay." Tabitha rushed in the door and moved quickly to the waitresses' station for her apron and to assess where she was needed the most.

From there, the restaurant was so busy, jumping from minute to minute as each of them fought to keep up with the crowd, that there was little time to think, or to consider the mess she had gotten herself into with Alex.

He'd worked her, her brother, and her cousins. She'd realized that over the past several nights, as he worked at his laptop at the table or disappeared into the room she had given him. He was still working her. Those dark, heated glances, the promise in his eyes that he was merely biding his time, that she hadn't quite escaped him yet.

"Janey, table fifteen has been overbooked." Hoyt rushed up to her, a frown on his face, several hours later. "The customers are lingering over desserts and the next reservation has arrived."

"Charge the table a fifteen-dollar overstay fee," she told him in frustration. "They know the rules. The reservation is for an hour and a half only unless they reserve for more. Have Tabitha prepare the extra table in section two and seat the others there."

She hated being forced to set up the extra tables. It added to the hostessing and waitressing duties, and once the table was there, they had to continue to fill it, otherwise word would get around that they turned away customers when there was an extra table.

She glanced to table fifteen and sighed at the couple there. They invariably kept their table longer and then protested the fee loudly. Tabitha would likely get shortchanged on her tip as well.

Shaking her head, she gathered menus for the additional table and approached the older couple, Charlene and Don Finmore. Don was on the city council and had once been a friend of Dayle Mackay's. At least, he had thought he was. He'd had no idea how Dayle had used him until it was over and the news of Dayle's arrest had come out.

"Charlene. Don." She smiled back at them as they rose from the upholstered, padded bench in the waiting area. "You're table's ready if you'll follow me."

Don was older, in his sixties. Charlene was close to his age, and Janey knew this was their anniversary dinner.

"Happy anniversary." She smiled over shoulder. "Forty years, isn't it?"

Charlene's pleased smile came and went quickly. "How did you know?" She asked suspiciously as Janey seated them and Tabitha moved forward.

"Charlene, I've known you two since I was a little girl," she reminded them. "Of course I remembered your anniversary. I was allowed to attend one of the parties you gave when I was a teenager, remember?"

Charlene's face softened for a moment. "You were fourteen," she recalled. "Your parents weren't going to bring you, until we insisted."

And Janey had paid for it later in a dark, cramped closet.

"I remember the cake," Janey told her, closing her eyes as though the memory were a good one. "It was delicious."

Don smiled then. "I had it ordered from Louisville, just for Charlie."

"And the icing was a family picture." Janey smiled. "I thought it was the most gorgeous cake in the world. Congratulations again, and please"—she leaned close to the couple—"dinner is on me tonight. Forty years together is a beautiful thing to see. I hope you enjoy your meal."

She drew back, whispered the order to Tabitha that the meal was on the house and to make certain the Finmores had the proper care for this special night, then moved quickly back to the reception counter.

The memory of that party was a haze in Janey's mind, but she had never forgotten that cake. A family picture. Parents and children and their infant grandchildren. To Janey at the time, it had seemed like watching a fairy tale come to life as she saw the family interact. And she had, even at that age, known her family was so different, monstrous even, compared to others.

The addition of the extra table allowed several walk-ins a chance at dinner, and allowed for a few extra reservation seatings. By the time the restaurant doors were closed and locked, Janey felt as though she had been through a war.

The waitresses and busboys were working to finish the cleanup, and in the kitchen Desmond and his staff were sanitizing surfaces and preparing to wash the last load of dishes.

"Go relax until everything's ready to lock up for the night, Janey," Hoyt told her. "We can handle the rest of it."

Janey slipped her shoes off as she slid onto the stool at the reservation desk and stretched her arches.

"We need more help." She sighed.

"We've been saying that for weeks," Hoyt reminded her.

"Have another ad put in the papers," she said. "I don't want a sign on the restaurant. I've talked to our other girls; maybe word of mouth will help as well."

Her waitresses made damned good tips for the most part, but the pace was a killer and the paperwork was getting out of hand because Janey was needed in the dining room as well.

"Okay, I'll see if I can make a dent in the paperwork." She rose to her feet, bent, and picked up her shoes, before heading to the office, where she knew what was waiting on her.

It wasn't just paperwork, but Alex.

She pushed her fingers through her hair as she moved closer to the room. He'd be lying back on that couch, reading some kind of magazine. His head would turn to her, that invitation in his eyes.

The invitation to let him take her, to let him stroke and pet her, touch her. Over the past three days her desire for that touch had grown to the point that it was turning into a driving, addicting need. Alex was turning into a need.

She unlocked the office door and stepped in, and there he was, just as she had known he would be. Stretched out on the couch, a computer magazine in his hand. His head turned, the dark shadow of a beard making his gray eyes seem more intense, more stormy.

"Things ran late." He sat up, legs spreading as he planted his feet on the floor.

Faded jeans and a gray shirt. Boots. Too sexy to be legal, as her friend Rogue had said.

"A little." She shrugged as she moved to the small refrigerator for a glass of wine.

She was exhausted and riding on nerves. Alex was making her crazy.

"You're not resting enough," he stated.

Janey almost snorted at that observation. No, she wasn't resting at all. She was tossing and turning, imagining Alex in the bed beside her and going crazy at the thought of the ways he would touch her.

That, added to the incessant concern Natches and her cousins were showing, was exhausting her. She loved them dearly. More than they would ever know, but she just wasn't used to this. Getting a handle on it wasn't easy, and she didn't feel as though she was even being given time to breathe.

"I'm fine." She poured her wine before returning to her desk and sitting down in the large, padded chair.

She tensed as Alex stood up and moved over to her.

"Don't harass me," she warned him with a sigh as she stared at the paperwork. "I have too much . . ." Her lashes feathered closed as his hands came down on her shoulders and his fingers began kneading.

Oh, yes. She almost melted. God, this was what a woman needed at the end of the day. She could have just sunk into her chair and become a puddle of goo at the intense pleasure that began to move through her.

His thumbs worked into the backs of her shoulders, then her

neck. He rubbed and caressed until she would have given him anything to continue. Until she was nearly a weeping mass of relaxed sensation.

And as the stress moved out of her, another tension invaded her. His fingers on the bare flesh of her neck, his breath at her ear as he leaned close.

"Unbutton your blouse," he whispered as he kneaded and manipulated tight, aching muscles.

She wasn't going to argue with him. Not even.

She forced her fingers to move, releasing the tiny pearl buttons and letting the material part over the white, lacy bra she wore.

Her breasts were hard, swollen, aching. She was so ready for his touch. So ready to be stroked everywhere, taken in every way.

Her lips were parting, her head turning for him, when a hard "Natches knock" sounded on the door.

Janey's eyes widened as Alex paused. She knew Natches's knock. She knew he didn't wait. She barely had the first few buttons of her blouse redone when he walked into the office from the outside door and came to a hard, shocked stop.

He blinked back at her as she flushed; then he glared at Alex before he slowly turned his back.

"One. Two."

Fuck, he was counting. She moved to hurriedly button her blouse and restore herself as she pushed at Alex's hands.

"Three. Four."

She had managed the final button when he reached five and turned back. His expression was dark, accusing, as he stared at Alex behind her.

"We need to discuss your assigned duties in this little matter," Natches growled. "Touching doesn't come under that list."

Alex grunted but moved back from her.

"You should wait for an invitation to enter," Janey informed him in frustration. "Geez, Natches. You don't just walk in."

"My name is on the deed, too." He used that as such an excuse and she knew it.

He moved into the room, wearing jeans and riding chaps and a thick leather jacket over the dark shirt beneath. Chaya should keep him locked on the houseboat so he didn't cause so much damned trouble.

"What do you want?" She lifted the wine and took a healthy sip. "Not that I don't enjoy seeing you," she assured him. "But midnight is an odd time for a visit."

"Not when your sister has a stalker." He flicked a look over her shoulder at Alex, then grimaced. "You know he's too old for you, right?"

She was in serious danger of breaking her one-glass-of-wine limit and going for the bottle.

"Natches." Her voice was warning.

He grunted. "I just came to see how you were doing." He shrugged his shoulders restlessly. "Chaya, Crista, and Kelly are doing some kind of girl thing on the boat, and Dawg and Rowdy were pouting in Dawg's. I didn't feel like putting up with the pouting."

"So they were picking on you, and you thought you would share the fun and pick on me?" she asked sweetly.

He grinned, then frowned back at Alex.

"The produce people called me today," he finally told her. "Manager was screaming something about an abusive foreigner cursing at him over celery. Said he lost the restaurant account."

Janey leaned back in her chair now. "So?"

He shrugged again. "The manager's a friend of mine. I just wondered what happened."

"You don't want to know anything about the restaurant unless it finally burns to the ground, remember?" she reminded him. "So why are you here about this?"

His eyes narrowed. "I just told you why."

"Tell your friendly manager to remember me the next time he

decides to send out inferior produce." She crossed her arms on her desk and leaned forward. "It was crap, Natches. I was getting the worst of the deliveries, deliberately, because of Dayle. They haven't figured out yet that the perfect Mackay princess was just as much a pawn in Dayle's games as anyone else was. I don't care about the comments, but I won't serve my customers crap."

Natches was still, silent for long moments. His expression never changed, but she watched his eyes, watched the slow burn of his temper.

"Look, I can take care of the business," she told him. "Desmond arranged a new supplier out of Louisville. We'll get produce later in the day, but we'll have it on time and we'll get it fresh. No big deal."

"The suppliers in Louisville charge more," he reminded her.

"I'm sure we can weather the small jump in cost," she breathed out roughly. "I'm not going back to your buddy for supplies, Natches."

"I wouldn't ask you to," he told her. "Why didn't you tell me what was going on?"

"Why don't you tell me every time Chaya chews your ass for being arrogant and full of testosterone?" she asked mockingly.

"But you're my business, too, and the problems you have here because of suppliers that I know is my business," he informed her, his voice a hard, lazy drawl. A dangerous sound. "Especially when I arranged with someone I called a friend to make certain you were given exactly what you needed."

"Maybe he didn't believe I needed anything better," she remarked, before pushing her fingers through her hair in irritation. "Look, it doesn't matter. It's business, nothing more. I wasn't satisfied with their product so I went somewhere else."

He nodded abruptly, before rising to his feet once again and heading for the door. As he opened it, he turned back to them, leveling a look at Alex.

"I'm going to cut your fucking hands off if I keep catching them on her," he growled. "Damn, find someone your own age."

He slammed the door before either of them could retaliate.

"One of these days, I'm going to cut his tongue out," Alex mused behind her.

"Better do it before he cuts your hands off." She almost laughed, before turning back to the piles of papers on her desk.

God, she wanted his hands on her. But it was do this now or it wouldn't get done at all.

"One hour," he told her, moving back to the couch.

She stared back at him questioningly.

"One hour for paperwork, then I'm dragging you upstairs." He picked up his magazine and stretched back out on the couch. "Better get used to it, sweetheart. Time's counting down."

Unfortunately, she spent more of that hour staring at his sexy body and that hard ridge under his jeans than she did focusing on her paperwork.

At this rate, Natches wasn't going to have to worry about burning the place down. She was going to end up destroying it herself from lack of paperwork completion and an overload of fascination for the man who seemed determined to drive her completely and totally insane.

SIX

Rule number one: He was too damned old for her.

Rule number two: He was too damned hard for a virgin, because nothing in his life had ever been as difficult as taking her nipples with slow precision.

He'd wanted to devour. He wanted to suck her hard and deep into his mouth, nip those tiny hard points and hold her to the couch while he buried his cock hard and deep between her thighs.

Rule number three: Never, ever get emotionally involved with a woman. And it was obvious she made him weak. Otherwise, he'd have never held on to that restraint.

Alex felt like a drowning man a week later as he paced his own house, waiting on evening to fall so he could slip back into her apartment. Ray and Rowdy's suggestion that Alex keep his presence at the apartment as secretive as possible made sense. But it left the whole day without her. He had no reason to linger around her, and no chance to figure out the enigma of Janey.

And he was no closer to figuring out who had left those letters than he had been a week ago.

He stopped pacing long enough to refill his coffee cup and rub at his thigh. Hell, it still ached, even a month later. The bullet that had torn into the muscle and nearly shredded it had been a bad fucker. Bad enough that Alex had put in for extended leave. Time enough to consider if he was returning or not.

He could cash out now with full benefits, no problem. He'd been in the Army since he was eighteen. He could take six months' active reserve and retire at thirty-eight. He'd been thinking too damned much about retiring lately.

Police Chief Harding was making a bit of noise about retiring, and Alex had already been approached about taking the position when he stepped down. Hell, it would beat dodging terrorist bullets and bombs and putting his ass in the line of fire continually.

He had a little niece or nephew coming in a few months. He'd like to have time to be an uncle. He didn't consider becoming a father himself. Not Alex. Hell no. He'd raised his sister, Crista, and swore at the time he'd never risk having kids himself. Shit happened, then your kids had to fend for themselves. Protect themselves.

He ran one hand over his head before rubbing wearily at the back of his neck. More and more often, he was thinking about shit he had no business thinking of. Especially in the past six months. Things like Janey, round with his kid. And this after telling himself all the reasons he had no intentions of having kids with any woman. Things like waking up in the morning, his arms around her. And Alex wasn't the type to enjoy sleeping with a woman. Fucking her, yes; playing bed games all fucking night long, he was all for it. But he didn't sleep as well with a woman in his arms.

Now each night he checked on Janey, turned the television off in her room, and risked that hissing cat taking a swipe at him as he pulled the blankets around her, he found himself wanting to curl around her. He wanted to hold her while she slept, because she didn't seem to sleep well.

At the sound of a car pulling into the drive, Alex moved to the window and looked out, a grin tugging at his lips as he saw Dawg and Crista.

He leaned against the window frame and watched as Dawg helped Crista from the passenger side of the truck. Dawg frowned. Shook his head. Then a male grimace of frustration pulled at his expression, before he leaned against the truck as Crista headed to the front door.

His sister looked maternal and happy. The baby bulge of her stomach gave her a cute little almost waddle. He'd considered teasing her about it, but damn, her temper had been a little iffy lately.

He moved to the door and opened it as she stepped up to the porch. Dawg lifted his hand in greeting, though he was still scowling.

"Dawg's not allowed to come in and play today?" Alex laughed as Crista stepped into the house.

Crista ducked her head and hid her smile as Alex closed the door behind her.

"Dawg's been playing games again." She rolled her eyes. "He's already avoided Natches's fist this morning. I don't want to risk you two fighting."

"Wouldn't be a lot of fight to it, sis," he promised her, kissing her cheek. "Want me to make you some decaf coffee?"

It was a tease. Crista hated decaf coffee. She glared at him for his efforts. "Don't start with me, Alex."

He held his hands up in surrender as he laughed. "So why is Dawg stuck outside while you visit me?"

Alex had a feeling his sister hadn't just dropped by to check on him.

"How's your leg doing? Did you go to the doctor this week yet?" she asked as she moved to the fridge, opened the door, and checked it out. She moved to the cabinets next. "You need groceries, Alex."

"I went to the doctor," he reported. "The leg is healing. And I haven't exactly been at the house a lot this week. I've been eating out."

She turned to face him, crossing her arms over her breasts and resting them on the bulge of her stomach as she leaned back against the counter. Her brow creased thoughtfully.

She finally nodded. "Janey's a good cook. Maybe she'll fatten you up some."

Alex's brows arched. "Janey doesn't cook."

Crista's lips twitched. "She's an excellent cook. The weeks she stayed with us, I swear I gained ten pounds."

Alex scratched his jaw. "She doesn't cook for me."

"You probably pissed her off," she teased him. "What did you do to her?"

Alex stared back at her. "Don't fish, Crista. Get it off your chest."

Crista nibbled at her lip. "Are you sleeping with her?"

"Would she cook for me if I were?"

She rolled her expressive eyes. "Probably. Dawg's convinced you're sleeping with her."

"It's none of Dawg's business."

"Janey's vulnerable, Alex."

"Crista, are you here to warn me out of Janey's bed?" He frowned back at her. "Because if you are, then I think I'd rather visit with Dawg. I can hit him if he pisses me off."

"Which is why I'm in here instead of Dawg," Crista pointed out.

"And it's the reason why you can trot your little butt right back out there with him," he told her. "For Christ's sake. I wouldn't tell you if I was sleeping with her. It's none of your business. Do I question you about your sex life?"

It was bad enough that he knew she had one. And even worse that she had one with one of the wildest men in the county.

"Well, she's not cooking for you, so obviously you're not exactly in her good graces." Crista laughed back at him. "So I don't have to worry about Natches castrating you and ending the Jansen line forever. Right?"

Alex stared back at her broodingly.

"You're not going to sleep with her, right, Alex?"

Sleeping wasn't exactly what he had on his mind. "I wasn't making any hard and fast plans in that direction," he finally said, sliding past the question. "Stop interrogating me before I call Cranston and let him know how damned good you are at it."

She was still watching him worriedly. "I talked to Janey this morning."

His brow arched. "Oh yeah?" Exactly how close *were* Janey and Crista?

"She hedged, too."

Alex ignored her and walked back to the coffeepot, where he refilled his cup before turning back to stare at her.

If there was one person in this world that Alex allowed himself to love, then it was this woman. His baby sister. She was everything that was good and right in his world. Damn if he wanted to hurt her, but she was poking her nose in too deep here.

"I don't want you and Natches to fight," Crista told him firmly. "I wouldn't be happy, Alex."

He set the coffee cup on the counter and tightened his lips. "Fine. I'll castrate Dawg. Since sisters are all off-limits here, I think I'm about due my pound of flesh." He nodded to the bulge of her stomach. "A lot of years overdue, Crista. Dawg didn't exactly do you any favors when you were eighteen, but I let him live."

A shadow of pain crossed her face. The night she had spent with Dawg when she was eighteen had resulted in another pregnancy. A child she had lost. It had nearly destroyed her, and caused her to leave home for almost eight years.

The fact that Dawg had been too damned drunk to even realize what the hell he had done hadn't mattered. The son of a bitch should have kept his head enough to leave her alone. But Crista had been an adult. Alex had raised her to be an adult. And as angry as he had been over it, in some ways, Alex had known the other man cared more for her than he had let on.

"You're fourteen years older than she is," Crista finally said hesitantly. "Janey hasn't had a chance to live yet, Alex."

"Enough."

"Alex, I know you," she said softly. "I can see it in your face. Something's going on, and I'm afraid it could end up hurting all of us."

"Only if Natches decides to make me his business." He stared back at her implacably.

"Janey's his business," she warned him. "I heard him and Dawg talking, Alex. He's not stupid. He knows something's going on."

"Crista, go home with your husband." He picked up his cup and moved to the sink, rinsing it out before laying it in the bowl. "Take care of Dawg and that little niece or nephew of mine and stay out of this. Natches and I can deal with each other without your interference."

"You're all my family now, Alex," she whispered, hurt filling her tone. "I know you and Natches both. He's just got Janey back in his life. He's like a father with her. He's already so full of guilt that he couldn't make things easier for her that it eats at him. And we both know you're not in love with her. If you have an affair with her and walk away like you always do, then you'll deserve the fight he brings you."

"Crista, go home."

He wasn't fighting with his pregnant sister, and he damned sure wasn't going to let the anger building inside him erupt against her. When the hell had the Mackays decided he had nothing more to do than use a tender, vulnerable virgin and then toss her aside like garbage? When had his own fucking sister decided to go along with it?

"Alex . . ."

"Do you think I haven't tried to stay the fuck away from her?" The words tore from him as he faced her, watching her eyes widen in surprise. "Do you think I got up one morning and planned to have a king-sized hard-on for that woman, Crista? What the hell is in your mind? Since when do you take me for some bastard that doesn't give a damn who he hurts?"

Her lips parted. "You are sleeping with her?"

"I'm not sleeping with her, Crista," he bit out. "Do you want me to swear I'm not going to sleep with her?"

She breathed out slowly. "Could you?"

"Not in this lifetime." He shook his head, knowing it was only a matter of time. "And Natches will just have to deal with it if it happens. Won't he?"

She stared back at him in surprise. "Are you . . . in love with her?" she asked hesitantly, then grimaced at the scathing look he tossed her. "Ah yeah. Forgot. Love doesn't exist for Alex Jansen." Then she grinned. And that grin was enough to make a smart man run for the hills.

Unfortunately, Alex was too pissed to be smart. It was bad enough the Mackays thought he was some bastard without morals, but his sister?

"Crista. Look. I have things to do, and making my pregnant baby sister cry isn't one of them," he assured her in irritation. "So why don't you go home with your husband, and stop worrying about Janey."

Her expression, surprisingly, brightened. She straightened from the counter, walked around the room, and before he could stop her she grabbed his wrists and burrowed against his chest.

Hell. He hugged her. Because she was his sister and she'd got him used to her hugs while she was still in diapers. Sometimes he even missed them.

"You know I love you, Alexander Jansen," she whispered as he let his arms tighten around her, just a little bit. "And you are the best brother in the world."

He grunted at that. "Yeah, well. You're not bad for a sister either." He kissed the top of her head and let her go, shaking his head at her moods as she left the house and moved along the walk to where her husband was cooling his heels at the truck.

Alex watched and almost chuckled. The fierce, devil-may-care Dawg Mackay was a fool for his wife. And it was a damned good thing; otherwise Alex really would have killed him.

Crista let Dawg help her into the truck, snapping her seat belt as he loped around the front of the vehicle and then stepped into the driver's side.

"Well, at least you're not crying." He sighed as he started the truck and pulled out of the drive. "You still should have let me go in. I could have at least made him mad before we left."

Crista chuckled. "He has enough problems."

"How do you figure?" He cast her a wary glance. "What kind of problems?"

"I'm not telling you." She laughed.

"Why not?" He glowered back at her. "We don't have secrets, Crista. Remember?"

Her lips twitched. "I'm not telling you, Dawg."

"Why?" he demanded incredulously. "I keep your secrets real good."

"But this is Alex's secret."

He frowned. "He's sleeping with her?"

"He's definitely not sleeping with her."

"He's doing something besides sleeping with her?" He slid her a look from the corner of his eyes. "Things Natches would go ape shit over?"

"Nope." She shook her head.

"Then what's the secret?"

She leaned closer and grinned. "That's for me to know, and you to convince me to tell."

Immediately, lust slammed into him, seared his guts and tightened his balls. Okay, he could play with that one.

"I'll make you scream it," he decided. "Oh, baby. This one will be fun."

"I'll never tell," she drawled.

"Ah, a challenge?" He headed for home. "I can deal with that. Now let's see if you can."

He knew a variety of ways of making his wife talk. And he knew she loved every damned one of them. Yeah, Dawg was so good when he was bad.

Janey slipped from her apartment that evening, made her way to the restaurant office, then sneaked back out the back door and onto the next street. She ducked into the pizza shop there and called a cab, waited impatiently until it pulled up outside, and then she was out of there.

Alex was due to arrive at dark, and it was almost that now. It was edging past five and she had agreed to meet Rogue at the bar outside of town at six. She would be a little early, but it would be worth it. She had a feeling Alex wasn't going to be all about letting her go barhopping with Rogue.

Strangely, despite the fact that Rogue had been injured six months ago because of the information she'd overheard in the investigation against Dayle Mackay, the other woman had still sought her out.

Rogue had come to the restaurant several times, made her friends come. All that leather in one place could be a bit intimidating, but Janey had liked her friends. The big rough-and-tough biker types. The ones Rogue rode with had hearts of gold, even if they were hard-talking and just as hard-drinking.

With her long red gold hair and violet eyes, Rogue wasn't a woman Janey would have imagined enjoyed the crowd she ran with. But there was no doubt she did.

She and Rogue had shared lunch several times in the restaurant before it opened, talking about Dayle and Nadine Mackay. Talking about Somerset. Rogue was better than a psychologist. And she had a way of getting to the heart of a matter without asking a single question.

Rogue reminded Janey a lot of herself, too. She wasn't the touchy-feely type, so Janey didn't have to worry about that. But she was fun, she liked to laugh, and Janey had never really had friends before. She could have friends now, she thought, as she paid the cabdriver nearly a half hour later and entered the bar. She had that option and she intended to take advantage of it.

"You're early." Rogue looked up in surprise from the bar where she was sitting. "And here I was afraid you wouldn't make it at all."

"I told you I wouldn't cancel out this time." Janey slid onto the barstool beside her friend and looked at the bartender. "A beer please? Very cold."

He nodded and turned away.

"Yeah, you said you'd be here," Rogue agreed. "But you've been really short on the phone when I call. I thought maybe you were rethinking our friendship."

Rogue's grin was knowing as she tipped her own beer to her lips and took a drink.

"It's been hell week," Janey muttered, gratefully accepting her beer and taking a long, cold drink.

Every night after dark, Alex arrived. The four days a week that the restaurant was open, he would wait in her office until she was finished for the night.

Those nights weren't so bad. Once Fat Cat ate, she and the cat retired to her bedroom, where they watched the news, often going to sleep while watching.

Each morning she awoke and the television was off. Which meant Alex must have turned it off sometime in the night. And that only pissed her off more.

He hadn't touched her again. He was quiet, often retreating to his own room, bringing his own food with him. He talked to her, very casually. Hell, one night they even discussed politics. Stupid frickin' politics. And she was dying. Tossing and turning at night, dreaming of his touch, waking wet and hungry for him in a way she had never imagined being for a man.

A week. There were no more letters so far. Nothing had happened. She was throwing him out tonight. She'd already made that decision. When she got back, she was kicking him right out the door.

"It looks like hell week doesn't describe it," Rogue drawled. "Sweetie, you forgot the makeup. And the skirt."

No kidding. She might have forgotten her brain in her rush to get away this evening.

"I was in a hurry." Janey shrugged.

"You never get in too big a hurry for your makeup. Grab your beer. We'll run upstairs and fix you up, then come back down after the band gets started."

Janey grabbed her beer, but she wasn't so sure about this.

"Do I look like a hag?" she asked the bartender as Rogue dragged her away.

"Naw, you look sweet." He grinned. "Sweet don't do well in here, sugar."

Great. Now she looked sweet.

"What does he mean by that?" she asked as Rogue dragged her behind the bar and through the Employees Only–marked door.

"He means you look like a fresh-faced virgin." Rogue laughed. "Virgins scare men, Janey. Big boys get all kinds of messed up when it comes to a virgin. So we're going to liven you up some."

"That's a scary thought." She sighed as Rogue dragged her up the stairs. "Liven me up?"

She didn't want to look like a virgin. She didn't want to act like a virgin. She wanted to have fun. To just be Janey. To let free all the bold, vibrant dreams she had held trapped inside her so long.

"Make sure you have fun?" Rogue threw her a laughing glance as they entered the small apartment upstairs. "Come on in. I think we even have some decent clothes."

Janey looked down at her jeans and blouse. "What's wrong with my clothes?" she exclaimed.

Rogue turned back, pursed her lips, and narrowed her eyes. "Janey, haven't you ever wanted to be just a woman?" Rogue asked softly. "Not Natches's sister, or Dayle Mackay's daughter." She grinned. "Or Alex Jansen's responsibility?"

Janey stared back at Rogue suspiciously. "What do you mean by that?"

"Deny Alex is babysitting you right now," she dared Janey. "Now, I doubt many people know about it. But I just happen"— she looked her nails smugly—"to be a little smarter than most people. Besides, I overheard a little comment Natches made to Dawg last week while I was out on the docks at a friend's boat. Something about murder, babysitters, Janey, and Alex. I'm good at the whole two-and-two-equals-four thing."

Janey hesitated.

Rogue smiled back at her. "I'm not asking questions. But a hundred bucks says we have three Mackays and one Jansen that walks in the bar tonight. Now tell me. What do you want them to see? A little girl waiting to be collected? Or a grown woman taking her life back?"

She craved to take her life back. Or rather, to have the life she always dreamed of having. One where she made her own choices, decided her own destiny.

Janey frowned back at her. "I'm not a little girl, Rogue."

"No, you're not." Rogue's expression hardened a bit. "But that's how they see you, isn't it?"

"How do you figure that?"

Rogue crossed her arms over the snug leather vest she wore in lieu of a blouse or shirt. "I know Alex, Janey. And I now his habits. He comes in wounded, finds himself a little plaything, and has hot and heavy fun while he's home before he ships out again. Sometimes he finds a few women to play with. He's as hard and sexual as any Mackay male. And no"—she grinned—"I haven't fucked him. But what I know is that this time no one else has either. And I know he's been staying in that apartment of yours with you, *babysitting*." She rolled her eyes. "Since when are you a baby, honey?"

Janey's lips thinned. "What's in this for you, Rogue?" She wasn't the trusting sort, no matter how much of a baby people wanted to think she was.

Rogue's expression turned bitter for the slightest second before it smoothed out. "Because I've been where you are." She turned and moved to the closet on the far side of the room. "I was sweet and innocent and thought everyone was a potential friend." Long red gold curls moved across her back as she shook her head. "Someone taught me better."

She pulled several hangers from the closet and turned back to her.

"Try these on." She tossed the clothes to the bed. "You have a few more curves than I do. They're loose on me, so they should fit. Daddy didn't check for the correct sizes when he bought them."

Janey tentatively touched the short leather skirt and brilliant red camisole. "Your daddy?" She looked at Rogue in shock.

"I do have a daddy." Rogue laughed. "I wasn't hatched, Janey."

"But he bought these?" She held up the silky stretch camisole. It would be snug. Scandalous.

"He knows what I like." Rogue shrugged. "Get dressed. I have stockings here somewhere. And I know I have heels. Let me find them."

Rogue spoke fondly of her "daddy." How odd would that be, Janey thought. To have a father who bought pretty clothes, provided affection and support. Whatever shadows lingered in Rogue's eyes, they weren't because her father didn't love her. Janey knew from the few conversations she and Rogue had had that the other woman treasured her father.

As far as Janey was concerned, she herself hadn't had a father. Or a mother really. She may as well have been hatched.

She stared at Rogue as the other woman moved into the closet, mumbling about her own clumsy habits.

Janey looked at the clothes again. The leather skirt was very short. To-her-thighs short at least. It would flash stockings. There would be no way to wear a bra with that top. Could she do it?

She had dreamed of wearing clothes like this. Of being confident, feminine. A female force to be reckoned with.

And Rogue was right. Before the night was out, her brother, her cousins, and one irate babysitter would enter that bar. Did she want to look like a child or a woman? Did she want to be herself, or the responsibility everyone else saw when they looked at her?

Hell no. For once, for one night, she was going to let all that wild freedom, all that need inside her, free. If Alex was going to come looking for her, then she'd make damned sure he found the real her this time.

"Do you have red heels?" Janey called out to Rogue.

Rogue popped her head out the closet, her eyes twinkling. "Honey, I have three different shades of red. But I thought you'd go for black."

Janey shook her head. "If I'm gonna be bad, Rogue, let's go all the way."

Rogue's eyes twinkled. "Now you're talking. And you've come to the perfect source, sweetie. Rogue knows exactly how to be bad." She winked, turned back into the closet, and, a second later, emerged with red shoes to match the top.

"Red stockings?" Rogue asked.

Janey shook her head. "Black. Net."

Rogue pursed her lips in a soundless whistle. "Oh man. Things are definitely going to get interesting tonight."

SEVEN

When Alex arrived at the apartment, it was empty. He used his key to slip in. The place was as silent as a tomb. On the landing outside, the cat meowed plaintively but wouldn't come in.

Alex set the food bowl on the balcony, locked the apartment back up, then rushed to the office. He slipped in there. Checked the restaurant. It was still and silent. No sign anyone was there or had been there.

Moving back outside, he jerked his cell phone from his hip and punched the sheriff's number.

"Yeah?" Zeke answered quickly.

"Janey's missing."

There was silence for all of two seconds before Zeke let out a virulent curse. "You called the Mackays yet?"

"That's my next call. There's no sign of struggle or trouble, but her car's still parked outside the office and her cat was waiting on her. Does she have any friends?"

"Not that I've heard of," Zeke bit out. "Call the Mackays. I'll get an APB out on her. Shit. Dammit all to hell."

The call disconnected. Alex punched in Dawg's number. He didn't want to deal with Natches yet.

"What's up?" Dawg answered, his voice a slow, easy drawl that almost had Alex wincing. He knew what that sound meant.

"Janey's gone."

There was silence. "What do you mean, gone?" Dawg's voice wasn't lazy anymore.

"I mean I just checked the apartment and the restaurant. Her car is still here and she isn't," Alex snapped, fury burning in his gut. "Get your asses in gear."

He disconnected as he ran for his truck. God, where was she?

She didn't have friends. He'd watched her in the past week; other than a few business calls, she didn't chitchat on the phone. No one visited. She worked, she ate, slept, went to bed. She didn't socialize and she didn't just disappear.

Pulling out of the driveway, he called her restaurant manager, Hoyt Napier. The son of a deceased vet, Hoyt was quiet, steady. But he hadn't seen Janey since work the night before.

Where the hell could she be? He pulled to a stop at the intersection to the main highway, his hands gripping the steering wheel, his teeth clenched.

The ring of the cell phone had him flipping it open quickly at the sight of Dawg's number on the display.

"Did you find her?"

"Are you fucking insane?" Dawg growled. "It's been three fucking minutes. Uncle Ray and Rowdy are heading around the lake to look for her. Natches is already in the parking lot gunning that fucking cycle of his. Someone tell him it's cold. I'm about halfway down the dock still trying to pull my fucking boots on, goddammit."

"And you're wasting my time why?" Alex pulled into the traffic, his gaze canvassing the sides of the busy streets as he began weaving through the traffic.

"Because Natches is losing his fucking mind, maybe? Chaya and Crista are heading to Kelly's car with her. Dammit all to fucking hell. They won't stay home."

"Dawg, I'm not chitchatting with you, dammit," Alex yelled. "Tell me where to look for her. Son of a bitch, where would she have gone?"

He could feel it building in him now. Fear. Complete, unadulterated fear. He should have known better. He should have stayed on her ass twenty-four-seven. He knew better than to let her out of his sight.

"One nutcase at a time, Alex," Dawg growled. "I already have Natches freaking out here. Don't join the party."

"Get fucked!"

"Not by you, asshole," Dawg assured him. "Now, listen up. Janey wouldn't have gone anywhere with anyone easy. She'd have left something. Anything."

"Do you think I don't know that?" Alex yelled.

He was losing it. He could feel himself losing control. He hadn't lost control since he was sixteen years old and nearly fucking killed his father when he came home from school to find Crista running a 104 degree fever and dehydrated.

"Okay. She didn't leave anything," Dawg agreed. "We all said someone's just trying to scare her. She could have left on her own. Fuck, she's a Mackay, man, whether you or Natches, either one, wants to admit it. And she's a woman to boot. Expect the unexpected."

"She would have left a note."

Dawg snorted, but Alex heard the slam of his truck door and the squeal of tires.

"Janey hasn't had to leave anyone a note in her life," Dawg snarled. "Now, use your damned head. If Janey didn't leave a light on, she's safe."

"How the fuck do you know?"

"Because, that was our agreement with her when she moved out from Natches's boat. She has rules to live by, Alex. Didn't she tell you?"

"She would have to talk to me first." When he found her, he swore, he was going to make her understand *his* fucking rule.

"Okay, here are the rules. If she's forced from the office or from the apartment, she'll leave a light on. Otherwise, all off. Were they off?"

"They were all off. Completely. Not even the porch light was left on."

"So ninety percent chance she left on her own."

"Her car is there," Alex argued. "She didn't go on foot."

"And that's why we're all out running the roads like fucking jackasses right now," Dawg retorted furiously. "You sure she didn't have a date?"

"No. Fucking. Date." The thought of it had red edging at the sides of his vision.

Janey, on a date? With another man? He'd have killed the son of a bitch.

Fuck. Fuck. What the hell was he doing here? What was he thinking?

"Check the movie theater. Bookstores," Dawg ordered. "Grocery store. She likes to cook. Crista said she hasn't been cooking while you were there. She might have decided to. She likes to browse the mall. She could have taken a cab. Janey doesn't like driving if she knows she's going to be stopping somewhere to eat. She likes a glass of wine with her meal and won't risk driving. She takes cabs a lot."

Alex disconnected the call. He was getting ready to punch in the number of the cab company when the phone rang.

"What?" he snapped into the line, expecting it to be Dawg.

"We have a problem." Zeke's voice was almost amused.

"No shit!" Alex bit out. "What now?"

"I just talked to Natches. He called the cab company. Driver took her to that bar at the edge of town. You know the one. The biker bar."

Alex didn't say a word. He shut the phone, tossed it to the seat, and executed a U-turn in the middle of town before speeding through the traffic to the bar in question.

The biker bar. The one where Rogue Walker and her friends kept the town filled with gossip.

His jaw clenched as the phone rang and he ignored it. Dawg called. Natches called.

Ten minutes later he swung into the crowded graveled parking lot as the sheriff's cruiser pulled in behind him. Before Alex was out of the truck, Natches rolled in on his bike, Chaya, Crista, and Kelly pulled in, and Dawg eased his pickup in behind them.

Alex strode furiously to the door, jerked it open, and stepped into the raucous, smoky atmosphere. He hadn't taken half a dozen steps inside when he came to a full, hard stop and just stared.

He swore he swallowed his tongue. He heard Zeke curse behind him. Dawg was chiding Crista over something and Chaya might have been arguing with Natches. All Alex knew, all he saw, was Janey.

She was incandescent, and it wasn't that bright red, too-damned-snug, tiny, strapped little camisole top that made her light the room up either.

Her hair was straight, feathering around her flushed face, her reddened lips. Her green eyes glowed. Her arms were stretched over her head as she and Rogue rocked with some leather-clad dancer on the dance floor, both of them laughing and weaving, swaying seductively as the men around them danced with them. Old, young—they had the whole fucking bar rocking. There were other women on the floor. The women that ran with the bikers, dressed scantily, usually fighting. Not tonight. Tonight, they were dancing, and Janey was in the middle of it.

She tossed her head, shook her hips, and a vise tightened around his balls. She wasn't wearing a bra. She better be wearing panties.

That short black leather skirt flirted with the tops of fishnet stockings, and red fuck-me pumps graced her small feet.

And she was having fun.

Alex felt something clench in his chest, tighter than before. His guts felt twisted, his cock was a steel spike throbbing beneath his jeans, and his senses were so fucking scattered he didn't know how to sort them out.

He'd seen Janey as sweet, vulnerable. Someone he had to protect from life and from himself. Hell, he'd never stop thinking that. But that was a woman on the dance floor, and every male instinct raging inside him warned him that if he didn't take what belonged to him, then someone was going to take it away from him.

Tortured need clashed with the honor he had always demanded of himself. Dark, brutal, the memories of the past filtered through his brain as he watched her.

He'd almost loved once in his life. At twenty, two years after joining the Army. He was in Germany. His lover was an embassy liaison, and she had died in a back alley on her way home to her apartment. A victim of senseless violence. It hadn't been terrorists. She hadn't been a spy; she hadn't known any secrets. She'd been raped and murdered, and left in a filthy back street.

And Alex had protected his heart ever since. It wasn't just terrorism or betrayal that killed. Women died every day. Innocent deaths. Acts of God. In the snap of a finger all the happiness that could build inside a man could be snatched away just as easily.

He couldn't let himself love. But he couldn't walk away from the vision on that dance floor either.

Her green eyes shimmered between her dark, smoky lashes. Red lips curled with eager fun, not lust. Not invitation. Simple fun.

She bumped hips with Rogue before they turned and swayed with several other eager male dancers. She was laughing, keeping her distance; she wasn't touching. She was excitement itself, and he was going to come in his jeans just watching her.

"Natches, leave her alone," Chaya was ordering her husband behind him.

"Dammit, Chaya, they're bikers," Natches was arguing.

"She's having fun, Natches."

Alex swallowed tight. He moved through the crowd, pushing his way past them, and headed to the dance floor as the band slid smoothly into a slow, sensual tune. Janey laughed and shook her head at the men around her, pointed to the bar, and turned to leave.

He caught her at the edge of the floor. His arm slid around her waist, pulling her against him as she stiffened.

"Dance with me, Janey." He lowered his lips to her ear, feeling her soften, feeling her body flow into his.

Alex turned her slowly, pulled her into his arms, and, staring down at her, jerked her hips to his before he began swaying with her.

It always amazed him, each time he had her in his arms, how tiny she was compared to him. A good six inches shorter even with heels, her curvy little body fragile against him. His hands cupped her hips, slid to her back. He wanted to crush her against him. Lift her up and carry her away. Touch her. Fill her with the hunger raging, dark and brutal, inside him.

"I couldn't find you," he whispered against her ear. "I was worried."

Her hands smoothed over his shoulders, as though she enjoyed touching him.

"I left all the lights off," she murmured, letting her body stroke against his, caress him.

"You didn't tell me about the lights. And you took a cab."

"I don't drink and drive." Her hands ran over his black leather jacket.

"I'll drive." He brushed her hair aside from her ear with his chin and tasted the lobe of her ear.

He heard her sharp intake of breath, felt her soften further against him.

"I want to go parking." Leaning back, her smile drowsy, her cheeks flushed, she gazed up at him with enough hunger to fry his brain. "I've never been parking."

Parking with Janey? God, he hadn't taken a girl parking since he was sixteen years old.

"Janey, I'm a man . . ."

"Who's going to take me parking," she told him firmly, choosing that moment to rub her hips against his, to stroke over his cock with her lower stomach as her hands clenched against his biceps. "I've never been parking, Alex."

She was going to kill him. Because he was going to take her parking.

"You really want to lose your virginity in the front seat of my pickup?"

The thought of it had flames shooting through his mind. Hell. The image of that in his head would make him crazy.

"When I was seventeen, I was at the lake, remember?" She pushed her hands beneath his jacket, her fingers stroking over his chest.

"I was thirty-one," he reminded her.

"I wanted to leave with you. I wanted to jump into that pickup you had and just ride away with you. And I imagined you taking me parking." Her tongue licked over her lips. "I wanted you, Alex. I wanted you so bad."

He was fucking crazy.

"I'm not easy, Janey," he tried to warn her. "I won't be satisfied with a little stroke and tease."

"I'm a woman, Alex. But it doesn't mean I don't want to have fun."

One hand slid down his chest, his abdomen; her fingers curled beneath the band of his jeans and stroked over the throbbing, sensitive head of his cock.

He had to clench his teeth to hold back his cum. Still, his erection throbbed and a small spurt of silky release pulsed to her fingers from the tiny slit.

And what did the little witch do? With him shielding her body, she pulled her damp finger free, lifted it to her lips, and licked. Curled her tongue right around her damned finger and her lashes dipped in pleasure.

"We're leaving."

"I'm having fun, Alex," she murmured, but she didn't fight him when he gripped her upper arm and pulled her after him.

"Where's your coat?"

"Oh. Damn. I must have forgot to wear one," she said, too innocently, as they left the dance floor.

Fuck. He jerked his jacket off and pushed her arms into the sleeves, thanking God the bar was dim and it was dark outside.

"Wow, the whole family is here." Janey stared around Alex as she approached not just her brother and cousins, but their wives as well.

Rowdy, Kelly, Dawg, and Crista watched her and Alex with an edge of amusement. Natches looked thunderous, Chaya resigned.

"What the hell are you doing here, Janey?" Natches groaned as he jerked her to him for a rough hug. "You scared the hell out of me."

She wanted to roll her eyes. "Sorry. Did I break curfew?"

Chaya snickered. Natches didn't.

"Come on." Natches gripped her arm. "We'll take you home."

"Natches, I'm not sixteen." She pulled her arm back and almost glared at him. "Besides, Alex promised to take me riding around. I'm not ready to go home."

"Then you can come back to the boat," Natches gritted out.

"Chaya, take him home and give him some before he blows a gasket." She stared back at her brother in shock. "Natches, what is your problem? What? It's a sin for me to go out and have fun?"

"With him, it should be illegal." He glowered at Alex. "He's too old to be running the roads with you."

"Oh geez, am I still in high school?" Janey shook her head and stared back at Natches angrily. "Get a grip, Natches. Go home. Have a beer. I promise to be home in time for curfew. Oh wait." She widened her eyes. "That's right—I'm over twenty-one. I don't have a curfew."

Did his lips twitch? His eyes were narrowed, his lips tightly compressed, but she swore she saw them twitch.

"Damn, I think she's a Mackay." Rowdy laughed as Janey turned and stalked out the door, followed closely behind by Alex.

Boy, she bet he was enjoying having three Mackays at his back.

"Natches, you poke that fist in my back again and I'm going to break your hand." Alex's voice drifted through the night, a low murmur of danger as Janey felt him stiffen behind her.

"Alex, please don't break his hand." Chaya sighed. "I have several uses for it. Natches, stop being an ass."

"Yeah, really." Janey turned and stepped around Alex.

She caught him. Fist raised, Natches was getting ready to poke Alex in the middle of the back again. Actually, it was probably more of a full-fledged strike than a poke.

His fist stilled as he stared back at her.

"High school," she reminded him.

Natches dropped his fist, only to cross his arms over his chest.

"He's fired. Chaya and I will stay at the apartment with you."

Janey leaned back against Alex's pickup, sensing the tension running high between the two men. Because of her. They were friends. They had always been friends. Was she coming between that?

"Do you trust me, Natches?" she finally asked, needing to know.

She hadn't asked him that, ever. But suddenly, the need to know rose inside her like an illness.

"I've always trusted you, Janey." He frowned.

"Then stop," she said softly. "For my sake, Natches. Please."

He leaned closer. The moon added brilliance to his dark green eyes as they glittered in warning. "If he breaks your heart, I'll kill him."

"If he breaks my heart," she whispered back, "you'll never know."

Natches shook his head at that. "I'll know, Janey," he promised her. "Just like I've known other things for years." He looked at where Alex had been drawn aside by Dawg and Rowdy. He watched them, closely, but he couldn't hear the conversation.

Janey stared back at her brother coolly. "And what do you think you know?"

"That you think you've been in love with him since you were seventeen years old. And he hasn't been able to take his eyes off you in just as long. I'm not a fool. But I'm not a man who will sit back and watch a man his age mess with his kid sister and toss her aside. Remember that. Because you're right—you're over twenty-one. You're an adult. But you're still the baby sister I'd die for. Remember that."

Janey felt herself pale. She knew Natches meant every word. When she was eight, she had watched him nearly die at Dayle Mackay's hands as he beat Natches to the floor for daring to try to protect Janey from a slap.

Natches hadn't fought him back. He'd let Dayle expend his rage, and after he'd healed, he'd shown the man how he'd retaliate.

The bullet that had taken Dayle's car windshield out barely missed his head. Dayle had known who pulled the trigger, and he knew Natches would kill him, over Janey.

Yeah, her heart was at risk, but she had learned a long time ago how to hide her feelings. Natches might think he knew something, but unless he was certain, he would never strike out.

She patted his cheek lovingly. "I love ya, Natches. But my heart isn't going to be broken. You forget. I've had a lot of years to grow up. I know even more than you think I do exactly why my heart is going to stay safe. Don't worry. Love isn't a part of it."

And he didn't look any happier than he had when she first saw him at the bar. And Alex must have overheard, because damned if he didn't look unhappy, too.

And that was okay. Tonight, she had made a decision herself. She had been fascinated with Alex for far too many years, and the need she had for him wasn't going to go away.

For his sake, he was right; it was better no one knew he was staying with her. His reputation wouldn't suffer for having slept with the daughter of a traitor, and when this was over, maybe she would leave. Being alone in another city beat the hell out of being miserable here, knowing no one trusted her, that no one even considered the fact that she was as much a victim in Dayle and Nadine's conspiracies as anyone else had been.

But because she had played the dutiful daughter when he demanded it, now she would pay for that as well. No one wanted to see beneath the surface. No one except a bar full of bikers wanted to know the woman she was, rather than the woman they wanted to perceive her as.

Rogue had said once that this county had created her and she'd stuck around to rub their noses in it. Janey didn't think she had that much strength. Once Alex walked back out of her bed, she would have no choice but to leave. Because a part of her knew she had stayed to be with him.

"Are you ready to go?" He opened the driver's-side door of the pickup and helped her in, ignoring Natches and the others as he climbed in beside her.

A second later they were pulling out. Janey could feel her family's gazes on her as they left, and it left a heaviness inside her to know how worried they were.

Not about a potential stalker. They were more worried about the fact that it was Alex she was leaving with. Rather than gaining their trust to follow her heart as they had followed theirs, Janey instead felt their combined worry and concern weighing her down, pulling at her heart.

She wasn't used to that concern; at least she wasn't used to feeling it. She had been alone for so long that sometimes she didn't stop to wonder if it was natural not to let someone know she would be gone. Or what her plans were, or if she was happy or sad. No one had ever been in a position to support her, or to ease her through the hell her life had been for so long. Now Janey didn't depend on anyone but herself.

It was better that way. As Alex pulled from the bar and headed toward the lake, she told herself it was better knowing the terms and conditions of any relationship before one stepped into it.

Alex needed to protect his reputation. She had heard a few of the conversations at the restaurant. She knew the city council was hoping to get him in as the next chief of police. He couldn't risk a relationship, at least not a public one, with her. The daughter of a traitor. A supposedly once loving daughter.

Yeah, she had played that role well.

And now she was going to pay for it.

EIGHT

Alex pulled the pickup into a secluded clearing next to the lake, the same area he had first noticed the woman Janey was turning into, six years before.

The narrow dirt road that led to the tree-sheltered clearing and rocky beach was a favorite summer gathering place. During those warmer months, the lake level would be higher, the water warm and relatively safe to swim in.

Now the bare trees swayed in a cold winter wind, the lake was low, deserted, and the clearing intimate and empty of anyone except the two of them. He cut the lights and stared at the water spreading out before them.

"Natches has a right to be pissed," he finally told her softly. "You need someone who's going to fall in love with you. Someone who can give you a future."

And he couldn't. He couldn't give her the dreams he knew she had inside her. That happily-ever-after every woman deserved, especially this woman.

"I don't expect you to fall in love with me, Alex," she answered him, her voice somber. "I never asked you to."

He turned and stared at her.

She was watching the lake, her expression quiet, calm. That damned mask she wore had the power to piss him off more than Natches's barbed comments or the hard, warning fist he'd felt in his back earlier.

"Then why are you here with me, Janey?" he asked her gently, when the need, the hunger, powering through him was anything but gentle. "In six months you've not had a single date. You haven't made friends."

"Rogue . . ."

"Doesn't count." He sighed. "Rogue is a good person; don't get me wrong. But she's one person, Janey. One friend, and a wild one at that. The woman in that bar isn't you."

Her lips took a bitter edge. "That's where you're wrong, Alex." She shook her head, her hair brushing her face as she still stared at the lake. "So wrong." She looked at him then, and he felt a ragged, painful emotion tighten his throat at the expression on her face. "That's everything I've had to push back all my life. Dancing. Laughing. I had fun. It was fun. I want to be me, just for a little while. Just me. Without feeling the condemnation of a county, or the judgmental opinions of those who keep watching to see if I'm just as dirty, just as evil as what spawned me."

"Janey."

"I want to touch you, Alex." She turned then, shifted her shoulders, shrugged off his jacket. "I want to be wild with you. I want to be me with you. Is that so wrong? Is it so horrible?"

Pale skin shimmered in the moonlight. His palms itched to touch her, to feel her soft flesh beneath his hands.

"Alex. Just for a little while, pretend with me." He watched her eyes, saw the shimmer of tears. "Pretend I'm just a woman you want. That there's nothing wrong with me. That there's nothing dirty tainting who I am. Just for a little while."

Christ. She was going to cry. The tears were in her eyes, eyes naked with need. The need to be touched, held. To be a woman with the man she desired.

Then her words penetrated his lust-fogged brain. His gaze sharpened on her as he reached out, jerking her to him.

"Never let me hear you say something like that again," he barked ruthlessly as her eyes widened in shock and he gave her a quick, hard shake. "Pretend, your ass. For Christ's sake, Janey. I want you until I can't breathe for it. I have for years. And the only thing you're tainted with is my fucking touch. Because by God, I should know better."

The desperate, blinding need that exploded inside him, to wipe such a thought from her head, spilled through Alex. He ached; to the center of his soul he ached that she somehow believed she wasn't truly desirable, that she was tainted and somehow unworthy.

"Look at you." His voice was an agonized whisper as he wrapped his hand around the back of her neck, holding her as he moved, shifted, bending over her until she had no choice but to recline back on the bench seat.

God, now he knew why he hadn't wanted that fucking console in his truck. So he could do this.

"You make me so fucking hard I can't even think." He lowered his head and nipped her pouty lower lip.

Damn truck was too small. He shoved his knee between her thighs and braced his foot on the floor. But hell. He shoved his knee right against her pussy, watching that damned skirt slide up her thighs to reveal white lacy panties.

He was not fucking her in this truck, he thought. It wasn't going to happen. There simply wasn't enough room.

"Alex." She whispered his name, her hips moving, riding his knee as her arms twined around his neck. "Kiss me hard and deep. Like you're as hungry for me as I am for you."

Janey was dying inside. She needed him. She'd partied and had fun tonight, maybe had one beer too many, but she hadn't forgotten that she wasn't dancing with Alex. He hadn't taken her out; he wasn't holding her, laughing with her.

And then he had been there, like a fantasy come to life. Hard and warm, holding her in his arms, dancing with her, staring at her with all that hunger in his eyes, and all she wanted was one night. Just this one night to be more than the traitor's daughter, more than the responsibility he had to babysit.

She was no one's baby. Sometimes she felt as though she belonged to nothing and no one. Tonight, just for a little while, she wanted to belong to Alex.

She lifted to him, her thighs tightening on the hard width of his knee shoved against her pussy, and oh, that felt so good. Her arms tightened around his neck, her tongue licking out at his lips.

And then he was there. His lips covered hers with that hungry groan she loved so much and he was kissing her hard and deep. One hand held her neck, keeping her in place. The other gripped the hem of her skirt, jerking it higher, over the band of her stockings.

She could feel him all over her. From her lips to her legs. So warm and hard, like a living blanket filled with fiery heat.

"I'm not fucking you in a pickup." He groaned, sipping at her lips now rather than devouring them. Teasing her with his kisses. "I'm telling you now, Janey. I'm not doing it."

"Okay," she panted in excitement, her hands moving down his chest as he eased back, pulling the shirt from his jeans before her fingers moved to his belt. "We can do other stuff."

"Ah hell." His groan almost made her smile.

"I want to taste you again, Alex." She jerked his belt open, loosened it, then pulled at the metal button of his jeans. "I want you in my mouth, against my tongue. I want to suck you, taste you."

She slid the zipper of his jeans down, her eyes widening as his cock sprang free.

"Hmm, commando," she whispered breathlessly, using both hands to surround it, stroke it. "Alex. I'm scandalized."

"You're about to get more scandalized. Because, baby, you're gonna suck my dick until I fill your mouth."

She'd never heard that tone in his voice. It sent a shiver down her spine as he pulled back, sitting back in the seat to lean against the door, his cock rising from his jeans, thick and hard as he pulled her up between his legs.

One large hand circled the heavy stalk; the other clasped her neck again. She hadn't realized how sexy that was, how much she loved his strong fingers controlling her head, holding her wherever he wanted her.

Submission wasn't a game she played, but this, the firm, determined hold of a man who knew what he wanted, knew how to take a woman. Oh yeah, this she liked.

She tugged back, staring up at him as she knelt in front of him, her lips parting as she fought to breathe.

"It's awful big," she drawled before licking her lower lip. "Maybe I can't handle it."

The amused grunt that filled the cab almost had her grinning. "I'll teach you how to handle it."

He palmed the back of her neck, pushing her down. "Lift your ass while you go down on me, baby. Give me something to play with while you blow my mind."

Janey wrapped her fingers around the engorged shaft. Her tongue peeked out, licked over the damp crown, and she moaned at the taste of him. Moaned at the hard jerk of his cock, the rasp of his breath.

He reclined against the door, one leg on the floor, the other stretched out along the seat, and his cock really was big. She loved it. It was thick and long, and for tonight, it was all hers.

She pursed her lips, pressed them over the slit, then slid them down over the throbbing heat as she felt his hands, both of them, clench in her hair.

"Christ. Your mouth," he groaned. "Janey, sweetheart, you're going to kill me."

She was dying herself. She surrounded the thick crest with her mouth, remembering the taste of him in the bar, salty and male, dark and delicious. She wanted more. She wanted to feel him pumping in her mouth, filling her with his release.

She could feel her own pleasure building at his ragged, hoarse groans. Electric sensation whipped through her, sizzled between her thighs, wrapped around her clit, and tormented it with the need for orgasm.

"Damn. Baby. Such a sweet little mouth." His voice was harder now, darker. He was loving it. Loving what she was doing to him, and it filled her mind, intoxicating her. He was more potent than whiskey.

His pleasure tore through her mind, building her own. She was touching him. This hard, experienced man. A man she'd never believed she would have in her bed. Touching him and he was loving it. He was hard and hot in her mouth, his muscles tight, bunching each time she flicked her tongue over the broad crest and sucked him deeper into her mouth.

"That's it, Janey," he groaned. "Suck me slow and easy, baby. Damn you. It's so good. So sweet."

One hand moved from her hair, slid down her back. She felt the skirt rising, passing over her rear, exposing it, bunching at her hips.

"Damn you. Fucking thongs." His finger slid beneath the little strap that ran between her buttocks. "Oh, Janey, that's fucking wicked, baby."

He tugged at the strap, tightening the material over her clit as she moaned. Because it felt so damned good. Her thighs parted, and her mouth drew him deeper, sucking his cock head with hungry draws of her mouth.

Each time the pleasure tore through him, he rewarded her. He pulled on the strap, caressed her clit with the tightening fabric until her hips were rolling with each tug of the cloth, her moans building in her throat and passing by his cock.

One hand stayed locked in her hair. He moved her mouth on him, refusing to let her suck him faster, keeping her rhythm slow and easy.

"Yeah, that's the way, baby. Tease my dick. Pay me back now. Because when I get you spread out on a bed . . ." He groaned, his hips jerked, driving his cock against her almost involuntarily as she tongued the underside. "You little witch, when I get my lips on your pussy, I'm going to make you beg to come."

Oh well, that was going to take a long time, wasn't it? If she could force herself to let his cock go for a second, she'd be begging him now.

So she did as he suggested. She teased, licked, stroked. She used her admittedly limited knowledge and his groans of pleasure to guide her. She probed at the slit with her tongue, tasted him, and needed more. She sucked the head deep, firm, moaning, stroking the shaft.

"Ah yeah, baby, right there." He tightened violently as she rubbed her tongue under the head of his cock and sucked him deep. "It feels like you're going to swallow my dick. Fuck, that's good."

Alex was in hell. In ecstasy. Each ripple of her hot little mouth over the head of his cock was agonizing pleasure. Her hands stroking the shaft, the sweet, subtle scent of her pussy reaching him.

Hell, he was going to have a stroke right there in the front of his truck and he couldn't do a damned thing to stop it.

All he could do was hold her head, show her how to move to make him crazier, to make the pleasure better. Sweat beaded on his forehead, ran down the side of his face. It was cold as hell outside and he was burning up inside the truck. Burning in her mouth and fighting to hold back just a few more minutes. To let her torture him just a little bit longer.

"Ah, Janey. Baby."

She moaned again. Every time he used an endearment, she softened against him, and his heart raged with pain at the thought that no one called her anything but her name.

"Ah, there, sweetheart. So fucking good. Like an angel. Sweet, sweet Janey."

She sucked him like she was starving for him. Her lips, her tongue. She licked and sucked, stroked, and her moans rippled over the sensitive crest.

He tugged at the scrap of material that ran between the cheeks of her perfect ass. The thongs were snug; each tug he knew would caress her clit. Lift her higher, give her the smallest hint of the hell he was in right now.

Flames were erupting in his balls. Fuck.

"Janey, baby, I'm going to come," he groaned. "If you don't want your mouth full of me, then you better move."

She didn't move; she took him deeper, hungrily.

Alex shook his head and fought the release. Not yet. Ah hell, it was so damned good. He didn't want it to stop. Didn't want to lose the pleasure of her sweet, hot mouth consuming him.

His balls grew tighter, drawing beneath the base of his cock as electric tingles began to build at the base of his spine.

"Darlin'. I can't hold back." He couldn't fucking breathe. "Janey. Fuck. Fuck."

He arched his hips, held her head in place, and heard the ragged, hoarse groan that tore from his lips as fiery sensation raced up his spine and ecstasy erupted in his balls. He felt his cum spurting inside her mouth, filling it as her mouth worked to take him, swallowing as she moaned, cried out, licked, and sucked until he was spent. Until he had to pull her head back, because each stroke of her tongue was like a lash of agonizing pleasure on the oversensitive flesh.

He was breathing hard, sweating. Lifting her face to his, he stared into her dazed expression, watched as she licked her lips slowly, catching a final drop of his semen from the pouty curves.

Instantly, he was as hard as he was before he came in her mouth.

Sliding his hand between her thighs, his teeth clenched at the heat of her dampness against her panties. Oh yeah, she was wet, ready for him. Wild with the need. Too wild to wait.

"Lay back, baby." He eased her back on the seat, staring up at her as he slid her panties over her thighs, along the black stockings. Holding her feet in his lap, he drew the panties past the red fuck-me pumps and tossed them on the dash before spreading her thighs.

"Fuck. I bet those wild-assed Mackay women take you to the spa with them, huh?" He stared at perfect pink flesh, bare of curls, glistening and wet.

"I go by myself, too," she said breathlessly, a temptress smile on her face as he spread her legs wider and shoved the seat farther back toward the backseat of the dual cab.

Okay, that gave him some room. It was cramped, but God, he couldn't wait to get her back at the apartment. He had to taste her now. Just a little bit. Just enough to have her screaming in release as his tongue shoved up her pussy. Yeah. He could wait that long.

His lips lowered, his tongue parted silken, soft folds, and he licked up the narrow, snug slit of her pussy with a groan.

Had any other woman ever tasted so sweet? He knew none had. Silky syrup clung to his tongue as he circled her clit and moved back. It filled his senses, and he devoured each taste.

He licked at her sweetness, pushed his hands beneath the rounded globes of her ass, and lifted her to him, kissing her clit, pursing his lips over it and giving it soft, gentle little sucks as she writhed in his arms.

"Alex. Oh God. Alex. It feels too good."

Oh yeah, he knew too good. He remembered her mouth on his cock making him insane.

"Payback," he groaned against her clit and felt her shudder in pleasure.

He wanted her shuddering in pleasure. He wanted her screaming with it. He wanted her release spilling to his tongue and infusing his senses.

She was so fucking hot he was about to melt. His cock was pounding. It would be so easy. So easy to slide between her thighs and press inside her. To fuck her as hard and deep as he needed to fuck her.

His hands clenched around the cheeks of her ass, his tongue circled her clit and fought to snap the reins back on the lust lurching demandingly against the hold he had on it.

Fuck, he wasn't taking her in a pickup truck. He'd have her in her bed. With her legs wrapped around his waist like they were wrapping around his shoulders now.

Ah hell. Her hands were on his head, buried in the short length of his hair, urging him to her.

He sucked her swollen clit into his mouth, let his tongue press and ripple against it as she gasped his name, then nearly screamed his name.

God, he loved that sound. That surprised pleasure, the rush of sensation in her voice, the way her nails pricked his scalp.

She was close. So fucking close that he could draw this out for another hour or shove her into release now. If he let her have it now, he could take her home, he told himself. Take her back to her bed and spend the night fucking her.

But if he let her come now, he'd have to stop. He'd have to

drive them home. And he didn't want to let her go. Didn't want to lose the sensation of her in his mouth, her heated juices making him drunker than hell on her taste.

"Alex, please," she moaned, her voice throaty, so damned sexy.

He pleased her. He licked her little clit, drew it into his mouth. For a second. Until she tensed, tightened, that building pleasure racing through her. Then he drew back and licked along the folds again until he came to the tight, gripping entrance to her pussy.

He rimmed the opening, licked over it, and heard her cries fill his head, felt them stroke his senses. So close.

She was so close.

Janey couldn't think, couldn't do anything but feel. She shook her head as need exploded inside her, over and over, racing through her bloodstream as she felt the pleasure consuming him.

Oh God. It was so good. She hadn't thought it would be this good. She had thought it would feel like her own fingers, her own touch, not like this. His tongue was rough silk, and so hot. When it stroked over her, it flayed her with sensation. When he sucked her clit into his mouth, she was devoured by the pleasure. It was burning through her, licking over her flesh and making her crazy.

She needed.

"Alex, please," she cried out. "Oh God. Please let me come, Alex. It's so good. So good."

He groaned. His tongue probed at the opening to her vagina and she tensed and cried out at the pleasure. Then he was kissing her again. Deep kisses along the slit, his tongue licking into it before he came back to her clit.

He sucked it into his mouth and didn't stop. His tongue flickered just beneath it as he drew on her, and a thousand suns exploded inside her.

It couldn't get any better. She hurled through ecstasy, then it got better. His tongue thrust hard and heavy inside her, pumped inside her pussy, and she was screaming his name, detonations of pure white-hot energy flowing through her as she felt her juices spilling from her. And felt Alex tasting them, consuming them, groaning and fucking his tongue inside her, deeper, harder, until she collapsed in mindless pleasure. And he was still licking, still taking her, still groaning her name.

"I'm going to hell," he finally groaned, lifting his head to kiss her one last time, to purse his lips over her quivering clit before pulling himself up.

He was fixing his jeans.

"What are you doing?" She frowned. "You're not finished."

Alex had to grin at that demanding tone. A virgin she damned sure was, but she wasn't going to be one for long.

"I'm not fucking you in this truck, sweetheart."

Her lips parted at the endearment; pleasure filled her face. She loved it. And he loved that look on her face.

"Why not?" She stretched, arched, and he almost took her then.

"Minx." His chuckle was rough, strained. "Sit up. You'll be lucky if I can get us back to your place before I'm buried inside you."

"I could handle that," she promised with a smile, though she sat up.

He cupped her face, because he saw the edge of worry in her eyes, the hint of vulnerability.

"I want room, baby. Room to touch you. To suck those sweet nipples, to taste that pretty pussy again. Room to watch as I take you. I want that really bad, darlin'. I want to watch my dick stretch you open and take what no one else has a chance of touching. I can't do that in this fucking truck."

That glazed look of hunger and need filled her eyes, and he almost took her anyway.

"I can handle that," she whispered.

"Hell, let's hope I can handle it," he groaned, sliding behind the steering wheel and readjusting his seat. "You just might be the end of me. Because touching you, Janey, is hotter than hell."

He dragged her to his side and attached the middle seat belt around her rather than let her slide into the passenger seat. He wanted her against him. Wanted her right by his side, heating him, close to him.

He turned the truck around and headed back to the apartment, moving a little faster than he probably should have. He was definitely pushing the speed limit.

Driving with one hand, he tucked the other beneath Janey's leg, holding her close as her head lay on his shoulder. Fuck. This was insane, but he couldn't let her go. He hadn't done this since he was a hormone-crazed teenager with more dick than good sense.

And he swore, tonight, he was in just as bad shape as he had been then. More dick than good sense. Because tonight, he was taking her. All fucking night long. Because he had a feeling it would take a hell of a lot longer than he'd imagined to ever sate the hunger he felt for her.

He was suddenly worried he would never sate that hunger.

NINE

She had waited so long. Sometimes the need for touch, in the middle of the night, had nearly driven her insane over the past years. The need for Alex had dug sharp claws inside her, twisted into her womb and left her aching at the oddest times.

But at night. It had always been worse at night, whether in Somerset or at school. Huddled in her bed, staring into the dark, that need had been like a fever, an ache that built, night by night and, until six months ago, had left her sobbing with the need to be held.

There had always been something about Alex. He was sexy all over, but his arms had always drawn her. The powerful biceps, the strength that seemed to infuse them. If she just had his arms around her, she sometimes thought, then she could sleep rather than toss and turn. She could think rather than fight the fear.

Alex was the embodiment of strength to Janey.

As they drove through town, her head pillowed on one of those hard arms, his hand holding her close to his side, she almost regretted the miles the truck ate so quickly. She wanted to be home, because she wanted to feel him over her, inside her. But she didn't want to lose this. This feeling of security, of complete male power enveloping her.

It would end all too soon anyway. The night would be over, and come dawn, Alex would slip from the apartment, as he always did. She would put her mask back on and she would face the world again.

Could she do it, knowing everything she couldn't have?

She would, because she had to. But she had a feeling it would be harder. Because she wanted to hold on to this feeling right now. The feeling that she was normal, plain Jane. Not the traitor's daughter. Not a responsibility he had to look after. Just Janey, Alex's lover.

"You're quiet." His voice was a stroke of midnight across her flesh.

"I'm coming down." She grinned, a bit smugly perhaps, because her body was still humming with pleasure.

"Don't come down too far," he warned her. "I want you hot and ready for me, Janey. Trust me, sweetheart, once I get inside you, I'm not going to stop fucking you for a while."

He called her sweetheart. He called her baby. And he said it gently. Like he meant it.

How immature of her, she thought. She was worse than a silly teenager, but the sound of those endearments had her heart clenching with pleasure.

"Who says you have to stop?" She watched him take the turn that led to the apartment. "I bet I can keep up with you."

She looked up at him, watching his jaw tighten, the look of brooding lust he shot her from the corner of his eye.

"Oh, I have no doubt you'll keep up," he promised her with a wicked smile as he pulled into her driveway.

Pulling to a stop, he slid the truck into park and turned off the ignition. Then he surprised her. He didn't just get out of the truck. He cupped her neck in that way that sent tingles of pleasure racing through her, made her feel feminine and sexy, and lowered his lips to hers.

His kiss wasn't hard and deep. It was gentle, and hungry. His lips worked over hers, slanted over them, while his tongue pushed into her mouth and stroked against hers.

And oh God, it was so hot she felt blistered. She felt need shoot through her system like an intravenous drug, straight to her heart, then between her thighs, filling her sex with melting warmth.

"Christ, you make me hot," he growled into the kiss. "If I make it up those stairs without fucking you, it's going to be a damned miracle."

Then he surprised her again. He moved from the truck, pulled her across the seat, and lifted her against his chest.

"Legs around me," he groaned as he wrapped one arm beneath her ass and held her to him. "Hell. If I don't at least feel you, I won't make it."

Her legs wrapped around his waist. His hard abs flexed between her thighs as he slammed the truck door closed and moved for the stairs.

"People will see your truck in the morning," she reminded him.

"Fuck 'em."

A surge of emotion at the words caught her off guard. He wasn't worried that others would know . . .

"Zeke and his deputy are picking up the truck later anyway." She crashed. Like a balloon slowly deflating, Janey felt the joy that had surged inside her recede.

She was so stupid. How insane to let herself believe anything but the truth. She buried her head against his neck, though, her lips moving on his flesh until, before she knew it, Alex pushed her against the side of the building, halfway up the steps, groaning.

Only then did she realize she was biting him. Biting his neck, sucking at it, marking him as the pain rose inside her like a tidal wave threatening to destroy her.

She marked him as he gripped her hips and thrust against her almost violently. The wedge of his cock beneath his jeans was hard and thick, pressing into her as she cried out against the tough skin of his neck.

His hand held her head to him. His breathing was hard, fast, his hips grinding against her as she held on to him.

She couldn't let him go. She had to hold him. Needed to draw a part of him into her, to leave a part of herself that he could never be rid of.

"You're killing me." He bent his neck for her, giving her what she needed for long moments before pulling her head back and glowering down at her. "If I end up fucking you on these stairs, I'll spank your ass for pushing me that far."

"Be careful, Alex. I might enjoy it." She stared back at him fiercely. "We could try it and see."

He turned, holding her against him, and moved up the stairs fast. He was one raging hard-on. His dick was the only thing that mattered at this point, and it was demanding, desperate.

If he didn't get inside her, he just might end up coming in his jeans, and if that happened, then he was definitely going to spank her.

He shoved the key into the lock, only barely noticing that the cat wasn't around. It must have eaten its fill earlier. Then he pushed into the apartment and came to a hard stop.

Violent fury poured through him.

Turning, sheltering Janey, he ducked back out the door, slamming it behind them.

"Alex?" There was fear in her voice as he held her to him and all but ran back down the steps and to the truck.

"Get in." He shoved her back into the truck as he tore his cell phone off his hip and dug into the backseat for the Glock he carried.

He checked the clip quickly before snapping it back in place.

"Zeke." For the second time that night the sheriff answered his call.

"Get to Janey's apartment. There's been a break-in and there's a note on her kitchen table. Nothing was touched by us. I walked in, then pulled back."

"On my way," Zeke informed him. "I'm calling the Mackays, Alex. Sorry, man, they'll kill me if I don't."

"Hell," he swore. "And they can't seem to keep their wives at home. It's like calling the farce squad."

Zeke's hard laugh was amused and dangerous at the same time. "I'm heading your way. Stay covered. You should see my lights in seconds."

Zeke disconnected as Alex flipped the phone closed and leaned his head against the frame of the truck. He felt like pounding his forehead into the metal.

"We're in trouble." Janey sighed.

Alex lifted his head and stared back at her quizzically.

"I just left the hickey from hell on your neck, Alex; there's no way Natches can miss it. There's no way anyone could miss it." And she sounded damned pleased over it.

It still burned. His dick still pounded with the burn.

Hell, he should have just fucked her in the truck. At least then, when Natches killed him, he'd deserve it. Or at least, deserve it more.

Grinning, he arched his brow and drawled, "You're next."

But it didn't ease the fear from her eyes, or the rage burning in his gut. A second later the flashing lights of the sheriff's cruiser and two of the city's finest pulled into the parking lot.

Zeke and four officers exited the vehicles. The four officers, weapons drawn, started around the building as Zeke moved up to him.

"Dawg called in. They left the girls with Ray. The boys are heading in, though. We'll wait for them before we head up to the apartment."

"Her alarm hadn't been tripped," Alex told him, noticing the glance Zeke made to his neck, the slight widening of his eyes. "Don't start, Zeke."

"Fuck. I hope those boys ain't armed." Zeke shook his head as he glanced in the cab of the truck.

Alex had felt Janey move into the driver's seat; he could feel her against his back, peeping over his shoulder to watch the sheriff.

"I might have branded him, Zeke." There was a smile in her voice, despite the tension.

Alex could hear the fear in her tone as well. She was trying to cover it, to push it back, and that just pissed him off more. She shouldn't have to feel the need to hide her emotions, her fears. She should be safe, secure.

"Yes, ma'am, you did." Zeke nodded. "Do you think I can keep Natches from shooting him long enough to search that apartment upstairs?"

The joking was light, a tension easer, an attempt to still the fear Alex knew Zeke could see in her face.

"Sure. Natches isn't stupid. He just likes to play dumb sometimes."

Alex turned to her at the hint of tears in her voice.

"Hey. Stop worrying. It's going to be okay."

"Of course it is." Her smile was too bright, her eyes too green.

"Sweetheart, you start crying on me, and we're going to have problems. I don't have anyone to shoot yet."

Her smile trembled. "Don't worry about me. Crying isn't something I do very well."

But she turned her head, sliding back into the seat and moving back to the passenger side.

Alex whispered a curse. "I'll murder the bastard, Zeke."

The sheriff shook his head. "Don't tell me about it, okay? I'm the one with the badge. Some things I might not need to know."

"It's clear, Sheriff." One of the officers moved around the building. "We have the front and back entrance secured. We're ready to move inside."

"Let's check the restaurant first. Work our way up." Zeke looked into the truck. "You have the key, Janey?"

She shook her head. "I left those keys upstairs. All I have is the house key."

Zeke grimaced.

"Natches has the keys. He carries them with him all the time. Just in case," she told them. "If he's on his way."

The sound of the Harley racing through the streets could be heard.

"Sounds like him," she muttered.

Janey clenched her fists, grit her teeth, and forced the tears and the fear back into the dark, lonely hole where they couldn't feed, where they couldn't build. She could feel herself shuddering on the inside, freezing. So cold that even when she wrapped Alex's coat around her, she couldn't get warm.

She wanted to curl into a corner alone and scream. She wanted to hit. She wanted to howl out at the pain and find something to untie the knot of horror growing inside her.

This shouldn't be happening. She should be able to live in peace now that Dayle and Nadine were dead. She shouldn't have to be afraid again, shouldn't have to fear for those she cared about.

She shouldn't have to leave the town she loved to protect those who meant the most to her.

She pressed her knotted fists into her stomach as Natches moved up to Alex and the sheriff. Her brother's voice was hard and cold now. It wasn't angry; he wasn't acting the fool as he had at the bar. He was stone-cold serious, and the gun she glimpsed shoved into the holster at his side assured her of it.

Minutes later, Dawg and Rowdy were joining them, both of them armed as well. They weren't joking around. They were still considered agents, attached to the Department of Homeland Security, owing to their participation in the investigation that had revealed Dayle Mackay and Nadine Grace as members of a domestic terrorist group.

"Janey, I'm locking you in the truck." Alex turned back to her. "Keep the doors locked, no matter what. Do you know how to use a gun?"

She nodded bleakly. "I know how to shoot."

He reached over, popped the glove box, and drew out another, smaller automatic handgun. He checked the clip, then shoved the gun into her hands. "Use it if you have to, honey. You hear me?"

She nodded again, then turned to him. "Be careful, Alex. Please."

"Always," he said softly.

He moved back, hit the lock on his door, then slammed it closed. She watched them as they moved to the office entrance. Two officers were at the back stairs as the sheriff moved into the restaurant with Natches, Dawg, and Rowdy.

It was too dark back here, she thought. Too many shadows. Too many places for someone to hide. The officers left outside were cautious, wary. Their hands rested on the butts of their weapons as they watched, in different directions, their bodies tense and prepared.

Janey wanted to curl into the seat and just escape. Like she had escaped the day Nadine had touched her. She wanted to burrow into her own mind and pretend none of this was happening. But Alex and Natches were in there. Once again, someone else was protecting her; they were putting their lives on the line while she sat safely along the sidelines.

As she sat there, she heard a distressed feline wail. The officers jerked, turning toward the Dumpsters that sat along the fence on the opposite side of the truck.

"Fat Cat." She jerked the door open as an orange blur jumped from the ground into the truck.

He was wailing and meowing plaintively as he tried to burrow beneath Alex's coat.

Janey slammed the door closed and relocked it, then wrapped her arms around the heavy cat and stroked his fur.

"Where have you been, bad cat?" she whispered as he meowed again, a sound of mingled anger and fear. "Are you okay?"

She ran her hands over him, but nothing seemed hurt. He huddled at her side beneath the coat, his head sticking out, his topaz eyes glaring up at her.

"I know, I'm late. I'm sorry. Bad mommy, huh?" She stroked his head, almost smiling mockingly at her own words. "It's okay. I'll give you extra hamburger tonight. How's that?"

As though he sensed the little reward, he laid his head on her lap, but his heavy body still trembled. Fat Cat didn't like strangers in his territory evidently.

As she stroked him, she watched Alex, the sheriff, and Natches move from the office and head up the stairs to the apartment. They spoke briefly to the two officers; Rowdy and Dawg were still in the restaurant for some reason.

She stared at Alex as he moved behind the sheriff but in front of Natches, to the small landing. The door opened, a thin wedge of light spilling from inside.

That was what she hadn't seen earlier. There was a light on inside the apartment. And Janey had been careful not to leave any on when she left.

"Who was here, Fat Cat?" she asked the feline quietly, still stroking his fur as she fought the panic trying to rise inside her.

She was shaking as hard on the inside as the cat was on the

outside. And she was horribly afraid that her insistence on staying here, in Somerset, was going to end up hurting someone
other than herself. Natches or Alex would end up hurt. Or both.
And she didn't know if she could live with herself if that happened.

Alex shoved the Glock into the back of his jeans,
propped his hands on his hips, and glared around the room after
they'd finished checking the apartment. Natches and Zeke were
reading that letter, again. Alex didn't need to read it again. He'd
had enough of it when Zeke first unfolded it. The filth in it was
enough to make a grown man sick.

More of the same bullshit with a little addition about corrupting good patriotic men. Give him a fucking break.

The officers with Zeke were finished dusting for prints, and
Dawg and Rowdy were giving the restaurant a last check before
collecting Janey and bringing her up.

Zeke pushed the note into a plastic bag, secured it, and dated
and signed it before shaking his head and moving to the door.

Natches stayed. He turned, glared at Alex's neck, and crossed
his arms over his chest.

"Don't start, Natches," he warned him. "I'm not in a bullshit
mood right now."

"That's my sister you're jacking around with," Natches accused him.

"Yeah, and it's my sister one of you was jacking around with
last year," he bit out.

"Not me," Natches argued.

"Yeah, well, one of you is just as bad as the other." Alex sighed
in irritation. "Get the fuck off my back. Nothing you say is going
to change a damned thing."

"She's going to try to leave," Natches told him warily then. "I know her. She thinks I don't, because I let that bastard send her away. But I know her, Alex. She's going to try to leave, thinking it will protect us."

"She'll change her mind." Alex moved through the living room, pacing it off.

He could feel something teasing at him here. How the hell had someone gotten into the apartment without activating the alarm? There were no hidden doors. There was no other way in. All the windows were secure. They'd checked the closets, checked the walls themselves. Nothing.

"And what makes you think she'll change her mind?" Natches retorted. "That fucking hickey on your neck?"

Alex stopped and turned his head slowly. He stared back at Natches, feeling the itch under his skin, the need to loose the pent-up violence raging through him.

"Keep pushing me."

There was no "or else." They both knew the "or else." They could fight it out, but it wouldn't change a damned thing.

"Hell," Natches muttered.

They heard Dawg and Rowdy coming with Janey and that wailing cat. Hadn't Alex fed that little monster earlier?

Janey stepped into the apartment, ignoring the tension between her brother and Alex as Fat Cat jumped out of her arms and ran to his missing bowl.

"Bowl's on the porch." Alex looked at Dawg.

Dawg stepped outside, retrieved the empty dish, and set it down. Fat Cat smacked him, claws bared.

"Little bastard," Dawg growled. Then he snarled at the cat.

Janey picked up the bowl and moved to the fridge, where she filled it with the fresh hamburger she kept on hand for the cat.

She stayed silent. Fed the cat and filled his water bowl before turning and moving through the kitchen. She turned the corner and headed for her bedroom.

"Janey." Natches followed her to the hall. "We need to talk a minute."

"I have to change clothes." She shook her head, keeping her back to him. "I'll be out in a little while."

She closed the bedroom door and leaned her back against it, drawing in a shuddering breath. She could feel the sobs building in her chest and she hated it. Hated it. She hated crying, she hated the sense of helplessness it filled her with, and she hated trying, trying so hard to play the perfect little girl and never succeeding.

Shaking her head, she pushed Alex's coat from her shoulders and tossed it over the bottom of her bed. The heels and stockings came off next. Then the skirt and top. She only distantly realized she had forgotten to put her panties back on.

In the bathroom she showered, scrubbed the makeup from her face, and lathered her hair. She had to go shopping tomorrow, she decided. If being the good girl didn't work, then screw them all, she'd be who she wanted to be. She was tired of hiding. Sick to her back teeth of being protected.

Drying off, she moved back into her bedroom, and drew on the long cotton pants she used to sleep in. She hated those, too. The T-shirt. Tomorrow, she was buying gowns. Silky gowns. Sexy gowns. It didn't matter if anyone else saw them. She would see them.

Running her fingers through her hair, she left her bedroom, rather expecting her apartment to be cleared of Mackays. It wasn't. Ray and Maria were there as well now, Kelly, Chaya, Crista, and a concerned Faisal.

Faisal had moved into an apartment in town with a few other boys that the Mackays had taken under their wings over the years. The other boys were preparing Faisal for college. The incredibly bright, energetic young boy Natches and Crista had arranged to have brought out of the Iraq desert didn't look any happier than the Mackays did.

"Aren't you guys sick yet of dragging your pregnant wives out over nothing?" She threw Dawg and Natches a disgusted look.

"You're something to us, Janey," Chaya spoke up, her hand resting on the small mound of her belly as she sat on Natches's lap in one of the kitchen chairs.

"You're family," Crista finished for her.

She, too, was pregnant, about a month further along than Chaya was.

"Besides, we can't let the boys have all the fun." Kelly, Rowdy's wife, grinned from where she sat on his lap. "Otherwise, they might get spoiled."

Janey bit back a retort. Opening the fridge, she pulled out the wine, poured herself a glass, and pushed the cork back into the bottle. She left it sitting out as she turned and faced the crowd.

She wasn't used to this. It was too much. And there was Alex, doing nothing, not a damned thing, to hide that bite on his neck as he leaned against the wall and watched her.

"It's after eleven," she told all of them. "Nearly my bedtime." She gave them a false, bright smile. "I'm sure it's nearly yours as well."

She didn't want to deal with hours of placating the worry and concern she saw in everyone's eyes. She just wanted them to go away.

"Natches and I are going to stay all night, Janey," Chaya decided. "We're worried."

Janey inhaled, then lifted the wine. She took a long sip, staring at Chaya and Natches over the rim of the glass. Her brother's face was calm, but his eyes raged.

"I thought that was Alex's job?" She looked at Alex. A mocking half smile tilted his lips.

"Not tonight," Natches told her, his voice even.

Janey shook her head. "Fine, the two of you can stay and I'll get a hotel room. Not a problem."

Natches dropped his head back on the chair and closed his eyes as Chaya patted his knee.

"Janey, please . . ." Chaya began to protest.

"It's his apartment. It's in his name." She shrugged. "It's not a problem. I'll also be posting ads this week for a manager for the restaurant. I'm thinking about going back to college."

Strangely, Natches looked back at Alex. Alex stiffened, his eyes narrowing.

"Sudden decision, isn't it?" Alex asked.

"Not really." Janey shrugged. "I need a break . . ."

"Bullshit."

Alex's voice was carefully controlled, his gaze flat and hard.

She sipped at her wine again, her gaze locked with his.

"I'll find another manager before I go, but I'll be leaving within a few weeks."

Ray, Maria, Rowdy, Kelly, Dawg, and Crista rose from their seats as Alex's jaw tensed and Faisal watched the Mackays worriedly.

"Yeah, time for us to leave." Dawg stretched and wrapped his arm around his wife before heading for the door. The others followed. Chaya and Natches stayed in place.

"Come here and give us a hug, Janey," Dawg commanded.

"I, too, will leave." Faisal watched Natches in concern. "But I do not like the thought of Janey leaving this town, Natches."

Janey hugged Dawg as she listened to Natches and Faisal talking. She hugged Ray and took his kiss on the cheek, and Maria's. Kelly's hug was tight and hard, and Rowdy kissed her hair with a whispered "Nice try."

Crista smiled and hugged her, then Dawg wrapped her in his arms, lifted her against him, and almost made a tear fall with his muttered "Don't leave us. We love ya, ya know?"

"I know, Dawg," she whispered back. "College calls, though."

He chuckled at that. "You wish."

Faisal stood before her then, his dark face and gleaming black eyes concerned. "I would not enjoy losing the aunt I have come to admire as I admire you," he told her.

"You're a hell of a nephew, Faisal," she assured him with a quick smile. "Get back home. I'm sure you have classes tomorrow."

She closed the door behind him, then moved back to her wine.

"I'll go pack my bag." She finished her wine. "I'll call a cab from the bedroom."

Chaya stood from Natches's lap and curled into the corner of the couch as Natches lifted his head and stared back at Janey.

"Running away again?"

"Shut up, Natches," Alex said calmly. "Take your wife and go home."

Natches turned and gave him a long, level look. Alex missed it; his gaze didn't leave Janey's.

"Hell." Natches pushed himself from the chair and looked at Chaya. "You ready, honey?"

"Not really," Chaya said calmly. "I don't like how the two of you are railroading her. I think I'll stick around and play referee."

"Thank you, Chaya." Janey smiled tightly. "But I know how to fight my own battles when someone's not holding the threat of a gun to my brother's head."

Natches tightened, the reference hard to miss. Yeah, Dayle had made certain she understood exactly what stepping out of line meant.

"You should have told me he was threatening you with me," he growled.

She shrugged. "My bad."

"Your bad?" He blinked back at her, anger glittering in his eyes. "What the hell is up with you?"

"Me." She stared back at him, her lips firm, her gaze steady as she breathed heavily. "I'm tired of this, Natches. This isn't my home. No matter how much I want it to be, it's not going to happen. Now's a damned good time to accept that."

"Hell, Natches," Alex drawled. "I finally met a Mackay that knows how to quit. Now, here's one for the record books. Congratulations."

His gaze never wavered from her.

"Looks that way, doesn't it?" she retorted coolly. "You can leave, too, by the way. I don't think your services are required anymore."

"My services?" His brows arched. "Well now, ain't that too bad. But we can discuss that little particular after your brother leaves." His gaze moved to Natches then. "Or not. All according to how pissed off he wants to get tonight, I guess."

Chaya rose from the couch. "Yes, time for us to leave, honey." She caught Natches's hand as he glowered at Alex. "Now, Natches."

"We're going to discuss this," he warned Alex.

"Uh-huh. Add it to the rest of the subjects you've warned me we're going to discuss. I'm sure I'll get around to it later."

Janey watched, forcing back the trembling in her hands, feeling it settle in her stomach as her brother and sister-in-law left. Slowly. Natches was angry, but for once he was reining that anger in. That didn't bode well for her. Alex didn't move from where he leaned against the wall. His head tilted, his gaze growing curious as the door closed, and he reached out and slid the locks home.

"I asked you to leave as well," she told him, keeping her voice low, the quiver out of it.

"You sure did." He nodded his head slowly.

"Then why are you still standing here?"

"Because my dick's still hard," he answered her. "You made some pretty heavy promises tonight, Janey." He straightened slowly. "We'll see to those first. Then we'll discuss that insanity you just spouted about going back to California."

A shiver raced up her spine as he took a step toward her.

"I changed my mind about the supposed promises." She tried to sneer. "Sorry, Alex. Go find blondie; I'm sure she'll take care of that hard-on for you."

He smiled. And that smile sent a nervous reaction shuddering through her so hard that this time, her hands did tremble. Her pussy quivered. Her clit became so hard, so sensitive, she swore the rasp of her panties was going to cause her to come as the reaction punched into her womb.

He looked wild. Sexy. Dangerous.

"Doesn't work that way," he growled. "Oh, baby, not even in your wildest dreams does it work that way."

His arm snaked around her waist, jerked her to him. His hand cupped her neck, holding her in place. "Now I'll just show you exactly how it does work."

TEN

Alex couldn't explain, even to himself, why the hell the thought of her leaving, running, affected him like it did. It made him crazy, made him wild. Made him determined to show her exactly why she wasn't walking away from Somerset, or from him.

He'd warned her he was hard, warned her he wouldn't be an easy lover, yet when his lips came down on hers, he found himself pulling back, holding back, more eager for the heat and seductive pleasure than the wild, hard clash of pure lust.

There was something about her small, fragile body that made him feel bigger, stronger than he was. Something about the strength of her hunger that filled him with a sense of awareness, of the primitive possessiveness that he had been fighting for years.

Janey was different. There was something so special, so intrinsically unique, about her, that he knew she would never recede into the back of his memories as every other woman had.

Janey would always demand his attention. Without design, without even trying; if she was near, she would always enchant his senses.

A terrifying thought for a man who had ensured that no woman ever chained his soul. If he had enough sense left inside him to think.

The moment his lips touched hers, there was no thought. There was nothing but Janey. Her lips opening beneath his, wild and hungry as her arms curled around his neck and she all but climbed his body in her attempt to get closer.

He clasped her neck, feeling its fragility beneath his palm. He could feel her pulse pounding in the side of her neck, and beneath his fingers he could feel the tension building at the back of the slender column.

Her shy little tongue touched his, then licked, sucking his tongue into her mouth. She moaned as his lips slanted over hers.

She was as untamed as the wind. He had felt it in her, sensed it in her, even before he saw her dancing at that damned bar. Before he felt her body swaying, moving against his, and saw the exquisite joy she found in the dance.

Now he'd show her a different dance.

"You think it's so easy to walk away," he murmured against her lips. "Get up in the morning and walk away from this. I dare you."

He deepened the kiss, leaning her into the wall as he lifted her, forcing her legs around his waist and pressing his cock between her thighs as he braced her against the wall.

One hand held her neck, the other her ass. His fingertips caressed and stroked as his tongue commanded her lips, her mouth. Deep, wicked kisses. Kisses that seared his soul even as those desperate moans echoing in her throat became more imperative.

Her hands were at the back of his head, trying to hold him to her. Sharp little nails pierced his scalp, adding to the sensations. He could feel the dominance, the hard-core sexuality inside him rising to the fore. But it didn't overwhelm the kiss. Something else, a heavy vein of gentleness, a need for tenderness, tempered yet heated him further.

God, he was burning for her. His balls were on fire, his cock harder than it had ever been. If he didn't get her to a bed then, he was going to end up fucking her against the wall.

He moved, stumbled a bit, trying to kiss her and get them to her bedroom at the same time. He wasn't about to let her go yet. To release those lush, pouty lips that moved beneath his, suckled at his tongue and moaned with such earthy pleasure.

Damn her. She was twisting him in so many different directions he didn't know what the hell to do with the feelings he could feel breaking free inside him.

He'd never known this rich, desperate tenderness for any other woman. Tenderness mixed with a lust so overwhelming he wondered if he would survive it.

Laying her back on her wide bed, Alex rose over her, holding her hips to him as he settled against her, both hands clasping her head as he moved his lips from hers to her jaw, then her neck.

He could feel the mark she'd left on him burning against his skin. Her mark. A brand. He'd never allowed another woman to mark him. The primal wash of lust he'd felt when she had done it, though, nearly had his cock pumping his seed into his jeans. And it created a hunger. A hunger to mark her just as effectively. To brand her. To leave his stamp of ownership on her.

Her neck arched and tilted to the side as he felt her breathing become harder, rougher. His lips slid over her neck, moved to the juncture of her neck and shoulder, where he knew she was most sensitive. He licked the spot, kissed it, then opened his lips over it and drew the tender skin into his mouth as he bit down on her.

She jerked against him as though electrified. Her hips arched into his, grinding against his cock, writhing beneath him. She was like a living flame in his arms now, and he was desperate for more.

Pulling back, he felt his teeth clench at the sight of the mark on her pale neck. It was deeper, the small bite darker, than he had intended. The fierce male pride that surged through him shocked him.

He stared down at her dazed face and wondered if this was what she had felt when she had seen her brand on him. This primal, overwhelming need to possess. For a man who had gone through life swearing to never possess anything that could be taken from him, it was a frightening feeling.

"I marked you back." His voice was fierce, triumphant.

"You marked me long ago and just didn't know it."

Alex felt his abdomen clench at the declaration. If possible, he swore his dick thickened.

"You're dangerous, baby." He smiled down at her, hoping to take off the edge of near-obsessive hunger rising inside him as he levered up and forced himself to unbutton his shirt and shrug it from his shoulders rather than rip it off.

What the hell was wrong with him? He could be buried inside her now, pumping into that tight, hot little pussy and he was holding back instead.

It was that damned tenderness he couldn't seem to push aside. He wanted her aware of him, so ready for him that when he took her, the pain would be minimal. The thought of hurting her sent shards of tension radiating through his mind.

"I love your body." Her sigh was followed by the tentative touch of her fingers against his flexing abs. "So strong and hard. I wish I could wrap you around me."

Christ. Her eyes. Those light green eyes stared up at him, wistful and filled with something that went deeper than hunger. It made him want to wrap around her, to become her personal shield, her blanket, her fucking life.

He was losing his mind to her.

He watched her, forcing himself to stay still as she pulled at his belt.

For a moment, regret flickered in her gaze as she pulled the belt free, and he knew what was going through her mind. She thought she was going to leave. Thought she was going to leave him. Oh, poor little Janey. She had another thing coming.

"Take your shirt off first." He stilled her hands when she would have released his jeans. "I want to watch you take it off."

She paused, blinked up at him, and her eyes darkened with a hint of self-consciousness. But she did it. She reached for the hem of her shirt and slowly lifted it. Her softly rounded belly was revealed, her breasts, then she was tossing it from her head.

And Alex was still staring at her breasts. They were perfect breasts. Not large, just right. Swollen little mounds topped with pretty cotton-candy pink nipples that were stiff, hard.

"I want to suck your nipples until you come from it," he growled, and a flush worked over her breasts and up her neck. He couldn't tear his eyes away long enough to see her flushed face. Yet.

He loved her nipples. His mouth watered to taste them, to draw them in, play with the hard little tips with his tongue.

"Your nipples make me sweat," he told her roughly. "I want to suck them so bad it burns me alive."

As he watched, those hard tips seemed to flush further. Rising over her, he licked at first one, then the other as he toed his boots off and kicked them over the side of the bed.

He tore at the snap and zipper of his jeans, working them off as he sucked at each hard little point. She was going wild beneath him. Her arms hugged his head, trying to push all of her breast into his mouth. Incredible. She was making him crazy with the taste, with each little cry that fell past her lips.

When he was naked, he tugged at her cotton pants, pulling her panties with them. He wanted her naked, wanted her bare. He wanted to cover her, wrap around her. God help him, he wanted to fulfill that need he heard in her voice for security, for safety. For pleasure.

Jancy watched Alex's face. Pleasure came in surprising ways, she had found. Not just the touch of his hands, or his mouth, but the look in his eyes, the tight, hungry grimace that pulled at his lips.

When she stroked his shoulders, his lashes would lift. His cheeks hollowed as he sucked her nipples, but each caress she gave him, each new touch, brought him pleasure as well. Brought her pleasure.

It was so good. The sensations traveling from the hard tips of her breasts to her womb were sizzling. His mouth covered her nipple, his tongue rasped it until she was writhing beneath him, crying out his name in a need so vicious she didn't think she could bear it.

She felt as though she were burning up. That the heat in the apartment was too high. That some internal thermostat had stopped working.

"Fuck, your nipples are good, baby," he drawled, his voice rough, sexy, as his dark gray eyes stared up at her. "Hard and sweet."

As he spoke, one hand smoothed down her side to her hip.

"Almost as sweet as your pussy was in that truck tonight."

A shocking surge of pleasure clenched her womb, and he grinned with wicked, naughty intent.

"Are you wet, Janey?"

Was she wet?

"What do you think?" she cried out. "Alex, you're killing me."

She lost her breath as one finger, just one, slid through her cleft, gathering her juices and running around her clit.

"Ah yeah, sweet honey," he whispered. "You're so wet, Janey." His finger ran down the cleft and circled the entrance to her vagina as his lashes dipped over his eyes. "So tight."

His finger pressed inside. Janey gripped his biceps, felt them tensing beneath her and felt more of her juices meeting his penetration.

Oh, it was so good. So much better than her own fingers. His calloused fingertip rasped just inside the opening, stroking her internal muscles as she clenched around it.

Janey turned her head, lips parted, pressing to that heavy muscle in his upper arm as he stroked her, stretched her. She was only barely aware of biting into the tough skin, drawing it into her mouth.

Oh, she was so going to mark him again. Because it was mark him or scream.

She screamed anyway seconds later as he added a finger, stretched her, pressing inside her and stroking her to insanity.

"You're fucking tight, Janey. Do you know what this is going to feel like around my dick?" His voice was harsh, agonized. "You're going to make me crazy once I get inside you, baby. Once this sweet pussy is gripping me, rippling around my cock like you're rippling around my fingers."

Her hips arched as she tried to drive the penetration deeper. She needed deeper, needed more of this exquisite, burning sensation. She could feel the small, tight thrusts through her entire body. Each lash of pleasure whipped through her veins, burned her deeper, hotter.

"Ah, sweet baby." His head lowered, his lips roved over her breasts. He kissed, licked. He sucked at the mounds. Hard enough that she could feel it in her womb. Gentle enough that there was no fear, no pain. There was just Alex touching her. Touching her as he never had, as she had never believed he would.

"Janey." His voice thickened, became rougher. "Baby. If I don't fuck you, I'm going to come on your bed." He licked at her nipples again and his fingers pressed in farther, rotating and sending a flash of burning pleasure tearing through her.

Then another. Another. His fingers were sliding deeper, taking her, working inside her with slow, controlled twists of his wrist.

Janey moved her thighs farther apart, her feet braced on the bed as she tried to thrust into each penetration. Tried to take more than he was allowing her.

"Do something," Her head thrashed on the bed.

She was burning, burning inside and out. And he was as well. Her eyes opened to see the sweat as it ran in one small rivulet down the side of his face. His eyes were so dark, thunderous. His expression heavy with lust.

"Demanding," he groaned. "Keep giving me orders like that, Janey, and I'm going to come before I get inside you."

"Fuck me, Alex." She stared back at him, lips parted, her breathing harsh. Heavy. "If you're scared, baby, then lie back. I'll ride you."

Oh God, she hadn't actually said that, had she? Teased him when she was dying for him.

He froze, his face tightening, cheekbones standing out in stark release as primal, primitive lust filled his expression. His cheeks darkened, his lips looked heavier.

"Hell yeah." He suddenly grinned, and in that grin was teasing, wicked hunger.

She tried to hold him to her as he pulled away. Her hands slapped the bed as he eased from it.

"What?" she demanded roughly. "Where the hell are you going?" She came to her knees, struggling to find the breath to speak, to figure out why he had pulled away from her.

"Latex, sweetheart. I bet my left nut you're not on protection, are you?"

Janey stilled, her heart suddenly beating rough and hard as he reached down for his pants and pulled a foil pack free.

She lifted her hand, then dropped it, watching him, heart racing; the need to do it for him was killing her. She wanted to sheathe him. She wanted to touch him.

"You can, you know," he said, his tone still teasing, but growing rougher.

Her gaze jerked to his as he held the small square pack out to her. "Get me ready for you, darlin'. Show me how much you want me."

She felt her hands shake, excitement and fear pulsing through her. She had never done anything like this, had no idea what to do, how to touch him.

She reached out and took the small square of foil, then opened it carefully, until the latex disc was held gently between her fingers.

"Just roll it over my cock, baby."

She moved closer, holding her lower lip between her teeth as she watched his fingers curl around the heavy shaft.

And stroke.

It was so sexy. She could barely breathe. Excitement was racing through her now, her juices weeping from her pussy. She wanted him inside her. She wanted all of him.

She pressed the rolled condom against the head of his cock and unrolled it down his shaft carefully, watching as his fingers lowered, gripped his balls, and a groan filled the room.

His other hand tucked around her neck and lifted her face for his kiss. His lips were hard, hungry. They devoured as she held on to him, her tongue meeting his, dueling with it as she lifted against him.

"Christ, you make a man crazy."

He gripped her hips, lifting her against him as he moved to the bed again, propping himself back, arranging her legs to straddle his hard, muscular thighs.

Janey stared back at him in surprise. "What are you doing?"

"Take me." He smiled back at her, the curve of his lips tight, his gaze so dark, stormy. As though some hard, dark core was being restrained, pulled back.

She could sense it, but she didn't feel it. His hands were gentle, firm, and as he pulled her hips lower, she felt the broad head of his cock pushing against the entrance to her pussy.

"I want inside you so bad I'm about to explode just thinking about it." His hands clenched on her hips, then slid to the curve of her ass. "Take me, Janey. Go wild on me, baby. Let me see all that fire you're hiding inside you."

Janey shook her head. She knew what he wanted. He wanted all of her. She could feel it. If she gave it all to him, then how would she survive when he walked away? Alex always walked away, she knew that. No woman had ever held him more than a few weeks. No woman ever would. Especially not a traitor's daughter.

"I'm not taking you, Janey." His lips moved over her jaw, touched her lips. "If you want it, baby, you have to take it. Slow and easy, or hot and wild . . . Fuck."

She couldn't stay still.

Janey pressed down. She moaned as she felt the broad head part her, enter. She lowered her head, pressed her forehead against his shoulder, and pressed down more.

She was going to pass out. The blood pounded through her head. Pleasure was like a cascade of white-hot sparks, brilliant, electric, racing through her body.

He stretched her until she swore she couldn't take more. She followed his guiding hands at her hips, rocked against him, felt more slip inside her, and she was dying for even more.

"Alex." She moaned his name.

"Janey, baby." He was tense, his muscles rippling with restrained power beneath her. "Fuck me, sweetheart. Take what you want."

She wanted. Oh God, she wanted so bad.

She rolled her head against his shoulder, her hips flexing, moving jerkily, pushing down, feeling the stretch and burn.

"Help me," she cried out.

If he would just do it, then she could hold a part of herself back. She was certain of it. Just enough of her heart to survive.

"Give me your wild, Janey," he urged, his voice tight now, hoarse. "Give it all to me, baby."

She shook her head. She couldn't stop.

A whimper tore from her throat as she moved on him again, lifting and lowering, working him inside her. There was no pain, just that burning, stretching pleasure.

"Help me!" she cried.

"Fuck me, damn you! Take me, Janey!" The hard command in his voice ripped through her. It tore aside hesitation. It slashed through her brain, filled her with defiance, with challenge.

Her head jerked up, her eyes opened. And oh God, she should have kept them closed. His face was dark. Forbidding. His touch was light. There was nothing heavy, nothing forceful. But his face. The sight of all that lust, the heavy, brutal sensuality flickering in his eyes, tore through her.

"All of you?" She moved against him, her nails digging into his shoulders. "You want me to take all of you?"

"All the way to my fucking balls." His muscles were tight with restraint. His hands fell away from her, lifting to the back of the headboard. His fingers were pale with the force of the grip he had on the bed. His biceps flexed, rippled.

She wanted to bite him again.

"All the way to your balls, Alex?" She braced her hands against his chest, lifted, and slid back down. Slowly. So slowly.

His expression twisted. His head fell back against the bed.

"Fuck. I'm going to come so hard you'll feel it, Janey. You'll feel me pumping into that damned condom."

She pushed down farther, staring back at him, shaking, shuddering. It was so good. So fucking good.

"How bad will it hurt?" She whimpered. "I want all of you now, Alex. Tell me. How bad will it hurt?"

He drew in a hard, deep breath. "I took care of it, Janey. With my fingers, baby. No pain. No fucking pain. I can't hurt you, sweetheart. Not like this."

Her heart was breaking in her chest. She could see the need inside him, desperate, so male, dominant and powerful. And restrained. Holding back, so he wouldn't hurt her.

In that moment, she knew he already had all of her, no matter the consequences, and it didn't matter that she couldn't have him in public, that he couldn't claim her. Because of this.

She lifted, let her head fall back, and let all her weight go into the next downward stroke she made.

She heard herself wail. Felt the agonizing, burning ecstasy that filled her as she took him. All of him. All the way to his balls as he shouted her name.

His hands jerked from the bed to her ass. Gripping it, lifting her. "Janey. Fuck. Baby."

"Let me go." Her nails dug into his wrists.

It had her now. That hunger. That need. She was powerful. She was invincible. She held the most incredible strength she had ever known, deep inside her, for only a second.

And he was holding her back.

Her head lifted. "Let me go."

"Not so hard," he gritted out. "Fuck. You're too little to take me like this, Janey."

She leaned forward, nipped his lower lip, stared back at him. She'd read things. She knew some things. She let her muscles clench around the heavy crown still embedded in her.

"Don't take my choice," she whispered. "You said I could take you. I need you, Alex. All of you. Just like that."

Sweat dripped down his face now, dampened his chest.

"Your hands go on the headboard." She pulled them free, pressed them back.

She was shaking. From the inside out, trembling, clenching on him.

"You're spanked," he panted. "So fucking spanked."

Her pussy flooded around him.

"Maybe I want spanked."

She lowered herself and it began again. Lightning. A blaze of fire. The stretching fullness that didn't stop, wouldn't ease. It burned with pleasure. Ached with ecstasy.

She couldn't stop moving. She rode him hard and fast, feeling the pleasure building inside her. Taking her, overtaking her.

"God yes, fuck me, baby." He was straining beneath her now, his hips lifting with her, pushing his cock deeper, harder, inside her. "So sweet. So damned tight. So damned tight you're killing me."

She couldn't breathe. She could feel the sensations slamming through her now. She was dizzy, dazed. Her head lowered to his shoulder and she lost all control. She bit him and sucked at his skin, slamming her pussy onto the thick, throbbing cock penetrating her, fucking inside her until she screamed.

Her orgasm was alive within her. It raged through her, arching her back. It raced through her, pulling her muscles tight, clamping her pussy around him as she felt the hard, heated pulse of him inside her.

She was shuddering, writhing, twisting against him and dying from the pleasure. And he was right. She could feel him coming. Hot spurt after spurt as though it were filling her, heating her, sinking inside her and exploding through her womb.

It was brutal, it was terrifying and exhilarating. She wanted it again. Again and again. She didn't want to live without him inside her. She didn't want to exist without his kiss, without his hunger.

And when his head lowered, his lips covering hers, his tongue pushing hard inside her mouth as he growled her name, she knew she wanted all of him as well.

It wasn't pleasure. It went beyond pleasure, beyond ecstasy. For a moment, just a moment, she felt as though she belonged to him.

ELEVEN

Alex knew the moment it happened. The second he felt his sperm shooting from the slit of his cock, he felt the latex split. And he felt pure, undiluted rapture. The fiery heat, the wash of Janey's release, his cum spilling inside her, spurting hot and deep into the rich, fist-tight grip she had on him.

He'd never had a condom break. He'd always been on guard for it, until Janey.

He couldn't pull back, couldn't jerk out. All he could do was slam his lips over hers, holding her to him and trying to push deeper inside her. She took him to the hilt. He could feel the ultra-tight depths of her from the tip of his cock to the base; there was no place left to fill her. But he tried. Tried to get deeper, to fill her to her womb as his seed shot from his dick.

It was the most exquisite pleasure a man could know. More pleasure than Alex had ever imagined knowing, and he knew, when it came to sex, he had a damned good imagination. He was sure, sure to the depths of his soul that he had known every lust-filled, wicked, sensual sensation to be found.

Until this. The crown of his dick bare, buried inside her, feeling each desperate ripple of her pussy, each pulse of his cum and hers. Feeling her. Inside and out. And feeling the soul-deep knowledge that there was no chance in hell of walking away from her now.

He held her in his arms now. He couldn't let go of her. Couldn't make himself let go of her. He was buried in her, the latex spread away from the head of his cock, and he swore he felt her heartbeat in her pussy. Rocking, rippling around him. He felt it clear to his soul.

He leaned his head over her. Trying to surround her. His sweet Janey. She loved it when he held her, stroked his hands over her, and she tried so hard not to. He had seen it in her eyes, felt it in her. That need to hold back, to not be dependent, to not need anything or anyone. And now she was going to be stuck with him.

At least until he knew whether or not she was carrying his baby.

She was still shaking in his arms. He couldn't tell her yet. Her little nails were still digging into his biceps. For some reason, he thought, his arms turned her on. She was holding on to him there and she would get that little faraway look in her eyes, kneading the muscle. He knew it sure as hell turned him on. And when she had bit him . . .

He closed his eyes and leaned back against the headboard. Hell, he was hard as a rock again.

A little giggle passed Janey's lips. Alex opened one eye and stared down at her as she pushed herself up against his chest.

"I felt that." There was the slightest satisfied curl to her lips.

"I'd be worried if you didn't," he told her, then sighed heavily. "Come on. You're exhausted."

He felt her yawn, felt her leaning against him again. Hell, it hadn't been a good day for her. He'd tell her about the condom tomorrow morning. That was soon enough.

He slid from the bed as he lifted her from him. She burrowed under the blankets and snagged the pillow he had been leaning against before curling up and closing her eyes.

She wasn't running to the shower or running to clean the scent or feel of their sex from her body.

Alex shook his head, unrolled the destroyed condom from his erection, and padded into the bathroom. He used the toilet, washed up, and dried before flipping off the light and moving back to the bedroom.

He turned off the little low light on the night table before reaching for the blankets.

"Turn the light back on," she mumbled from beneath the blankets. "I don't like being alone in the dark."

He slid into the bed and pulled her into his arms, her back against his chest. "You're not alone."

She froze, as though she hadn't expected him to stay. Alex wrapped himself around her. Her head pillowed on his arm, his larger body framing hers. His erection pressed against the cleft of her rear.

A few seconds later she relaxed against him, though, and burrowed closer. He knew the moment she went to sleep. The wariness left her, slowly. Her breathing deepened, and Alex was left to stare into the dark, his arms around her, wondering what the hell he was going to do. Because holding her as she slept felt as natural as breathing.

Hell, he'd fucked up here. He should have gotten her on birth control before he let things go this far. He should have thought to ask her before tonight if she was on birth control. But he'd known. A part of him had already known she wasn't protected. And he was damned if he could find a moment's regret inside him.

He hadn't wanted to be tied to any woman, but he was also a man who well understood fate and destiny. Sometimes shit just happened, but it happened for a reason.

He brushed her hair back from her forehead, his lips pressing against her hair as he closed his eyes against whatever the hell it was raging inside him.

He'd never imagined he would be a father. A husband. He'd sworn it would never happen. There were too many things in the world that a man couldn't control. Acts of God a man didn't have a chance of avoiding.

He let his hand slide over her hip, his palm flattening on her stomach. She hadn't even washed. Maybe he should have told her. There were ways of attempting to stop a pregnancy. He could have had her try it. So why hadn't he?

Because he knew fate when it kicked his ass. In his entire sexual lifetime, he'd never had a condom break. Not once. But it had with Janey. With this one tiny, fiery woman-child, all his ideas about his future had been shot to hell.

He didn't have a choice. He'd have to marry her. He'd take the six months' active reserve duty and resign from the Special Forces. He'd had enough of blood and death anyway. He'd had a bellyful of it. He'd take care of Janey, and their child.

He was a damned good father. Hell, he'd raised Crista. She'd survived, even turned out to be a hell of a woman. He could do it again with his own. He was a man now, not a kid himself.

And he was rationalizing something that had a slow, steady burn building inside him. He wanted to jerk her closer, wanted to lean down and kiss her stomach, whisper to the life that could be growing there. He was going crazy and he hadn't even hit middle age yet.

And Natches would kill him. He almost grinned at the thought of that. Natches Mackay. They'd called him the ice man once. Now he was like an active volcano ready to blow at any moment. His wife and Janey were his trip wires.

"Hmmm." A little moan slipped from the woman he was holding as she moved against him again. Her ass wiggled against his cock and Alex ground his teeth together at the sweet pleasure that rocked through him.

He could have this, every night. Every day. Once they caught the bastard tormenting her, he'd show this county that Janey wasn't to be messed with. She had paid for being Dayle Mackay's daughter in ways that should have broken her years before. Should have turned her cold, heartless. Instead, the core of the girl she had once been had hidden behind an unemotional façade and cool green eyes. A façade that was slowly easing around him. Tonight, she'd gotten angry. Flushed cheeks, blazing eyes. Tomorrow, she'd likely scratch as deep as that damned cat of hers, once she realized he wasn't letting her go.

Try to run off to California on him, would she? His smile was less than amused. Like hell. His woman. His hand pressed her closer, felt the smooth roundness of her stomach. And, maybe, his child as well. She wasn't going anywhere without him.

"Again," she mumbled, surprising him, rubbing her ass against his cock, her hand covering his.

"Sleep, baby." He kissed her forehead, then groaned as her leg lifted, rested along his, opening herself to him.

"Again." Sleep-filled, demanding, the hunger in her tone undid him.

Alex moved, shifted, gripped the shaft of his cock in his hand and eased it against the snug opening of her wet pussy.

She hadn't cleaned their sex from her. That still amazed him. Their combined juices clung to her, slid against the head of his cock as he tried to ease into her.

One touch. That was all it took. Just one touch. She reached between her thighs, her fingers curling along his balls, and he lost his damned mind. Lost it. Lost it inside the tightest pussy he'd ever fucked, as he plunged half the length of his dick inside her. Pulled back, pushed in. He was moving inside her, harder than he should. He knew he was being harder than he should be.

But fuck. Christ almighty. She was lava-hot. His cock was bare, no latex, and it was the most exquisite pleasure in his life.

And he couldn't stop to savor it.

"Alex, it's so good." Her forehead pressed into his arm as her hand curled beneath it. There was an edge of a sob in her voice, desperate pleasure, rising need.

"Here. Over." He felt like an animal. Like a brute. He pushed her to her stomach, lifted her ass, and pushed inside her, hard and deep. "Touch your clit, Janey. Rub it. Make it better."

Her head was shaking against the pillow as he pushed inside her again and stilled. Tight, hot flesh rippled and contracted around him as he covered her, hovering over her, his lips at her ear.

"It'll feel so good." He kissed the shell of her ear. "Let your fingers caress your clit, baby. Surely you masturbate." There was no way she didn't.

"Not with you here." Her whisper was scandalized.

"It will feel so good," he crooned again. "When you feel good, your pussy gets hotter, tighter. When your clit explodes, your tight little pussy is going to grab on to me and suck the life out of me."

She whimpered, a sound of pleasure and need. Making Janey come out of that cool little shell of hers was going to be his pleasure. He could do it. She loved his touch. Needed it as much as he needed hers.

"Touch yourself, baby." He gripped her hand and pushed it beneath her body. "Think about me. Think about how crazy you're going to make me when your hot little cunt begins to quiver and tremble around my dick. I'll go crazy."

She moved and he felt it. Her fingers were on her clit, her moans rising beneath him as he clenched her hip with one hand and thrust against her, pulled back. He eased inside her again, and felt the ripple and shudder as he stroked her inside and she stroked herself outside.

"Damn, that's good," he said softly at her ear. He licked at the lobe, then nipped it and felt her panting for breath.

Alex dug his knees into the mattress and pumped her hard then. Fast, quick strokes before he stopped, stilled. She was crying out beneath him, shaking so hard in pleasure that she made him feel ten feet tall. And she was still stroking her clit, her fingers playing over it.

Janey was dying inside from the pleasure. She needed with a desperation she couldn't explain. As though in sleep, the hunger had risen inside her, biting into her.

"Does it feel good, baby?" Alex's voice sent tremors racing down her back. "You feel good on my cock. Like living fire. Come on, Janey, tell me you like it."

"Love it. Love it." She pressed her forehead into the pillow and lifted her ass for him. He stretched her wide, overfilled her, and she loved it.

"I could fuck you like this forever," he groaned. "Just pumping inside you, slow and easy, baby. Do you feel how hard your little clit is? How it throbs?"

"Yes. Oh yes." It was throbbing. Hard and fast. Like her heartbeat.

"I feel your pussy throbbing around my cock, too. You're getting close, aren't you? The closer you get, the tighter you get."

Explicit, demanding. The words fired inside her brain, sending electrical impulses of sensation racing to her clit, her vagina.

He felt huge inside her. He *was* huge inside her, and she loved it.

"Keep stroking, sweetheart," he crooned. "I want to feel you come around me."

She knew how to do this. This had saved her sanity. She stroked her clit, knowing it would never be the same again without Alex inside her.

"Feel good?"

"So good, Alex. So good."

He kissed her neck, her ear.

"Tell me to fuck you again, Janey. Come on, baby. Do you know how much I loved hearing that? Those pretty lips pouting, demanding I fuck you."

"Fuck me! Fuck me hard, Alex. I need it hard."

"Why hard, sweetheart?" A shiver washed over her at his voice. "Slow and easy lets you feel it. Lets you feel it build and tighten inside you."

And it let her need. It built on her memories. It would sear into her brain and into her soul.

"See how good slow and easy can be?" Slow and easy, one long stroke inside her. He eased back, leaving her desperate, empty. Aching. Then he filled her again, stretched her, revealed ultrasensitive nerve endings as her clit tightened with impending release.

"You take care of that pretty clit. I'll take of this sweet pussy."

Janey fought for breath. She couldn't believe it was this good, this soon. That it could get better than it had been the first time. That anything could do this to her, make her insane, make her drop her inhibitions, her fears. But Alex was doing it. With his hoarse statements, his crooning demands.

"Oh, you're close," he growled at her ear, nipped at it. "You're getting tighter." He was moving faster. That was what she wanted.

"Yes, faster. Oh, Alex. I can't stand it." The pleasure was whipping inside her, whirlpooling, sucking her into some vast, star-studded realm filled with racing pinpoints of ecstasy.

Her fingers rubbed over her clit, around it. Close. So close. Alex was moving faster, pumping inside her, shafting her with heavy, exquisite thrusts that pushed her higher.

"I'm going to come." The words whispered from her lips and he groaned again. "Oh God, Alex. I'm going to come."

"Come for me, baby." He fucked her harder, faster. "Come for me, Janey, all over my dick. Let that sweet pussy suck me tighter."

She exploded. More from his words and the heavy, pummeling

strokes inside her than because of her fingers. But it was white-hot, brilliant. She screamed into the pillow and felt the violent, shuddering tremors jerk through her body, quake her womb, and throw her, helplessly, into a fire that consumed her and tossed her, left her writhing and convulsing beneath him as she heard him groan her name and stiffen behind her. His cock seemed to swell further, pulse, and spill a blaze of heat inside her as the sensations rocked her again.

She was lost in it. Lost in the feel of him over her, like a powerful blanket, covering her, pumping into her as she slowly, so slowly, drifted through a shower of pleasure.

She collapsed beneath him.

Long moments later, she felt him move, leave the bed. And then a warm damp rag ran between her thighs.

"No," she mumbled, more asleep than awake. "I like you there."

He paused and kissed her hip, and she swore she heard him curse. But sleep smothered her, dragged her in, and wrapped her in bliss.

She felt him pull her against him again, distantly, in her sleep dreamscape, his arms living warmth, his leg over hers keeping the nightmares at bay. She swirled on the edges of her subconscious, but his hold on her kept them back. His palm flattened on her stomach again. And she liked that. A kiss pressed to the top of her head, and it was the last thing she knew.

TWELVE

Alex wasn't in bed with her when Janey woke the next morning, but she hadn't expected anything less. Dusk to dawn. He couldn't be seen.

She stretched beneath the blankets and a small smile curved her lips, despite the flash of pain at the thought that he couldn't be seen with her. It hurt. It clenched inside her like an open wound, but oh, her body had the most pleasurable ache in it. She felt rejuvenated. Impossibly energetic.

Fat Cat was at the bottom of her bed, curled into a tight little ball. He must not have come to bed until after Alex left. Janey wrapped her robe around her, then lay down across the bed, creeping up to him as he lifted his head and glared at her.

"Aww, Momma's sorry, Fat Cat." She propped her chin on her hands, inches from his face, and smiled back at him. "But Momma got stroked last night. And mighty well. Surely you don't begrudge me just a little bit of petting for myself?"

He blinked his eyes, narrowed them.

"It was really nice, Fat Cat." She sighed. "All over. I could swoon at the thought of it, you know."

He blinked and watched her almost curiously. As if he actually gave a damn, she thought, though it was a kind of happy thought.

"I wondered why you finally started demanding the petting," she said softly, reaching out with a finger to stroke his nose. He liked that. Being stroked from between his eyes to his nose. He purred a little bit. "I want to curl into Alex's lap and let him just pet me all night long, too, now."

Fat Cat gave a disgusted little feline *pfft*. Janey let a laugh tickle her throat as the cat edged just a little bit closer.

"It was almost perfect," she told the cat. "He was very naughty, Fat Cat." She scratched under the cat's chin as he listened.

"I was purring, too," she drawled. "Well, maybe I was scream-ing more than I was purring. He's really good, you know. Excel-lent, Fat Cat. How many virgins have you heard of actually coming their first time? And no pain." She smiled. "He made sure it didn't hurt."

Another disgusted little rumble from the feline male.

"Now, we have a nice little trade going here, cat." She rubbed around his ears. "I feed you ground steak and you listen to me talk. Look at it this way, it's a damned good trade. I'd listen to Alex talk forever." She sighed. "If he would just keep touching me."

The cat rolled over on his back.

"Mushy talk means belly rubs, huh?" She laughed, scratching at his belly as he batted at her hands. "You're spoiled, cat, you know that?"

He meowed sweetly.

"I love you, Fat Cat." She whispered the words. "I've never told another living soul I love them. You know what happens when you love, don't you?"

But she did love. She stared at the cat, watching those wise topaz eyes as she played with him. She did love. She loved her brother and her cousins. She loved this ragged old cat. And she loved Alex. She knew last night, taking him into her body, that she loved him.

"Time to get up, big boy." She lifted him to the bed, stopping as Fat Cat jumped to his feet and arched before rubbing his face against hers. A soft purr rumbled in his chest and she wanted to hold him to her. Wanted to grab that chubby little body and rock him against her chest. And she couldn't even explain why.

"Be good, cat," she whispered. "Momma has to shower."

She moved from the bed to the bathroom, shedding the robe and closing the door behind her.

She didn't see the bedroom door push open, and Alex thanked God for it. The cat brushed past him with a growl and headed to his food bowl as the man stared at the closed bathroom door silently.

God, she made his chest hurt. Made his heart feel as though it were breaking inside his chest.

She talked to a fucking cat. He'd bet a hundred bucks she had never talked to another human like that in her life, and he realized he wanted her to talk to him like that.

It would have been dangerous if he hadn't already decided the course he was taking. She would fall in love with him easily, he thought. He'd like having Janey's love. And he'd make sure she never lacked for the petting she needed. Or someone to talk to. To dream with.

He'd filled her twice last night. Pumped his cum inside her until he thought he was dying from his release. He'd found her little calendar that morning in a kitchen drawer. Organized little thing that she was, she had the first and last day of her most recent monthly cycle marked.

She was in the best possible time of the month to conceive. There wasn't a chance in hell that she wouldn't.

He ran his hand over his hair. Zeke had picked him up at dawn as arranged, and Alex had returned to the house for his laptop and a few more changes of clothes. When he wasn't on a mission, he liked to dabble in Internet security, tracing and hacking the secured sites he was paid to try to crack. It was a nice sideline.

He'd been working on one of the new sites when he heard Janey talking in the bedroom.

He hadn't expected her to be talking to that damned cat. And he hadn't expected the loneliness, the need to share that he had heard in her voice. She was telling that cat secrets that she should have been sharing with close friends. Women needed to share those things; he knew that from raising Crista. They needed a shoulder to cry on and an ear to listen.

And that was something Janey had never had.

He sat back down in front of the laptop at the kitchen table and turned his attention back to hacking into the site he had pulled up. The owners were worried that several new programs might have created some vulnerabilities. Alex hadn't found any yet, but he'd reached the third level into the secured areas without too many problems. That wasn't a good sign. It wasn't the programs that were the issue so much as a lack of dedicated attention to keeping certain areas of their network blocked.

He was backing out of the programs when he heard Janey in her bedroom, teasing Fat Cat again. He wondered if that scruffy, fat-assed feline had any idea how lucky he was.

Securing the laptop and closing it up, he looked up as she rounded the corner into the kitchen and came to a dead stop.

Light green eyes widened as a rosy flush filled her face. She was wearing an oversized T-shirt and a pair of socks. He doubted she was wearing panties, and the thought of it had his cock hardening again.

Unfortunately, they needed to talk before he took care of that.

"What are you still doing here?" She tucked several curls behind her ear as she moved past the table and glanced at the half-full coffeepot. "Coffee still fresh?"

"Coffee's fresh." Alex leaned back in his chair and watched her, hiding his smile as she let her gaze lick over him. "We needed to talk, though."

Her gaze became shuttered as she shrugged and moved to the coffee. "What do we need to talk about?"

Janey couldn't imagine anything from the night before that needed discussing. Repeating, maybe, but not discussing. And finding him in the kitchen this morning made her nervous, especially considering the fact he probably heard her talking to the cat. His expression was too stoic, his eyes too watchful.

"What are your plans for the day?" he asked her.

Janey shrugged. "Restaurant opens at four. We have a full reservation list. I need to type up the ad for the newspaper, call the college."

She'd cemented that idea in the shower. As much as she loved being home, being around her brother, she was bringing too much grief to all of them. She'd return to California and see if it wasn't easier there. Maybe a few years down the road, she'd manage to find someplace that reminded her of home.

"That's not going to work, Janey." His voice hardened.

"Of course it is." She set her coffee on the table before reaching into the cabinet for the pack of sticky cinnamon rolls she kept there.

Pulling it down, she stared at the nearly empty pack before turning narrowed eyes to Alex. "You ate my rolls?"

His grin was unapologetic. "I was hungry. I worked up an appetite last night."

And her face flamed again. Damn him.

"And that's one of the things we need to talk about," he told her as she set the package on the table and pulled out a chair.

"Why dissect it?" she mumbled. "Leave me alone."

He leaned forward, braced his arms on the table, and stared back at her, his expression hardening now.

"The condom broke, Janey."

She shook her head, feeling her brain go numb. "You're not serious."

He leaned back in his chair. "I'm very serious. It ripped to hell. Now we need to deal with it."

She swallowed tightly. "It was just one time . . ."

"Twice."

"It ripped twice?" Her eyes widened as she grappled to understand what he was saying.

His lips tilted in a strange half smile. "No. I just didn't bother with one the second time." He lifted his coffee mug and sipped as though they were talking about nothing more important than the weather.

She was in shock. There was no other explanation for it. Janey felt her lips go numb, but she felt a wild, impossible surge of excitement racing through her. She did a fast mental calculation and knew, she knew the chances of her becoming pregnant couldn't be any higher than right now.

She licked her lips nervously. "Was it my fault?"

She had rolled the condom onto his heavy erection. She had loved doing it, but it wasn't as though she had any experience at it.

His brows lifted. "How could it have been your fault?"

"Well." She swallowed tightly, feeling the blush burning across her cheeks as she lowered her eyes to her coffee. "I put it on you."

"It wasn't your fault."

Was there a vein of amusement in his voice? She couldn't lift her eyes to see. Confusion jumbled through her mind. She hadn't expected that. She wasn't certain what he wanted her to say or what she was supposed to feel. She had a feeling this hard surge of joy, anticipation, wasn't it.

"It doesn't change anything." She lifted the cup of coffee and sipped at it, ignoring the heavy silence that filled the room then.

"Excuse me, but I could have sworn you just said it didn't change anything," he stated, his voice dropping, lowering.

Janey forced herself to lift her gaze, to meet his hard, flinty one.

"That's exactly what I said. If I'm pregnant, I'll deal with it."

"And how exactly will you deal with it?" His lips thinned. "You wouldn't consider getting rid of my baby, would you, Janey?"

Shock raced headlong through her. She stared back at him for a moment in disbelief. It took critical seconds for the accusation to fire inside her brain and disbelief to burn away beneath anger.

Cold, brittle mockery curled at her lips. "Your opinion of me sucks, Alex." She pushed back from the table, abandoning her sweet breakfast as anger curled through her. "No. For your information, I'd never consider harming our child."

The accusation hurt. It sliced through her soul with a ragged edge and left her bleeding, aching in pain. She had forgotten; she had let herself forget to hold back with Alex. She had slipped up last night. Realizing she was in love with a man softened a woman. Made her weak.

"Good. Then I'll talk to Natches tonight. We can get married in the morning after securing the license at the courthouse."

He crossed his arms over his chest and stared back at her coolly. None of his emotions showed; she had no idea, one way or the other, what he even thought about a child.

Janey looked at the cup of coffee, wondering for one insane moment if it had been drugged. Or if Alex had just lost his ever-lovin' mind.

"No," she finally said carefully. "We're not getting married."

This was happening too fast. Too many emotions were crowding inside her now, racing through her brain, making it impossible to make sense of everything.

For one moment, wild, impossible joy had filled her. Alex wanted to marry her? She could keep him, hold him close to her. For how long? Until he realized the cost of marrying her? A woman everyone in the county wanted to convict as a traitor? How long would it take him to hate her?

"Janey." He came out of his seat, his finger pressing into the top of the table, so commanding, so dominating. It was equally sexy and irritating. "I won't allow my baby to be raised without me. Period. You don't want to test me on this."

"Until we know whether or not there's a child, the point is moot." She had to force the words past her lips. "Until then . . ."

"Until then, I'll be fucking the hell out of you daily," he growled, moving around the table to jerk her into his arms. "And I think I'm addicted to the feel of your pussy bare, Janey. There won't be any more condoms. How long do you think it will take you to get pregnant if you're not already?"

"I think you're crazy," she gasped. "Listen to yourself, Alex. This won't work. You know it won't work."

"Why?" He pushed her against the wall, not ungently actually, the move too damned sexy. It made her wet. Made her want to weaken, to surrender to him then and there. "Tell me why it won't work, Janey."

"Do you love me, Alex?"

Janey already knew the answer. She knew, but it still tore a hole in her heart to see the answer in his face.

"Don't believe in fairy tales, sweetheart." He sighed, touching her cheek with his fingertips. "Sometimes I forget how young you are."

How young she was? As though age had anything to do with love. Since when?

Janey jerked away from him, barely restraining the urge to throw something at him. Glaring at him instead, raging inside, she faced him, her fists clenching at her side.

"Well then, remember," she said scathingly. She wasn't going to bother to even try to hide the anger. Screw it. She'd been in Somer-

set six months, and hiding beneath that damned mask of uncon-
cern wasn't fooling anyone, least of all Alex. "Remember how
young I am, Alex," she told him, mocking anger twisting her lips.
"Because I won't marry a man who doesn't love me. Screw it. You
and this damned town. I deserve better than a man who thinks loving a woman is a fairy tale or a town that thinks I'm such a tramp
I'd sleep with that disgusting excuse for a father that I had. You
know what? You can all go to hell."

His arms went over his chest as he stared back at her silently,
coolly. She recognized that posture. Did he really think that flashing those impressive biceps of his was going to change her mind?

From the corner of her eyes she caught a glimpse of that bite on
his neck, and the shiver that rushed through her, barely hidden, almost weakened her knees. She had one on her neck as well. Her
shoulder, across the tops of her breasts. Her stomach.

Her breathing became shallow. Okay. They'd snacked on each
other like ravening beasts the night before and broken a rubber. She
could deal. That didn't mean she was going to marry a man who
didn't love her.

"You know it's not going to be that simple." He finally spoke,
and when he did she wished he had just kept his damned mouth
shut. His tone was implacable, his expression determined.

"Yes, it is going to be that simple," she informed him. "Starting
today, Alex, my life is going to simplified exponentially. Number
one"—she held up one finger—"I'm no longer pretending to be
some damned robot that doesn't mind the little strikes and barbs
that come my way. Number two"—she held up the second finger—
"I'm not going let you or anyone else dictate to me how I walk,
talk, dress, or act. And number three"—before she knew it, she had
her finger buried in his chest and her voice had risen—"I will not
marry any man who doesn't love me." The finger came back to her,
to her chest, and determination struck a hard, fierce blow there.
"I'm not unworthy of love, no matter my age or who the hell my

biological parents are. So stuff that along with your arrogance and go straight to hell."

She turned on her heel and stomped to her bedroom. She had work to do. She'd wasted too much time in the past months letting people, people she didn't know and who didn't matter to her damned life, affect her. She loved Somerset, but she could leave. She could go anywhere she wanted to go now, and there was nothing and no one to stop her.

Except herself.

She slammed the door shut, locked it, then leaned against it and slowly placed her hands over her stomach as her eyes closed.

She could be pregnant. That changed her plans. Until she knew for certain, Alex was right—she couldn't leave. But if she was pregnant, there was no way she could stay either. She wouldn't let her child be subjected to the prejudice and cruelty this county was heaping on her. Especially Alex's baby.

Alex was considered one of Somerset's favorite sons. A Special Forces soldier who had survived untold wars. He returned home wounded, healed, and went out to fight again. He was a hometown hero, sleeping with a traitor's daughter.

Funny, how those same people saw Natches as a hero as well. Well, not funny perhaps. They had stood aside all those years that they knew Natches was getting the hell beat out of him at home. When Dayle had disowned him, many had turned their backs on him as well, until Dayle's arrest. Now he was a hometown hero, too, and they'd found someone new to punish.

She pushed her fingers through her hair and fought back the anger rushing through her. Anger wasn't going to help her. Pride, determination—screw all of them.

She stalked to the closet, drew out the clothes she'd already chosen to wear today or this evening. The restaurant opened its doors at four, but the employees arrived hours before that. She needed to be downstairs, overseeing everything within the hour.

She usually enjoyed her coffee and rolls first. But no, this morning Alex just had to drop his little bombshell before she could even get that first jolt of caffeine into her system.

She had no doubt it was deliberate.

Her hands were still shaking with anger as she rolled sheer black stockings up her legs and attached the lacy elastic band to the straps of the matching garter belt. Black panties came next, the thong eliminating any hint of panty line beneath the black mid-thigh-length silk skirt.

From her dresser she pulled free one of her favorite bras. One she had rarely worn outside the house. The demi bra gave her breasts a little added volume and, when paired with the violet short-sleeved silk-lined knit sweater she wore, made her feel sexier, more in control.

She buttoned the tiny violet buttons that ran up the sweater, buttoning it far enough that only a hint of cleavage was left showing, and Alex's bite marks were well covered.

There was no way in hell to hide the one on her neck completely. She applied her makeup then, following Rogue's laughing advice, applied the heavy cover base to the mark before using a touch of foundation to blend it in against her skin. It was still there, but it wasn't glaring.

Hell, if she couldn't hide it, she may as well own it at this point, she told herself. But as she stared into the mirror and brushed her hair to curl around her neck, she couldn't find it in herself to be ashamed of it. Simply wary. Alex didn't want others to know where he was sleeping at night, and she didn't want to harm the reputation she knew he had in the county.

Thankfully, the cut and style of her hair helped to hide the mark. She knew it was there, though, and she had the memory of how it had been placed there. The mark on Alex's neck couldn't be hidden without a ton of makeup, she thought, as she applied her lipstick and stared at her own kiss-swollen lips.

What the hell had she been thinking when she'd done that?

Oh, she knew what she was thinking. Ownership. If only for a few days, however long it took for the mark to recede, everyone would know he had been claimed. It didn't make a whit of difference, because no one would know who the hell had claimed him. But she knew. She knew, and each time she thought of it her stomach clenched at the memory.

Finishing up, she slid her feet into three-inch black heels, made certain her hair was still curled over the side of her neck, then left the bedroom.

Alex was still there.

He rose slowly from the kitchen table, where he was working on the laptop, and stared at her, his expression granite hard now, his eyes flat, distant.

Poor little Alex, the stupid little girl he was having to watch over wasn't obeying him near as well as he would like. She almost snorted at the thought.

"I have twenty minutes to get downstairs," she told him, moving to the fresh pot of coffee just finishing in the maker. "Can I drink this cup of coffee without being harassed?"

He closed the laptop slowly as she turned back with a full cup and lifted it to her lips. His expression was nerve-racking. She had never seen him look like that.

Pissed, obviously, she thought. That was too bad, because now she was pissed.

"It's harassment to ask for one logical reason why you won't marry me?" His hands were placed carefully on the table. Broad, calloused, strong male hands. Yeah, she loved those hands, too.

"I told you why. It was a completely logical reason." She'd lived without love for most of her life. She wanted love. She needed it.

"I care for you, Janey." He sighed. "You'd never have to worry about me cheating on you or hurting you."

He'd already hurt her, more times than she could count. The

very fact that he went to such lengths to keep anyone from knowing he was staying with her had the power to rip at her heart if she let herself think about it too often. And she thought about it often.

She loved him. As she stared back at him, she realized, in some ways, she had loved Alex for years. Every time Dayle had allowed her to come home, she had looked for him, asked about him. She had been fascinated with him. That fascination hadn't changed.

She lifted her coffee to her lips and sipped, hoping the caffeine would clear her head. Despite the years she had spent keeping herself alone, isolated, giving Dayle no one he could use to strike out at her, Janey had managed to retain a few dreams. And one of those dreams was love.

"I deserve more than just a man who cares for me," she finally told him. "You can care for a pet. I want to be more than that to someone, Alex. I need more than that."

He wiped his hand over his face and exhaled roughly. "Janey, sometimes you're so damned mature you frighten me, then times like this you make me feel like a fucking cradle robber." He rose from his seat, frustration lining his face now as she watched him carefully. "Sweetheart, listen to me, what you're looking for doesn't exist, and you're only going to get your heart broken looking for it." His face hardened then. "And if you're carrying my child, then that baby will suffer the effects of however you hurt yourself. Is that what you want?"

"We'll discuss that if it happens." Her voice was a hell of a lot calmer than she was.

"It will happen." His arms bracketed her, his hands slapping against the counter beside her. "Trust me, sweetheart, if it didn't happen last night, then it will tonight or the night after. Because fucking you without latex is too damned good to give up."

"I hope you've had blood tests lately," she stated calmly.

Janey was anything but calm. She could feel her nipples beading,

her pussy heating. Hell, she could feel her womb shaking in anticipation at the sight of the lust flickering in his gaze and his tight,
forbidding expression. If she looked, lowered her gaze to his jeans,
she knew what she would see. If she gave him the slightest go-
ahead, he'd be buried inside her.

So thick, so hard. He would push between her thighs, stretch
her, burn her with pleasure.

"Look at your face," he said, his voice rougher now. "I can see
the need in your eyes, baby. You want me, again. Pumping inside
you, filling you with my cum. It was hot, wasn't it, Janey? So hot
it's addictive."

Oh yes, she did want him. The want was like a fever inside her.

"It was hot," she whispered back, moving to set yet another
unfinished cup of coffee on the counter.

"You want me, Janey."

She turned her back to him, gripping the counter with desperate fingers as she closed her eyes and fought the need. No, she didn't
want him; she loved him. She loved him with a strength she hadn't
believed in herself. That was, she'd loved him until this morning.
Until he had offered her marriage, without the love.

"Want isn't enough." She shook her head, feeling him behind
her, feeling his breath at her neck.

"Do *you* love *me*, Janey?"

She blinked against the tears that would have fallen. She wasn't
going to cry for him.

Turning back to him, she lifted her gaze to his, forcing the emotion back, forcing the pain back. It didn't matter what she felt, she
told herself. It never had. All the wanting in the world wouldn't
change that. "You don't believe in love, Alex. So it doesn't matter
one way or the other, does it?"

THIRTEEN

Mackay's Café was packed. With the addition of new chefs, a decent kitchen staff, and serious managing, the restaurant was attaining a reputation not just for the fact that it was run by the traitor's daughter, but for its food, its service, and the fact that Janey allowed herself to be on display.

She had watched Dayle Mackay's haphazard management of the restaurant for years. It was no more than a front then, a way to launder the money the militia filtered through its ranks. Now it was kicking some serious ass.

At eight that evening they had a full house, tables filled no sooner than they were emptied and cleaned, and a small waiting list on the off chance of a cancellation.

Janey was kept on her feet, moving through the restaurant, seating customers, fielding questions and comments. And compliments.

She was seating a table of six when she knew the night was going to go to hell.

It began with Natches and Alex walking up to the hostess station and standing, rather patiently. Natches wasn't always patient. He was wearing his motorcycle chaps and a leather jacket, his hair was windblown, his face roughened from the cold. Alex was dressed in jeans and the long-sleeved gray striped shirt he had worn that morning, boots, and a hip-length leather jacket that absolutely did not do a damned thing to hide from Natches that hickey on his neck.

"I hope you enjoy your meal." She smiled to the occupants of the table as they sat down and accepted their menus. "Your server will be right with you."

She turned, caught the eye of the waitress for that section, and motioned her over to the table before moving to the reception area.

Natches had that look in his eyes that warned everyone around him not to push him. Alex's expression was pretty much as it had been when she left him that morning. Stony. Cool. He wasn't pleased with her and that was just too bad.

"I don't have any tables free, Natches," she told her brother. "You and Alex will have to eat in the kitchen if you're hungry."

"I own the place. Surely I can have a table," he drawled, drawing the attention of everyone close enough to hear them.

Hoyt spoke up behind her. "Ms. Mackay, we have a cancellation on table fourteen in twenty-five minutes."

"And we have a waiting list." She turned to her manager with a bright smile. "Perhaps you should call the Daltons and let them know we have a table if they can be here in time."

Hoyt stared back at her helplessly before glancing to Natches and Alex. The younger man hero-worshipped both Natches and Alex. Turning them down would break his heart.

She rolled her eyes. "Fine. They can wait for the table in the office." She turned back to Natches. "You can wait in the office."

"You can come with us."

Before she could avoid him, he had hold of her arm and was pulling her through the restaurant to the short hall and the large office past the restrooms.

Oh, this so wasn't good. Natches hadn't dragged her around like a puppy since she was five years old.

Unlocking the office door, he pushed her inside before following. At least he released her before moving into the well-appointed room with a disgusted breath.

"Bastard liked his comfort, didn't he?" He stared around the office at the leather seating arrangement and glass table. The desk was Janey's addition. Scarred and comfortable, it beat the contemporary modern glass one Dayle Mackay had had before his arrest.

"And I like keeping myself in comfort." Janey propped her hand on her hip, flicked her gaze to where Alex leaned against the wall, his eyes narrowed on her, then back to Natches. "What the hell is up with this? I have work to do if you don't mind, and dealing with you in a snit isn't conducive to that job."

"Stan Johnson called from the newspaper a few hours ago," he informed her as he took a seat on the corner of her desk. "Says you put an ad in the paper."

Janey lifted her chin before shooting Alex an accusing glance. "He wasn't supposed to tell you."

Natches shot her a hard grin. "He's more scared of me than he is of you, sis. He squealed like a rat."

Janey grimaced at the image. Actually, Johnson probably reminded some people of just that rodent.

"And how is this his business?" She nodded to Alex.

"You carry matching hickeys," Natches snapped. "You made it his business."

Great. She barely managed to keep from lifting her hand to cover the mark everyone had been staring at that evening.

"Like hell." She shot Alex a scowl.

"We're not going to argue over this," Natches told her coldly. "I've done had my spat with Alex; I'm not following up with you. I'll tell you the same thing I told him."

"And that is?" She jerked her head to him, feeling the anger beginning to clench inside her.

"When you hire a new manager, this place closes down," he told her. "I'll burn the bastard to the ground as I should have six months ago. You got me?"

"You're not the only owner, Natches." Janey could feel it. She hated it. She could feel the anger beginning to build, to crash past the shield she kept around it. "Don't walk in here and think you can order me around, because I won't fight with you. I'll call your wife."

There was a long, slow blink of outraged green eyes.

"You did not just threaten to tell Chaya on me," he growled.

"It wasn't a threat. It was a promise." She shrugged. "Now I need to get back to work."

"Janey." His voice stopped her. It was somber, serious.

"What?"

"You wouldn't actually leave me, would you?"

She looked away, then breathed out roughly. "I don't know, Natches," she finally whispered, shaking her head. "Right now I just don't know. I know when I open the banquet room for more tables, I'm going to need more help. If I give up the managerial side and just take over the paperwork and other business areas, then it will free my time up some. I'm not thinking past that right now."

She couldn't, until she knew if there was a baby or not.

"She's not going anywhere. I told you that," Alex stated, still watching her.

Natches flicked Alex a look, then turned his gaze back to her.

Thoughtful, almost calculating, his silent regard made her nervous as hell. Natches crossed his ankle over his knee and watched her intently.

"I have work to do."

"We're talking," Natches informed her tightly.

"No, we're not talking. You're trying to intimidate me. Both of you are and I'm not having it." She rounded on him, anger pulsing in every beat of her blood now. "Why? Last I heard you wanted me away from him anyway because he was too old for me." She pointed imperiously to Alex. "So why the hell are you letting a damned hickey decide if he gets to watch you knock me down a peg or two?"

Hurt resounded through her. She felt berated, humiliated, like a child that had stepped out of line. And he had done it in front of her lover.

"Janey, that isn't what I'm doing." Natches stiffened as Alex frowned back at her.

"That's what both of you are doing," she rasped. "Treating me like a child who doesn't have the good sense to run her own life. I don't need you to tell me where to stay or how to make a decision, Natches. And I sure as hell don't need you telling me how to do it." She turned to Alex, angrier at him perhaps than she was at Natches.

Natches was her brother. He just didn't know how to act any other way. But she had expected more from Alex. Expected him to let her be a woman, his woman, if only for a little while. But one who had his respect if nothing else.

"Janey . . ." Natches was rising from his chair, that determined look in his eyes again.

"Go to hell," she muttered. "Burn the damned place to the ground. See if I care what you do with it. But right now I have a job to do. And that doesn't include fighting with you."

He jerked to his feet.

"The next moron that grips my arm and drags me somewhere

is getting clawed," she warned him furiously. "Touch me, either one of you, and I swear to God, I'm going to get violent."

She had to fight the tears, the sob that trapped in her throat, because her brother was doing the one thing guaranteed to come between them. He was trying to control her.

She strode quickly to the door, aware of Alex straightening, his body tense. Jerking it open, she turned to him, staring up at him, hurting inside so bad she wanted to find a corner to hide in rather than face everyone who had watched Natches drag her around like a little kid.

"Sleeping with you doesn't make me your puppet," she told him roughly. "Never imagine it does, Alex. And the next time you sic my brother on me, then you won't be anywhere near me. I don't care if the entire Army National Guard is stalking me."

She stepped back into the hall, slammed the door furiously behind her, and walked quickly back to the restaurant.

As the door slammed, Alex turned slowly to Natches. He was standing in front of the chair, his expression heavy, lined now with something akin to grief.

He'd had no idea what the other man was doing. Natches had called as he arrived at the restaurant with a brief "We have a problem. Meet me at the restaurant."

Hell, he should have demanded explanations first.

"I should kick your ass, Natches," he growled. "What the fuck was in your mind? Did you really think this was going to get me thrown out of her life without hurting her?"

Natches ran his hands wearily over his hair and scowled back at Alex. "Maybe I wanted to see if you were willing to fight for her. You're just going to let her walk away, aren't you? Fucking tough-assed Alex Jansen. Doesn't need any one woman. You're going to break her heart."

Alex shook his head. "If I break her heart, she'll survive it. If you break it, it will scar her forever. Is that what you want?"

Alex didn't know whether to hit the other man or feel sorry for him. Natches looked as though someone had just dropped a boulder on him. Alex understood the feeling. Janey had managed to do the same damned thing to him that morning.

Natches sneered back at him. "She wasn't like this until you came around. She used to listen to me."

"And now she doesn't obey you so well, is that it, Natches?" Alex asked, his tone acerbic. "Pull this shit on her again, and I'll send you home to Chaya with a few less perfect fucking teeth. Now I'm going to go try dinner."

"Alex."

He paused before turning back to Janey's brother.

Natches was a man tormented, and Alex understood it, to a degree. Alex's sister had married into the Mackays eventually. But he'd had to watch a part of her die for years when she was younger, because of the very same man she had ultimately married. He hadn't forgotten what it felt like.

He shook his head. "I'm serious about this, Natches. Just as I'm serious about her. I didn't walk into this intending on walking away later."

"You love her?" Natches frowned, an edge of disbelief in his voice.

Love. Son of a bitch. That word was being thrown around like a bone to a favorite hound.

"As much as I can love anyone," he finally stated wearily. "I'm committed. That's going to have to be enough for you."

He was going to have to find a way to make it enough for Janey.

Janey wasn't in the mood to be pacified. She was aware of Hoyt showing Natches and Alex to the table they had been given, close to the hall that led to the restrooms and then the office. Just as she was aware of the waitress that rushed to serve them.

The little blonde was a favorite of customers at the restaurant. She was chatty, just a little flirty, and always polite. Tonight, she was more than a little flirty. She was all smiles and batting eye-lashes. It was enough to have Janey gritting her teeth in irritation. Not that either Natches or Alex seemed to be encouraging it. Alex watched Janey. Natches glared at Alex. And weren't they all just having a damned good time.

Shaking her head, Janey turned the hostess station over to Hoyt and made her way back to the kitchen to check things there. Desmond was a godsend. Though he was originally from New York, she'd managed to snag him when she caught a sniff of a rumor that he was looking to take over his own kitchen, to rule his own roost, so to speak. She'd made him an offer, done a lot of begging, and promised him total control if he would pay attention to more country cuisine than international and find a way to blend them when possible.

The dishes he came up with astounded her. Fresh greens fried in garlic and olive oil rather than the traditional country favorite of boiling them down first. Fried fresh, tossed, and served with crisp fried chicken, rolls, and mashed potatoes with a bit of cheddar cheese and sour cream added.

Traditional and unique. It was becoming one of the favorite dishes prepared there.

As usual, the kitchen was running like a well-oiled engine. The staff was too scared of the short, volatile little Italian-American to let it run any other way.

"Desmond, you're my angel," Janey declared, grinning as he turned and swatted at her, though his black eyes glinted with mis-chief as his wife, Angelina, rolled her eyes.

"Janey, his ego is bad enough." Angelina laughed.

"And his food is perfect." Janey blew him a kiss. "Besides, we both know you love his ego." She wagged her brows suggestively, then ducked out of the doorway as Angelina laughingly threw a dish towel at her.

Moving through the dining room, she stopped at several tables, chatted, and made certain everything was running smoothly there before making her way back to the hostess station to relieve Hoyt.

"Everything okay?" she asked as he eased back from the small, waist-high counter and the electronic table display that sat on it.

"Everything's running smooth," he assured her. "Natches and Major Jansen are enjoying their meal. I replaced their server with one of the young men." He frowned. "I've warned Tabitha about her flirtatiousness, if you don't mind."

Janey stared back at Hoyt's sincere, concerned expression and had to bite back a protest. Hoyt thought the Mackay cousins and Alex Jansen were some kind of superheroes.

"Fine," she finally said. She'd talk to Tabitha before she left. The girl was one of her better waitresses, and it was her friendliness and outgoing personality that had many customers asking for her by name.

Hoyt nodded and returned to the checkout counter while Janey turned and tried not to stare at Alex. He was obviously enjoying his steak. No doubt on the house and compliments of Natches. She shook her head. At least she didn't have to worry about feeding him later. But it didn't solve her more immediate problem of how exactly to deal with her new lover.

It was a problem that continued to plague her, especially while Alex and Natches lingered, talking to Hoyt in the lobby as Tabitha covered the register.

They lingered too long to suit her. They made her nervous. Thankfully, there were no comments that could cause Natches to lose his temper. Or Alex. She knew what Natches was capable of. He would break bones. Alex, she wasn't as certain of. There were times she wondered if he wasn't the more dangerous of the two.

She knew he was.

Once they were gone, she breathed a sigh of relief. And hours later, her calf muscles aching from strain, she turned the final lock on the doors and headed back to the office. And hopefully a glass of wine.

She could feel Alex waiting for her before she ever reached the office door. She could feel her body, as tired as it was, preparing for him. Standing outside the door, she pressed her forehead against the wall, closed her eyes, and tried to force back needs that she'd never had to fight before. Feelings she hadn't known before.

Right now all she wanted to do was curl in his arms, have him hold her. Then she wanted him to fuck her until she was screaming, begging for more. And she wanted to feel him coming inside her again. Feel that heated wash of possession, even knowing the danger of it.

Tomorrow, she was going to have to call the doctor, and get in quickly. If she wasn't pregnant now, then she soon would be. She had a feeling Alex's little soldiers were just as effective at their job as he was at his.

She pressed her hands against the wall, palms flat, and reined in the tears that wanted to escape. She was finally free. She could finally feel a measure of security, and what had she done? She'd gone and let herself love a man who didn't believe in love. Who didn't believe in giving himself, only his body.

And Janey didn't think that luscious body was going to be enough to ease the ache building inside her. Because she wanted, hungered for, so much more from him.

And yet he was offering so much more than she had ever expected. A husband, children of her own, a chance to build the life she had dreamed of—if only she could ignore the fact that he simply "cared for" her.

She felt the sigh that eased from her chest. It felt lost. She felt lost. Amid a county that wanted to fry her for her father's sins, simply because there was no one else to torment, and emotions she couldn't seem to control anymore, Janey could feel herself spiraling out of control.

It wasn't hysteria rising inside her. It wasn't anger. It was something so deep, so primitive, that she couldn't explain it, couldn't describe it, even to herself. It was a need to mark Alex, to imprint on him in the same way he had on her.

A damned love bite on his neck wasn't enough. She wanted his heart.

She lifted her head and pushed back from the wall. Gripping the handle, she turned it slowly, opened the door and stepped inside.

And there he was, waiting for her. Stretched out on the couch, one arm behind his head as he read some kind of electronics magazine. And it must have been damned stimulating reading, because he was hard.

Janey closed the door and leaned against it, staring at the thick wedge of his cock beneath his jeans as he laid the magazine carefully on the glass-topped table.

"What do you want, baby?" His voice was a growl, a hard, rough rasp of male heat.

What did she want? Oh, she knew what she wanted, and she knew in what order she wanted it.

She licked her lower lip. "I want you. In my mouth."

He rose to his feet. "Let's go." He held his hand out to her.

Janey shook her head. "I don't want to wait. I want you here. Right here."

He moved to her, slowly, as her gaze lifted to his. "Do you want to get naughty, sweetheart?"

Her lips tilted. "I'm a Mackay, Alex. I don't want to get naughty; I'm naughty by birth. By genetics. Remember?"

She wasn't talking about her parentage. Her cousins were considered three of the wildest men in the state of Kentucky until they fell in love. And she, the lone female, had been left behind. Forced to hold herself back. Not from sex, but from being herself. From letting that core of the woman she was free. And with this man, it could be free. She might have to protect her heart, but he held her body in the palm of his hand. And she was determined to hold at least that much of him.

"And how do you want me?" He stopped before her. Tall, broad, powerful.

"In my mouth. I want to feel you in my mouth, Alex. I want to taste you." She wanted to own his heart, but she would make do, for tonight, with his cock. "All of you."

"Then take it, Janey," he ordered her softly. "If you want it, baby, take it." He paused, then whispered, "Own it."

FOURTEEN

Own it. Oh, she wanted to own it, but there was so much more she wanted.

"I had a fantasy once," she whispered.

He was breathing harder, definitely. "Really?"

"Really. Remember the night you caught me sneaking into the bar when I was eighteen?" One of the few times she had managed to get up the nerve to slip away from Dayle Mackay's house while he was out of town, and have fun.

His lips twitched. "I remember."

"You were furious."

"I was so fucking hard my balls were blue." He stood in front of her, not touching her, watching her. "I wanted to fuck you so bad I couldn't breathe."

Janey licked her lip, her stomach clenching at the knowledge that even then he had wanted her.

"I came home and touched myself," she whispered, laying her fingers on his chest. "I was so wet. My clit so hard."

"You're killing me."

"I imagined you were really furious," she continued. "You tore your belt off and lashed my hands behind my back. And told me you were going to teach me what happened when good girls went to bad places."

"Fuck." His eyes closed; lust filled his features.

"Once you had my hands secured behind my back, you pushed me to my knees." She could barely speak. Excitement was racing through her body, tearing through her mind.

"Janey. This is very bad." He inhaled roughly. "You don't want to start sex games with me, baby. I'm a fucking master. And you're too damned tender."

"You pushed me to my knees, and I couldn't touch you," she continued raggedly. "Then you pulled your cock from your un-zipped jeans, pulled my hair with your other hand, and fucked my mouth while you whispered very naughty phrases. And when you came, you pulled back, because you wanted to watch your cum shooting in my mouth. You wanted to see me taking it, accepting you. And I wanted it," she breathed. "I still want it."

It had been one of her favorite fantasies for years. Alex, his gaze thunderous and hard, his expression tight with sexual hunger.

As her hand trailed down his abdomen, he caught her wrist, drawing her gaze back to his.

"Playing games with me might not be a good idea," he warned her. "Especially this kind of game, Janey."

"Come play with me, Alex," she murmured, hunger and need clashing inside her. "Let me be your fantasy, too."

It slammed into his gut. It sent arcing though him a wave of heat so powerful that Alex wondered that he didn't come in his jeans that second.

Lust. A lust unlike anything he had ever known. Hunger he'd

beaten down over the years, determined to conquer. Because in the back of his mind, he'd always known he'd have her. And he didn't want that part of himself interfering. He didn't want to frighten her. Didn't want to ask more than most women wanted to give.

And now it raced through his system like a runaway train, determined to have its way. He watched her eyes, his body stiffening, his dick tightening until it felt as though it would burst.

She wanted the games? The hard edge of a sexual intensity so sharp it cut through the senses like a blade? Oh, he could give it to her. Give it to her and make her love it, if it didn't destroy both of them first.

Before she could counter, he twisted her around, pressing her firmly against the door as he felt her gasp.

"Once you open the cage, the animal doesn't go back in," he growled at her ear. "Be sure, Janey."

"Are you scared, Alex?" Her ass ground against his dick.

"*You* should be scared." He held her wrists in one hand and jerked his belt loose with the other.

His cock was throbbing now; he could feel the pre-cum dampening the crown. The thought of what he was about to do tightened every muscle in his body and had his balls tight with lust.

Hell, this went deeper than lust. It was a craving. A fucking addiction. One of the wildest damned fantasies he had ever known.

He looped the belt around her wrists, tightened it, and secured it. She couldn't get loose unless he let her go. She would be restrained, helpless. He could have her any way he wanted her.

"That Mackay courage is going to get you in trouble, sugar," he drawled, nipping her ear, tangling his fingers in her hair and tugging her head back. "You have no idea what you're asking for."

Her lashes lifted; sparkling green eyes, so light they were almost colorless, looked back at him as her pouty lips parted, her tongue stroked over them.

"You have no idea how much more I want."

Damn. Hell.

The rasp of his zipper was the only sound in the room. He didn't loosen his jeans, just the zipper; then he drew the swollen shaft of his cock free.

His dick was violently engorged, the crown so fiercely swollen it felt bruised.

"I'm going to fuck your throat," he growled, his hand tightening as he held her hair, turned her, and pressed her down.

Wild, wanton, she went to her knees, staring up at him, her eyes flashing with color, darker green and lighter green swirling together in an incredible hue as the pupils dilated.

Alex held the shaft of his cock in his hand, pressing it against his lower stomach as she licked her lips. Eyes narrowed, jaw clenched, he used the hold he had on her hair to pull her to his tortured ball sac.

"Lick my balls. Suck them. Nice and easy, baby."

He almost shouted in pleasure when she did just that. Watching him, her eyes on him, her tongue swirled around the tight flesh before she drew first one tortured sphere into her mouth, then the other.

He was stretched on a rack of pleasure so intense he didn't know if he could keep from coming then and there. He'd never seen anything so beautiful as Janey caressing, licking, kissing his tortured balls. But he was about to see something a hell of a lot prettier.

He took the agonizing pleasure for as long as he could. His head falling back, his neck tightening as he felt perspiration glaze his face. Fuck, this was good. So good.

Too good.

He pulled her head back.

"Open your lips. Give me your mouth, sweetheart."

She loved the endearments. He watched her pupils dilate, her lips part. Sweet pink lips. Holding the shaft of his cock, he rubbed the head against them. Over them, letting her hot tongue lick over it.

She curled her tongue beneath the sensitive spot underneath the head, rubbed at it, licked at it.

"So naughty." His jaw tightened as he pulled back. "But it's not just those pretty lips I want."

He tucked the dark, engorged crown between her lips and pressed inside. Slow and easy. He wanted to watch. Wanted to see her suck his dick into her mouth.

It wasn't just sexual. The intimacy of the act slammed into him. This wasn't an experienced woman who knew exactly how to work a man. This was Janey. She'd been a virgin for him. She was innocent, fragile, and blowing his mind as her mouth tightened on the swollen crown and sucked with wicked, sensual pleasure. Shafts of brilliant sensation tore through the head of his cock, raced to his balls, and ran up his spine. She sucked with hungry, fierce draws of her mouth. Taking him deep, working her tongue over him. He could almost feel the back of her mouth, and when she swallowed, sweat dripped down his cheek.

"Oh, you've been very bad, darlin'," he groaned, his hand tightening in her hair, drawing her back, then forward, moving her on his cock. "Flatten your tongue and breathe in." He pushed in a little deeper, watched her eyes widen, water. But she took him.

He pulled back, his heart racing, his breathing tight and restricted. Hell, he didn't know how long he was going to last.

"You practiced," he accused her with a tight smile, sinking inside again. "Did you have a toy, baby?" Her pupils flared again.

Janey wouldn't have taken another man like this, not without giving him all of her herself. No, this belonged to him, just him, and whatever toy she used to fulfill her fantasies.

"Let's see if we can give you what a toy can't." He held her head still. "Breathe in, sweetheart." He sank in, watched her eyes water as the head of his cock touched her throat, then pulled back.

"Next time, breathe in and swallow." He took her mouth again, sank in, and a snarling groan tore from his chest as she did as he told her.

Her eyes watered, but her face flushed as she swallowed and then moaned in protest as he pulled back. Alex had to shake his head to find one last thread of control. This was destroying him. Janey on her knees, his hands tangled in her hair as he fucked her throat.

"I'm going to come, baby," he warned her as he sank in again and the pressure nearly ruptured his balls. "One more stroke. When I pull back, open your lips. Let me see my cum fill you."

He was twisted. He was fucking insane. He sank in again, and when she swallowed, he let go. Stroking the shaft of his cock, he pulled her head back, watched, and couldn't hold back the throttled yell that tore from his throat.

"Fuck yes. Take it, Janey. All of it." He filled her mouth, watched each spurt of his seed filling her mouth as tears rolled from her eyes.

They weren't tears of pain, physical or emotional, but the sight of them struck at his chest.

"Now suck. Swallow me, baby. Swallow all of me." He pushed the head of his cock past her lips again and gave one last pulse of release as she swallowed, sucked, and moaned around the sensitive crown, and tore another groan from him.

He wished he could curb the need. Pulling her to her feet, he knew there wasn't a chance in hell. He was still dying for her. Dying for more.

Catching her around the waist, he moved her to the chair next to them, pushed her to her knees in the seat cushion, and pressed against her shoulders to lean over the back. Gripping the belt around her wrists, he held her in place as his knees bent and he pressed the still-hard, violently sensitive crown between the bare, soaked lips of her pussy.

Intense heat encased his cock. Slick, fiery syrup. He could hear her crying, begging for more. But he wanted this to last. Wanted to feel every ripple of her pussy as he pressed inside her. Feel her tight.

"Ah God! Janey, baby." He bent his knees, worked in deeper, deeper, and felt every cell in his body catch fire as he lodged to the hilt inside her. "Sweet, sweet Janey. God, I love this. So tight. So fucking hot."

Janey was drifting in a haze of pleasure and need. Her pussy throbbed, flexed. Her clit was tortured. Behind her, Alex held on to the belt with one hand as she felt the fingers of the other slide around her hip, pushing between her thighs.

"Poor little clit," he groaned at her ear. "Poor sweet pussy. What do you need, Janey? Slow and easy? Or hard? Fast? Do you want me to pound inside you, or slide in long and slow?"

She shook her head. She was supposed to decide? She wanted both. She wanted it all. Her head hung over the back of the chair as she panted, just trying to breathe through the pleasure.

"Do you need a little more burn, sweetheart?"

He was buried full-length inside her. How could he burn her more?

His hand rubbed the side of her ass; her eyes widened.

"Yes. Oh God, Alex. Yes." Her back arced, and a cry strangled from her throat as his hand landed on the side of her ass.

Again. He pulled back and his hand landed, not too hard, hard enough to burn, hard enough to send explosions of brilliant pleasure racing through her.

"So fucking pretty." He smoothed his hand over her, then lowered it, pressing her thighs farther apart.

His fingers rasped around her clit; then he was gripping her hip and plunging inside her. As though he couldn't go deep enough, couldn't fuck her hard enough.

Janey felt her muscles clamp down on him involuntarily, trying to hold him inside her, tightening on him seconds before the most incredible orgasm tore through her.

It lit up her mind. It sent brilliant shards of heat and light racing through her body as she screamed his name, cried, felt the tears that rolled from her eyes at the sheer, perfect brilliance of a release that soared through every fragment of her being.

She was pulsing around him. He slammed in deep, yelled her name, and she felt him, spurt after spurt filling her again, sinking deep inside her as her pussy flexed and tightened around him.

She was left limp, ragged. Her only tie to earth was his grip on her hip and the warmth of his body behind her. Because nothing in this world, nothing else, mattered in this single moment, but this.

It was after midnight, and Natches was still awake. He paced the living room of the houseboat, feeling the chill wind outside, though he knew it hadn't penetrated the heavily insulated interior.

It was a chill he couldn't shake inside.

Clad in jeans, barefoot, a longneck bottle of beer in his hand, he paced back to the closed shades of the door and paused. He took another drink of the beer, then paced back to the table. To the picture and the note.

She was the devil's whore and now she's breaking a good man. Your sister. Your responsibility. Take care of her as you took care of her bastard, incestuous lover.

God, this was insane. He stared at the picture. It had been taken from the second floor of the building across the street from the restaurant. The window there looked directly into Janey's window. Through the sheer curtains Natches could see the two forms. Alex and Janey. Alex was too damned big. Too fucking old for her.

He wiped his hand over his face and turned away. It looked as though Alex were forcing an embrace on her. Natches finished the beer and only barely managed to keep from throwing it at the wall.

"Natches."

He turned, watching as Chaya moved into the room from the back bedroom. She swayed with maternal, sensual grace. The hard mound of her belly poked out ahead of her, and she was the most beautiful thing he had ever seen in his damned life.

His Chay. She moved into his arms, and he held her and their child against him, closing his eyes, praying to God he could protect them better than he was protecting his sister.

"Have you called Alex yet?"

She knew about the picture. She had been there when the plain manila envelope had been delivered by Ray after he found it on the front seat of his pickup that evening as he was leaving for home.

Natches's name was printed on it in large letters, obviously computer-generated. She had been there when he pulled the picture free.

"He wouldn't hurt her," he said heavily. "Tell me again it's not what it looks like."

"Natches." Her hands rubbed against his back as her head lifted from his chest. "You know Alex. You said that yourself."

"A lot of years," he admitted, moving away from her. "He's a good man. A good soldier."

But was he a tender lover? The kind of lover his sister needed? It was bad enough the son of a bitch was fourteen years older than she was.

"You need to call him," she told him again.

Natches nodded. He knew he did. Alex had been sloppy closing only the sheers like that with a stalker obviously watching Janey. If this had happened after they learned about the stalker.

Alex had come to him with the information. Zeke had told Alex. Zeke would have had a reason for doing that. He would have had to have seen something, known something. And Janey had been wary, but it had been her idea for Alex to stay.

Or had it?

Alex was more than just a fucking soldier; he worked with the Department of Homeland Security and was one of the most manipulative special agents employed there.

Shit. He couldn't think like this.

"Natches, if Janey were being forced into anything, she would tell you," Chaya told him again.

Natches shrugged, appearing to agree with her. He tried to tell himself. Hell, she had snapped his and Alex's head off that evening. She wouldn't have done that if she was scared.

"I'll go talk to them in the morning," he said.

"You're worried about more than just this." She moved to him again. "What's wrong, Natches?"

She saw so much of him. Sometimes it amazed him, humbled him. She was his second breath. Hell no, she was his first breath. He couldn't live without her.

"I hurt her tonight," he finally admitted, before explaining what happened. "She wouldn't speak to me before I left."

"Oh, Natches," Chaya groaned. "You can't play games with her. She's too smart for that and you keep forgetting it for some reason."

He frowned at her chiding voice. "She's my sister, Chaya. My baby sister. I have to watch out for her."

"She's an adult, Natches." It was the same argument they had visited for the past six months. "Let her decide on her own."

"Hell, Chay, she's talking about leaving." He pushed his fingers through his hair roughly. "I'm just getting to know her. I don't want her to leave."

Chaya sighed. "Natches, you have to let go eventually. What are you going to do if we eventually have a daughter?"

Chaya was left speechless, lips parted, as Natches swung around and capped his hand over her mouth. He was pale, honest to God white, around the eyes, with a sick look on his face.

"Don't say it," he hissed fiercely, his green eyes bright, terrified. "Don't say the D word, Chay. You gotta promise me. Promise me. We're only going to have boys. Swear it, Chay."

She blinked back at him as he lifted his hand just enough for her to speak. "Swear it. Right now."

She chided him gently. "Natches, I can't do that."

"Don't tempt fate by talking about it, then," he growled. "I mean it, Chay. We're having boys. Just boys. I understand boys."

He didn't feel nearly as vulnerable at the thought of a boy for a child, she knew. The thought of a daughter still had the power to send Natches into a panic.

Chaya sighed. Maybe tonight really wasn't the night to tell her husband that the tests the doctor had done were definitely showing a girl.

She looked at his face again. No, it wasn't the time.

"I'll meet Alex in the morning when he goes to his house," he said and nodded, turning away from her. "Not tonight." He shook his head and groaned. "Hell no, not tonight. Swear to God, if I have to look at that hickey on his neck one more time, I'm going to kill him, Chay."

"I understand, Natches." She kept her expression serious, somber, as he swung around her. "Really, honey, I understand." She held her hand out to him. "Will you come to bed now? I'm lonely."

His gaze flared; his body tightened instantly.

"I thought you were tired."

"Natches." She grinned. "I'm never that tired."

He took her hand and let her lead him back to their bed. He

made love to her. Slow, easy love. And later, when she was drifting off to sleep, he held her in his arms, stared up at the ceiling, and that picture flashed before his eyes again.

God, there were some things an older brother just didn't need to know.

FIFTEEN

Alex stared at the picture and the note that Natches slapped on his kitchen table the next morning.

"Why the hell aren't you at the apartment?" Natches bit out. "Whoever's watching her is close, Alex."

"She threw me out," Alex murmured, staring at the image someone's camera had captured. Janey, locked against him, his hold dominant, appearing forceful. It looked bad. It had been hot as hell when it happened.

"And you're not covering her ass? You didn't call any of us?" Natches stomped around the kitchen. "How do you know she's safe?"

"I called in backup and told Faisal to keep an eye on her. That boy is hell in a fight, you know." He stared at the letter, a frown brewing on his brow. "What the fuck is this?" He slapped the paper to the table. "They think she's somehow corrupting *me*?"

"Yeah, go figure," Natches sneered as he threw him a hostile look.

"And this was waiting in Ray's truck last night after hours?"

"That's what I said." Natches was livid. A livid Natches was not a comfortable sight. "Who's watching Janey?"

"Tyrell Grayson and Mark Lessing. And as I said, Faisal is inside." Alex stared at the picture again. "This was taken from across the street, wasn't it?"

"Good guess, Sherlock," Natches grunted.

Alex's lips thinned. "Natches, work with me here."

"I worked with you when I mistakenly thought you were looking out for Janey, rather than looking for a way into her bed," he snarled. "Hell, Alex. How would you feel if those were pictures of Crista? What would you have done if you had had photos of the night she spent with Dawg when she was eighteen? Would you have been a happy little camper?"

Alex clenched his jaw. Hell no. He hadn't had pictures and he hadn't been a happy camper.

"Some things a brother doesn't need to know, or see. Hickeys on her lover's neck, a man too old for her to begin with. And pictures of him manhandling her."

"Fuck you," Alex growled.

"Not in this lifetime, hotshot," Natches snapped back.

Alex ran his hand over his head. Natches had to be one of the most stubborn, difficult bastards he had ever run across.

Natches was an aggravation. This picture was dangerous.

"I've had Tyrell and Mark watching the apartment when I'm gone since the night we found the note in her kitchen. So far, nothing's happened. No one's been overly curious, and no one's been following her."

"Where is she now?" Natches glared back at him.

"I talked to her just before you arrived. Called her cell phone. She was getting ready to go to the office to get some work done."

"Your men check the office and restaurant?" Natches's voice was hard, cold.

Alex nodded at that. "They have a key to the office as well as the apartment. They finished checking it out just before I left. They have surveillance set up on the three entrances and are watching Janey specifically."

"You brought in two of your men," Natches growled. "Your gut's crawling, aint it?"

Yes, it was. It had been for days.

"I'm moving in with her tonight for good," he told Natches. "There will be no more leaving in the morning. I'll set up there, keep a better eye on her."

"Shit." Natches braced his hands on the counter and stared out the kitchen window. "Hell, Alex. She was supposed to be safe now."

"She will be." Alex wouldn't have it any other way. "She is safe, Natches. And she's damned careful. Janey's no one's fool. Pay attention to something more than your pride sometime and you'll see that."

Tyrell and Mark had noticed it. Staying out of sight, Mark had reported, was becoming increasingly hard. Janey was sharp, and she watched people, cars. She wasn't the least bit casual about her own protection.

It was something Alex had noticed as well. That picture was an anomaly. Normally, Janey was very careful about pulling her curtains closed once they entered the apartment. He'd distracted her that night.

"This is bad," Natches finally said, his voice weary, worried. "This is bad, Alex. Whoever's doing this is serious."

"We already assumed that. That's why we're seriously watching her, Natches." He turned to the other man, seeing the tense set of his shoulders. "But if you don't get off her ass and let her live her own life, when it's over, she's going to walk away."

Natches knew that. Alex knew he knew it. But it bore affirming.

Natches finally shrugged. "You're still alive."

"Barely," Alex grunted as he collected the picture and shoved it into the envelope Natches had handed him. "I'm going to keep this. Check a few things."

Natches shrugged and turned back to him as Alex picked up the extra bag he had packed that morning. Clothes, a few extra weapons. He was prepared to move into the apartment that night, despite Janey's objections.

"You going to show her that picture?" Natches asked, nodding to the envelope.

"Why wouldn't I?"

Janey deserved to know. It was her life, her protection. She had to know to be on guard.

"You going to tell her where you got it from?" Natches asked.

Alex flipped the envelope around to show his name on the front. "What do you think?"

"Bastard!" he snorted.

"Why didn't you bring this to Janey?" Alex leaned against the table, curious. Natches was fierce in his protection of his sister, but Alex hadn't seen a lot of interaction between them.

Natches shrugged. "Look, Hickey Man, keeping her ass safe is your job." He glowered at Alex's neck.

"No, it's her job as well," Alex pointed out. "She can't be on guard if she doesn't know what the hell is going on. If she knows, then she knows to help me protect her."

"No shit," Natches muttered.

Damn Mackays. There wasn't a one of them that was easy to deal with.

"What do you want from me, Natches?" he asked. "You want me to walk away? Leave her unprotected?"

"What I want isn't the question." Natches shook his head. "Time for me to go."

"Why don't you try talking to your sister, Natches?" Alex asked as he headed for the door. "Is it that hard?"

Natches paused at the door, staring out the window, tense. Angry.

"She doesn't talk to me," he finally said. "I get yes. No. Okay. Whatever. I get polite smiles and noncommittal answers." He turned back slowly. "Does she talk to you?"

Alex felt it then. The thing he couldn't put his finger on since staying with her, since touching her.

"She talks to her cat," he finally admitted. "She doesn't talk to me."

He could hear her mumbling every morning to that damned cat, behind the closed bedroom door after he left her. She snuggled it in the evening, fed the little bastard ground steak, and pampered it so much Alex actually felt a little jealous at times.

Natches grimaced. "Well, hell. I don't feel so damned pissed off now. At least I'm not alone."

Which didn't make Alex feel any better.

As he opened his lips to return a mocking retort, his cell phone rang. Having checked the number, he answered it quickly.

"You're calling me," he murmured, turning away from Natches. "Is everything okay?"

Janey had never called *him*.

"You know a lot about computers, right?" There was an edge of frustration in her tone.

"A little bit." He arched his brows. "What's wrong?"

"My computer, obviously." She sighed heavily. "There are files missing, jumbled. I can't make sense of half of what's on here. Can you come look at it? I need to locate my suppliers file and bills I do through my accounting software. It's messed up, Alex. Bad."

"I'll be right there," he promised her. "Keep the chair warm for me."

There was silence on the line.

"Are you cold?" There was an edge of amusement in her tone, but also confusion.

"I could be."

"I'll turn the heat up," she promised. "See you soon, Alex."

She disconnected the phone as he pulled it back and stared at it with a frown. Hell, she didn't talk to him or flirt with him. Damned stubborn Mackay female. He glared at Natches.

"Let me guess. Janey?" Natches flicked the phone a brooding look.

"Her computer's messed up." He shoved the phone back into its holster before gripping the duffel bag and moving to the door. "I promised her I'd come look at it."

"Is she going to keep your seat warm for you?" Natches mocked angrily. "Moron."

"Asshole," Alex growled back at him, though he couldn't help the grin that tugged at his lips. "I hope that kid of yours is a girl."

Natches stopped on the sidewalk. A full, hard stop as Alex turned back to see his pale features.

"Take that back," he seemed to wheeze.

"What?"

"The D word," Natches bit out. "Take it back, Alex. You little bastard, don't make me kill you."

Alex laughed. "Scared, Natches?"

"Shaking in my fucking boots," Natches whispered, slowly moving again, heading for his motorcycle. "Oh Lord, I'm shaking in my fucking boots."

"I swear, Janey, I think either your computer has been hacked or someone managed to get into it." Rogue stepped back from the desk, a cup of coffee in hand as Janey disconnected the call with Alex.

She looked at the security system next to the door of the office thoughtfully. She knew Alex had tweaked the security, said it would be harder to bypass now. Someone had gotten into her apartment easily enough; it would be entirely possible that the stalker had gotten into her office.

"This is going to turn into a headache." She sighed as Rogue brought her coffee over to the seating area and lounged back in the very same chair Alex had taken her in the night before.

She was so glad she had thought to use cleaner on the leather furniture. She could just imagine her horror if Natches had sat in it before she cleaned it. Oh Lord. Her head was a mess. Alex had messed her up bad last night and she wasn't recovering very well.

"I can see you're enjoying cohabitation with the luscious soldier you're hiding upstairs." Rogue grinned, glancing at her neck. "You did a good job masking it. Almost."

Janey rested her elbows on her knees and pushed her fingers through her hair in irritation. "Thanks, Rogue," she muttered.

"Come on, Janey. It's cute." She laughed. "But I hear his is even better. A real branding."

Janey groaned. "Stop. He's on his way over here. He'll know we've been talking about him if you keep this up."

"He reads minds?" Rogue's brow arched.

"Probably." She restrained a shiver. Last night, he'd sure read hers. He'd taken what she'd given him and built on it until it blew her mind. Now here she was, a mindless waste without a hope of repairing the damage before he walked through the door.

"Gossips are going crazy, my friend," Rogue drawled. "No one's figured out who's doing you yet. It's killing them."

"The gossips are always going crazy over something." Janey shook her head and stared back at Rogue.

Long red gold curls seethed from the crown of her head and flowed down her back. Dressed in jeans, boots, and a long-sleeved T-shirt, she looked like a wild, untamed pixie.

"Yeah, but this gossip is getting weird." Rogue shook her head in confusion. "I'd have expected that little manager of yours, Hoyt, to be accused of it, but no one breathes his name."

"Hoyt?" she gasped. "Hoyt's a sweetheart. Everyone loves him. Besides, he's too young for me."

"He's your age, Janey." Rogue laughed. "You're just too fixated on that whole older-man thing."

No, she was fixated on Alex. That was her problem.

She groaned in frustration. "I should have stayed in California."

"And miss all the fun here?" Rogue laughed. "Really, Janey, that's so selfish of you, wanting your privacy and peace over our entertainment. Alex should spank you."

She flushed to the roots of her hair as Rogue squealed in glee.

"Oh my God, has he spanked you?"

"No!" She glared at her friend. "Leave me alone. You're too bad, Rogue."

"You liar." Rogue laughed, amusement sparkling in her violet eyes. "He spanked you, didn't he?"

Did those few little slaps last night count? Oh hell yes they did, because she wanted more.

"He didn't spank me. Now stop. This is embarrassing."

"Only because you never had a real friend before." Rogue waved her comment away as she propped her feet on the glass coffee table and wagged her brows suggestively. "You should give me all the deets, you know. That way, I can look bored and uninterested when all the good juicy gossip pours in. I can be a mystery, and let everyone think I know absolutely more than they do, which I will. It ups my standing in the little demi-community I live within."

The demi-community, as Rogue called it, consisted of bikers and misfits, criminals and troublemakers. Somehow, Rogue knew all of them.

"I think you can manage to make them believe you know even when you don't," Janey pointed out. "You don't need deets."

"But deets make it much more fun." Rogue sighed heavily. "Oh well, since you refuse to accommodate me . . . Do you think Alex will bring that sexy sheriff with him?" She lifted her brows suggestively.

"I'd guess he'll bring Natches with him if you saw his motorcycle in Alex's driveway this morning."

"Yes. I did. All that testosterone in one place." Rogue gave a false shiver of pleasure. "It's enough to make a woman have naughty thoughts."

"Try living with all that testosterone." Janey sighed. "You'll change your mind fast."

"No doubt." Rogue cocked her head and listened as Janey heard the deep throb of a Harley pulling into the back lot. "Sounds like that testosterone is about to invade your office."

"They fight," Janey muttered. "They're making me crazy."

"Like two little boys over a toy." Rogue's laughter was light and compassionate. "Poor Janey. All that love and she doesn't know what to do with it."

Janey gave her a sharp look. Rogue grimaced and rolled her eyes. "Yeah, that's all my bitterness coming out. Ignore me."

It wasn't the first time Rogue had made a remark, or given that explanation for it. Rogue had her "daddy," who sent her presents, gifts, and pretty clothes. And he left her in Somerset to face the hell Nadine Grace had built for her when Rogue first arrived in town, as a teacher of all things.

Lena Rogue Walker had come into town as a high school teacher, and her first day on the job, Nadine Grace had invaded her schoolroom, along with the principal, demanding to know if Rogue was related to the Walkers that lived near the county line. Rumored moonshiners, a hard-drinking, rough-living lot that Johnny Grace had once tried to steal from.

Unfortunately, Rogue had been related to them. Her father was one of them, though he had left before the trouble with Johnny, and made a small fortune in electronics and the stock market.

What happened in the months after that had become Rogue's personal nightmare, and still had the power to leave her shaking in fear, Janey knew.

Maybe it was the reason they were drawn to each other as friends. A similar hell. Nightmarish visions they couldn't always separate in their dreams, and couldn't forget while they were awake.

Whatever the reason, they had survived, and despite the other woman's harder edge, Janey was coming to trust her as the only true friend she'd ever had.

Rising to her feet, Janey smoothed her hands down the sides of her jeans and straightened the snug T-shirt she wore before opening the door.

Right on time. Natches and Alex walked into the office. Both were scowling and neither seemed in a pleasant mood.

"Rogue, how did I know the two of you would end up hooking up?" Natches grinned when he saw the other woman. "Come here and give us a hug, sugar."

Rogue was out of her chair and squealing like a little girl. "Oh boy, when the hags in town hear you gave me a hug, they're going to be so green."

She all but jumped into his arms as he laughed at her. When he set her back on her feet, he wagged his finger at her. "No gossip. Chaya will kick my ass."

"You'll love every minute of it." Rogue wrinkled her nose as she turned away and lifted her bag from the coffee table, before turning to Alex. "Hey, stud, someone either hacked her 'puter or they manually inserted a bad boy virus that's fucking with her. It's beyond me."

Alex paused at the desk and turned to Janey, his expression tight and controlled. "You called her first?"

Janey shrugged. "She was coming over this morning anyway."

The look in his eye assured her that he wasn't pleased that she hadn't called him first.

"Looks like Rogue kept your chair warm for you, Alex." Natches poked at him with a gleeful laugh.

"I am so out of here." Rogue laughed as she turned to Janey and shook her head in sympathy. "Good luck, girlfriend. I don't think I envy you after all."

The door closed behind her as Janey watched Alex and Natches. Tension was riding high between the two men, and it had the power to make the back of her neck tingle.

"What's going on?" she asked her brother.

Natches ran his hand over the back of his neck as he turned to Alex, glaring at him.

Janey felt like shaking her head as Alex stared back at her brother coolly.

Alex shook his head as he came around the desk, pulled a folded envelope from the pocket at the side of his duffel bag, and handed it to her as he pulled his jacket off.

Staring at the two men suspiciously, she lifted the envelope. "What's this?"

"Someone left Natches a picture of us," Alex told her quietly. "The night I went up to your apartment with you. They snapped a picture from the empty second-story room in the building across the street."

The abandoned store across the street. Okay, this shouldn't be too bad. A picture of them. They had kissed, but nothing else.

She glanced at Natches's closed face before drawing the photo free from the envelope. She stared at it silently.

Oh, that didn't look good. Her lips twitched at the sight of the hold Alex had on her. It was dominant, powerful. She lifted her eyes to him. "You're still walking. Chaya must have a good influence on Natches."

Alex grunted at that. "Read the letter."

She was pulling the letter free. She blinked at the words and then lifted her gaze back to him and drawled, "I'm so naughty. Should I be spanked? Or killed?"

Natches's muttered curse almost had her smiling, but the tight knot of fear growing in her stomach wouldn't allow for it.

She tossed the papers to the table and pushed her fingers through her hair as she sat back on the couch and breathed out roughly.

"So what do we do now?"

"You come back to the boat," Natches bit out.

"And endanger your wife and child?" she asked him.

He stared back at her in disbelief. "Excuse me here, Janey? Mackay Marina. Smack-dab in the middle of the Mackay dock? I don't hardly think so. No one would dare try to strike out at you there, and we'd catch whoever was watching you."

"Well, let's see," she mused. "There's the drive to work. And back. Back is the kicker. Sometimes I don't leave this office until after one. Then there's the fact I have to be here early for deliveries. Speaking of which, I hope you have some cash on you. Desmond's fresh vegetables are due any minute, and I don't have my computer running for the check printout." She looked at Alex as he stared back at her, his expression brooding. "Is it running?"

"Not yet." His smile was hard.

Janey looked at the computer and back to him with a sigh.

"I need some money, Natches. I have several deliveries coming in this morning and no way to pay for them."

Alex moved to the computer as her brother glared at her.

"Moving from here isn't an option," she told him firmly. "We've discussed this."

He sat down in the chair across from her. Thank God it wasn't the one Alex had done her in.

"I'm worried, sis," he said softly. "This isn't good. Someone has focused their crazy on you, and I can't figure out who it is."

"Obviously someone who respects the hell out of you and Alex." She flipped her fingers to the letter still lying on the table. "They need someone to hate for what Dayle did. They don't know me. You were responsible for catching him. They just need to let off some steam."

"You know better than that," Natches said.

Alex watched the exchange closely. He could see Natches's fears, his guilt that Janey was being targeted. Brother and sister both were fighting against a barrier raised between them, one Dayle Mackay had placed there. Natches had taken the beatings until he was twenty, to ensure Dayle never abused Janey. And she knew it. Her guilt was like a cancer eating inside her. Natches had watched out for her from afar, bullied friends into helping him when she went away to school, and generally made himself crazy because Dayle had still managed to hurt her six months before. He hadn't been able to protect her, and his guilt added to that barrier.

"I know I have to deal with this on my own." Janey shook her head. "If it gets too bad, then I'll leave."

"And when you do, whoever it is will follow you. And there will be no one to protect you," Alex bit out. "Is that what you want?"

He thought of the child he'd almost bet she was carrying. His baby. The hell she was leaving.

"You have a better choice?" Janey asked, that damned remote mask of hers slipping into place.

"Exactly what we are doing," Alex growled. "Whoever it is will mess up. When he does, I'll be here."

The look she gave him made him hard as hell. There was the barest flicker in her gaze of heat, of knowledge. She knew exactly what they were doing. Fucking themselves to death if they kept up the way they were.

"Enough!" Natches snapped. "Enough of the looks, okay?"

"Natches, you seem to have a problem with me having a life. Period." Janey surprised him. Him and Alex.

There was the barest edge of stress in her voice, just the lightest hint of mockery as she stared back at her brother. "I'm over eighteen, remember?"

"And we both remember how we failed to protect you six months ago," Alex told her as he rebooted her computer and moved to counter whatever was distorting her programs. "We don't intend to let that happen again."

Natches scowled at him. "Yeah, what he said," he growled, then muttered, "Didn't ask his opinion, though."

Janey narrowed her eyes between the two men. "Is this normal?" She finally asked.

"What?" Natches scowled.

"The way you two are bickering?"

"I bicker with Dawg constantly," Alex told her absently as he worked at the computer. "Crista lets him get away with too much. Someone needs to point it out."

Natches's scowl deepened.

"Okay," Janey said slowly. "Tell you what, I'm going to go to the kitchen and let Desmond know the veggies are definitely a go." She rose from her seat.

"Janey, why don't you have the cash to cover the deliveries?" Natches asked softly. "You get a salary as manager."

"Locked in the computer." She shrugged.

"She's lying to you," Alex stated, frowning at the computer as she whipped her head around to glare at him. He knew her too well.

"Janey." Natches's tone was warning. "What's going on?"

"I had bills to pay. I paid them." This was a discussion she didn't want to get into.

"Your apartment is free." Natches began ticking off her bills. "No car payment; I gave you that car. Electric, water, et cetera, are in with the restaurant, so that's covered. Groceries are your main concern." He raked his gaze over her. "You're not exactly eating a lot."

"Go to hell." She moved for the door.

"When Alex gets that computer up, I'll check your salary," he said lazily. "Maybe we need to discuss what you're making."

"I hope you have a daughter," she muttered, jerking the door open and slamming it behind her as she stalked into the hall.

Natches glowered at the door, then turned to Alex as he chuckled.

"I thought she loved me." Natches sighed. "I really thought she loved me."

Alex sat back slowly from the computer. "She's been hacked. A virus was inserted and all her information wiped from the surface. I think I can retrieve it, but someone knew what they were doing. This is serious, Natches. Someone wants to destroy her."

Natches stared back at Alex and breathed in heavily.

"I'll kill them," he said softly.

To which Alex replied, "You'll have to beat me to it."

SIXTEEN

"You're going to have to talk to your brother eventually, you know."

Of course, Alex was waiting on her when she trudged back into the office after making certain everyone was finished for the night and locking up. It was almost midnight. The late crowd hadn't dwindled out until after eleven, and the restaurant had stayed busy.

"Did you get my computer fixed?" She ignored his comment about Natches.

"Everything's running smooth." He pushed back from the computer. "I even worked up the payments you had listed for today and have everything ready for you to sign. I input your invoices, listed your deliveries, and you should be good to go for the night." He laid to the side the stack of papers awaiting her signature.

"Regular little secretary, aren't you?" She eased into a chair, slid her heels from her feet, and stretched her arches.

She was exhausted. She needed another manager. It was obvious she was going to have to open the extra dining room if she wanted to increase profits from the popularity of the restaurant. And the newspaper was refusing to run the ad without Natches's okay. That pissed her off.

"I try to please," he drawled, leaning against the table on the other side of the desk.

A minute later, a steaming cup of fresh coffee was at her elbow. Janey stared at the coffee, then up at Alex.

Before she could turn her head, his palm cupped her neck, and the way he did that was too dominant and too sexy for words. Then his lips stole a long, melting, tongue-licking kiss that just about stole her mind.

When he lifted his mouth and moved back, a confident smile on his face, she frowned back at him.

"I've detected a pattern here." She sighed. "You kiss me and give me coffee before you start harassing me."

"Janey, I never harass you," he said mockingly. "I merely state my opinions."

"Well, tonight I don't want to hear your opinions." She lifted the cup and sipped, almost moaning at the rich, dark taste. But it still wasn't as good as his kiss.

She turned back to the computer, going through her accounting program, checking the work he had done that day. Not that she didn't trust him. She was anal; she admitted it.

He'd of course done everything perfectly.

"Tabitha mentioned you were talking about opening the banquet room for reservations in a few weeks," he stated as he poured his own coffee. "You can't handle it alone."

No kidding. She almost snorted at that statement.

"I'm not begging Natches to approve a general manager," she told him with an edge of anger. "The newspaper won't even run my ad now."

"Talk to him, Janey," he stated again. "He thinks you're going to leave. And that thought is your fault."

"Staying here might not be an option." She lifted her shoulders negligently. "Either way, the restaurant needs to stay open. To take advantage of the popularity right now and continue to grow into the future, it needs to maintain a daily reputation. Poor service or shutting it down for a period of time will only destroy any future earnings for it."

"I have a feeling we both know Natches doesn't give a damn about this restaurant," Alex said. "I'm wondering why you do."

"Income."

"Bullshit." His tone was sharp. "Don't lie to me, Janey. I don't like it."

She wanted to know how he knew she was lying, but she refused to ask. She was almost afraid to know.

"I always loved the restaurant," she finally said, hating to admit to anyone that anything was important to her. "Every time I came here I could see how to make it work. I knew what it needed." She stared at the computer screen. "And it ate inside me because it was nothing but a means to an end for Dayle. I hated him for that alone."

The restaurant became a symbol to Janey, and she knew it. Something that could endure with the proper care and staff. Something she could build her life around.

"Does Natches know how you feel?"

She turned and looked at him curiously. "Why do you care? Why are you suddenly so damned concerned about my relationship with my brother?"

"Because he's going to end up hitting me out of frustration," he growled. "He can't figure shit out with you, so it makes him even more pissed that I'm sleeping with you, because he thinks he's losing the sister he never had a chance to know, before he has a chance to get to know her. It's a male thing."

She stared back at him suspiciously. "A male thing?"

He rubbed at his jaw. "I would really hate to have to fight Natches, Janey. But you're his baby sister. The baby sister he was never able to be a brother to. He doesn't know things that brothers think they should know. Now he's getting even more pissed that I'm sleeping with you, because he thinks I'm coming between the two of you."

"And this is a male thing?"

"It's a male thing." He nodded. "We're not just possessive over our lovers or wives, but we have this thing about our baby sisters, too. It's our job to make sure they don't get hurt. Physically or emotionally."

"And you're aware that's totally asinine, correct?"

He grinned. "Oh yeah, we know that with our heads. But our hearts are another matter. That's where it's our baby sister's responsibility to figure out the problem and fix it."

Janey bit her lip. Hard. It was that or tell him exactly how ridiculous the whole baby sister/older brother thing sounded.

"So, I'm supposed to what?" she finally asked. "Ask him nicely to let me hire another manager? Beg him, maybe?"

"Or sit down and tell him that restaurant means more to you than some fly-by-night hole-in-the-wall you can walk away from. Because we both know you won't walk away from it short of death. Be honest about that much, Janey."

"I would walk away from it before I'd see you or my brother hurt because someone wants to hurt me," she stated, staring around the office, thinking about the dining rooms outside. "It's not worth that."

"You're not going anywhere." He crossed his arms over the white shirt he wore and stared back at her implacably. "Admit it."

"Why are you harassing me? Go away, Alex." She turned back to the computer and shut it down. "I have paperwork to do."

She was lifted from the chair and tossed over his shoulder.

"What are you doing?" she screeched, bracing her hands above his butt and staring down. "Let me down."

His hand landed on her ass in a quick little slap that had her eyes widening.

"You're done for the night," he told her, striding to the door.

She heard him setting the alarm, then the lights flipped out and cold air was swirling beneath her skirt as he stepped outside.

"You're crazy." She throttled the yell that the accusation should have been. "Certifiable. Dammit, Alex, I have work to do."

"Yes, you do," he drawled, moving up the stairs. "You have a hell of a job ahead of you and it involves my hard dick. I'd rather take care of that in a bed if you don't mind."

Arousal should not have slammed inside her. She shouldn't have just let him cart her around like a sack of potatoes because his dick was hard and he wanted a bed to fuck in.

But she did. Because she wanted him. She loved him. Because she wanted as many memories as she could build before she had to force herself to let him go.

"Here we go." He set her on her feet at the door, then moved in front of her to unlock it and push it open.

It was silent as a tomb inside. He flipped the kitchen light on and moved inside, pulling her into the kitchen and closing the door before punching in the code for the security system.

Janey stayed in place as he pulled the handgun from the holster he wore behind his back and moved through the apartment.

He flipped lights on and off as he moved through each room, finally returning to the kitchen, his tall, broad body moving with a male grace and power that never failed to make her heart race.

"It's clear?" she asked as he pushed the gun back into its holster.

"Clear." His gaze flickered over her. "Those short skirts are killing me, you know. Knowing what you're wearing under them. Smoky stockings and a black garter belt. It makes me hard, Janey."

"Everything makes you hard." She pulled the gray silk blouse from the band of her skirt and began unbuttoning it slowly.

"Everything about you makes me hard," he agreed, his expression beginning to tighten as he loosened the reins on his arousal.

"Just me?" She leaned against the wall, watching him closely, knowing she was pushing, and in pushing would most likely end up with a broken heart.

She couldn't just let things ride, could she? No, she had to have more. She had to push for an emotion she knew he didn't feel.

"Just you," he surprised her with his answer. "I haven't wanted another woman since you came home, Janey."

But was it enough?

She left her blouse unbuttoned as she moved her hand to the little clasp and zipper at the side of her skirt.

"Do you give me all of you?" she asked him softly, promising herself that she was not going to mention love.

His hands fisted at his side. "What do you want?"

"The one thing you want to give me the most," she whispered.

"Do you know what that is, baby?" His voice roughened, lowered. "You don't know what all of me can be."

Janey licked her lips as she let the skirt slide over her hips and pool at her feet. His gaze flared, became thunderous, his cheekbones darkening as arousal tautened his features, making them sharper, more savage.

"Maybe I need to know all of you, Alex. You take all of me. You come inside me without protection, knowing what could come of it. You want more from me than you should ever have the chance to demand. Maybe I want to see what I'm getting in the bargain."

As though something had flipped a switch in his expression, it became more intent, his eyes darkening. His fingers uncurled, but he didn't come closer. He didn't move to her. He stared at her, his gaze tracking over her body, heating her, making her want more than he had ever given her. She wanted the parts of him that he held back, the parts he hid from her. She wanted as much of him as he demanded of her, but she would take this, for now.

"Janey, I can get nasty," he warned her then. "Some things need to be worked into."

Her lips curled knowingly. "You and the Mackay cousins were close growing up, weren't you, Alex?"

"You know we were."

"Did you join in their games?" Games where they took women together. The Mackay cousins had been known for sharing their lovers until they fell in love. "I won't be shared."

"I'd kill the man who tried to touch you now." He moved to her, one hand cupping her neck, holding her in place. Did he know how that turned her on? Made her crazy for him?

"But you did it," she murmured. "All those things they did."

"What do you want, Janey?" His other hand tightened at her hip. "Tell me. I'll give you what you want."

"The wildest thing you ever imagined doing with me." She wanted to be wild with him. "That's what I want, Alex. The most wicked, sexual thing you ever thought of if you could get me in your bed. What would you do to me? How would you make me scream for you?"

"Don't." His hand tightened at her neck.

"What was it?" She turned her head, kissed his wrist, then nipped it, all the while watching him, trying to tempt him. "What could be wilder, Alex, than tying my hands behind my back and making me suck your dick?"

He jerked her hips closer. His head lowered. His lips, they were fuller, more kissable, sexier. She wanted him to kiss her like he was now. She sensed, knew, it would be hard, rough. All of him.

"Burying my dick in your ass would be wilder." His hand slid into her hair, tangled in it. "Listening to you scream, beg, because you don't know if it's the most incredible pleasure in the world or the most painful." His lips touched hers. "Feeling you fuck yourself with your fingers while I slam my cock inside her ass, knowing you're so gone with the pleasure, my touch, your needs, that nothing matters but feeling my cum bathe you there. Milking it out of my balls and making it yours."

Oh God, she was supposed to breathe now? She stared up at him, panting, but still not drawing in enough air.

"You're huge," she whispered breathlessly. "It won't fit."

"Is that a dare, sweetheart?" Male challenge, male dominance, pure male hunger washed over his features. "Darlin', you don't make dares like that with the big boys. Because trust me, they take you up on it."

Her lips parted to protest. It hadn't been a dare. It was a statement. But as they parted, his lips slanted over hers, took them in a deep, tongue-thrusting kiss that had her going to her tiptoes, desperate to get closer.

Janey slid her hands up his arms, to his powerful biceps. She loved the heavy muscles there. The way they flexed and rippled with the control he exerted over himself. The way he fought to make certain he didn't hurt her.

She wanted his control in ashes. The way hers stayed around him. She couldn't deny him. She knew, each time he pumped his seed inside her, that he wanted her to carry his child. It wasn't love. It couldn't substitute for love, so why did it affect her as it did? She couldn't deny him. She ached for the feel of it. Ached to feel him inside her, spilling the liquid heat of his lust, giving her a part of himself he had never given another woman.

He was building silken threads around her soul, and she couldn't stop it. She knew only one way to combat it. To build them around him as well. And each time Alex lost himself inside her, she swore she felt the threads twining around him.

"You don't know what you're asking for." He swung her up in

his arms. As though she weighed nothing. As though she were delicate, as though he liked holding her.

"I'm asking for you." She licked his neck, caught a bit of flesh between her teeth, and sucked it into her mouth playfully.

She loved marking him, but she needed to mark him elsewhere, where it couldn't be seen. Where only they knew it was there. A brand he would feel, but one others could only guess at.

He entered the bedroom, closing the door behind them, because Fat Cat was in the apartment. Evidently Alex had let him in earlier and fed him.

A second later he laid her on the bed, drawing back from her as she stretched beneath his gaze, feeling her breasts swell, her nipples hardening further as he stared down at her.

"We're going to leave the garter belt and stockings on," he told her.

She bent her leg, trailed her fingers over her bare stomach to the low band of her panties, and watched as he all but tore his shirt off. Her hand slid beneath her panties as he jerked at his belt, her fingers dipping into the hot, liquid cleft and pulling back.

Slick, shining with her juices, she lifted her fingertips to her lips and licked over them.

"You little tease," he growled, but she knew Alex liked this. He loved it.

Janey smiled and ran her fingers down her neck before lifting and sliding the blouse over her shoulders as he jerked his jeans off.

His cock was iron hard. The thick crest was dark, flushed with blood, a bead of pre-cum pearling at the tip, making her mouth water.

He turned to her nightstand, and she watched in surprise as he withdrew a small tube of lubricating gel.

"Prepared, were you?" she asked, surprised at the husky, sexual tease in her voice.

"It has other uses," he assured her. "Tonight, though, we're going to use a lot of it."

She expected him to turn her over and just take her. She didn't expect him to rise over her, for his lips to slant across her and his kiss to become wild, primal. It was more than foreplay; it was a psychological branding, this kiss.

Her arms wrapped around his neck as she felt the straps of her bra lower over her arms. His hands, they were so strong, so broad, long-fingered, and calloused. Male hands. A man's hands. Hands that knew where and how to stroke.

The front clasp of the garment loosened and he drew it away from her. Where he tossed it, she didn't know and she didn't care.

"Alex." She whispered his name as his lips slid from hers to her neck. Teeth raked, tongue licked. "What you do to me . . ." She arched closer.

"What I want to do to you is probably illegal in every state of the union." He bit her shoulder, then licked the little wound. "I want every part of you, Janey."

She breathed through the sob that wanted to work from her chest. Every part of her? Did he want the heart that already belonged to him? The soul that opened up for him?

"Damn, I love your nipples." His tongue stroked over them. "So hard and sweet." He sucked one into his mouth, licked it with his rough velvet tongue and had her toes curling as he suckled her with heated hunger.

He touched her, stroked her, drew on her, as though starved for the taste of her in his mouth. He drew the tip between his teeth, stroked it with his tongue, and she swore she nearly came from the excitement of it. Then he was sucking the hard tip again, sending flares of sensation racing to her pussy as his fingers stroked her thighs, parted them, and trailed to the swollen band of her panties before pulling back again.

"That's so good," she cried out. "I love my nipples in your mouth, Alex. I feel it all the way to my clit."

He jerked against her, groaned low and deep before he pulled her hands from his shoulders and drew back.

"Play with them," he ordered her roughly. "Let me watch you play with your nipples while I eat your pussy, Janey. I need the taste of you in my mouth. All that sweet syrup, sliding over my tongue."

A hard spasm gripped her muscles, jerking her up to him as pleasure shot through her system. Her fingers moved to her nipples, grabbing them, rolling them as he tugged her panties over her thighs and down her legs.

As he'd threatened, he left her garter belt and stockings on. His fingers played with the elastic garters. His lips kissed above the frilly, lacy bands.

"All I can think about, knowing what you're wearing under those skirts, is how sexy you look just like this." He pushed her legs apart, lifted her knees until her thighs were spread wide, her pussy open to him. "All I can think about is getting my lips in this sweet, hot flesh."

His tongue licked through the cleft, a quick, hard stroke that had her gasping and lifting to get closer to him.

She felt his fingers, easing below, spreading her juices from her cleft to the tiny opening of her rear.

He didn't push inside her, just teased her. Pressed and made her want more. She had never imagined wanting this, until now. Until Alex—as fantasies drifted through her mind during the day, wondering just how much of his sexuality her lover was holding back.

"The taste of your pussy makes me insane." The rough vibration of his voice against her clit had her jerking, gasping.

She rolled her nipples, her back arched, her head lolled against the pillow. The pleasure. Sweet, sweet heaven, so much pleasure.

"I'm going to fuck your ass until you're screaming for me, Janey," he warned her.

"Alex." She was ready to scream already, as two fingers pressed inside her vagina, working in, screwing against the sensitive muscles and stroking them erotically.

She could come now. Just a little bit more. Just the right stroke.

"Oh, that's not a scream, baby." The primal sound of his voice was a caress by itself. "But you're going to scream."

His fingers pulled back, coaxing her juices from her, letting them ease along her flesh to her rear. Lifting one leg, he pressed her foot to his shoulder, and the fingers of his other hand were pressing against the other entrance.

He was playing with her. Playing her body. His lips were on her clit, licking around it, providing just enough pressure to make her completely insane, as two fingers thrust inside her sex again. They worked inside her, twisted, stroked a spot inside her so ultrasensitive that she lost her breath.

As she gasped, she felt a slick, cool finger slide inside her rear. Just that easy. It pushed against the tiny opening as heat burned through her nerve endings.

"Oh God! Alex. Alex." She was chanting his name as the finger pulled free of her.

"Sweet and hot. Your ass is so tight, Janey. When I take it, it's going to feel as though every part of you is filled with me."

When his fingers returned, they were slicker, cooler. The heavy lubrication was eased just inside her. Then his lips pursed over her clit, and two fingers from the other hand pushed inside her pussy again. Deep.

She inhaled roughly and the finger at her rear slid inside again. He repeated it. Moving back, lubricating his fingers, sliding one inside her as he pushed two deep into her vagina and he tormented her clit with his lips, his tongue.

Janey could feel perspiration building on her skin now. The flames burning inside her were racing, licking over her body as he continued to push her higher, stroking her deeper.

The next time he penetrated her rear, there were two fingers. The burn grew, the pleasure became mindless. When he eased three fingers inside her ass, she was bucking against him, her head thrashing, her fingers digging into the blankets rather than playing with her nipples.

His tongue was a demon of pleasure as it licked around and over her clit. The fingers in her pussy were torturous, ecstatic. She was lost in so many sensations—pleasure, pain—feeling them burn inside her until she was begging for more.

"There, baby." There was something in his voice as he eased from her then. "Come here. Turn over for me, love."

Love. He called her love. He didn't love her, but he called her love.

Excitement, pleasure, and need a vicious heat searing her, Janey let him guide her. She rolled to her stomach, coming to her knees for him, feeling his hands easing over the cheeks of her rear.

"Almost ready, sweet love," he crooned, his fingers pressing against her opening again, lubricating her more. "Ah, Janey, you're going to kill me. I want you so fucking bad. Right here."

She stilled. She could feel her juices easing from her vagina, and the thick, swollen cock head Alex thrust against her back opened her.

"Slow and easy, darlin'," he whispered, pressing the cheeks of her ass apart. "We go slow and easy. Breathe in for me. Deep, Janey."

She breathed in and nearly shattered. She felt him pushing inside her, stretching her, hot and throbbing as unbreached tissue began to burn, nerve endings rioting with sensation.

Janey could feel the scream building in her lungs.

"Inhale, baby." His hand smoothed down her back as he stilled behind her. "Slow and deep. Now. Janey."

She inhaled, then a wail tore from her as she felt the heavy, tight muscles stretching open for him.

He stopped. She could feel him behind her, breathing hard. Deep. She could feel his muscles straining, the edge of his control disintegrating.

"Ah God, you're so fucking tight," he breathed out roughly. "Milking my dick like the hottest fist in the world."

"Alex. Alex, what do I do?" She cried out at the wild, unrelieved hunger clawing at her now. "I can't stand it. Please."

His hand landed on the side of her ass. A brief, light little slap that felt too good. Too hot.

"Breathe in. Deep. Every time you breathe in, I can go deeper." He panted. "Breathe. God, Janey, I have to fuck you. Breathe, damn you."

She breathed in, inhaling when she wanted to exhale on a scream as the head of his cock popped past the tight ring of muscles that would have held him back.

Then she screamed. Or she tried to scream. She couldn't breathe. She couldn't think. He was working inside her in slow, easy thrusts that pushed him deeper, deeper inside her, until she felt the slap of his balls against her pussy.

"Son of a bitch," he cursed behind her.

She felt moisture drip to her back, knew he was sweating. She was moist with perspiration. Dying for more.

"Touch your pussy," he ordered roughly, his hands clamping on her hips. "Fuck yourself with your fingers now, Janey. Let me feel you riding your fingers, because I'll be damned if I'm going to last long."

She was crying, begging. She pushed a hand between her legs and buried two fingers inside her sex, immediately clenching, tightening on them as he jerked behind her and pushed in deeper.

"Fuck. Fuck." His voice was harsh. "Ah hell. Janey."

She felt his control snap. She felt it in the hard grip on her hips, in the jerking motion of his hips. Then he was fucking her. Taking her ass with deep, powerful strokes as her fingers filled her pussy.

She could feel him. Every throbbing, heavy vein, every powerful inch of flesh stroking inside her. She felt it in the burning stretch, the driving thrusts. His control was gone, and her sense of reality exploded as her clit rubbed against her palm and her fingers stroked her pussy to orgasm.

She was screaming for him, feeling the orgasm that tore through her, quaking through her nerve endings, harder, deeper. Her release was so powerful, so vibrant, that she felt every hot spurt of his seed filling her rear. Each drop of his cum pumping inside her as she wailed out her pleasure.

She was crying, limp and trembling, shuddering with the aftermath of a release so intense, so deep, she couldn't seem to gather her shattered senses in order.

Alex still covered her, still filled her. His heavy, warm body was like a blanket over her, like a shield between her and the world, holding the pleasure inside her, keeping the warmth around her.

And she couldn't stop shaking. She couldn't stop tightening around him. Exhaustion seeped inside her, and yet she could feel adrenaline racing through her.

"Ah, baby. My Janey." His voice was a low, sated rumble at her ear as he kissed her neck, the cheek turned to him. "My sweet love. So sweet. So fucking good."

She gasped as he pulled back, easing from her.

"Come here, love." He pulled her against him, his hands stroking down her back, over her arms as he held her against his chest. "There, darlin'. Just lay here."

Alex couldn't hold her tight enough, couldn't get her close enough to his chest. His heart was beating in slow, heavy thumps, the release that had powered into her body having shaken him. The strength of it, feeling as though it jerked more than just his seed from him, had nearly destroyed him.

He needed to get up. He needed to clean her, clean himself, but he couldn't let her go. He wrapped himself around her. He had to shelter her as close inside himself as he could get her.

And yet he could feel the need for more. It wasn't sexual. It wasn't physical. It didn't make sense. But he knew he needed more.

SEVENTEEN

The cell phone ringing brought Natches awake. He stared blearily at the clock by the bed, then at the window. Hell, it wasn't even fucking dawn yet.

Pulling the device off the nightstand, he checked the caller ID first. Unknown name and unknown number? That wasn't possible. This was a DHS-equipped phone. It showed everything but what the caller ate last.

He flipped it open. "Yeah?"

He was already moving from the bed when the voice came over the connection.

"You have e-mail." It was distorted. He knew the sound of electronic voice distortion. He pulled his jeans over his legs, zipped them, delaying as long as possible.

"Did you hear me?" Anger snapped across the line.

"Who is this?" He let his voice sound drowsy, sleepy.

"A friend," the voice announced. "Check your e-mail. It's important." The voice cracked. "I wanted to be nice about this, but you have to see what she's done to him." There was a hint of tears in the voice.

Natches headed to his computer, feeling the hairs at the back of his neck lifting as Chaya moved from the bed.

"What are you talking about?" he asked the caller.

There was a tearful sniff. "Do you see?"

"Takes my computer a minute to boot up," he stated.

That was a lie. The computer was on; a flick of the mouse and e-mail was up, complete with the attachment.

He opened it and felt his head explode. Behind him, Chaya gasped in shock and he couldn't blame her. There was more than one picture, but the first was enough. Natches couldn't stand to look further. He couldn't do it. The first one showed a curved feminine rear spread apart, pink and pretty, and filled with a thick, engorged cock.

He turned away, swallowing against the bile in his throat. Fuck, he knew who it was and he could feel an almost killing rage building inside him. That was Alex and Janey. Fuck. Fuck. That was his sister's butt. He was going to be sick. He was going to kill Alex.

He turned to Chaya and mouthed, *Call Alex. Cameras in bedroom.*

She nodded quickly and rushed to the phone by the bed.

"What kind of e-mail?" He closed his eyes and fought to sound sleepy, not quite aware of what was going on.

"You have a lousy computer," the voice sneered. "Are you playing me, Natches?" There was an edge of hurt. "Don't play me."

"I'm not playing you." He closed his eyes and fought to breathe. "E-mail." He paused. "Shit. What is this?"

"Look what she did to him!" the voice was furious now, filled with pain. "Look what he's doing, Natches. She's making him like

Johnny was. She's taking away his manhood by making him do that to her. Do you see it? Do you see what she begged for? How she's corrupting him?"

"How did you get these pictures?" He flipped through just enough to identify Alex and Janey's faces, nothing else. That camera was in their bedroom. Right across from the bed, in the vent in the wall. Son of a bitch, how had that bastard gotten in the apartment?

"He's gone now," the voice whispered. "I saw him leave the bedroom."

Natches turned to Chaya, fear beginning to rise inside him.

"Now, let's settle down. Let's talk a minute."

"I gave you the chance to take care of this," the caller screamed. "I sent you the picture. I showed you how she was making him act. She's a slut. A whore. Her father taught her how to be a whore and she's corrupting Alex. I told you."

"Let's talk about this . . ." Fear rose inside him. He could feel it, oily, weakening. The bastard had finally lost his fucking mind.

"Alex, get Janey out of the apartment. The bedroom has cameras. Natches has pictures and he's on the phone with your stalker. Get her out of there."

Alex was moving from the table as Chaya's frantic, low voice came over his cell phone. Moving quickly, he pushed back from the table and rushed to the bedroom.

Janey was playing with the cat when he left. The fat little bastard was on its back batting at her fingers. He'd left them in peace, knowing the cat still hadn't adapted well to his presence.

"He has more pictures. Natches will kill you," Chaya was hissing as Alex rounded the hall and jerked Janey's door open.

Her head lifted from the bed in shock.

"Let's go." He didn't wait for questions. He yanked the cat up as he grabbed her arm and pulled her from the bed.

"Alex . . ."

"Move!"

Adrenaline surged through him as he heard Natches screaming, "Get her out. Get her out."

He pushed her through the door, the cat tearing at his arm as he heard a window shatter. Then all hell exploded around them.

He felt the force of the blast shake the apartment as the cat jumped from his arm with a squall. Janey screamed as he threw her to the floor.

Searing, brilliant pain lanced his shoulder as he landed on top of her, dragging her beneath his crawling body, fighting to get her to safety as lights flickered, shattered, and the apartment went dark.

He still gripped his cell phone in his hand. He could hear Natches screaming. Blood was gushing down his arm, but Janey was alive.

The living room window had shattered. He had a second. Only a second. He had lifted her and thrown her into the kitchen doorway, to the other side of the wall, when another explosion shook the apartment. Shrapnel exploded through the wall overhead as he protected her with his own body, curling around her as she screamed his name. He felt something else bury in his shoulder and gritted his teeth against the pain.

Hell, it was Iraq all over again. The explosions, the sound of nails and glass exploding around him, as sirens wailed in the distance.

"Safe," he yelled into the cell phone, Natches's screaming voice still echoing from the connection. "What the fuck is going on? I need the outside secured before the son of a bitch throws something through the fucking kitchen window."

He dragged Janey across the room and jerked open the pantry closet beside the refrigerator, before shoving her into the narrow entrance and hunkering down beside her. He jerked the fridge door open, sheltering them with the heavier metal barrier rather than the thin wood of the pantry closet door.

"We're coming. We're coming." Natches was yelling into the phone. "Zeke and the police are on their way. Chaya called from her cell. Fuck. Fuck. Alex, is she okay?"

"Alive," Alex snapped. "Get me some fucking backup. I'm not taking her out without it and we're too vulnerable here."

He was bleeding like a stuck pig. Alex could feel the blood pouring from the sharp objects buried in the shoulder that he kept turned carefully from Janey's huddled form.

"Is Janey wounded?" Natches was screaming.

"Negative." God, he wished he had a weapon on him. "Natches, get here now."

There was silence.

"You're wounded." Natches's voice was lower. The other man was an asshole when he wanted to be, but he was sharp.

"Confirmed," Alex breathed out roughly. "Get here, man. I'm unarmed. All weapons are in other areas. We're shielded in the pantry closet with no more than the fridge door. I hear sirens approaching, but we don't know who the hell or what the hell."

As he spoke, the back door shattered. Alex braced himself for more trouble. He disconnected the call and waited.

"Major. You in here?" Mark Lessing's voice sounded from outside the door.

He remained silent, pressing a hand back to Janey in warning. He trusted his men with his own life. He didn't trust anyone but himself and the Mackay cousins with Janey's.

"Major, I'm sliding a weapon through. It will move beneath the refrigerator door." Mark stayed in place, his voice military cold and efficient. "Clip is loaded. Tyrell and I have the door covered. Here it comes."

He waited. A second later the Glock slid to his feet. Alex picked it up carefully, checked the clip.

"Did you catch the bastard?" he called back.

"Negative. We gave chase, but he got away. We came back in case we were needed here."

"Mackays are on their way," Alex told him. "Tyrell, cover the stairs. I'm not moving her until I have clear protection on all sides."

The sirens were getting closer. Alex could hear Janey behind him, her breathing erratic. He knew she wasn't wounded; he'd checked as he held her beneath him and again as he threw her into the closet.

"The first blast in the back distracted us, Major," Mark bit out. "Hell, we've been out of action too long."

Mark Lessing and Tyrell Grayson had quietly left the Special Forces when information that they were lovers had leaked to the head brass. They'd been out of the forces for several years, but they were still as sharp as any man on his current team. Whoever did this was just that fucking good.

"Alex, you're bleeding. I can smell it." Janey's voice was faint behind him. "I need something to press against the wound."

Hell. Her voice was thick with fear. He could feel her tension behind him, the fear that spread through her like an oppressive cloud. But damn if she wasn't holding it together. There was no panic, not yet. She was shaking in shock, but holding back, waiting.

"There's shrapnel still lodged in the wounds." He suspected nails. "Help will be here soon, baby."

Janey wiped at her tears, barely holding back sobs. She could feel them tearing at her chest, but she couldn't distract him, not yet. Horror filled her at the thought of the blood she could smell. And she could see it from the dim light the refrigerator cast, the shadow of it running down his side. She wanted to touch him. Oh

God, she needed to touch him, to make it stop, and she didn't dare move.

He had already proven he would shield her from death, take it himself first. If she distracted him and caused him to be hurt more or, worse, killed, she couldn't live with that.

So she capped her hand over her mouth as she had learned as a child. The tears fell, but she kept the sobs inside. She kept the fear and the pain inside, hid it where it couldn't distract him, couldn't cause him to be hurt worse.

She used to do that when she was small. Sobbed inside while she held everything back. Dayle didn't hit Natches as hard if she didn't cry. If she didn't seem to care.

But she couldn't stop the tears now. Alex was bleeding, and he was bleeding bad. He had been hurt trying to protect her, just as Natches had been so many times. The reasons why didn't matter. The fact was, it was all her fault.

"Mackays are pullin' in, Major," Mark Lessing called into the kitchen. "We have four coming in hell-for-leather, sheriff and city cops behind them."

Janey could hear the commotion outside now. Tires screaming, sirens blaring. Alex was leaning against the doorframe, but he held the handgun easily and his body was tense, on guard.

"Alex, we can go out now," she whispered, swallowing back the tears that would have filled her voice.

"Not yet." His voice was hard.

"You're bleeding to death on me," she snapped. "Stop being so stubborn."

"I know what I'm doing, Janey." His voice was hard, forbidding.

A sob escaped her. She couldn't help it. She couldn't hold it back. "Alex, please," she cried, her voice ragged with pain. "Please, Alex, don't bleed to death on me. Please."

Alex turned slowly. The dim light from the refrigerator shadowed across her face. Tears ran from her eyes like small streams. The green was darker, filled with horror and fear. And with pain. Because she could smell his blood, because she knew he was hurt.

She wasn't sobbing; her breathing was rough, labored, but there were no sobs. The tears were all the more heartbreaking for the lack of sound.

"Come here, baby." He angled his body, still sheltering her, but allowing his good arm to wrap around her and pull her to his chest. "I'm okay."

"Where is she?" Natches's furious yell penetrated the dark room. "Janey!"

The closet and refrigerator doors were jerked aside as Alex came to his feet, dragging Janey with him. Then a dark shadow reached for her. Hands gripped her, trying to pull her away from Alex.

"No!" She couldn't see who it was. A part of her knew it was Natches, knew he was trying to drag her away from Alex, but the insanity building in her mind locked in place. "Alex!" She tried to hold on to him as she fought the hands dragging at her, kicking out, sobbing, trying to wrench away and stay by Alex's side.

"Dammit, Natches, let her go." Alex curled his arm around her chest and jerked her to him.

Natches froze, the serious end of Alex's Glock in his face, hard, brutally flat gray eyes locking with his.

"She's in shock. She's terrified. Let her fucking go."

Natches released his sister carefully. He could see the other man's pale features, the blood that ran down his arm, the glitter of pain in Alex's eyes. But he was holding Janey to him as though she alone could keep him on his feet.

"Hell!" Natches moved back, aware of his cousins, Sheriff Mayes, and the city cops behind them. "Zeke, we have to get them to safety. He's wounded."

"Ambulance is en route."

"No ambulance," Alex growled, stepping from the closet, aware of his own bare feet, and of Janey's.

"Mark, you and Tyrell have your ride?"

"Right outside," Mark confirmed. "Ready to roll."

"Natches, you and Dawg head to my place and secure it. Rowdy, you'll go in front of Mark's vehicle, Tyrell will cover from the back."

"Dammit, Alex," Natches protested.

"Alex, the EMTs will be here in minutes and we need your statements," Zeke snapped.

"Then you can get them at my house," he snarled, keeping Janey close with his good arm as he felt the blood trickling down his back. "Take a look at this fucking apartment, Zeke. She's not safe here and someone is deadly serious about this. My house is safe."

Natches and Dawg were already leaving. He could hear Natches cursing as they ran down the stairs, promising to gut and castrate him, but they were going.

"Alex, that shoulder's bad," Rowdy told him calmly, his dark green eyes concerned. "Let Mark patch you up in my truck and Tyrell can follow us in. Zeke can wait for the investigator. After they finish going through everything, they can come to the house."

"Please." Janey whispered the word against his chest. He could feel her tears, hotter than his blood, against his flesh.

"Let's go!" He nodded before turning to Zeke. "Cover us to the truck. Bring the investigator when you're finished here. First blast was in the bedroom. Second was in the living room. He had time to run to the front after tossing the first device. First landed on the bed is my guess. Second landed in front of the couch."

Janey held on to Alex as they moved for the door. She kept her arms around him, terrified he was going to fall on her, that he had waited too long, bled too much.

But he didn't let her go, and he wasn't weak. Despite her efforts to help him, he practically lifted her off her feet as he rushed her down the outside steps. And he didn't let her go. Not once did his arm relax from around her until he was pushing her into the back of Rowdy's dual-cab pickup followed by Mark Lessing and a blurr of orange fur as Fat Cat wailed plaintively and planted himself on the other side of Janey.

Mark had a heavy bag in his hand. No sooner had the door closed behind them than Rowdy was pulling quickly out of the parking lot and Mark was pouring something over Alex's shoulder.

"You son of a bitch!" Alex went taut, every muscle screaming in pain as the antiseptic ran over his shoulder.

A light flicked on.

"I'm putting a clotting powder on it until we're at the house." The sound of a package ripping had sweat popping out on Alex's head. "We know how much you like this, Major."

Bullshit.

He jerked his arm away from Janey, clenched the back of the driver's seat and the back passenger seat.

"Hurry!" he barked.

He kept his head down as agony lit every nerve ending he possessed. A growl tore from his throat and he heard Janey choke back a sob as the cat hissed.

The clotting powder was hell. He nearly cracked his teeth holding back a furious yell as the pain lit a red haze in his mind.

"Fucker!" he bit out. "Your turn is coming."

"Like hell." Mark grunted. "Tyrell and I got out of this shit for a reason. Remember?"

He remembered. Hated it. But he remembered it.

Breathing in roughly, he lifted his head and stared back at Janey. She was paper white, her eyes dilated, but damn was she holding up. Her robe was belted tight around her; she was shivering, but watching him with sharp, assessing eyes.

Her hair was mussed around her face, tears streaked her face, but by God, she was alive. She was living and breathing, one hand on the bunched biceps curled against the seat behind her, the other pressed against his chest as her lips trembled.

"Don't die on me," she whispered, and another tear slipped past her eyes. "Please, Alex."

He forced his lips to kick up in a grin. "Can't get rid of me that easily, can she, Mark?"

"Hell no, Major," Mark answered. "You're like fucking Superman. Made of steel." Mark's voice was heavy with sarcasm.

"Ignore him. He's jealous. He just wishes he had all my scars."

Mark snorted beside him.

"Come here, love." He wrapped his good arm around her, pulling her close. "Right here." He kissed the top of her head, tucked her close, and stared out at the night as the pickup erased the short distance between the restaurant and his house. "I have you, Janey. I'm not letting you go, baby. I have you right here."

EIGHTEEN

Natches and Dawg had the house secured when Rowdy pulled into the drive and brought the truck to a stop at the back door.

Mark jumped from the passenger-side door, while Alex eased back, pulling Janey with him as that damned cat cried out pitifully.

"Here, Mark." With his good hand, he lifted the surprisingly docile feline to the other man. "There's cat supplies in the cupboard in the kitchen. Never did get rid of the shit after Crista's cat ran off."

So long ago. Hell, he could feel every damned year of his life weighing on his shoulders right now.

"Hold on to me," he ordered Janey, lifting one of her arms around his neck as he gripped her waist with his good arm. His left arm was practically useless at this point. He suspected a nail was lodged inside it, though Mark hadn't said anything either way. Alex could feel the shrapnel that was going to have to be dug out.

Bastard. It could have been Janey's tender flesh riddled with the sharp projectiles. If he hadn't been there, that first homemade bomb would have landed in her bed, taking her out immediately.

He had to fight back the fury at the thought of what they would have found. There would have been nothing left of the woman he held in his arms now.

"You can't carry me, Alex." Janey tried to pull back, tried to keep him from exerting the hard muscles of his back and shoulders as he lifted her.

He did it anyway. His arm tightened around her hips, holding her to him as he nodded to Mark. Rowdy moved in front of them; Mark, carrying the cat, took up the rear as another man moved from the vehicle following them.

The back door opened quickly and Alex rushed her inside. He ignored Natches and Dawg's expectant looks. "Mark, I need you and Tyrell with us in the bedroom. Now."

"Fuck that." Natches moved behind them. "You're not keeping me out, Alex."

Alex kept going. He didn't give a damn if Natches was there for now. Janey needed something, someone to hold on to, but God help Natches if he suggested taking her out of the house.

"Do you need your team, Major?" Tyrell asked, his voice chilly as they filed into the bedroom.

Alex shook his head as he set Janey on her feet and glanced at the other man. "They're on assignment."

He'd let the team go when he'd taken that last hit to his leg in Iraq. The missions were getting longer, the danger becoming less adrenaline- and more ennui-infused. He was losing the drive and he knew it. As he looked at Janey, thought of the baby she could be carrying, he knew he wasn't going back.

"Sit!" Mark Lessing, medic's bag in hand, pushed Alex to the heavy kitchen chair Tyrell had dragged in.

"Janey, fix us some coffee," Alex ordered her as he straddled the chair, knowing what was coming.

"Come on, sis." Natches wasn't mocking or his normally over-bearing self. His arm went around her shoulders.

She shrugged it off and glared back at all of them.

"Natches can make the coffee."

Alex closed his eyes as he propped his good arm on the back of the chair and watched her. "You don't want to be here for this," he told her, knowing what was coming, knowing that when Mark began detailing exactly what was buried in his shoulder she wasn't going to be strong enough to handle it.

She was a woman. Tender. Sweet. She had no business here. He looked at Natches. "Get her out of here."

"Try it and find out just how well those self-defense classes I took work," she warned her brother.

She wasn't going anywhere. Janey moved slowly to her lover, staring at him, aching, hurting. She could feel the pain and the fear for him cutting through her like a dull, jagged knife.

"Don't make me leave," she whispered as she stood in front of him. "I should be here."

His gaze was flat. His soldier gaze. Hard. His jaw like granite. His gaze sliced to Natches.

"I'll stay," Natches said quietly behind her. "If she wants to leave, then I'll get her out of here."

Silence filled the bedroom as Mark moved behind Alex.

"Here's what we have." The medic sighed. "You got whiskey, Major? You're going to need it."

"Kitchen cabinet." He nodded to Natches.

The other man moved quickly back to the other room.

"We have two six-inch nails buried in, almost to the bone, I'm guessing. They have to come out. Looks like a metal shard protruding from the fleshy part of your shoulder, deep, but thin. We have puncture wounds, no slicing. We have some shredding flesh, a few burns. We have to get the projectiles out first and we'll go from there."

Alex stared up at Janey. A tear slipped from her eye. A single tear as she touched his face with trembling fingers and Natches moved back into the room, the fifth of whiskey in hand.

Alex grabbed it, tipped it to his lips, and took as much as possible in one gulp. Damn, he needed to be drunk. He pushed the boundary with the liquor, consuming quite a bit of the liquid before handing it back to Mark.

"You should have gone to the hospital, Major," Tyrell snapped.

"Too many reports," Alex replied. "We can't let the attacker know I'm weak. Get to it, Mark. Let's get it over with."

"Alex." Janey whispered his name as Natches pushed a chair to her.

She sat down in front of Alex, leaned her head against his good arm, and touched him, held on to him. God, he should push her away. He needed her out of here.

Agony streaked through him as Mark doused the area with the liquor and went to work. He was quick, efficient. The nails and shrapnel were pulled out within minutes. The longest fucking minutes of his life.

He kept his head on his arm, snarled in fury at the pain, cursed the bastard responsible, and swore he was going to fry him and feed him to the dogs at the local humane shelter.

"All out," Mark announced. "Shouldn't need stitches. We have straight punctures. I'm going to clean them, bandage your shoulder up, and inject an antibiotic. You're going to have to sleep soon, Major. You're going to fall on your ass if you don't."

"Soon." Alex knew sleep wouldn't hold off much longer. The wound as well as the adrenaline crash would get him. Before it did, he'd make certain everything was secure to protect Janey and himself while they slept.

Janey held back more tears as he rose to his feet as though nothing was wrong, no pain, no wounds. As though he hadn't shielded her body with his, as though it didn't matter.

"There's coffee in the kitchen if someone wants to make it."

Janey turned to Natches, meeting his brooding gaze, the worry she saw there.

"Let me get Janey some clothes and we'll be right out," Alex announced. "Close the door behind you."

Natches stared back at her for long seconds before he moved out of the room, followed by Mark and Tyrell.

"Here."

She caught the T-shirt he tossed her as she turned around.

"Crista left some sweats in here, too." He moved to a dresser, rummaging through it until he came up with a pair. "Get those on and we'll figure this out."

He moved to the closet and pulled out a shirt. As Janey dressed, she watched him ease into the shirt, button it, then sit down in the chair to tie leather athletic shoes on his feet.

"When we walk back out there, you're going to play real nice," he finally announced as he rose to his feet.

"What do you mean?" Janey watched him warily now.

"There were cameras in your bedroom. That's how Natches knew to call. I'm guessing he got some real pretty snapshots of us earlier." Anger filled his tone as Janey stared back at him in shock.

"Of us? You mean . . ." Her face flamed in shock. "Earlier."

"No doubt," he bit out, his expression tightening in anger. "He's going to drag you out of here. And I'm telling you, Janey, you try to leave with him, and there will be hell to pay."

She shook her head before glaring at him. "You think I'd take this danger to Chaya or Crista and their babies?" she asked him incredulously. "You think Natches is that insane, Alex? Or that I am?"

"I think Natches is terrified for you." He ran his hand around the back of his neck in frustration. "And I think you're starting that whole internal argument where you can't let someone be hurt because of you. I'm letting you know right now, Janey. Leave this house and when I find you, I'll paddle your ass."

Her eyes widened. "What is this, another of those male things?" she argued. "You're in pain, therefore you can start ordering me around like one of your soldiers?"

"Pretty much." He grimaced as he moved to her, jerking her against him, holding her to him as he stared down at her.

And he was hard. Janey noticed that fact first. The second was that his eyes glittered now with almost fevered intensity.

"You're mine, Janey."

Before she could argue, his lips were on hers, his kiss hard, heavy, his tongue filling her mouth, pumping inside it as her fingernails rasped against the heavy cotton fabric of his shirt where it covered his rippling abs.

"Now, don't argue with me in there," he breathed out roughly. "Where you're concerned, I'm not nearly as in control as I act, and I'm sure as hell not rational."

"Yeah. Try insane," she accused him. "Evidently nails buried in your shoulder isn't enough for you to figure out how much trouble I am."

His eyes darkened, flared with anger. "Six months ago I carried you out of Dayle Mackay's house, and I made myself a promise."

"That you could save me?" she sneered. "Like a child."

"Is that what you think?" The tight curve of his lips was in no way one of amusement. "Oh no, baby, that wasn't it. I promised myself you were going to belong to me. One way or the other. No matter what it took. I didn't come back this time with pure intentions, Janey. Not by a long shot. When I came home this time, it was with every intention of getting you into my bed and keeping you there. Forever."

Her eyes widened. "You're lying, Alex."

"I don't lie, Janey." His expression was savage, his eyes thunderous. "And this, I sure as hell aint lyin' about. Get it in your head, baby. You're not going anywhere. Once this is over, I'll go back to trying to convince you that this is where you want to be; until then, it's where you're staying. Period."

"Whether I want to or not?" she cried out. "Do you ever listen to yourself, Alex? You don't believe in love, but by God, I belong to you." She mocked him furiously. "You don't care that I want more than a man who's settled for me, or decided he wants to own me. No, that's just supposed to be enough for me."

"You love me," he stated.

Janey stared back at him. That statement destroyed her. She felt the pain lance though her heart, through her mind. It dug into a part of her that she always fought to protect and ripped a jagged wound across her soul.

Yes, she loved him. Loved him until she wondered if she would survive what he was doing to her.

"That doesn't mean I don't need your love, Alex," she whispered. "That I don't need a man who knows how to love. You like the sex. You like having a woman you think you can control with sex. And you like the thought of being a daddy." She continued to mock him. "But you don't love me. And I need love."

"Janey." His voice was warning.

"I've lived without love all my life," she stated roughly. "My entire life, Alex. I'm not willing to live the rest of my life wondering what it would have been like to be loved."

She felt her lips trembling, her fists clenching. "Damn you! Damn you to hell for making me care. For touching me. For showing me everything I can't have!" She was screaming at him, enraged now. "You play the big, tough soldier who gets nails pulled out of his shoulder without a whimper. But you're a fucking coward."

"That's enough, Janey."

"The hell it is." The tears were running down her face again;

sobs were tearing at her chest. "You won't love me. You can't love me. You can't even let anyone know you're fucking me!"

Janey swung away from him as those words tore from her lips. She capped her hand over her mouth, fought back a sob. Fought back the pain.

"What did you just say to me, Janey?" His voice was dangerously soft.

Turning back to him, she realized the bitter smile that shaped her lips was rife with mockery.

"You hide through the day." Her breathing hitched. "When I have to go out, my brother or cousins follow me; you can't. You pace my fucking apartment. Wouldn't do for the future chief of police to be caught screwing a traitor's daughter, would it?" She had to fight to breathe past the tears now. The hurt. "Look at you." She yelled back at him. "You nearly bled to death in front of me, and now you're stating ownership like you bought me on an auction block. You don't own me."

She was shaking. Shaking so hard she felt as though she was going to come apart. She could feel her heart shattering, all the pain, all the years that she had been alone, too afraid to care, too afraid to love, slicing through her.

"I didn't let anyone know we were lovers because I didn't want your stalker to know someone was plotting to catch him," he said softly.

His expression was frightening. It was hard, flat. His eyes were brutal, spearing into her.

"Good excuse." She wiped the tears from her face. "Really worked, too. You almost died!" Her voice rose again.

His finger stabbed at her. "We're going to fight this out later," he promised her, his voice furious. "When your brother isn't standing in the kitchen listening to us argue like idiots."

"There's no fight." She caught her breath on another sob. "There's no fight, Alex, because in the end, it's not going to matter either way. You won't love me. That leaves us at a dead fucking end."

"Janey, dammit, do you think I don't care for you?" His voice rose now, his eyes dilated, the color darkened. "Do you think you don't mean more to me than any woman in the world outside my sister?"

"That's not love!"

"I wouldn't fucking breathe if anything happened to you," he yelled back furiously, crossing to her and jerking her against him. "What the fuck more can I give you, Janey? Damn you, I couldn't live in a world without you in it."

She buried her head against his chest, sobbing. Breaking down. Feeling the anguish of so many years rising inside her. All the aching loneliness, the nights she stared into the darkness and wouldn't let herself cry.

"It's not love," she cried desperately, holding on to him, wanting to sink into the floor and curl into herself as the rage and the pain raked through her with angry talons. "Oh God, Alex. I can't walk away from you. I can't tear myself away from you. And you're going to destroy what's left of my soul."

Because she needed to be loved. Just once. To hear the words *I love you.* Words she hadn't even heard from her brother since he was a boy. Words she had never heard since then from anyone, male or female. She needed, no, she hungered to be loved, and unfortunately, Janey knew, no other man's love but Alex's would do now. And Alex didn't believe in love.

"Janey." His arms were around her, both arms. He held her against his chest, one hand covering the back of her head to press her against him. "Baby. You have everything I am," he whispered against her hair. "Everything, Janey. I'd never cheat on you. I'll never hurt you. Nothing matters past you. If I could give you more, I'd give you more."

Janey shook her head, pulling back from him. "Let me go."

"I can't let you go." He cupped the side of her face and lifted it, touched his lips to hers. "Janey, you might walk away from me, but I'll never let you go." His eyes stared into hers, and inside, she felt that secret, hungry part of herself open again, gasping, grasping for any part of him she could get.

"And I have no choice but to accept that," she said hollowly. "Because you're right, Alex. I do love you. I love you so much I can't bear what I'm doing to both of us now. If I could walk away and take all the danger with me, I'd do that. Because I hate myself for this. I hate myself for being here. And I hate knowing you're in danger because of me." She jerked away from him, forcing him to release her. "But you'd follow."

"I'd follow," he said quietly. "To the ends of the earth, Janey, I'd follow you."

She glanced over at him, drying her face. She hated crying. She hated the sense of helplessness, of hopelessness, that it filled her with.

"Do you know how to love babies, Alex?" she whispered then. "Am I supposed to accept that you can't love at all? Or just that you can't love me?"

She touched her stomach, wondering. Hating herself because she loved him too much, and she knew it. She loved him with everything inside her soul. And he didn't know how to love.

"Watch you touch your stomach, Janey," he said gently, "as though already imagining our child there. Do you think for a moment that you and that baby won't fill my world?"

"Babies need to hear *I love you*." Her chin shook as she tried not to cry anymore. "Even from their fathers."

What the hell was he supposed to say? Alex stared back at her, suddenly feeling an edge of helplessness. He couldn't explain to her what he felt for her, what he felt at the thought of having children with her. Holding their child. Seeing both of them in a new life they had created.

His throat locked up at the thought of trying to explain it, tightened with emotion he didn't know how to describe. This wasn't what he had heard love described as. This wasn't what he had seen love to be. He wanted to protect her, yet he wanted to watch her be herself. He wanted to surround her in security, and at the same time, he thrived on the flashes of independence he saw within her.

"Teach me how to love, Janey."

He watched the surprise that filled her face, the shock.

"Alex, you don't just teach someone how to love," she said miserably.

She didn't know how much her pain struck at him, how it destroyed him. Seeing her eyes so filled with shadows and hurt enraged him.

"Why not?" he asked her then. "You have a man willing to give you his life if it will protect you from a single scratch, a single tear. If you're that important, why can't you teach me how to love?"

Her expression clenched, a flash of bemusement filling her gaze.

"You're crazy," she finally accused him, but she didn't fight him when he pulled her back into his arms, and she didn't cry.

God, her tears destroyed him. Seeing her sob, feeling her refusal to let him comfort her—she had no idea what it did to his insides. He felt as though his chest and his throat were shredded with emotion, with fury. He wanted to kill at the sight of her tears, the sound of her sobs. Because Janey just didn't cry. She was stronger than that. She'd held her tears back when he was certain she should have been sobbing over the past weeks.

But she cried now, because he didn't know how to love. Because he didn't believe the love she was looking for existed anywhere. Except in a woman's soul.

Maybe that was it. Hell if he knew. Right now he just wanted to hold her. He just wanted to curl up in his bed and go to sleep with Janey in his arms and forget the past few hours and the terror that had filled him at the thought that Janey could be taken from him.

"Zeke and the investigator will be here soon." He lifted her head, kissed her lips, felt the little shudder that raced through her and rested his forehead against hers. "It's going to be over soon. I promise. You'll be safe, and we'll get this all worked out."

She nodded slowly, her lashes fluttering closed as she let her head rest against his chest for just a second. Just a second.

Then he felt her backbone stiffen and she was moving away from him, straightening her shoulders and breathing in deeply. Damned stubborn Mackay pride. He almost smiled as he watched her.

Damn, she kept him off balance. Right when he expected one thing from her, she showed a reservoir of strength that astounded him and gave him something else.

"You know, Janey," he told her softly, waiting till she turned to him, "if the love you're talking about exists, then there's nothing less that I feel for you. You own me. For now, can we let that be enough?"

She tipped her head again, and for a second he saw the way her eyes flashed with knowledge, more like her brother's than was comfortable for Alex. Then a small smile, one that made his dick pound, edged her lips.

"Yeah," she finally said, a breath of sound that wrapped around him and eased something that had been tightening inside him. "Yeah, Alex, we can let that be enough for now."

NINETEEN

"Whoever made this baby knew what the hell he was doing." Alex surveyed the damage in the bedroom as Mark, Tyrell, and a less-than-cooperative police detective picked through the rubble, sorting through it for pieces of the bomb and the shrapnel it contained.

"Any six-year-old can put one of these together off the Internet," the detective informed him hostilely.

"Off the Internet, any six-year-old can't set a timer to it and give it the exact amount of time needed to get away from the window," Mark stated coldly as he used a large set of tweezers to lift another piece from the carpet.

He looked at the part of the device he was holding, turned it and considered if for long moments. "Hell of a timer, Major."

Alex inhaled slowly, his nostrils flaring in rage. "So we have an explosives expert to find. Someone who's obviously native to the area."

"Lots of explosives experts around the world," the detective muttered. "Not everyone that wants to kill comes from Somerset."

The detective, Joey Runyon, was a Somerset native. At five-ten and forty-seven years old, he was a veteran on the force. His shoddy work wasn't an example of his past record.

"Detective, do you have a problem with this job?" Alex leaned against the doorframe and watched him with cool curiosity. "Because I can make damned certain you're reassigned."

Detective Runyon rose to his full height, not that it did him any good. Five-ten wasn't six-plus feet no matter how much a man threw his shoulders back and lifted his chin.

Mark came to his feet, laying the piece of the timer in the shallow plastic container used to collect the shrapnel and debris from the bomb.

"You're not police chief yet," Runyon sneered. "And after this, it's doubtful you will be. Everyone knows Jane Mackay is nothing like her brother. She was her daddy's little pet whenever she was around. Sleeping with her isn't going to gain you points—"

Alex didn't have to jump for the man. He took one long step, his arm snapping out, his fingers latching around the other man's neck as he slammed him into the wall.

The detective's eyes bulged, and his face paled as he struggled against Alex.

"I really want to kill you," Alex said softly. "If we were anywhere else, I'd cut you in tiny pieces, Runyon, and feed you to the local wildlife. Is that what you want?"

"Major Jansen, what have I told you about harassing local detectives? Son, it's bad for the Department of Homeland Security's image. You know that. Let the little fart go so I can have his ass fried with his superiors. That's always so much more fun."

Alex's teeth clenched at the sound of the familiar voice. He should have expected it. Why hadn't he expected it? Timothy Cranston, special agent in charge of the investigation that had been responsible for cracking the theft and potential sale of weapons in the Somerset area two years before.

"Come on, Alex, let go of the little fucker's neck. You know how much I enjoy breaking careers." Timothy patted his shoulder as he stepped farther into the room.

"Man, you are so fucked-up." Alex sighed as he stared back at the detective. "I would have just killed you. The Rabid Leprechaun over there will make you wish you were dead. Over and over and over again."

He released the detective.

"Detective Runyon," Cranston drawled. "You were in the military, weren't you?" Cranston flipped open the little notebook he never left home without.

Runyon rubbed his skinny little neck and glared back at Cranston. "Yeah. I was."

"Runyon worked with explosives, Major Jansen," Cranston drawled, his brown eyes flicking to the detective with malevolent humor. His chubby face was wreathed in a devil's smile, his hair almost standing up in spikes.

"Then he should have known any six-year-old couldn't have built this explosive," Mark commented.

Cranston turned to Mark with a frown. "You're not supposed to be here."

Mark grinned. "I'm the ghost of explosives past, just lending a little wisdom here and there." He arched his blond brows expressively.

Cranston sighed and turned back to Alex. "Is this the best you could do on short notice for a team? Son, call me next time; I'll send you a team."

"Special Agent Cranston." The detective spoke up then; evidently he knew Cranston. It seemed sometimes that everyone did.

"Don't talk to me, asshole. You don't exist." Cranston frowned back at him heavily, his shaggy brows arching like little demi-horns as he turned back to Alex. "How did you get stuck with that prick?"

"Cranston, you don't have jurisdiction in this case." Runyon stepped forward aggressively.

Alex stepped back cautiously. Because Timothy smiled. A real-life honest-to-God filled-with-amusement smile as he rubbed his hands together in glee.

"So report me," Timothy drawled, his brown eyes sparkling in childlike pleasure. "I dare you."

Runyon finally had the good sense to swallow nervously.

"This isn't a federal case." Runyon was obviously restraining his own sense of self-importance.

"Hey, dickhead, there was an attempt on a military officer's life, one assigned to the Department of Homeland Security—that makes it a federal case," Timothy growled in disgust. "Alex, where did this little turd come from?"

Alex winced. He'd rarely seen Timothy so pissed off. This was Timothy carrying a load of pissed, and the dumbass detective was about to get the brunt of it.

"He was the first one on the scene last night." Alex lifted his good shoulder in a shrug. "Besides, the chief and I are friends. I figure there had to be something good about him somewhere."

"I'd question that friendship if I were you." Timothy turned back to the detective. "Get your bony ass out of my investigation, you incompetent little prick. And pray to God I don't decide to see if I can't pin this explosion to your sharp little nose and throw you behind bars for a nice little vacation."

Runyon stepped back.

Alex shot him a compassionate look and shook his head warningly. "Go, Runyon. I'll see if I can't settle him down and save your job." Alex grinned. "At least until I'm your boss. Then we'll talk."

Runyon stalked out. Seconds later the front door slammed as Timothy cackled.

"That little prick." The special agent shook his head. "He's got issues. I'll have him checked out."

"What the hell are you doing here, Timothy?" Alex watched curiously as the special agent stared around the room slowly.

Timothy shrugged. "Forced vacation. They were making me take a break until this came across the wire. Since I handled the investigation here, they let me come back to work."

Alex's brows arched. Timothy didn't take breaks. He was always manipulating, conniving, and catching criminals. It was all he lived for. He'd die in the line of duty, Alex was convinced of it. Likely from a stroke.

"I don't need any help, Timothy," Alex told him firmly. One had to be firm with Timothy. "I have it covered."

"I'll just make sure of that." Timothy shoved his hands in his pockets and turned back to him. "Report says you've been living with that little Mackay girl, Natches's sister. You like living dangerously, don't you, boy? I'm surprised he let you live."

Alex's lips quirked as he rubbed the back of his neck. "It's been touch and go, the letting me live part."

"She's a good girl." Timothy nodded slowly. "I had a full investigation done on her. Damned shame how Dayle Mackay tried to use that kid against Natches all those years."

"She's survived." Alex had to fight the anger that threatened to return.

"Survived only to come home and face this bullshit." Cranston stared around the room again. "You know what, Alex?"

"What?" Alex's eyes narrowed on the other man. His expression was heavy, his gaze dark with grief.

"She looks like my baby girl," Cranston said softly. "My little Maria. She was in the Federal Building with her mother when that terrorist's bomb hit, you know."

Shit. He hadn't seen the vague resemblance. "Yeah, she does, Timothy," he said gently.

The agent had lost his wife, his daughter, son-in-law, and new granddaughter in a strike by homeland terrorists. Cranston had taken every terrorist-related assignment he could get since. He didn't rest. Alex knew he would never rest.

"She looks like her," he repeated as he turned back to the bedroom, his expression twisting for the slightest second in rage and pain. "Bastard tried to blow her to little pieces, didn't he?"

"He almost managed it." Alex had to grit his teeth against the rage.

"And almost took out my best fucking team commander," Cranston snarled. "Where's your mind? I got the papers the other day that you're not returning? What's with that shit?"

Alex grinned. "Bum leg." He rubbed at his thigh.

"Lying bastard." Timothy stared around the room again, his attention shifting from the window to the bed. He pursed his lips as he measured the distance. "Five-ten, maybe," he murmured. "Your perp. Not a big boy. Didn't take a lot of force, but he would have had to put everything into it. Jerked a little; aim was a little off when it came through the window, I bet."

Alex looked between the shattered window and the hole in the bed where the bomb exploded. "How do you figure?"

"Placement." Timothy shrugged. "It came in high, dipped, and missed the exact center. He wasn't as strong as he thought he was."

Timothy was fucking scary.

"I think he's right." Tyrell moved into the room as Alex turned to him. "I was checking outside. Found some prints in the yard that were a little off. Ground is still damp where she uses the sprinklers in the evening. Someone dug in deep at one spot, braced, and threw, I suspect. Footprint is small, likely size eight to nine. Zeke is casting it."

"Where's the Mackay girl?" There was the barest edge to Timothy's voice. Sorrow mixed with concern and the cool disinterest he wanted to portray.

"In the restaurant." Alex grimaced. "Chaya showed up, and last I heard Natches was cursing a blue streak. Janey just smiles at him and does what the hell she wants to."

Timothy chuckled at that. "She's a good girl, but she's got no business here. It's like a fucking war zone." He stared around. "I'm pulling your team back. They're on training missions at present so it's not going to affect anything important. I want enough men to cover this. We place them right, pull in a few of our female agents from Louisville, and we should be able to catch him fast."

"This is personal, Timothy," Alex warned him. "The department's going to slap you over it."

"Hell, won't be the first time." Timothy grinned. "And it's not personal. Attempting to kill one of my boys is serious shit. Department takes it serious." Timothy turned, looking around the room again. "Did you find all the cameras?"

"There was one in every room except the kitchen. There's no overhead vent there," Alex told him.

Timothy moved beneath the vent, turned, looked at the side of the bed, and tilted his head before moving through the apartment. Alex followed after him.

"Your report said her apartment was broken into with no signs of a breach in her security system?"

"None I could find," Alex agreed.

"Hmm. Thought you were good at that stuff."

"So did I." Alex grunted as he followed Timothy through the apartment.

There were two bedrooms, two baths, closets in each room and the bathrooms, and a hall closet for linen and towels that Janey never used because she never had guests stay overnight. Living room, kitchen, pantry closet. Timothy checked it all, then turned and paced back to the hallway, scratching his grizzled cheek.

"What do you see, Timothy?" Alex knew him. He'd worked with Timothy for ten years now; in the past years his team had been under exclusive DHS authority, and Timothy was the primary agent he worked with.

"Doesn't work out," Timothy muttered.

"What doesn't work out?" Alex shifted his shoulder, trying to relieve the ache in it. The nails had gone deep, and Alex had felt the wounds breaking open and bleeding throughout the afternoon.

He moved back to the closet at the end of the hall, slapped the back, and frowned. The wall was solid. He stepped into Janey's bedroom, looked around, then went to the guest bedroom, looked around it. Alex looked but couldn't see whatever it was Timothy was looking for.

"You think there's an entrance to the restaurant below?" Alex asked.

Timothy counted steps across the bedroom, along the width of it. He moved back to Janey's bedroom and into the bathroom. The bathroom was on the other side of the closet.

He was frowning as he moved back to the hall, stared at the closet again. "Four feet difference."

"How the hell do you know this shit?" Alex growled. "I don't see it."

Timothy shrugged. "You're not trained to see it the way I am. You haven't had to rip out walls and dismantle homes to find them. Question is, where is our door?"

The bedrooms weren't even. The guest room door was close to the closet, while Janey's bedroom door was closer to the living room. The bathroom to the guest room had another door from the hall into the bathroom as well as one into the guest bedroom.

Timothy ran his hands over the wall, tapped and knocked, listened. It all sounded solid to Alex. He and Natches both had checked the walls the same way just after the break-in.

"Bathroom," Timothy spoke more to himself. "It has to be in the bathroom."

Alex was in complete bafflement as he followed Timothy back

to Janey's bathroom. The other man tapped, listened, pressed, and moved until he was squeezing himself into the narrow space between the wall and the claw-foot bathtub. And there he found it. He tapped the wall, pressed down on one of the tub's clawed feet, and Alex watched as the end of the bathtub slid to the side and the entrance in the floor slid seamlessly open.

"Damned ingenious." Timothy stood staring at the narrow staircase that led downstairs. "It goes straight down. Think and tell me where this will end."

Alex moved to gaze into the darkened interior. "The other side of the restaurant, away from the office. The banquet room. Janey's been wanting to open it for seating."

"Anyone fighting her over it?" Timothy asked him quietly.

"Tabitha, one of the young waitresses. She works as hostess when Janey's dealing with other things."

"Not her." Timothy shook his head. "Tabitha Cooke is a kid. A little flighty, low grades but social. She doesn't have the intelligence. Anyone else?"

Alex shook his head. He bet Timothy had files on every damned citizen in the county memorized from the investigations he had run in the past two years.

"Everyone else seems excited by the prospect," Alex told him. "Why didn't I find this? Natches and I both went over this room and the other bedroom."

"Some of the ways they do it would amaze you." Timothy shook his balding head as he backed away and slid the tub back in place. "There's a locking lever on the foot of the tub." He pressed it with his foot. "Not easy to accidentally activate. I saw something similar at another place. The whole shower stall slid out like this. This one just slides around, leaving all the pipes intact. Very good."

"Someone had access to her all along." Alex could feel the adrenaline racing through him now, fury igniting in his head. "Son of a bitch, it's a wonder they didn't kill her in her sleep."

Timothy shrugged, the wrinkled sleeves of his gray suit jacket shifting around him.

"Stalkers are odd creatures," Timothy said. "From the report the sheriff sent me, it's only started escalating since you showed up. The pictures, this attack. Natches told the sheriff the stalker was upset, crying, because you were, ummm, getting a little nasty. She was corrupting you. Making you unnatural." Timothy's brows wagged. "Really, Alex. Anal sex?"

Alex refused to blush. Dammit to hell. It was bad enough Zeke saw those pictures and knew just how fucking hot Janey was; having Timothy know was damned uncomfortable.

"Timothy, don't make me murder you," Alex sneered.

The special agent in charge of making Alex crazy snickered.

"Come on, let's go see Natches and Chaya, then." Timothy hitched the band of his pants and moved through the bathroom. "And let's keep that little passageway our secret for the time being, at least until we're away from the restaurant."

Alex followed, more anxious to check on Janey than he was letting on. After letting Mark and Tyrell know they were heading to the restaurant, he and Timothy had left the apartment and were headed down the stairs when they heard Janey, obviously arguing.

"I don't care if you do burn it to the ground. As long as it's standing and open, I'll do what the hell I want to do."

"Are you trying to die?" Natches was leaning over her desk, his hands flat on the surface, tension filling the air as Janey held the identical stance, her hands on the desk, almost nose to nose with him.

"I'm not shutting down. If I shut down, I'll never regain momentum. It doesn't work that way."

"You stay open and someone's going to kill you." Natches's voice rose in anger as Chaya sat on the leather couch with her legs propped on the table, staring up at the ceiling as Alex followed Timothy into the office.

Chaya took one look at Timothy, lowered her jean-clad legs, and stared back at her former boss dismally. "Oh hell," she muttered. "What are you doing here?"

Janey's gaze jerked from her brother's furious one to see Alex walk in behind a short, squat little man. He looked like someone's favorite uncle or grandpa. His face was lined, there were traces of sorrow in his eyes, and his thinning hair looked as though he ran worried fingers through it much too often.

The bright smile on his face was forced, and the mockery in his eyes was brittle, hiding things, she was certain, he didn't want others to see.

"What the fuck do you want?" Natches snarled at the little man as Janey came from around her desk.

"Natches!" She stared at him, shocked. "That's rude."

The little man snickered. "Yeah, Natches, don't be rude."

On first hearing, the comment could have seemed snide, but Janey heard the underlying affection in his voice. She knew it, because she had heard the same tone in her own voice. It kept others off balance, at a distance.

"Chaya, Natches really needs to go home for his afternoon nap." Janey smiled tightly at her brother. "He's getting cranky."

Chaya's laugh earned her a brooding look from her husband as she shook her head. "Don't worry, Janey. Natches and Timothy don't actually come to blows; they just threaten to."

Alex moved over to Janey, and surprised her when, with a grin, he lowered his head and caught her lips in a quick kiss.

"Timothy, this is Natches's sister, Janey. Janey, meet Special Investigative Agent Timothy Cranston from the Department of Homeland Security."

"Hello, Mr. Cranston." She gave him her hand to shake, and was not in the least surprised by the firm warmth of his handshake or the flicker of amusement in his gaze.

"Miss Mackay, it's a pleasure to meet you." He nodded, then

pulled back, rubbed his hands together with an air of glee, and looked at Alex and Natches. "We're going to have fun, boys."

Janey noticed that neither Alex nor Natches looked comfortable with that proclamation.

Natches ran his fingers through his hair in frustration before turning to Alex. "She won't close the restaurant down," he stated furiously as he shot her another glare. "I'm half-owner."

"And you promised you'd be the silent half," she muttered, moving behind her desk again. "Let it go."

"Shutting the restaurant down is the wrong move." Timothy shook his head, then turned to Alex. "Have you checked this room for the cameras as well?"

Alex nodded. "We found two cameras in the overhead vents. They were accompanied by voice-activated recorders. It was simple, not as professional as the bomb, but effective."

"Can I look around the restaurant?" Timothy turned to Janey.

"No." Natches turned to Janey then. "Tell him to go home."

Janey felt like rolling her eyes as she stood to her feet, thankful she was wearing comfortable clothes rather than the hostessing attire she usually had on by now.

"A quick tour." She smiled at the other man. "Then I have to get dressed. The restaurant opens in less than three hours and I have a feeling we're going to be packed."

"We'll just keep my investigative status between us if we meet anyone," Timothy told her as he held out his elbow for her to take. "I must say, Ms. Mackay, I believe you may have gotten all the politeness and hospitality in your family. Natches *can* be a little cranky."

"Yeah, like a five-year-old." She shot Natches another glare as they moved to the door. "If we have time, we'll stop in the kitchen. Desmond loves giving out samples of what he's working on for the evening. Perhaps he'll have time to fix you a quick lunch."

Timothy's smile was pleased, his gaze warming as he patted her hand while moving into the hallway with her. "I'd very much appreciate that, Ms. Mackay."

"Janey." She liked this little man. He had a charm and a flare that immediately put her at ease, and an underlying sadness and warmth that touched something inside her. "Please, call me Janey."

Alex followed behind them silently, almost grinning as Natches and Chaya followed. Natches was pissed. Alex glanced back at the other man, to see the dark, suspicious frown he leveled on Cranston's back.

The Mackays butted heads with Timothy too often to see the almost pure genius behind the man's maniacal façade. Alex had worked with him enough to understand it, respect it, and be very wary of it.

"So, this room isn't used?" Timothy was walking around the banquet room after Janey had opened it, so innocently unaware that she had been maneuvered. "Why aren't you using it?" He turned back to Janey with a curious look.

"Because my coowner refuses to authorize an ad for a general manager." Janey crossed her arms over her embroidered shirt and glared at Natches. He grunted in reply.

Timothy tilted his head, rather like an inquisitive, eager hound, and regarded them both somberly. Alex held back his wince.

"He'll change his mind," Timothy promised her with an almost besotted smile. "I'll discuss it with him, my dear."

"Thank you." Janey bestowed one of her sweet, perfect smiles. Alex's dick hardened. Cranston blinked, and for a second, Alex saw the emotion in the other man's eyes.

Janey resembled the child he had lost. And Alex had the uncomfortable feeling that she might have just gained a father figure.

TWENTY

Janey paired three-inch-heeled knee boots with the black leather skirt she hadn't been able to wear before, nude stockings, and a shimmering violet blouse for the night.

Beneath it, she wore a violet push-up bra and matching thong that she knew Alex had seen her bring down from the apartment upstairs to change into.

Thankfully, most of her clothing was intact, as well as her precious store of shoes. Within hours the restaurant was packed, with the waiting area filled. There weren't enough tables, and Janey was watching money flow out the door with each couple that gave up on getting a place between reservations. She was desperate.

Cell phone in hand, she sent Tabitha to seat the next couple and made a desperate call to Rogue. "Get dressed and get over here. I need a waitress."

"Darling, leather is in." Rogue sighed. "I can be there in twenty minutes, but take me as I am."

"Get here," she begged, then turned to Hoyt and Natches. "Open that banquet room now. Hoyt, get the linens and silverware and get it ready."

Hoyt and Natches exchanged alarmed looks.

"I said now," she hissed as she grabbed menus. "Right now."

"The register." Hoyt looked frantic.

"Timothy." Janey threw the agent, who had lingered around, a hopeful look. "Can you run a register?"

"In my sleep." He smiled his patient grin. The one he kept giving Natches as he moved behind the counter. "Go, boys. She told you what to do." His voice became commanding, in charge. God, if she wasn't already in love with Alex, she might have had to fall in love with Timothy. Or make him adopt her.

"Thank you." She gave him a quick kiss on his rough cheek and turned back to the waiting area. "If you'll be patient," she announced. "We're opening the banquet room. Seating will be available soon." Then she rushed back to the kitchen.

A frantic, vocal argument with Desmond had him placing a call to extra staff and getting them in, followed by a slamming of pans and Italian curses. But his eyes had glittered at the challenge.

"I hire my assistant tomorrow," he announced. "He'll be here by evening. No arguments."

"No arguments, Desmond. I swear."

Janey rushed back to the dining area, apologized to the waiting couple at the reservation counter, and led them quickly to their table.

Rogue showed up, dressed in leather pants, though a silk blouse topped it off and three-inch heels made her look like a goddess as her hair flamed around her.

Thankfully, Rogue understood the reservation computer, and

she went to work as Tabitha, Janey, and the other waitresses fought to handle the additional seating and orders. Two more waitresses and three busboys were called back in. Within the hour, the banquet room was filled, as well as well as the reservation area.

Janey was rushed, stressed, and loving every minute of it.

Desmond was her angel, though he was cursing like a sailor. His wife and the additional sous-chef were working the kitchen; the extra stoves were in use for the first time since Janey had taken over the restaurant.

She was in heaven. Natches was even cleaning tables, beneath the eagle eye of his wife, and Timothy Cranston was working the register with patient confidence.

It was nearing ten when Janey had to begin turning away customers. Her legs were shaking with fatigue, and Rogue and Tabitha were looking beautiful but harried. Reservations ended at ten; they couldn't possibly take in more after that.

"I'm sorry." She shook her head at the group of three men who'd just arrived, dressed in business attire and obviously a little too drunk to be in public. "Seating is closed for the night."

At the head of the group, the older male, possibly in his thirties, frowned back at her, then leered. "That's not possible. You can take three more."

Behind him were a few other couples. "I'm sorry, sir. If you'd like to make a reservation for tomorrow . . ."

"Bitch. I'm here now." He kept his voice low, a warning hiss that had her flinching at the virulence in it. "Find a table."

Janey looked around. Timothy was buried at the register, and Natches was busing a table while Alex quickly helped him. Hoyt was across the room helping wait a table. She didn't have time for this.

"You don't want the kind of trouble you're getting ready to start here," she said quietly. "I think you and your friends should leave."

He sneered. "Trash like you doesn't tell me when I can leave. Now find me a table."

The other two moved, blocking her from sight of Timothy. Gossip was good for business, but a fight wasn't.

Alex looked back to where Janey stood at the reservation counter. At first, it looked as though she were merely talking to the businessmen standing around her. But something warned him, some instinct told him she was frightened. It was in the line of her shoulders, the tensed set of her head, and the indication that her arm was at an unusual angle in front of her body.

"Trouble," he told Natches quietly and headed her way.

He could see Timothy trying to peer around the register and becoming concerned.

"This is a really bad idea." He caught her words as he neared her.

"You traitorous little cunt," the older of the men rapped out, jerking her wrist, pulling her hard into the counter. "Give me the fucking table before I show you what a real man would do for you."

A red haze of primal fury enveloped Alex. It washed through his mind, shattered decades of control.

He knew Natches heard; Timothy heard. They moved for the group, but it was Alex who took on the one that had dared touch his woman.

Alex's hand slapped over the little prick's wrist, exerting enough force that his fingers immediately loosened. His arm went around the bastard's neck and he jerked him back, smiling at Janey's surprised face over his shoulder. "Be back in a minute, baby," he ground out furiously. "You just wait right here for me."

Natches had the other man in a similar grip, but Timothy was a brutal, sadistic son of a bitch. The third man was purple, gasping, as Timothy led him through the shocked bystanders, his fingers curved around the taller man's balls as he forced him to walk.

Janey stared, wide-eyed. The glass door closed, and seconds later those in the waiting area were rushing for the door as well.

"Now, that was interesting," Rogue drawled as she eased up behind her. "You do know Alex and Natches left their table unfinished, right?"

"They'll kill them." Janey started for the door.

"Oh, no you don't." Rogue caught her arm as Chaya looked up from where she had taken over for Timothy at the register.

"Rogue, Alex will kill them," she whispered. "I know Natches will."

"Then we'll send flowers." Rogue rolled her eyes. "Give it a break; let the men do their thing. We'll do ours and coo over their little boo-boos and tell them how heroic they are."

Janey swung around in outrage. "You're as crazy as they are."

To which Rogue pouted prettily. "Now, Janey, let's not bring the question of sanity into this." Then she grinned. "And I'm proud of being crazy, remember?"

A yell filtered in from outside, laughter, a whoop.

"Damn. I'd like to see that fight." Rogue sighed. "I'll go finish their table; you stay put." She glared at Janey. "Don't challenge Alex when he's in defensive mode." She grinned. "Unless you want a little some-some against the wall rather than a bed."

She sauntered off then, waving a busboy over and putting him to work. She marshaled the waitresses and busboys as though she had been born to give orders.

Janey turned to Chaya as the customers rushed outside to watch after paying for their meals.

"Stay," Chaya mouthed with a fierce look.

Stay? Like she was a puppy. A dog.

"This isn't going to be good for business, Jane," Hoyt spoke behind her.

Turning, she stared at the young man who didn't have a hope of managing the restaurant by himself. Hoyt was capable, but even with the two of them, they couldn't keep up.

He was frowning, his gaze disapproving.

Janey pasted on a smile. "That's what I thought about the bombing of my apartment last night." She flinched as another whoop filtered through. "I bet we're packed tomorrow."

She turned away from Hoyt and rubbed her wrist, then flinched at the sound of a siren in the distance. God, just what she needed. She breathed out wearily. She needed more help, because sure as hell, tomorrow was going to be even busier.

Alex stood back as the sheriff and two city cops arrived. Three less-than-courageous jackasses were writhing on the blacktop as he, Natches, and Timothy leaned against a nearby car.

The crowd that had gathered to see a good, brutal bloodletting was mumbling in disappointment. It didn't take long to put three soft-core little bastards to the ground.

Mark and Tyrell were inside watching Janey. They'd slipped into place as Alex, Natches, and Timothy headed outside.

As the sheriff's car and the city cops pulled in, Timothy stepped forward, badge in hand.

"Special Agent Timothy Cranston." He smirked at Zeke as the sheriff bit back a curse. "Cuff 'em and take 'em in. I'll follow along behind later."

"Charges?" Zeke sighed as the two police officers moved to cuff the three men despite their protests.

"We'll start with endangering a federal agent and move on from there." Timothy hitched his pants and grinned placidly back at Zeke. "Is that a problem?"

"Probably," Zeke bit out. "Cranston, I'm just about tired of you trying to run my county."

Timothy waved the objection away. "Don't worry. The chief of police really likes me. I can just deal with him."

Alex stared at the dazed assailant who had dared to bruise Janey's delicate wrist. He could feel his shoulder throbbing; he was bleeding again, but fuck it. His fist in that little asshole's face was worth it.

Adrenaline was still surging through him, though. There had been no outlet for the fury that pounded through him, and now it was turning into something more. Another man had dared to touch Janey, to insult her. He turned his head and glared at the crowd gathered around.

"Natches"—his voice was overly loud—"the next asshole that touches my woman may never be found again."

Natches stared back at him in mocking disbelief. "Yeah, well, I might help you hide the body."

Zeke rubbed his hand over his face in frustration as Timothy chuckled. Alex stared at the crowd. He couldn't forget Janey's accusation, her belief that he was ashamed of her, ashamed of his relationship with her.

The thought slammed into his mind. Blood surged through his veins. He left Natches and Timothy to deal with what he could see was Zeke's anger building. He pushed through the crowd, aware of several couples following him out of the cold.

He entered the restaurant, his gaze meeting Janey's, seeing the worry, the concern, the acceptance that he was going to pretend he was doing no more than defending a friend.

Fuck that.

He stalked to her, pulled her from behind the reservation counter, and as he curved his fingers around her neck and her lips parted, he pressed his lips against hers. His tongue delved inside her mouth, taking her gasp and filling her with his lust.

He felt her hands press against his abs, her fingers curling, her lips softening. And he pulled back.

"Next time, yell for help, dammit," he snarled. "And the next bastard that tries to manhandle you might not survive it."

He moved her, gently, back behind the register counter, then parked himself directly behind her. Fuck it. Fuck everyone that wanted to gossip. Screw the bastard watching her. At least now he knew Janey wasn't undefended. And as far as Alex was concerned, she never would be.

TWENTY-ONE

"That was so wrong, on so many levels." Janey slammed the office door closed after Alex passed through it behind her, just after midnight.

He hadn't left her side. If she went to the kitchen, Alex went to the kitchen. His hand would lie low on her back, or curl around her neck. He'd touched her often enough that she was one big, blazing hormone by the time they walked into the office, and pissed off over it.

"What was wrong?" He arched his brow and crossed his arms over his white shirt. He'd rolled the sleeves back, displaying his muscled forearms. His biceps bulged beneath the sleeves. She just wanted to jump his bones right now, but she was mad him. Furious with him.

"You beat those guys up," she snapped. "All you had to do was push them out the door. You didn't have to hit them."

"I wasn't alone," he pointed out mildly. "Natches and Timothy helped, you know. You're not yelling at them."

"Natches wouldn't listen if I did," she argued, then gave him a scandalized look. "And you want me to jump on Tim? Geez, Alex, that's like jumping on Santa Claus or something. He's a sweetheart."

Alex stared back at her in horror. "My God, don't put Santa Claus and Timothy's name in the same sentence. That should be illegal, Janey."

"Don't be mean to Tim, Alex, and it's totally beside the point. You did not have to go out and fight. It was insane and so completely unnecessary," she retorted furiously, thrusting her fingers through her hair in frustration. "Do you think it's the first time it's happened?"

She didn't expect his reaction. Before Janey could respond, he had her against the wall of the office, lifting her, pulling her to him.

"It's the last damned time it's going to happen," he bit out, practically snarling in her face.

"I don't need you babysitting me, Alex." She would have pushed at his shoulders, but she was afraid of hurting the wound. Instead, she tried to push at his chest, and he wasn't moving.

The problem with Alex not moving was that the arousal that had been building all day was only growing worse now. With his body pressed against her, the feel of his erection pressing into her lower stomach, she was beginning to burn for him.

"I'll be damned if I'm going to let those jackasses talk to you that way." Anger filled his voice, his expression.

His hands gripped her hips, no bruising, but firm as his gaze lit with fury.

"For God's sake, Alex. It won't be the last either. You can't just beat everyone up."

"Watch me!" His head lowered, his expression furious as his lips pulled back from his teeth. "Oh, baby, you just fucking watch me."

Her lips parted to argue. She had the argument on the tip of her tongue, and it was a damned good one. Something about him just being one man. But he stole the words. He stole her thoughts. His lips covered hers and he stole her senses in a kiss that sizzled clear to the soles of her feet.

She said she owned him; perhaps she owned his passion, his sense of responsibility. She couldn't forget the fact that he had been doing everything possible to ensure that she conceived. As though the thought of a baby with her pleased him.

The distant thought whispered through her head, that she make it be enough. She loved him so much, ached for him, needed him. Surely she could make what she had of him, which he swore was every part of him, be enough.

She couldn't help her arms from curling around his neck, her hands from splaying through his hair. She tried to breathe, but breathing was just a waste of time when she needed to feel his kiss, deep, as deep at it was. His lips slanted over hers. One hand held her head in place, and his tongue delved into her mouth like a stroke of hot, dark velvet.

He tasted of a hint of whiskey and pure dark male lust. He held her easily, despite the wounds in his shoulder, and within seconds nothing mattered more to Janey than getting closer. Tasting more of his kiss and feeling him in every cell of her body.

"You're mine, Janey," he groaned as his lips pulled from hers.

Scattered, hot kisses moved over her neck. Tiny bites. She'd be marked again and she didn't care, because she fully intended to mark him again.

She lifted her legs, encasing his thighs, then his hips as he jerked the skirt over hers. One hand moved between them, releasing the zipper of his jeans and the hard, engorged length of his cock.

"This is crazy. You're hurt," she gasped.

"Go easy on me, then." He nipped her collarbone as he jerked her shirt from her skirt. "Think about my wounds. Fighting me could make them bleed, Janey."

Disbelief mixed with excitement, anger, arousal. He was outrageous. Wicked.

"Get ready." He licked over her collarbone before lifting his eyes to hers. "I'm ripping those damned panties off you."

Her eyes widened at the sound of cloth rending, then there was nothing between her and the thick, heavy length of his cock.

"Ah hell yes." The hot shaft pressed into the wet folds as he gripped her butt and rode her against him. The silk-over-iron erection rubbed against her clit, stealing her breath as her head fell back against the wall.

Alex had never seen anything so beautiful. Janey's face was flushed with pleasure, with arousal. Her green eyes were darker, her black hair feathering around her face in silken ribbons where she had straightened it.

She enchanted him. Like some damned witch. She cast a spell over him that he couldn't escape—hell, didn't want to escape.

"Alex." Her hands spread out over his biceps and he swore her nipples beneath the silk blouse were harder for it.

Damn, he'd never been proud of his body until now. The bunch of his muscles, the hardness of them, she loved it. Her fingers flexed against his upper arms and her breathing heightened, her gaze became hotter, her pussy became wetter.

"Oh, Janey, I'm so gonna fuck you hard." He watched her eyes, watched them dilate as he lifted her, his fingers clenching her ass. "Put those pretty legs around my hips, baby."

He felt her legs lock at his lower back as he moved her, shifted, his cock pressing against the tender opening of her pussy.

Her juices eased over his dick, lubricating the engorged head as he began to push inside her.

Sweet, blistering ecstasy began to wrap around the head of his cock. Pleasure, sensations so rich, so fucking strong he could barely stand it, began to sizzle across his nerve endings.

"Damn, this is sweet." He pressed deeper, feeling sweat pop on his forehead, his back. She was like a supernova, so hot she burned inside and out. "Sweet and tight. Ah, Janey, it's like fucking pure paradise. Like possessing fire."

He didn't know how to be a poet, but damn if this feeling wasn't worth rhyming. He wanted inside her forever. For the rest of his fucking life, buried right here.

Gritting his teeth, he surged deeper, deeper. Bending his knees and holding her fast, he pushed every hard, aching inch of his cock and balls deep inside her and let out a hard, harsh groan of triumph as he felt her flesh rippling around him.

Her pussy milked him in slow, long contractions from base to tip. Tightened on him like a vise as little sobs tore from her throat. Her nails bit into his shirt, kneaded his biceps like a little cat.

"Don't stop." Her head rolled against the wall, her hips writhed, her pussy gripped until he thought he was going to go insane from the sheer pleasure of being inside her.

Pulling back, he let his lips catch hers again. Her kisses enflamed him. Sweet, silken lips, her curious little tongue dueling with his, fighting for dominance. Challenging him, even here.

He pushed inside her hard and deep, groaning at her shattered cry of pleasure. He didn't have to hold back with Janey, didn't have to force himself to handle her like glass. She gave what she got, and demanded more in return.

Turning, he carried her to the table, pushed aside the papers in the middle, and laid her back. Oh, fucking perfect.

He spread her thighs, stared at where he penetrated her and pulled back again. Sweet syrup clung to his cock, shimmering and hot. He pushed inside her again, watching the swollen folds of flesh part, watching the hard throb of her clit.

And his mouth watered. Watered for the sweet taste of her, the feel of her pleasure against his lips and tongue.

He didn't know if he had the strength to pull back, to ease from the wicked, brutally pleasured grip she had on his dick.

But he needed to taste.

Janey jerked, lifting to her elbows as she felt him release her. His cock slid from her, the incredible stretching burn easing. She watched, gasping as he knelt in front of the desk and his lips and tongue buried into her tormented sex.

"Oh God, Alex," she cried out as he let her watch.

He stared up at her, his tongue running over the desperately aching flesh, circling her clit, rimming it with fire before he pursed his lips and sucked at it gently.

"I can't stand this," she whimpered. "I need you again. I need you fucking me."

"Not yet," he groaned. "Let me taste you, baby. God, it's like an addiction. You're so damned sweet I want the taste of you in my mouth forever. Every second, Janey."

His tongue licked through the narrow cleft, lapped, moved to the opening, and plunged inside.

Janey shrieked out his name, her legs lifting until the tips of the black boots rested at his shoulders, opening her farther.

"Oh hell yes." His grin was wicked as he pulled back, his hands running up the thin leather of the boots. "Fucking sexy legs. Stay just like that, baby. Just like that while I eat the sweetest pussy in the world."

His hands gripped her ankles, his lips lowered again, and he was devouring her. Licking and sucking until nothing mattered but his lips, the pleasure, the tormenting licks of his tongue and the need rising by the second.

Janey pushed her top over her breasts, pulled her bra over the swollen mounds, and heard his heated growl as her fingers began pulling on her nipples.

Oh yes, so good. She was so close. The additional sensations on the swollen tips added to the fire burning in her clit. She was arching, her juices spilling, begging with every cry for release.

His lips moved to the hard, tortured nub of her clit, surrounded it, and sucked it. His tongue rasped around it, and Janey felt herself unraveling from the inside out. Her fingers tightened on her nipples, a wail spilled from her lips, and she exploded in a shower of brilliant, blazing light.

As she exploded, the pleasure imploded as well. Alex thrust inside her, one hard, deep thrust that speared into the gripping, tightening tissue of her pussy and pushed her further.

Her upper body jerked up as he held her legs over his arms and gripped her hips, jerking her forward. She gasped for breath, her eyes widening, her gaze dimming as he pounded inside her, pushed her higher, even as the first orgasm continued to wash over her. Only to throw her into another—higher, harder, brighter.

His name was a breathless attempt at a scream as she felt the rocking, desperate pulses of release tearing through her. It was a plea, a tormented cry as she flew outside herself, surrounded in ecstasy.

She could feel him, burying himself in her one last time, his own release spurting inside her as his male shout filled the room.

"Fuck!" His head tipped back, the tendons sharply defined in his neck. "Janey. Ah God. Baby."

His hips bucked, and his seed spilled inside her, unprotected, blasting hard and heated into the depths of her body as he finally collapsed over her.

Janey found herself collapsed back over the desk, her arms lying weakly at her sides, her legs still held in the crook of his arms as his lips moved between her breasts, over the curve. He licked at a still-hard nipple and she jerked at the torturous pleasure of it. Every nerve ending in her body was hypersensitive; even breathing was an agony of sensation, of pleasure.

She was drowsy, exhausted, and ready to curl into bed with him. Unfortunately, her bed was a little destroyed. That meant getting up, cleaning up, and making the trip back to Alex's house.

"I don't wanna move," she moaned as she felt him ease back slowly. "Don't make me."

He chuckled. But he didn't make her move. He lifted her in his arms and carried her to the couch before moving to the private bathroom.

She lay there, listening to water running. A second later he was kneeling by the couch, pressing her legs apart to clean her with a soft cloth.

He'd straightened his clothes, but his expression was still drowsy with sated lust, his movements slow and lazy. Tender. Gentle.

"I wrecked your pretty clothes," he drawled, and looked way too proud of himself as he straightened her bra and shirt.

"The clothes are okay." She covered a yawn as she settled back against the cushions of the couch. "You've exhausted me, Alex."

He reached up and touched her face gently. "If you don't talk to Natches about the general manager position tomorrow, then I'm going to do it for you."

"Dammit, Alex, you're messing with my wave here." She threw her arm over her eyes, blocking out the sight of his determined expression. "Leave me alone."

"This isn't going to go on, Janey."

She did not like the air of command in his voice. It was that military background, she knew. He just popped out orders like they were his to give.

"Don't tell me what isn't going to go on, Alex." She moved her arm and sat up with a frown, tugging her leather skirt back into place.

"You can't run both dining rooms without larger staff. And you can't go until midnight or after and still manage to get any rest for the next day."

"I was doing fine until you ended up in my bed," she muttered. "You keep me up all night."

He grunted at that. "Want me to stop fucking you?"

She pursed her lips and sat back against the couch, considering that option.

She finally shrugged. "You wouldn't."

Not that she had a problem with it, but it seemed Alex was damned determined to be a "daddy," no matter what. She was just having more trouble figuring why, and why her. Any single woman in the county would have spread her legs for him gladly.

Not that she didn't do it gladly.

She was making herself crazy. Janey pushed from the couch, ignoring his brooding look before moving to the bathroom to finish cleaning up. Of course, she didn't have extra panties in her office. They were now at his house.

She needed a general manager. But she needed Natches to sign off on it. She couldn't do it without his cooperation. And he wasn't giving it.

Okay, so it would help if she would just tell him she wasn't leaving. She braced her hands on the sink and stared at her own reflection. She was honest with herself at least; she wasn't leaving. Alex would follow her, and no doubt, the danger would follow her as well.

But she hesitated to tell Natches she wasn't leaving, because even now she sensed a reluctance in her brother. Perhaps a lingering fear that she was like Dayle? Sometimes she caught a look in his eyes, as though he were assessing her, watching her, for something. And she was terrified he was watching for signs that she truly was the daughter Dayle had everyone convinced she was. Or maybe he was truly so worried she would leave? But that didn't make sense, because she had never been a part of his life anyway.

Behind the closed bathroom door she wiped her tears away at the thought of that. Because she realized that she didn't know how to be a sister either. And catching on to the intricacies of being a lover to a man like Alex was more complicated than she had anticipated.

At least the restaurant was thriving enough so that maybe one day she could put other plans in place. Some days, she dreamed of a lunch crowd, a seven-day-a-week open door on the restaurant. It wasn't just the money; it was the vision. It was the ability to do all the things she had once believed the restaurant was capable of. Of making it a thriving, popular venture.

She washed her face and sighed wearily at the dream that might never be. She had the chef. She had staff. She had a full house every night. Should she ask for more? Should she ask for love and laughter on top of that?

She let her hand touch her stomach. She didn't feel pregnant. She didn't feel different. She felt like a lover, not a woman confident in her man's love. She was confident in Alex's commitment to her. She knew he'd stand by his promises no matter what. But she wanted more from him.

She owned him, she reminded herself, because he had made the conscious decision to belong to her and that she would belong to him.

But she loved him. Loved him until he filled parts of her that she hadn't known actually existed. Parts of herself that still ached in lonely pain, not because they were empty, but because she still felt that aching void. That lack of not just loving but being loved.

Was she asking for too much? God. She had Alex. He had promised her, and Alex didn't break promises. He'd given himself to her; did she have the right to ask for more, especially in light of the fact that she loved him until she felt as though her heart were breaking with it?

The questions tumbled through her mind, one after the other, always the same, until she felt as though she would lose her mind if she stood there contemplating them much longer.

Breathing in deeply, she smoothed a final tear from her face, a lone droplet of moisture that lingered on her cheek. She had more than she had ever thought she would have. For now, for tonight, she was going to have to let the rest of it be, because there were no answers, not yet, and she knew it.

Teach me how to love, Janey. The words whispered through her mind. Alex's words. She bit her lip, remembering then just exactly how much he had pledged to her.

Teach me how to love.

Could he love her? One thing was for sure—until they could both sleep without fear of bombs, it was a question that neither of them was going to be able to answer.

Until Alex was confident she was safe, he wouldn't let his mind be distracted from her protection to consider any emotions he might possibly feel for her. That meant the stalker would have to be identified and caught. She would have to face, eventually, whoever wanted her dead.

Someone wanted her dead.

Pretty much the story of her life, she decided, as she opened the bathroom door and returned to Alex. Someone wanted to own, control, or take the life she envisioned for herself.

Just as Dayle had wanted to do.

Her stalker had only taken his place.

TWENTY-TWO

Three nights later Hoyt collapsed onto the stool behind the register, and Rogue lifted her tired feet to the small cushioned settee in the waiting room and rested her head on the cushioned back.

Timothy was sprawled in a chair; his gaze was lively, though, and filled with mirth. Natches was cranky but appeared in better spirits after Chaya arrived with Ray. Maria, Ray's wife, had helped wait tables for two nights; she was beside him on a long bench, while Desmond and the rest of the staff were resting wherever they could before heading home.

"I would say it was a very productive four nights." Timothy rubbed his hands in obvious glee. "I have to say, Janey, this is the best vacation I've ever had."

With the staff present, Alex had already warned her that no one should know Timothy was part of DHS or a part of the investigation.

Mark and Tyrell were there, leaning in a back corner, supposedly simply friends Alex had pulled in to bus tables.

It was almost funny watching the women lust after the hard abs and tight bodies of her new busboys. Unless they were staring at Alex. She'd had problems with that.

"I'm exhausted." Janey draped her arms over the reservation counter and laid her head in them. "Oh God. I just want to sleep."

"I finished up your paperwork earlier," Rogue said and yawned. "Really, Janey, you need to get organized. Once I had it in the proper piles, it went quickly."

"You're hired," Janey mumbled into her arms.

Rogue's laughter was amused, but Janey wasn't joking. In four days, Rogue had managed to do the impossible. She had organized the paperwork. Janey lifted her head and stared back at her friend silently.

Rogue rolled her eyes, then stared around the room. "Who's giving me a ride back to the bar? Janey sent her monster sheriff after me this afternoon."

"Only because you swore your bike was broke," Janey accused her.

Rogue flipped her red gold curls and gave her an innocent expression. "Sweets, it's Saturday night. I was supposed to have fun tonight, remember?"

"You did. Three men pinched your butt, one gave you a fifty-dollar tip, and you managed not to break your legs in those heels."

Timothy smiled with rich amusement.

"If you didn't have fun," Janey concluded, "I had fun watching you."

"God save me," Natches muttered as Rogue's laughter tinkled through the waiting room and she stretched her legs before pulling out her phone.

"Watch this," she drawled and made her call. "Zeke? It's Rogue."

Her voice became heavy, tired, languorous. "The cabs are all busy and I'm so tired. Please pick me up." She waited, and Janey watched as her expression flickered with something not so innocent. "Do I have to ride in the back?" She waited, then drawled, "Will you use the handcuffs?"

Pure wicked laughter fell from her lips as she flipped her phone closed. "He'll be here in ten minutes."

"Is he using the handcuffs?" Timothy asked with a little too much curiosity.

Rogue pouted. "He said only if I break the law. As though I want to get caught doing that." She winked at Timothy before rising to her feet and moving for the door. "Nite nite, folks."

"Are you serious about hiring her?" Hoyt asked as the door closed behind Rogue's leather-clad form.

"If she'll take the job." She looked around at the staff still lingering. "Any objections?"

"She's fun." The waitress Tiffany shrugged as she moved to Rogue's seat.

"She's smart," Desmond stated. "Our new sous-chef arrives Monday; this will give me time to prepare him for the rush that comes on Wednesday. His wife is an excellent waitress as well. Opening the new banquet room should be no problem."

"I don't think we're ready for that," Hoyt argued. "We're moving too fast, Janey. The banquet room wasn't even prepared properly this week. The reputation we're building is going to suffer."

"Ridiculous," Desmond snapped. "Quality has not suffered, neither in customer care nor in the food. We've made certain of this. And the profits have surely risen dramatically." He turned to Janey. "I have run kitchens for years; our output was exceptional as was our quality."

"And our profits." Janey nodded. "We did more business in the last four nights than we've done in a month. And I agree with the quality."

"We can't keep it up," Hoyt argued again, his expression creasing in concern and a hint of anger. "Janey, this restaurant doesn't just reflect your name, but your brother's. You should remember that. When you can't keep up, the restaurant's good name will go to hell as well. Just as it did before."

Janey stiffened at the reference to Dayle Mackay.

"I'm aware of what can happen if we don't prepare properly," she stated coolly. "But I think we're able to handle the additional customers. We'll have an added waitress Monday with Desmond's additional chef. Tiffany's sister has agreed to waitress until we can find more staff, and Rogue will cover for us at least until we can find a general manager, if she doesn't take the job herself."

"We don't need a general manager; even Natches agrees with that." Hoyt looked to Natches for support.

"That wasn't what I said, Hoyt." Natches frowned. "I said we're not hiring one if it means Janey will try to leave."

"You're leaving?" Hoyt's head jerked around, his gaze narrowed. "You didn't mention that."

"I'm not leaving," she muttered, well aware of Alex watching her silently. "If I left, Natches would burn the place down."

"I would," he agreed with a mocking smile. "And we both know how much that would break my heart."

His voice was sincere. The look in his eyes wasn't. He'd love nothing better than to burn the place to the ground, and Janey knew it.

She stared around the waiting room at the curious gazes watching them.

"She's not going anywhere," Alex stated before she could speak. "Except home to sleep. I locked up the office; everything's ready to go whenever you are."

The kitchen was secured, everything prepared. All they had to do was walk out the front door.

"I still think this is a mistake," Hoyt stated as he moved from behind the register. "We're not ready for this move, and Janey doesn't have the experience for the job."

Yeah, she'd been hearing that argument out of him for months.

"She has the experience, but does she have the stamina?" Tiffany pushed herself to her feet. "God, I'm exhausted."

"She's got the guts to do it," Desmond argued, looping his arm around his wife's shoulders. "She'll do."

Janey smiled at his statement. "We have a day off. Let's see what we can do with our time then to rest and get ready for next week. Before opening we'll meet for any further ideas or objections."

"Why? You don't listen to them." Hoyt pouted.

"She listens when you agree with her," Natches snorted. "That should be close enough."

"You always disagree with me," she told him as Alex helped her with her leather jacket.

"And you never listen." Natches glared at her as Chaya gave a low, amused laugh.

"Poor baby," his wife murmured. "Come home, darling. I'll listen to you all night long if you want me to."

"Really?" Natches's expression perked up. "Interesting."

Laughter echoed around Janey as everyone filed outside and she and Alex set the alarms and locked the doors. Janey touched the glass of the door and stared into the darkened restaurant then.

Alex's heart clenched at the wistfulness in her expression. She had dreams. He heard them in her voice, saw them in her eyes. Dreams of a future here, dreams with him. He knew she had those dreams because he saw them in her eyes when she turned and laid that small hand on his arm.

Leading her to the truck, Alex could feel the fine hairs at the back of his neck lifting in warning, though. He'd felt it for the last two nights, the malevolent gaze focused on Janey, the threat of violence swirling in the air around her.

They were playing a waiting game.

He could feel Mark and Tyrell backing them as Alex kept her close to his side, sheltered by his body, the vehicles and the shadows around them.

What would he do if he lost her? He hadn't been lying to her when he told her he would cease to exist. When he'd been wounded, he'd come home with one thought in mind. Janey. Touching her, having her, relieving the unrelenting hunger he'd had for her for far too long. He hadn't returned with the best of intentions. Because seducing her had been his plan, not finding himself bound to her by emotions he couldn't explain, justify, or make sense of.

As they neared the truck, Mark and Tyrell moved ahead of them as Timothy eased in behind Janey. The older man was softer around Janey. Hell, that whole daughter thing. He'd worked in that restaurant like a pro the past few days. And if Alex wasn't mistaken, he had enjoyed it.

"Clear," Mark murmured after he and Tyrell checked the vehicle for explosive devices.

"This is ridiculous," Janey muttered. "All of you putting your lives on the line like this, Alex."

She was frightened. She hid her fear well until they left the restaurant each night, but until they were safely behind the locked doors of his house, she trembled with the terror of someone being hurt because of her. The fear wasn't as much for herself as for others.

"It's our job." Timothy beat him to a response. "And trust me, every time we win, every child, husband, daughter, or sister we save makes it all worth it."

"And I don't let anyone take what's mine," Alex told her softly as he lifted her into the truck and watched her slide to the middle of the seat.

She sat beside him; she never slid to the other seat anymore. He liked that. Liked the way he could curl his hand around her leg, above her knee, and touch her warm skin as he drove. He liked having her close to him, feeling her, knowing she was safe.

As they drove away from the restaurant, he felt the tightness in his neck increasing. The closer they got to the house, the more he could feel the danger approaching. Once they got in the house, it would ease. Whoever her stalker was, he hadn't figured a way past Alex's security yet.

It was impossible to toss a handmade bomb past the wrought iron that blocked the windows. His bedroom had steel shutters on the inside that further protected the room. Those had been installed immediately after he'd brought Janey home.

Dark blinds and heavy curtains further shielded the other rooms. Windows and doors were secured, and outside, Mark and Tyrell took turns sleeping in their truck and watching the house.

The waiting game was ending, though. Alex could feel it.

"Something's wrong," Janey whispered. "I can feel it."

She was staring out the truck window, her hands clasped tightly in her lap, as they turned onto a side street and headed to the house.

Alex never took the same route, never allowed anyone to know which way they were going.

"We're okay," he promised her.

He checked the rearview mirror. Mark and Tyrell were right behind them; there were no other vehicles following, and none in front of them.

"This is insane." Her voice was thick, worried. "I used to get like this, before moving here. I always knew when Dayle was going to show up, when he was going to try to pressure me into marrying one of his buddies." She sneered the last word. "I always knew when he was going to find a way to hurt me or Natches."

"Dayle is dead, Janey. I saw the body when Natches was there. He's gone."

She swallowed tightly. "But he left something," she whispered. "Someone who hated him enough that they think punishing me will get back at him."

He breathed out roughly, checked the mirrors, watched the street carefully as they neared the house.

"Someone crazy," he told her. "And no one is going to hurt you."

He turned onto another side road. It didn't make sense. No one was following them, but he could feel the sights on the truck, feel the danger rolling around them like a dark, oily wave.

He looked out the windshield. There was no place a shot could reasonably come from, not with the shelter of the buildings and the trees.

He turned down another street, coming from another angle into the street his house sat on. The closer they got, the thicker was the feeling of danger.

He pulled off into an alley, stopped the truck, and shut off the lights. Mark and Tyrell moved in behind him.

"Stay here." He opened the glove box and pulled free his backup weapon. Checking the clip and flipping on the safety, he handed it to her. "You know what to do?"

She nodded, staring back at him with wide, fear-filled eyes.

"Good girl. I'm just going to talk to Mark and Tyrell. I'll be right back."

She licked her lips nervously but nodded.

"Stay safe for me, baby." He cupped her cheek, bent his head, and kissed her quickly before stepping from the truck. The dome lights were disconnected; there wasn't even a glimmer of light as he stepped from the truck.

"I wondered if you felt it." Mark was armed. He carried his automatic rifle close to his leg, between his body and the truck. "Closer we get, the thicker it is."

"Question is, how many are we dealing with?" Alex murmured.

"Can't be more than one." Tyrell rubbed at his jaw. "Every indication we have is a single stalker. Whoever it is has some serious shit going on, though. I've been feeling this since we left the restaurant. We were followed, somehow. When you started cutting through town and taking other routes, it eased. But the closer we get to the house, the more nervous I'm getting."

Alex nodded and glanced around the alley. Instinct, they called it. A sixth sense for danger that made no sense to anyone except those who had managed to survive because of it.

They were sheltered by the garage at one side and a stand of pines that bordered a yard across the alley. It was a short, narrow little road protected from all sides. Alex's house was on the next street over. There wasn't a lot of cover going in, but there weren't a lot of places to hide, unless someone was stalking from the neighboring trees and yard.

"We could call the Mackays in," Tyrell suggested. "Have them come in quiet."

Alex shook his head. "If we don't show up soon, the stalker could get spooked and run."

He was torn. Catching the stalker while they had the chance was imperative. He was waiting on them at the house. Slipping up on him would be easy, Alex thought. Alex knew this place like the back of his hand. It was home territory; he knew the shadows and how to move within them.

"Other options?" Mark questioned him.

"Send Janey to the marina and we go in on foot," Alex murmured.

"Think she'll go?" Mark asked.

Alex sighed. "No." He looked back in the truck and met her worried, concerned gaze. She didn't like being out of this conversation.

"Stay with her and we'll check it out," Mark suggested.

Alex shook his head and stared around the alley again. He was the best tracker there, and that left only a few options. They had a chance to catch the stalker here and now, or they could wait and let the bastard surprise them another day. But he had Janey with him.

"Mark, do you still have the extra communication sets you stole from headquarters?"

Mark stared at him blankly, then grimaced. "Fuck, how did you know I had those?"

"Are they in the truck?"

"In my travel bag." He sighed. "Backseat of the truck."

"Get them."

Mark loped back to the truck and eased the back door of the dual cab open as Alex turned to Tyrell. "You and I are going to scout around a bit. We'll leave Mark here with Janey. He's good at feeling trouble. If the stalker doubles back, he can get her out."

Tyrell nodded. "We need to get her to our truck, though. You're blocked here."

Alex opened the door quietly and motioned Janey out. As she eased across the seat, he picked her up and carried her to the other truck.

"Don't leave me here without you, Alex. Please," she whispered as Mark jerked the front door open and he slid her inside.

He and Tyrell took two of the communication sets and slid them into place on their ears and at the sides of their necks. Testing reception between the three of them, they nodded quickly.

"Alex, please," she whispered again.

He turned to her, touched her cheek, and stared into her worried eyes. "It stops here, Janey. You'll be safe with Mark. I promise."

Her eyes closed as a pain-filled grimace contorted her face.

"I love you," she whispered when her eyes opened, the soft, fierce words striking into his soul. "Do you hear me, Alex Jansen? I love you. Don't you let yourself get hurt again."

God, she filled his soul. How the hell was he supposed to handle this kind of emotion?

"I'm yours," he whispered. "I'll always come back to you, Janey."

Then he turned away from her. He had to, or he'd never be able to leave her there.

"Keep her safe, and call the Mackays. We'll be back within twenty," he told Mark. "I want this bastard tonight."

He had the most experience. As Mark had stated before, he and Tyrell had been out of the game for a while. They didn't have the reflexes or the sense of predatory awareness Alex still possessed.

Mark would protect her with his life, Alex had no doubt of that. But Tyrell had always been a natural at the hunt, while Mark's instincts had been more refined. He could sense it coming, but he wasn't as good at pinpointing the direction it was coming from.

Alex would have been a hell of a lot more confident with a Mackay here. Natches would have been nice. He didn't like trusting her to anyone else. But the stalker couldn't know where they were. Whoever it was was watching his house, not the trucks.

The dome lights to the trucks had been disengaged weeks before, so no one could have detected their presence. She would be safe here.

"You be careful." Mark nodded to Alex before turning to his lover.

His lips kicked up in a knowing grin as Tyrell, just as broad, as tall, and as strong as the other man, lifted his fist. Mark and Tyrell touched fists, but the gesture was strangely intimate despite the fact that it was the same action often used between soldiers in the field.

This had a gentler quality to it. Male to male, lover to lover, their smiles a bond that went deeper than some male/female kisses Alex had seen.

It blew his mind every time he saw it. Until Mark and Tyrell had come to him years before and revealed that they were lovers, he had never guessed.

"Weapons." Mark turned from Tyrell and reached into the backseat. He returned with knives, handguns, ammo clips, and backup ankle weapons.

Alex and Tyrell weaponed up before Alex dipped into the front door, jerked Janey to him, and took his kiss. A deep, tongue-thrusting kiss despite her whimper, her attempts to hold on to him. Pulling back from her, he pressed his fingers to her lips. "Twenty minutes," he whispered. "Do as Mark says, Janey. Stay safe for me."

She nodded jerkily.

Janey could feel the fear shaking her apart from the inside out. She moved across the console to the passenger seat as Mark eased into the vehicle and closed the door softly behind him.

Darkness surrounded them. Janey had lost sight of Alex within seconds of him moving away from the truck.

Mark flipped his cell phone open and hit speed dial. "Natches. Back street across from Alex's house. Come in quiet, lights off. We have the stalker on-site and Alex and Tyrell are moving in." He was silent for a second. "Confirmed. I have her with me and we need backup." He flipped the phone closed and turned to grin at her. "Cavalry is coming."

"Alex should have waited," she said worriedly, fighting the fear and the tears that would have escaped.

"He and Tyrell are the best at this that there is," Mark promised her, flashing her a smile. "They'll be back in twenty, your stalker bleeding and moaning in pain, and everything will slide back to normal for all of us."

She gripped the gun Alex had given her, staring around in fear. It was too dark. There were too many shadows. And Alex wasn't with her. He was out there, in danger.

Mark tried to reassure her again. "The major has always known what he was doing. Trust him."

"I trust him." She trusted him with her life, but he wasn't here and she couldn't see him. She had turned and was staring through the passenger window, her gaze delving into the darkness, when she heard the windshield shatter.

TWENTY-THREE

Janey felt the pinch of something in her shoulder as she turned to Mark. His head had slammed back, his eyes widening in shock, a dart buried in his neck.

Janey reached, scrambling to the side of her seat to jerk it out. "Mark. Oh God. Mark."

He was struggling to start the pickup, the motor cranking as Janey felt dizziness sweep over her. The gun fell from her hand and terror swept over her as she heard the locks to the truck disengage. She felt around her shoulder and pulled out a dart embedded there.

"Comm." Mark's voice was raspy as he struggled to pull the small, black communications device from his neck. He shoved it at her. "Alex. Move. Move."

Janey struggled against the darkness trying to sweep over her. Reaching over Mark's now-still figure, she fought to reengage the locks, to secure the truck. Her shoulder throbbed. She felt as though she were moving through water, weighed down, her vision and her tongue thick as cold air swirled into the vehicle.

"Move, bitch!" Hard hands gripped her hair, jerking her back, pulling her along the seat and through the door until she collapsed to the ground.

Alex would be coming. She knew he was. He would be running. She just had to delay.

"Get up or I kill that little fairy in the truck. Fucking queer. He doesn't deserve to live."

The pressure against her scalp was agonizing. Janey cried out with the pain, struggling to her feet and fighting to hang on to the slender communications device Mark had pushed at her.

Her hands were shaking, a sense of vertigo slamming through her as she lowered her head to hide her efforts to tuck the device into the band of her jeans, beneath her shirt.

"God, this was almost too easy." The voice, disguised somehow, was gloating. "I knew where they'd come in at. I knew where they would park. I was smarter. I was better."

Janey struggled against the hold as she was dragged through a yard. It was dark, late, for some dumb reason no one on this street had a dog in their backyard; now, how stupid was that?

She could feel the edge of hysterical laughter bubbling in her throat.

"Don't worry, bitch. He walked right into my hands." The voice was familiar but she couldn't place it. She shook her head, praying she had activated the right button on Mark's communications device and that Alex was able to track her.

If he didn't track her, she was dead. Hell, she was probably dead anyway.

"If you don't step it up, I'm going to just shoot you and get it over with," the voice snapped. "And I would, except that spineless little brat of mine needs to understand success. Stupid little bastard. He's so fucking weak. Always arguing over what I want to do."

Augusta Napier, Hoyt's mother.

Janey could feel her body trying to shut down, her mind fighting to escape the reality of the knowledge. Augusta was a friend of the Mackays. She knew the other woman was ill. Hoyt had said she was sick; everyone knew she had been battling cancer. How had she found the strength to do this?

"Almost there, you little tramp." Augusta pushed her through a dark, tree-sheltered yard. "Your lover had no idea how close I was, did he? And I outsmarted him. Sometimes it's just too easy to outsmart a man."

Janey couldn't quite make her senses work. She stumbled at the sound of a heavy door lifting, then she was tumbling, falling. She hit the stairs and rolled down them, feeling the painful bite of each strike of wood against her body.

The door was closing then. A cellar door. Many of the houses on this side of town were older, the cellar doors built on an angle outside the house and leading to the basement or storm shelters.

Beneath her cheek was cool cement. The dank, musty smell of the air clogged her nostrils and had her choking, fighting to breathe.

"Come on." She was picked up and tossed onto a couch. "You need to put some weight on, girl. You're too skinny." Then she cackled. "Oh well, too late to put some weight on. Tonight is the last night of the rest of your life."

The electronic edge of the voice was gone now.

"Augusta, why?" She moaned painfully. "Where's Hoyt?"

"Hoyt!" Augusta yelled out his name as Janey lifted her head, turning her body enough to allow the link to work, if it was working, for Alex to know where she was.

Another door opened.

"Mother, what you doing in the basement? It's time for your medication."

A light snapped on, nearly blinding as Janey jerked in reflex and pulled the edge of her jacket over the communications device.

God, she wanted Alex. She was terrified.

Squinting, fighting the mind-numbing drug that had obviously been in that dart in her shoulder, Janey tracked the other woman in the basement as Hoyt moved slowly down the stairs.

Augusta wasn't very old. Forty-five or forty-seven, Janey forgot which. A tall, raw-boned woman with sharp cheekbones and dull hazel brown eyes. She had been pretty once, before the death of her husband several years ago in Iraq. Janey had heard Augusta had gone a little crazy at the news of his death. Evidently, it wasn't just a little crazy.

"Oh, Mother, what have you done?" There was weary resignation in Hoyt's voice now as he stepped into the basement.

Janey noticed he didn't get there in a hurry. Not at work, and not here. He moved slowly to the couch and bent beside her, brushing her hair from her face and checking her pupils.

"You drugged her?" he accused.

"Your father's dart rifle." Augusta shrugged her shoulders beneath the man's heavy jacket she wore. "He always said I would never know when I needed to use it. I guess he was right." Her laughter was evil, slightly crazed.

"Hoyt. Help me," Janey whispered desperately. "You're Alex's friend. Natches's."

"Stop trying to use your wiles on him, bitch," Augusta barked. "Trust me, Hoyt's not going to listen to you, are you, Hoyt?"

He lifted his head and breathed in roughly, sorrow and weary pain mixed in his expression as he rose to his feet.

He was still wearing the slacks and shirt he'd worn at work. His black leather shoes were dusty and scuffed.

"How long have you not been taking your medication, Mother?" he asked her.

"You sound like your father." Affection and amusement filled Augusta's voice. "I don't need the medication, Hoyt. I just need her dead. That's all. Kill her and everything will be right again."

"Do you really want to hurt Alex like that, Mother? I told you; he cares for her."

Augusta paused, her gaze flicking over Janey. "I helped Alex raise Crista." She smiled fondly. "Those stupid parents of his were never there to help him or to help him with Crista. I'd watch her if he had to do something of the evenings. Alex is a good boy." She frowned. "Too good for the likes of you."

"Alex loves her," Hoyt stated. "You should see them together, Mother. I think we're wrong about her." There was a hint of misery in his expression as he turned away from her. "And Natches, he's her brother. He loves her like a brother. She doesn't act like Dayle."

"We can't take the chance." Augusta shrugged her jacket off, revealing a man's flannel shirt and jeans. She wore military boots, and there was a handgun holstered at her side. "Besides, I didn't agree to anything."

"You didn't take your medicine."

"Get off my back about the medicine, Hoyt," she snapped, brushing back her brown hair. "I told you, we can't let her infect the lives of those we care about. Alex is almost like a brother to me. He hasn't even come to see me because of her." A thin finger pointed accusingly at Janey. "And the gossip is already flying. He'll never make chief of police with that bitch on his arm, and you know it."

Janey watched Hoyt. She kept her eyes on his face, pleading. He looked saner than his mother, but he looked resigned. As though he knew he couldn't keep Janey alive.

"Oh, Mother." Hoyt raked his fingers through his hair as he sat down on an abandoned kitchen chair and glanced back at Janey.

His gaze flickered to her waist, and misery was reflected in his face. He saw the communications device. She knew he did. Her heart was in her throat as he shook his head sadly.

"Hoyt, you know what's going to happen. We've discussed it."

Augusta meant to kill her and Janey knew it. She could feel her stomach cramping with the fear. Fear for Alex, because she knew he was looking for her. Fear for the child she might be carrying, because if she died, so did the baby Alex wanted so desperately. Desperately enough to pledge himself to her.

"You promised you would let it go." Hoyt sighed wearily. "After you nearly got caught tossing those bombs in her house, you swore you would let it go."

"I can't let it go," she yelled furiously, her lined face twisting in anger. "I waited at his house with the tranquilizer gun. I wasn't going to hurt him. He would have slept right through her death. But he had to try to trick me. Him and those queers he's running with. You saw the pictures, Hoyt. She's making him just like those two men are. Fucking her ass like some fairy. He's losing his manhood."

Augusta paced the basement now. She tried to push the fallen strands of brown hair into the clip at the top of her head, but they kept falling free. Her face was flushed with fury, her hazel eyes were flat, dead. The anger was more a show for Hoyt. The woman facing them was cold. Hard.

"You're nothing like your father, Hoyt," Augusta sneered then. "When Jimmy and I were in the Army, he was the strongest man in his group. He taught me everything he knew and he tried to teach you. I tried to teach you. What happened to you?"

Hoyt shook his head. "I'm not a killer, Mother."

"Your father wasn't a killer; he was a patriot," she yelled.

Hoyt stared around the basement, his expression so filled with grief that Janey felt tears fill her eyes. She had always liked Hoyt. He was a hard worker, quiet. But he'd never seemed crazy; he'd never seemed devious.

"Mother was in the Army for a while," he told her quietly. "Her and Dad worked together sometimes. They were a helluva team."

Pride transfused Augusta's face. "Jimmy was so strong, wasn't he, Hoyt?"

Hoyt nodded. "Yes, Mother, Dad was very strong."

"Until he died." Her face twisted in grief, her hazel eyes finally lit with emotion, with pain. "They took him away from us in Iraq. Bitches like her!" She pointed a sharp, thin finger in Janey's direction. "Traitorous sluts."

Hoyt looked back at Janey. "They made it look like Father was having an affair." Bitter knowledge glittered in his eyes. "He was found in a bed in a filthy little hovel with a young Middle Eastern woman. They were both dead."

Janey swallowed back the bile in her throat.

"Traitorous slut! Black-haired little whore. Your father wouldn't have touched her, Hoyt. That little tramp lured him there and he killed her for it." Augusta swung around to Janey. "And her father put her up to it. Just like yours put you up to destroying Alex and Natches."

Janey shook her head. Everything felt detached, wavy. Whatever had been in that dart, she hadn't jerked it out fast enough. It was distorting reality, making her weak.

"I did . . ." She swallowed against the thickness in her throat. "I tried to protect Natches. I did what Dayle told me to to protect him."

"She's a liar!" Augusta snapped.

Hoyt drew in a deep breath and rose to his feet. "I'll get your medicine, Mother."

"Hoyt, don't betray me." Augusta slid the weapon from her side and aimed it at her son. "I told you, son, you're going to have to choose sides. Now's the time to choose."

"He's your son," Janey whispered tearfully. "Augusta, he's your only son."

The other woman swung around to her, eyes blazing now, fury filling them. "Do you think I don't know that, you little tramp? But every man has to choose sides. His daddy told him that. I know he did."

Hoyt lowered his head and Janey saw the misery, the knowledge on his face. His mother was insane. As crazy as Dayle Mackay had been.

"Mother." Hoyt stepped toward her. "Come upstairs with me. Let's get your medicine and we'll talk about this. You said it was easier to talk when you take it. Let's discuss how to do this first."

For a moment, Augusta's face was transformed. She looked younger, almost vibrant in her love for her son.

"You were such a disappointment to your father," she whispered. "But I always loved you, didn't I, Hoyt? I always took up for you."

"Yes, you did." Hoyt blinked against the pain.

"Even when he hit me for it, I defended you, didn't I, Hoyt?"

He nodded slowly. "You did, Mother."

She lifted the pistol. "I never realized how right he was," she sneered then. "You're pathetic." And she pulled the trigger.

Janey screamed and launched herself from the couch. Stumbling, she threw herself at Augusta as the gun discharged and Hoyt slammed backward.

"You bitch!" Augusta backhanded her as Janey scrambled to hold on to her gun arm.

"Mother, stop!" Hoyt's voice was weak. At least he was alive.

Janey gripped Augusta's arm, fighting to hold it out of the line of fire in Hoyt's direction, or hers.

Augusta wasn't as strong as she looked. She was angry, though, and Janey was drugged. She was crying, fighting to breathe, when she felt herself jerked back and heard a weapon discharge again.

She watched the dark, neat little hole that bloomed in the center of Augusta's head as she flew into the shelves behind her, then slowly slid to the floor, leaving a trail of blood on the wood.

"Janey. Baby. Oh God. I'm sorry." Alex was holding her, turning her into his chest, one broad hand pressing against the back of her head. "I got here as fast as I could, baby. Hell. I'm sorry. Janey, I'm so sorry."

She held on to him, feeling the weakness she had been battling rushing through her now.

"I think I'm gonna pass out," she mumbled.

She felt her legs go first. Her arms. She slumped against him, darkness closing around her as she heard him curse.

"She's fine." Mark was still groggy as he checked Janey after Alex laid her back on the couch. The adrenaline he had managed to inject into himself after Janey was dragged away had kept him conscious, but weak. He'd managed to drag another communications device from his bag and follow Janey's assailant on foot while directing Tyrell and Alex his way.

He'd been hit with the dart first, and a moment later the second had pierced the side of Janey's shoulder. Mark had seen her jerk the dart from her arm after pulling the one from his neck. It could have killed him. She had saved Mark, and she had saved herself. And Alex hadn't been there when she needed him. He'd never forget that.

Outside the house they heard the scream of tires, the slam of doors, a siren blasting through the night. Hell, this was happening too damned often in Somerset. Fucking stalkers, homegrown terrorists, and insane citizens.

"Fuck." Alex looked to where Tyrell was checking on Hoyt.

Augusta had shot her son in the chest, though not directly through the heart. Alex hoped one of those sirens was an ambulance.

"I tried to stop her." Hoyt's muffled sob was painful to hear. "She went crazy when Dad died. As long as she was medded up . . ." He coughed. The sound wasn't pleasant. "As long as she stayed on the pills, she was okay."

"Rest, son," Tyrell told him gently. "Help is coming."

"I told her about the stairs at the restaurant, in the banquet room," he wheezed. "Then she started slipping in there when no one was looking. When she used the bombs, I knew. I couldn't stop her. I should have said something."

"Hoyt, hang on," Tyrell growled. "You have to hang on for us, son. We need to know what happened."

"Nothing can help. Journal. My journal has it all," Hoyt whispered and coughed again. The rattle in his breathing had Alex cursing. He moved to where Tyrell was trying to stabilize him, and watched as Hoyt stared back at him. "I'm sorry," he whispered. A second later, Hoyt Napier took his last breath. The young man's face lost its somber, worried expression. It filled with a sense of peace as Alex hunkered down beside him and glanced at Tyrell.

The other man's face was heavy, lined.

"This is why I wanted out," Tyrell whispered heavily. "Kids dying in my arms. Fucking crazies filling the goddamned world." Anger colored his voice. "This is why we left, Alex."

Alex gripped the other man's shoulder before rising and making room for Mark. The other two men didn't touch. They didn't embrace or cry. But the bond between them was so damned strong it was almost humbling. And for a second, just a second, Tyrell let his head rest against Mark's hard shoulder as they stared at Hoyt.

As raised voices and the creak of the cellar door were heard, they straightened and rose to their feet, tucking their weapons out of sight. State police officers were the first to rush into the cellar, followed by a harried Timothy. Behind him were the Mackays and the sheriff.

Timothy moved straight to Janey and stared down at her, his expression creasing in concern, eyes twitching as his lips thinned and a sense of fear filled him. Alex had never seen Timothy frightened.

"Janey!" Natches was pushing through, his expression tormented, his green eyes dark with rage and worry as Dawg, Rowdy, and Ray followed behind.

Alex lifted her from the couch. "She's drugged," he told them, refusing to give her to Natches as he tried to take her from Alex's hold. "Is the ambulance outside?"

"This way, Major." The first officer waved him back to the cellar doors. "Agent Cranston filled us in on the way. We have an ambulance waiting on the street."

An ambulance, several more cruisers, and every damned citizen on at least four city blocks were crowding the area now.

As he carried Janey to the waiting ambulance, he wondered if there was any damned way to get her to close that fucking restaurant down long enough for him to get his head back on straight.

He'd nearly lost her. Hell had opened up in his mind when he'd heard her being taken and realized he wasn't close enough to protect her, that he might not be able to get to her in time.

The communications device she had taken with her had been erratic, staticky, making it hard to determine where she was. But she had kept her head. She'd used the device the best way she knew how. He was going to have to teach her the proper way.

As the EMTs moved aside to allow him to lay her on the gurney, he detailed the possible injuries and handed them the dart he had picked up off the truck seat earlier. He touched her hair, kissed her brow, then pressed his head beside hers as he fought the fear tearing through him, even now.

He had promised to keep her safe. Sworn it. And still, she had nearly died. He had nearly let her be taken from him because he hadn't stayed with her. Because he had let someone else watch over her.

"It wasn't your fault," Natches growled behind him.

Alex lifted his head as an IV was being attached to Janey's arm and the medics prepped her for transportation to the hospital.

"I left her," Alex whispered, shaking his head.

"With a damned able soldier," Natches argued back, his hair mussed, his eyes still wild. "She's alive, dammit. And when she wakes up, she's not going to need a guilt-ridden lover. And she better fucking have a fiancé, not some son of a bitch ready to walk out on her."

Alex's lips twitched and he shook his head slowly. "Not in a million years, Natches. Not a million years or a thousand stalkers. She's mine."

Natches's eyes narrowed on him. "You love her?"

"She owns me."

Natches smiled. "I'd suggest telling her the love part. Those are the only words women understand, you know."

Alex shook his head. "She knows. It goes deeper."

Natches snorted. "Dumb-ass. Tell her." Then he sighed and reached out to touch Janey's limp hand. "Tell her, man. Because I think its something we both forgot to do."

Teach me how to love, Janey. He'd asked her that once, and he hadn't realized just exactly how both of them had misinterpreted what he did feel for her.

It went deeper than anything Alex had ever imagined love could be. Calling it love seemed almost trite, like saying he merely enjoyed being a Ranger when it had been his life for so long.

Until Janey. Janey was his life now, and his dedication to her went far beyond the dedication he had given his unit, his career, or even his life. It went beyond love. But if she needed the words, then he'd make sure she got them.

TWENTY-FOUR

Janey hated the hospital, and no one would let her leave. She was stuck there until they determined the effects of the drug in the tranquilizer and how her system was dealing with it. She had nearly died with the drugs Dayle had given her six months before; no one was taking chances now. And no one was leaving her in peace.

The whole Mackay clan was there; if they weren't in her room, they were outside her room. Taking turns coming in, watching her carefully and making her crazy. It went on all night, until by the next morning she wanted to scream in frustration.

Thankfully, Timothy Cranston arrived, ran everyone else out, and gave Alex a hard look when he nearly refused. Janey was surprised to see him go.

"He's a damned good man." Timothy ran his hands over his thinning hair as he sat in the chair beside her bed and watched her with heavy eyes.

"He is at that."

Janey watched Timothy. There was so much grief inside the other man that her heart ached for him.

"I had a daughter once," he finally said. "A family."

She felt tears flood her eyes and barely kept them in check.

"A little granddaughter." He smiled sadly, then ducked his head as he rubbed at his chest and inhaled hard. "I lost them in a terrorist bombing. My son-in-law, my daughter and grandchild, and my wife. I was supposed to be there, but a case was coming together and I wouldn't leave."

"And they died," she whispered.

He nodded. "Yeah. They died." He lifted his head again. "You look so much like my baby girl," he said then. "My little Maria. The first time I saw you, I knew your heart, everything you were, would be sweet and kind. And I was right."

Janey watched him silently.

"I don't have family," Timothy said then.

Janey reached out and touched the hand that lay on the bed beside her. "You're wrong."

His head lifted.

"Natches doesn't fight with people he doesn't care for," she told him softly. "Dawg calls everyone he loves names. And well, Rowdy, he just wouldn't speak to you at all if he didn't like you. And you remind me, Timothy, of everything I ever wished for in a father."

"I'm not the nice man you want to see." Timothy grimaced. "Every one of those boys out there will tell you that."

"Alex says you're a genius," she told him. "And I overheard Natches and Dawg talking after you left at Christmas. Natches was disappointed you hadn't stayed for dinner."

There was a flicker of something in his eyes, an emotion, almost a hunger that filled him. A need for family. The family he had lost was gone, and he knew it, but Janey saw that need inside him for something to replace it.

"Hang around awhile." She tightened her fingers on his. "Don't run off on us, Timothy. We miss you."

He sighed again. "Yeah, well, DHS has suspended me again." He grinned, like a little boy that had been caught doing something naughty. "They don't like my methods."

She grinned at that. "They're crazy, then," she decided. "But that's all the better for us."

He scratched his cheek. "Alex wants to be chief of police."

She nodded at that. "He'll get it, too."

"Well, of course he'll get it." Timothy's grin widened. "How much you wanna bet I can't win the next election for mayor, though?"

Janey stared back at him in shock, then in amusement.

"You wouldn't dare. He'd die."

"I know how to boss him around," Timothy chortled. "Trust me, Janey, he won't get bored at his job."

He rose to his feet, and his expression became serious once again as he reached out and touched her hair. "You're too old to adopt." He sighed. "Too bad. I'd have enjoyed holding a shotgun on Alex."

Janey shook her head before patting his hand and staring up at him gratefully. "You're a good man, Timothy."

His shoulders shifted, his wrinkled suit jacket bunching around his neck. "I better go. Alex will be getting antsy."

"Timothy." She stopped him as he moved to turn away.

"Yes?"

"You're part of my family," she told him then. "Admittedly, those Mackay boys are hard to get along with, but I have a feeling you enjoy that part of it."

His grin was mischievous. He finally grunted. "It's the only reason I didn't slap their asses in jail last year. They're good boys. Damned good boys."

"And we'll see you soon?" she asked, looking for promises. She felt the need for promises right now. She didn't want to lose anyone else she cared for.

"Yeah." He nodded slowly. "Yeah, Janey. You'll be seeing me more often than Alex might like."

With a final grin, he left the room. Silence surrounded her for the first time in too long, and before she knew it, her eyes drifted closed and sleep was finally attainable.

No bitching cousins, no worried brother, no sister-in-law hovering anxiously. She missed Alex, but she knew he was close. She could feel him. She let her head sink deeper into her pillow and let sleep wash over her.

She felt the kiss at her brow and almost smiled. Heard the soft whisper of her lover's voice, and almost woke. But it was quiet here, peaceful, and warm. And she let the warmth wash over her. Just for a little while.

TWENTY-FIVE

Hoyt's journals, and there were many of them, detailed a young boy growing into a young man aware that he had disappointed the father who'd expected him to be taller, broader, and stronger. He had a mother who had loved him with almost fanatic intensity, and he'd had the knowledge, even as a boy, that there was something not quite right about the parents he loved.

The past six months, the journals had been filled with fear as well. Attempts to make certain his mother took her pills, even hiding them in her food, melting them in her coffee. But nothing could have stopped Augusta Napier's insanity.

The fact that Nadine Grace and Dayle Mackay had always been her enemies didn't help. For years she had hated Natches, and only after word had circulated that it had been Natches who revealed his father as a traitor had Augusta decided he was a man worthy of her love. He and Alex, they were like her husband, she had decided. Strong and brave.

The man Jimmy Napier had been was just average. A soldier who had taken every tour he could get to escape his wife. A man rumored to have had a different lover in each different area he had been assigned to. His last lover, the daughter of a terrorist, had been his downfall. He had died in her arms, literally.

He'd been a good soldier, a loyal soldier, but he'd never advanced because he didn't have the drive, or the strength, to go higher. Or the trust. He wasn't known for keeping his word. Jimmy Napier hadn't just broken promises to his wife and son.

It was a sad tale.

Three days later, Janey stood beside Hoyt's casket before it was lowered into the dark wound in the earth created to hold him. She didn't bother to wipe her tears away, because she wondered if anyone had ever cried for Hoyt.

She laid a rose on his casket, touched the cold metal lid, and whispered a last good-bye to him. The young man who had supported her from the first day in the restaurant, the one who had given his life to save her from his mother, wouldn't have the chance to realize the dreams he had written in those journals. Nor would he have the chance to realize the vision he had shared with her for the restaurant.

Her throat was thick with her tears as Alex held her against him, his arm tight around her, his warmth seeping past the layers of clothes to protect her against the harsh bite of the early February air. There wasn't even a hint of spring. Hoyt had been buried on one of the coldest days that the month of February had known in decades.

And that somehow didn't seem fair. There should be a hint of warmth, a hint of newness in the air somehow. Something to give her hope that Hoyt knew he had been loved by those around him.

Swallowing tightly, she let Alex lead her from the cemetery back to the truck. And from there they drove to his house.

The Mackay family had gathered around her for three days. All of them. Her brother and his wife, the cousins and their wives, and Uncle Ray and Maria. But they were alone now as Alex pulled the truck into the driveway of his house.

Alex had been quiet for the past few days. Too quiet. She could almost feel him drawing away from her, and it rocked her to her soul. She was safe now, so how much of him would she still own now that there was no danger of anyone killing her or his potential child?

He unlocked the kitchen door and stepped in, still cautious, before he let her into the dimly lit house. It was overcast outside; the forecast was calling for snow, perhaps sleet along with it. It was brutally cold, but inside, the warmth seemed to seep around her.

She liked Alex's house. She would regret leaving it.

"The construction crew says the apartment will be finished in a few weeks." She shrugged her jacket off and hung it up with her purse on one of the coat hooks by the door.

"Really?" he drawled. His voice was cool, distant. "That's fast work."

She nodded slowly. "Yeah. Natches signed off on it immediately. I was surprised."

"Did you talk to him about a manager?" he asked.

She shrugged. She hadn't yet. Maybe she was afraid to.

"Why haven't you, Janey?"

She looked up at him, feeling uncertain, a little lost.

"Maybe," she whispered, "as long as he's not signing off on it, it means he wants to keep me around."

She'd done a lot of soul searching after Zeke allowed her to see Hoyt's journals. It had made her think of her own dreams, her own needs that she had hidden over the years, even from herself. Especially here in the past weeks spent with Alex. She had hidden from herself the knowledge of what it would do to her if she lost him.

She loved him past reason, and she knew it. Loved him enough that she knew she would never fully let go of him.

Alex sighed heavily. "Janey, he did everything he could to protect you for the better part of your life. What makes you think Natches doesn't want you here? That he would ever want you out of his life?"

"He doesn't know me." She looked up at him cautiously. "And that's my fault. Sometimes I fear he'll look at me and see Dayle. Or our mother. And I get scared inside that I'll do something or say something, and he'll see them. Or he'll remember the beatings he took for me." She shook her head as she moved to the table, staring down at the dark wood with a frown. "I played Daddy's princess, and hated Dayle, and myself, for it."

"Why did you do it?" He didn't move closer to her; he stayed distant, and she ached.

"Because I knew he'd strike out. He was waiting for a reason. He knew Natches would come running. And he knew then that he'd have the excuse he needed, possibly to kill him."

She shook her head again, fighting the tears. She was fighting tears so often in the past few days.

"Then you were protecting him as well, Janey," he told her quietly.

He moved to her then and his arms went around her. "Baby, you're one woman. One tiny, fragile little thing. Did you think you should be using your fists like Natches did?"

She nodded against his chest, her fingers curling into his suit jacket as her breathing hitched. "I should have fought. I should have found a way to protect myself. I shouldn't have depended on Natches. I should have been stronger, Alex."

"You should have been just the way you are," he whispered. "The woman who threw herself from the couch to attack a crazed woman with a gun, before she shot her son. Because you knew she would shoot you next. The woman who tore a dart out of Mark's neck before it could kill him, and still managed, despite the tranquilizer in her system, to grab a communications device and hide it on herself so she could be found. Nothing you've done has been unworthy in my eyes. Or in Natches's."

"Hoyt's dead, because of me." Her stomach cramped with that knowledge. "I saw his journals. His dreams. He'll never know them."

"Ah, Janey." His hand curled around her neck, so strong, his fingers against her skin, curling from the side of her neck to the back, made her feel feminine, protected. "Hoyt wouldn't have blamed you. Did you read the final journal? How he talked about how hard you worked, the dreams he knew you had? How he wanted you to succeed? Hoyt doesn't blame you, sweetheart."

"Maybe I blame me." She blinked back her tears.

"You will." He nodded, surprising her. "Just as I blame myself that Augusta Napier was able to get to you."

"No . . ."

He laid a finger against her lips. "I left you in the truck, without me. I didn't trust my own instincts that night, Janey. All I thought about was catching the person trying to hurt you, and stopping it. If you want to blame anyone for Hoyt's death, sweetheart, then blame me."

"You won't let me take responsibility for anything." She pushed away from him, suddenly angry. "You're like Natches. You make excuses for me. You pamper and baby me, and sometimes I want to scream with it."

"Oh, I blame you for plenty," he growled.

She swung around, eyes suddenly narrowing. "For what?"

"My hard dick. The fact that I've gone three days without fucking you because *your* family was crowded into my house like a fucking Mackay invasion. Oh yeah, Janey, there's some blame that lies directly on your pretty shoulders. But Hoyt isn't part of it."

Her breath locked in her throat for long moments before she swallowed past her own need and fears.

"You haven't acted like you wanted me."

He stared at her in disbelief. "I had your whole family in here, Janey, and Timothy glaring at me like he's adopted you. Hell. Do you have any idea how many times the difference in our age was mentioned and how no one had better hear *sounds* from our bedroom?"

Her lips twitched. "Sounds, huh?"

"Janey, *sounds*. And, baby, when I touch you, I do want to hear your sounds."

"So I can take the blame for your hard dick, but not my own weaknesses?" she said roughly.

"God, don't say the word *dick* unless you're trying to get into my pants." He sighed. "It just makes me harder." He caught her arms, sliding his hands to her elbows then back to her shoulders. "And, baby, you're fragile, not weak. Not unworthy. And you're human. Hoyt knew what his mother was and he didn't warn anyone. He could have. He should have. And he didn't. That isn't your fault."

A tear slipped free. "He loved her."

"Yes, he loved her," Alex whispered. "But no matter how much you love me, you would never stand by and allow me to do something you didn't agree with, would you?"

She frowned back at him. "You're arrogant, not mean."

"I beat those drunks up for insulting you." His smile was slow and wicked. "And you didn't even kiss my scraped knuckles."

She scowled at that. "I should have boxed your ears. They were drunks."

"They'll think before they insult another woman while they're drunk," he argued back. "But you let me know exactly how much you didn't like it, didn't you, baby?"

"You didn't listen." She pouted.

"Sure I did," he drawled. "Next time, I'll be real nice about it and just knock their heads together. I'll be nice and gentle."

Janey had to fight her smile as she felt his hands slide to her dress, pulling it up slowly.

"Are you trying to undress me, Alex?"

He huffed in exasperation. "I'd really like to see what you're wearing under that dress, Janey. And you said the word *dick*. You owe me now."

This she had. She lifted her head as his lowered, parted her lips, and took his kiss, even as he took hers. Lips and tongues touched, played together, stroked, and stoked the flames building inside them now.

She had his desire. Perhaps his distance had been because she had been surrounded by her family. And Natches had growled a lot. Timothy had doted on her and glared at Alex several times.

She had to let herself believe she could make this work. She had to let herself believe he loved her, and just didn't realize it.

"Say it again," he growled against her lips.

"Say what?" She was breathless, dazed with the need for more of his kisses, more of his touch.

"The word." His lips roved over her jaw. "Talk about my dick. God, you make me hot, Janey, when you talk dirty to me."

"You're so naughty." A breathless laugh left her.

"Yeah, and so are my intentions toward you." He nipped at her ear. "Come on, talk dirty to me. Let me hear it so I can fight coming in my pants. I love it when you make me ready to come in my pants."

Her head tilted back. "I want to suck your hard dick," she whispered. "All the way to my throat."

"Fuck!" His voice roughened.

"I want to do that, too." She pushed at his jacket, dragging it over his powerful shoulders to touch him, feel him. "I want to fuck you, Alex. I want to ride you like my own wild stud. Feel you hard and thick inside me, slamming into me."

"Hell." He lifted her from her feet and carried her through the short hall to their bedroom.

When he released her, he was tearing at his clothes, his cheeks flushed, his eyes thunderous. "Take your clothes off."

He tore off his shirt and yanked at his belt as she reached back and unzipped her dress.

"Can I suck your hard dick, Alex?" she whispered.

"God, you can suck any part of me you want." The hunger was brighter, stronger in his face than she had ever seen it. As though something had stripped away the last layer between man and lust.

She dropped the dress to her feet, leaving her clad in the black bra, thong, and smoky black stockings she wore with her pumps.

"Oh, sweet mercy." He toed his shoes off and pushed his pants and boxers from his muscled legs. "Get over here, baby. Suck my dick. Show me how much you want it."

She moved to him, slowly, watching his hands clench at his sides. His expression was tight, his cheekbones sharply defined and flushed.

"I love sucking your cock," she whispered, loving the freedom to be naughty with him, to love him as she needed to.

Her hands flattened against his chest, smoothed down the tight, rippling abs as she went to her knees and let her hands encase the thick, throbbing shaft.

Alex watched her, both bemused and so fucking turned on by the sight of her that it was all he could do to hold back the cum threatening to spurt from the tip of his cock.

Small beads of it formed despite the ferocious control he held over himself. She licked those drops away and murmured her appreciation with a little moan. Her lips opened, parted, encased the engorged, darkly flushed crest, and she sank her mouth onto it.

Alex's head fell back on his shoulders as a groan tore from his throat. Her mouth was like hot silk and velvet, her tongue rasping over the ultrasensitive head, curling over it, licking and tasting him as she sucked at the engorged flesh.

The fingers of one hand moved between his thighs and cupped his balls, her palm rolling against them in a way that, fuck, his toes were curling into the damned carpet it was so good. He almost yelled out at the pleasure. He might have, if she'd left him enough breath to do it. Instead, she seemed to suck that out of his lungs with the same hungry intensity that she was sucking the control from his mind and the cum from his balls.

He couldn't touch her. He had to force himself not to touch her. Not her hair, her face. His hands were curled into tight, knotted fists as he fought back the urge to touch.

If he touched, he'd lose it. He'd have her flat on her back, with him buried inside her and pumping his release into the hot, liquid depths of her body.

He adored her. Adored her lips, her tongue, her little moans, her silken hands, and the hunger that blazed in her eyes. But as he watched her, he knew he adored her spirit, her fire, and the woman who was so afraid of losing what she loved.

He saw it in her eyes. He'd heard it earlier in her voice. And he still couldn't figure out how to convince her that nothing in this world or beyond could mean to him what she did.

"Sweet Janey," he groaned, staring down at her, watching her consume him, steal his soul one soft lick, one deep draw of her lips, at a time. She had stolen his soul just as easily as she stole his control.

He could hold back only so long. His hips were moving against her lips, his eyes watching as he fucked her mouth, watching the damp moisture glistening on his cock as he pulled back, watching her lips take him as he buried the head of his erection between them once again.

His fingers uncurled, then locked in her hair. He felt his arms bulging as he fought to hold back, felt his abs flexing, his balls tightening further.

"I'm going to come, Janey," he groaned. "Ah hell. Enough."

He pulled back, holding on to her head as he forced her to release the bloated crest of his dick. Damn, he needed to fuck her. Needed to be buried inside her.

He lifted her to her feet before picking her up and carrying her to their bed. He laid her back and unclipped the little clasp of her bra before drawing it from her. He was dragging it over her shoulders when the sight of her tight, hard nipples became more than he could resist.

Janey arched, crying out his name as his lips covered a hard, sensitive nipple, pulling it into the hot depths of his mouth. He sucked her with hungry draws of his mouth, sending pleasure shooting from the tight tip to the needy depths of her pussy.

She writhed against the bed beneath, her legs parting as his thigh pushed between them. The hard muscle ground against her clit, and she felt the tightening, the erotic flames of pleasure beginning to sear her.

The sensations raced from her nipples to her womb, curled around her clit, and struck inside her sex. She could feel the clenching, building need. The desperate pleasure that she knew would only grow, only become deeper, hotter, until he filled her, until he triggered the explosive ecstasy she knew she would only feel in his arms.

"I love how your nipples taste," he growled as he moved from one to the other. "So tight and sensitive." His teeth rasped one; his tongue licked, and a lightning stroke of white-hot sensation whipped through her body.

She could feel the perspiration gathering on her flesh. The need tearing through her. She had to have him, soon. If she didn't—oh God, she couldn't bear it if she didn't.

Her head thrashed on the bed as his lips moved from her nipples.

He kissed the underside of her breast, sucked a bit of the flesh into his mouth, and she knew he'd marked her again. Knew it and loved it.

Then his lips were moving lower. His tongue licked down, his lips kissed, his hands parted her thighs farther as his head came between them. And he licked her pussy. One long, slow lick through the saturated cleft. When he reached her clit, he licked around it. Never enough pressure. He blew a heated breath over it, kissed it, and she nearly exploded into a million fragments.

His chuckle was wicked.

"You're going to tease me," she gasped.

"I'm going to adore you," he drawled. "Soak every taste and touch into my soul, Janey."

He licked and sucked. He kissed and had her screaming his name.

"Oh yeah, ah, baby, I love your sounds. Your cries and screams."

He stabbed his tongue inside her clenching sex and she nearly came undone then and there. She could feel the tension building in her womb, in her clit. The pleasure was so intense, so brilliant, it was nearly painful, and she wanted more. She craved more. She gripped his head, her fingers digging into his scalp as she arched to his lips. Her head thrashed. Her legs tightened around his head.

Groaning, he moved to her clit, licked around it, kissed it, then sucked it into his mouth as his tongue flickered, hot and quick, over the tender bud and left her screaming through her orgasm.

"Now ride me." He pulled her over him before the last waves of pleasure were finished rushing through her.

She still had her shoes on, her stockings. She had no idea what had happened to her panties or when he'd torn them off her. She was sure he must have torn them. He seemed to really enjoy tearing her panties off her body, and she loved it.

"God, I nearly came when you threatened to ride me like your own personal stud," he groaned as she straddled his hips. "Do it, baby. Ride me straight to paradise."

She gripped the base of his cock and eased over him, pressing it against her, her eyes closing, her head falling back as she felt him stretching her, filling her.

She was slick and wet; he was hard and thick. Like heated, silk-covered iron impaling her, stroking once-hidden nerve endings and sending sharp, intense flares of sensation racing to her womb.

She took him in one long stroke, easing down until he filled her completely, burrowed so deep inside her that there was no beginning, no end to either of them.

"Oh yeah, honey." His lips pulled back in a snarl of pleasure as his gaze narrowed. "Now ride me." His hands clenched her hips. "Damn, you look pretty like that."

She followed his lead, lifting and rising, grinding against him and crying out his name as the pleasure began to build again, the heat surging through her.

It was pleasure and pain. It was agony and ecstasy. It was like belonging. Like finally discovering the one place in the world where she knew she could find that elusive happiness that had never seemed quite real. Until Alex. Until he touched her, held her. Until he let her own him.

She would teach him to love her. Eventually.

For now there was this. Taking him as he took her, loving it. Riding him, rising and falling on the stiff length of cock, until they were both crying out with the release rushing through them.

She tightened on him until her muscles seemed to lock. Inside her, his cock swelled thicker, throbbed harder, and the heated, harsh spurts of his release pushed her own climax higher.

Sweat covered them, slickened their bodies as she relaxed against him. It was a damned good thing breathing was natural, because Janey wasn't certain she could have found the strength to draw a breath if it wasn't.

"Oh man, that was so fucking hot." He breathed out roughly. "I want to do it again."

Her muscles were shaking. He was practically draped on the bed beneath her. She could barely manage a laugh.

"Right now?"

He grunted. "A few minutes, maybe."

"Minutes?" She couldn't move yet. She was so limp, so weak, she just lay against him. He was still buried inside her, still hard, though without the steely strength of moments before.

"Okay, tens of minutes, maybe." He tried for a laugh as she groaned and lifted herself from him, collapsing on the bed beside him.

"Maybe I'll let you nap first." He turned to his side and wrapped his arms around her. "For a little while."

She smiled and kissed his chest, feeling him relax against her. He hadn't slept well while the Mackays had invaded his home.

She cuddled closer and let her eyes drift closed. Just for a little while, she told herself. A nap. But the nap became deeper, stronger. In his arms, safe, she let herself relax, and it was hours before she awakened. The day was surrendering to night and she couldn't seem to get comfortable again.

Pushing away from a still-sleeping Alex, she forced herself from the bed, stretching, trying to ease the aching tightness that perhaps the position they had used had put in her hips.

Smiling at the thought, she went to the bathroom. She needed to shower, then maybe she would fix dinner. She was getting hungry. She hadn't really been hungry in days.

She dampened a washrag, cleaned between her thighs, and when she pulled it back, she froze at the slightest blemish of a stain on the rag.

Agony rushed through her. It clenched her chest, her stomach. It burned through her with a blaze of pain so sharp, so fierce, she wondered if she would survive. She dropped the washrag and slid slowly to the floor, her head on her knees as she fought not to howl with the ferocity of the anger and the hurt that tore through her.

Between one second and the next, fate had destroyed her, and she didn't know if she could survive it.

Alex wasn't certain at first what brought him awake. But his eyes jerked open, and his hand went automatically to where he knew Janey should be.

She wasn't in the bed beside him, but he could hear her. Something he had never heard from her—muffled, soul-shattering sobs.

His heart went to his throat as he jumped from the bed. He didn't bother with his pants but moved quickly to the bathroom, where he found her, crouched in the corner where the sink and the wall met, her head buried in her arms, her knees pulled up to her breasts.

Beside her lay a damp washrag, the faintest hint of her feminine cycle staining it.

He'd known she would start. The tempting sweet taste of her earlier had been earthier, the sweet syrup a little sweeter. He'd known by the changes in her nipples, the tighter grip of her body.

"Janey." He knelt beside her, running his hands over, making certain she wasn't hurt. "Sweetheart. Talk to me. Tell me what's wrong. Are you hurt?"

She shook her head, but the sobs were heartbreaking. They were wounding his soul.

"Baby. Come here. You have to talk to me." He picked her up, despite the stiffness in her body, and carried her back to the bedroom, where he sat down on the bed, holding her close.

"This isn't like you, Janey," he whispered. "Why are you crying, darlin'? You're breaking my heart."

She cried harder. The sobs were heartrending, torn from her, despite her attempts to hold them back, and Alex had never felt so helpless in his entire life. He searched his mind frantically. Had he hurt her during sex? Said or done something to hurt her feelings?

Were her emotions just messed up? That happened that time of the month, he knew, but he had never expected it to be like this from Janey. Not that he minded, but he had to blink back his own tears at the sound of her sobs, and real men didn't cry like this.

"I'm sorry." She turned into him, curling against him like a frightened kitten, her arms tight around his neck, her body shuddering as her sobs became harder. "I'm so sorry."

"God, Janey, why?" He held her as tight as he dared, and yet he had a feeling she needed more. "Sweetheart. What do you have to be sorry over?"

"I'm not." Another shudder and sob. "I'm not pregnant, Alex. I'm not having your baby." And the tears flowed hot and filled with pain against his chest. "I'm sorry. I failed. I failed."

Alex frowned. He gripped her chin and lifted her face, his chest clenching at the agony in her green eyes, and then he knew. He knew why she was crying; she was so filled with pain that Janey had finally, truly cried.

"Do you think a baby was all I wanted from you, Janey?" he asked, his voice husky. Dear God, how had he allowed her to believe something like that?

When she didn't answer, his voice hardened. "Is that all you think I need—a fucking breeder?"

He was close to anger with her. The tears still fell, and her beautiful eyes were shattered. Because she thought that was all he wanted from her.

"We had a deal." Her breathing hitched. "You wanted a baby."

He laid her back on the bed carefully and rose. He took his time pulling on his jeans, keeping his back to her as he heard her breathing again on a sob.

"I love you." He said the words slowly, keeping his back to her, because he knew what he felt was so much more. But Natches had said sometimes they needed the words. He'd give her the words.

"You liar."

Alex turned in time to see her grab a glass he had set there earlier and throw it at him. If he hadn't ducked, it would have probably laid him out on the floor.

But she wasn't crying anymore.

"I don't lie, Janey," he snapped. "And the next time you throw something, I'm spanking you."

"Your spankings make me come," she sneered. "Big whooping deal. Just let me put my shoes on so I can shake in them."

He propped his hands on his hips, glaring at her as she moved from the bed. She threw him a furious look. She didn't bother to dress. A second later, a slender little finger was poking in his chest.

"You kept me because you thought I was pregnant," she accused him. "You gave yourself, committed yourself to me just like you committed yourself to the military all those years."

Alex blinked back at her. "I left the military, Janey. I wouldn't leave you."

Her eyes flamed in green fire. The light green darkened, sparked, raged.

"I'm not pregnant, Alex. You don't have to let me *own* you anymore and you don't have to lie to me."

"Accuse me of lying to you again, and I promise you, the spanking you get won't make you come, baby," he warned her, his voice quiet. "I said I love you. I didn't keep you as you call it because I thought you were pregnant."

"Then why else?" She sent him a scathing look. "The daughter of a traitor, remember, Alex? Daddy's perfect little girl that smiled sweet and did what Daddy told her to do. Why the hell do you think Augusta Napier thought I was corrupting you?"

"Hell if I know." He pushed his fingers roughly through his

hair. "Because honestly, I was thinking I was corrupting you, while I had my dick shoved up your ass."

She stilled. Narrowed her eyes. "Don't be a smart-ass, Alex."

"You know what?" He crossed his arms over his chest. "You're right."

"Yeah, I usually am," she sneered. "What am I right about this time?"

"I don't love you."

She froze and stared back at him.

"Love is just a pale fucking word for what I feel. I've watched love die. I've watched couples drift apart and love fade like a memory." He shook his head. "I don't love you, Janey. When I said you own me, I meant you *own* me. Heart. Soul. My hopes, dreams. My life. Because I'd die for you. What the hell more can I give you?"

Janey stared back at him. When he'd said he loved her, she'd realized the lie for what it was. There had been no feeling, no strength in the words. And there was now. There was the intensity in his voice that she had always associated with Alex and emotion. His emotions. His voice deepened, became rougher, when he let emotion slip free.

"Son of a bitch, I'm fourteen years older than you." He sighed. "We see things different somehow."

"Throw your age up to me again and I'll spank *you*." She told him fiercely. "Age has nothing to do with this."

She could feel something building in her now, glowing within her, taking hold of her and heating her, warming her in places she hadn't imagined would ever be warmed.

"I . . ." She swallowed tightly. "I really own you? All of you?"

"Janey, sweetheart," he groaned, moved to her, framed her face with his hands, and stared down at her. His expression was filled with emotion now. His eyes raged with it. "I could say I love you until hell freezes over, and I'll never say it enough to make myself feel as though I've told you how I feel for you. I'm a loner, baby.

I always was, until you. No one has ever owned any part of me, until you. Janey, I live for you."

He lived for her. He loved her past loving her. And she owned him. The tears fell again. Freely. She'd never been allowed to cry as a child or as an adult. But Alex had let her cry. He'd dried her tears at the funeral. He'd held her when she needed to be held. He'd let her be free, but she had always known his arms were right there, ready to curl within.

"I live for you," she whispered, those tears running over his hands now. "Alex, I love you so much it eats me alive because I've been so scared. So scared of losing you. Of not having you in my bed ever again, or not having your touch."

He pulled her to him. Right there, against his hair-roughened chest, his big hand covering the back of her head, making her feel sheltered, strong, and yeah, she was owned as well.

"I breathe for you, Janey." He whispered the words against her forehead, then tipped her head back and breathed against her lips. "You own me."

His lips covered hers, gently, tenderly, with hunger and with possessiveness, with all the emotions she had always dreamed of suddenly swirling between them.

They could have a baby later, if it happened. For now, she had Alex. And having Alex was everything her soul had despaired of ever knowing.

"You own me, too," she whispered, staring back at him. "All of me, Alex. You have owned me for so long."

His thumb smoothed over her cheek, wiped away the last tears.

"Are you going to talk to Natches now?" he asked, a hint of a smile at his lips. "Because we both know, Janey, you're not leaving my side."

"Ever," she promised. "Oh, Alex. I'll never leave your side."

EPILOGUE

Four Days Later

Janey was waiting nervously in the office when she heard Natches pull into the back lot. Alex was upstairs overseeing the repair on the apartment; she suspected he might actually be helping. He'd come down earlier looking all sexy and sweaty and she hadn't been able to take advantage of him. Dammit.

She hated her monthly cycle. She was definitely doing something about this.

But for now, she had a brother to deal with. A stubborn, possessive, sometimes too domineering brother. And one she loved.

A hard knock sounded on the door before it pushed open and he strode into the office dressed in his motorcycle leathers and tugging off black gloves.

He was really too damned good-looking for his own good. Impossibly charming.

"What's so important you had to e-mail that little order?" He frowned at her as he threw himself in the chair in front of her desk.

Janey leaned back in her own chair.

"I love you, Natches," she said softly.

He stared at her for long moments. She could see the emotions in his eyes now, where in the past she had never been able to.

"Yeah." He nodded. "I love you, too, Janey." He rubbed his hand over his cheek. "Where's Alex?"

Like her, emotion still had the ability to make him slightly nervous. They'd been raised to hide everything; sometimes that wasn't so easy.

"You and I have ground rules to settle. We don't need Alex for that." She leaned forward, picked up the legal agreement she'd had made, and pushed it toward him. "Sign it."

He looked at the papers, then back to her.

"Was the 'love you' stuff to butter me up?" His lips quirked.

"No." She shook her head. "It was a promise, Natches. We're family. You're all the family I have, and I don't want to lose you. But I'm not butting heads with you over this restaurant any longer. And I'm not coming to you for permission for everything I need. Alex is my soul, and I love him more than I thought I'd ever love anyone besides you. But this restaurant has always been my dream. Not yours. Mine. I don't want your part of it, but I will have control of it."

He looked around the office somberly before meeting her eyes again. "I hate this fucking place," he finally said. "I prayed you'd hate it."

She sighed at that. "It's not Dayle's place any longer, Natches. It's mine. As far as I'm concerned, Ray has always been the father we should have had. He's a Mackay, and he wears his name with pride. I won't do anything less."

He slapped his gloves against his hands and stared at the papers. "Burn the place," he whispered. "Start fresh."

"Why?"

He looked back up at her, his gaze heavy, filled with sadness.

"Neither of us would ever have to remember him again if it were gone."

She shook her head. "He made us who we are. And, Natches, we're damned fine people." She smiled through her tears. "We're good people. Chaya and Alex wouldn't love us if we weren't. And we wouldn't have survived otherwise."

He sighed heavily. "Stubborn," he muttered.

"A trait we share." She pushed the papers to him. "Give me control, Natches. Let's show Dayle what he missed out on. Mackay's will be the finest restaurant in the state, and one day, no one will even remember who he was."

He pulled the papers to him and signed them, then pushed them back and stood up. "I promised Alex I'd help him upstairs," he stated. "Dawg and Rowdy will be here in a minute to help, too."

Janey stared at the papers, then back at Natches. "You didn't read them. You should."

He shrugged. "They just say you have control, right?"

She nodded slowly.

"I trust you, Janey." He stared back at her, and that trust was in his expression, in his eyes. "I always trusted you."

"Always?" she whispered. Even when Dayle was beating the hell out of him because she had done something wrong?

He moved around the desk, bending until he was hunkered beside her chair. "Always. Even when you were a black-haired, squalling, red-faced brat pissed off with the world. When you were a toddler just realizing what kind of monster sired us, and a young girl trying to be so good so Dayle wouldn't erupt. Janey. I always loved you. You were always my sister. And you were always right here."

He lifted her hand and placed it on his chest. Over his heart. She placed her other hand atop his. "I always loved you, Natches."

He nodded and rose to his feet. "I owe you, though," he promised her.

"For what?" She stared back at him bemused.

"For hoping I have a daughter." His grin was rueful, but filled with laughter. "Chaya keeps throwing out hints. I bet I end up with a black-haired, green-eyed, wild-assed girl I don't have a hope in hell of keeping up with."

"You should only be so lucky." She laughed.

At that, he grinned, then nodded. "Yeah. I should only be so lucky. But she might change her mind when I'm running all the boys off."

"She'll love you. You'll be a good dad, Natches."

"You're damned right I will be." He nodded, determination filling his face now. "Now, you be good. Make us money or I'm burning the place down."

But he grinned as he stepped through the door. And Janey sighed deeply. She ached from head to toe; she hated her cycle, but Alex had promised her a back rub.

She put the papers to the side. She didn't need them. The lawyer didn't need them. It was the gesture that mattered to her, because she and Natches both knew the papers weren't legal. Not really. Because she hadn't signed them herself.

Fuck it. She stuck them in the shredder and listened to them grind away. Hell, she enjoyed the fights with her brother, just as she enjoyed her confrontations with her lover.

Speaking of her lover . . . She stepped from the office into the dining room, where Rogue was directing the staff like a general, dressed in leather, long red gold curls spilling around her back.

"Faisal, you're too damned good to be hiding in the kitchen." Rogue was arguing with Natches's adopted son. "I need your ass out here helping me oversee everything if we're going to pull off that four-day-a-week lunch crowd."

Faisal crossed his arms over his chest, a scowl on his face, and for a moment, just a moment, Janey could see the incredible influence her brother had on the young man.

"You are like a despot," Faisal accused her, his black gaze flickering over her expression with a hint of anger. "You order. Order. Order. I don't like your orders, Rogue. You do not ask."

"But, honey, if I ask, you tell me no," she drawled before her expression firmed. "So I'm telling you. You are officially my assistant. Get used to it."

Faisal turned to Janey furiously, his black eyes snapping. "You do something with her. I like the kitchen."

"You hate the kitchen," Rogue snapped as she turned to Janey. "Tell him he hates the kitchen, Janey."

"I'm leaving." Janey laughed. "You two can fight this one out on your own."

Rogue's eyes narrowed as her lips twitched.

"Go." Rogue waved her away. "We're good."

And they were. She smiled. Yeah, things were going to work out just fine. And Alex had promised her a back rub. She'd steal him from the carpenters and Cranston just long enough. And her smile grew brighter. Long enough to touch him, taste him, and get that back rub. Then he could go play sweaty male games with her brother and cousins.

First, he had fiancé things to take care of.

The diamond on her finger winked. The promise he had made to her filled her heart. Yeah, he owned her. And she owned him. And what was more, she realized as she left the office, she did deserve him. Tall, proud, and dominant. She deserved every inch of him.

Stepping into the apartment she caught his eye. He looked at her, his grin slow, knowing. He looked around. Everyone was working, grumbling, laughing, and he slipped away from them.

They snuck from the apartment to his truck and back to their home. And spent hours touching, loving. They didn't have to do more. It wasn't about the sex, or the very naughty intentions she knew their relationship had started with. It was about this.

He touched her face, her lips. He held her to him and rubbed her back, her shoulders. She sucked his release from him and felt her own pleasure detonate inside her from the excitement. It was about this. They were a part of each other. Heart, body, and soul. And that knowledge saw her into the nap she needed and the gentle kiss he laid to her lips as he held her.

Love didn't describe it, but it came the closest. They loved beyond love.

Lora Leigh lives in the rolling hills of Kentucky and is often found absorbing the ambience of this peaceful setting. She dreams in bright, vivid images of the characters intent on taking over her writing life, and fights a constant battle to put them on the hard drive of her computer before they can disappear as fast as they appeared.

Lora's family and her writing life coexist, if not in harmony, in relative peace with each other. Surrounded by a menagerie of pets, friends, and a teenage son who keeps her quick wit engaged, Lora's life is filled with joys, aided by her fans, whose hearts remind her daily why she writes.